"What will you name this child?" the druidess asked.

Daeghrefn stared more deeply, more intently, out the cave opening into the raging storm. Yes, now was the time for names. A time to answer his wife in kind for her cruelty and betrayals. He thought of ice, of loneliness, of forbidding passage.

Winterheart? Hiddukel?

He smiled spitefully at the second of the names. God of injustice. The broken balance.

But, no. There was a certain evil grandeur to the names of the dark gods. He would confer no grandeur on this child.

As if it had been summoned, a large tomcat, lean and ragged, slinked out of the inclement darkness, snow spangling its half frozen fur. Daeghrefn regarded the creature in horrified fascination. This is the omen, he thought. The name is about to come to me. The cat carried something large and limp in its mouth—a dripping entanglement of matted fur and dirt and torn flesh.

A winter kill. A rat or a mole, perhaps. Something tunneling blindly beneath the snow, scratched from the hard earth, chittering and scrabbling in its dark nest.

Daeghrefn closed his eyes, warmed by his bloody imaginings. "Verminaard," he announced proudly. "The child's name is Verminaard. For he is vermin, dwelling in darkness and filth like his damned father. . . ."

Saga

From the Creators of the DRAGONLANCE® Saga

VILLAINS

Before the Mask
Volume One—Verminaard
Michael and Teri Williams

The Black Wing
Volume Two—Khisanth
Mary Kirchoff
Available in September, 1993

Emperor of Ansalon
Volume Three—Ariakus
Douglas Niles
Available in December, 1993

DragonLance® Saga

VILLAINS
Volume One

BEFORE the MASK

Michael and Teri Williams

DRAGONLANCE® VILLAINS SERIES
Volume One

BEFORE THE MASK

Cover art by Jeff Easley. Interior illustrations by Karl Waller.

Author photo by Terri Miller.

First Printing: April 1993
Printed in the United States of America
Library of Congress Catalog Card Number: 92-61084

9 8 7 6 5 4 3 2 1

ISBN: 1-56076-583-6

TSR, Inc.   TSR Ltd.
P.O. Box 756   120 Church End, Cherry Hinton
Lake Geneva, WI 53147   Cambridge CB1 3LB
United States of America   United Kingdom

For Lisa, Colleen, and Bonnie, the first friends to listen to my stories. And for Terri, Brad, and especially Michael, who listen to them now.

— T. W.

For Phil and Ann Swain.

— M. W.

Acknowledgments

Thanks to Margaret Weis for her kind, generous, and supportive spirit.

Mary Kirchoff was of great help at the outset of the project; we wish her all the best in upcoming projects of her own.

Pat McGilligan has been there for us over the last four years with a steady, no-nonsense brilliance, shaping rough work toward vitality and life.

Scott Siegel, our agent, continued to believe and to pound the pavement ingeniously.

Pat Price's erudition and insight steered us to several invaluable sources on Teutonic rune-lore. Our version of this is impressionistic and no longer resembles its ancient original. But we would never have found the way without Pat.

Kim and Sammy Soza ran the most hospitable convention in the Southwest—Ziacon I. Stay in the saddle, folks!

Thanks to Terri Miller for our wonderful portrait photo on the inside back cover.

Thanks also to David Kirchhoff, Dorothy Westcott, and especially Mort Morss—all of Daylily World in Sanford, Florida. They were ever ready with solid, detailed information and superb plants. In the fall of 1993, Mort will introduce his new "Runemark" cultivar—the daylily upon which the flower in our book is based.

Finally, to our community of faith, thanks for your continued support and prayers. God bless all of you.

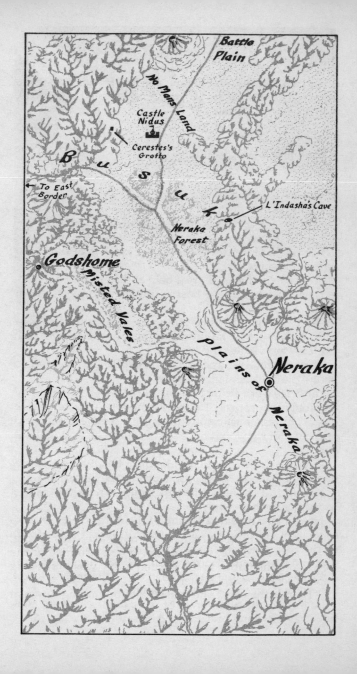

Prologue

In the small patch of cold sunlight on the hill above her cave, the druidess L'Indasha Yman bent to the spring planting with a worn-out spade and a weary heart. For three thousand years, winters had ended in jubilation for her. When she set the season's first seed into the newly turned ground or found the first shoot of returning growth in her daylilies, she would forget utterly the cold, the storms, her hunger for green, for bloom.

But this year, the winter would not leave. This spring, there was little pleasure for her in the promise of the seeds, and her labor in the garden today was producing mostly scratches and blisters.

"There's the rub," she mused aloud, looking down at

the splintering oak handle of the spade. "I should have mended you long ago. Five hundred years of gardens can be too much even for oak."

And too much for me, she thought. I will go on and on and keep the Secret and all the world will change, is changing—but in me now there is no change. My life is a removal. But I chose it full knowing.

She turned to a clump of daylilies and sat back on her heels, peering into the lavender blue face of an early bloom. At Paladine's command, she had planted these everywhere she lived or traveled. They were her particular love in the green kingdoms, for every morning, there was a new, extravagant grace and outpouring of beauty in their flowers, a grace and beauty that would last only for the day. She traced the triangular bloom with her finger and left a trail of silver light in the air.

To her surprise, the light spread, filtering through the careful rows of emerging sunflowers to the distant new leaves of the encircling vallenwoods, until the garden was aglow in silver and white.

"Cheer up," said a voice from the lavender-blue heart of the lily. "All of this mutter about loneliness and beauty that will fade is matter for bards, not gardeners."

L'Indasha smiled. "I've missed you. How long has it been?"

"But a day," the lily replied. "You've just been listening to your own world-weary drone. I was here yesterday, but you didn't look at me. See that shriveled flower to my immediate left? I waited all day in there for you to sit down and stop moping. Two bees and a grasshopper came by, though."

The eye of the lily winked at the druidess, and then she felt a hand on her shoulder.

Whirling about and rocking backward, she looked full in the face of a kindly old man, white-haired and bearded, a silver triangle pinned to the crown of his broad-brimmed hat. A gaudy purplish smear colored one side of his nose.

"Lord Paladine," L'Indasha began reverently. "You—"

The old man raised a finger to his lips.

"Hush," he breathed. "You'll wake the neighbors."

"I just wanted to tell you that—"

"Shh." The old man sat down on the freshly hoed furrow, his silver robes swirling with sun and shade. "A change has come," he announced quietly, smiling. "I'm sending you a companion. Some help."

"Some *help?*"

"Oh, not that there's aught wrong with the work you've done. I'm really very pleased. Thirty centuries, and Takhisis has not unmasked the rune. It's a splendid job, my dear. Worth enduring this long, wearisome immortality."

He held up the daylily bloom, now somehow missing its blue-purple center. He grinned.

L'Indasha cleared her throat. "Lord Paladine, I simply wanted to tell you . . . "

"Your helper is coming," he went on, "coming by a roundabout way. Well, *very* roundabout—twenty years in the doing. These things take time—growth—due season, you know. But *that* will be clear to you soon enough. And when help arrives, there will be important choices to make."

"Twenty years?" the druidess asked apprehensively. Twenty years seemed like days, even hours, after her vigil of three millennia. "How? Why?"

Lord Paladine waved his hand. "The Dark Lady's spies are everywhere. So my devices move slowly and quietly these days." He pointed to an overhanging vallenwood. "Like the growth of a large tree."

"I see," the druidess replied. "Rushed and suspicious eyes will not notice."

Lord Paladine nodded. "You be patient as well. Remember how I love you."

"How much shall I tell when the helper comes?"

L'Indasha asked. "Surely not everything."

"Oh, goodness, no!" the old fellow exclaimed. "It'd take forever, and my borscht recipe would get out!"

L'Indasha chuckled. "As if anyone would want it."

"Well, perhaps not," he mused, "but someone wants the Secret. More than at any time since I first hid the symbols on the faceless rune from her—from all the world—and entrusted them and that Keeper's pendant to you."

L'Indasha glanced down at the blue-purple stone about her neck. The warding stone that kept the Keeper.

Then all merriment vanished in Paladine's bright eyes. "Double your vigilance. Plant against famine and fire and the next winter. The barren season will last a very long time indeed. Unless . . . "

"Unless?"

Paladine crouched beside the druidess. "Unless the ages are accomplished," he whispered. "Soon the faceless rune will have two faces. They will be opposites, and they will be the same. If they balance each other, work together in their opposition, your job will be done. They can receive the Secret from you and defeat darkness forever. For they are Huma's kin."

"Children," the druidess breathed. "From the line of Huma . . . it will be full circle then. So these are the last of my quiet days."

The old man nodded and rose. The sunlight faded and dappled as a roiling cloud bank moved overhead. In the distance, heat lightning flashed, followed by a low rumble. "Provide. The storm is coming."

He turned to go, but L'Indasha beckoned him gently once again.

"Lord Paladine . . . ?"

"Yes?" he asked.

"You have lily on your nose."

Chapter 1

The winter of the old man's warning came even more quickly than she had expected, collapsing the autumn of that peaceful year into a matter of days, freezing the unfallen leaves to their branches.

This day, from her sheltering cavern, L'Indasha Yman kept vigil with the rising new storm. Harsh winds from the west—from Taman Busuk—whipped through the Khalkist Mountains, bringing dark, churning clouds and the faint, watery smell of winter lightning.

The druidess peered deeply into a bucket of cinder-clouded ice, rapt in her winter auguries. Somewhere out in the mountain passes—somewhere north and west, she could tell by the smoky crazing of the ice—someone was trudging through the biting snow, through the plunging cold and the rising night.

Darkness would soon overtake him, whoever he was. And with the darkness, the infamous Breath of Neraka—the murderous mountain night winds. On nights such as this, the Breath of Neraka was cruel . . . merciless. Horses froze in midstride. Trails vanished in sudden avalanches. Once, not long after she had moved here, the high winds had sealed an entire party of bandits in an impenetrable shell of ice.

And that was part of it, too—part of L'Indasha Yman's unsettled vigil in the oncoming night. Between the cold and the brigands, this was deadly country, these mountains between Neraka and the plains of Estwilde, mountains that encircled the shrines of the ancient gods.

What was it the old texts had said?

Forbidding. Impossible passage.

And yet someone was trying to pass.

The wind switched directions near the entrance to the cave. Dry snow whirled in thin columns, spiraling upward into the darkness as two icy gusts seemed to war for the waning light. Then one gave way to the other, and the snow began to settle and drift as total darkness sealed over the Nerakan passes.

L'Indasha pored over the ice. It was her particular divination—the old word for it something like *gelemancy*, something about the memory within ice. She kept the bucket of clean water by the mouth of the cave, and on cold nights, when it glazed over, it captured the past and the present in glittering strata. Tonight the ice was difficult to read. The sudden wind had brought ashes from old fires, the obscuring haze of cinders and burning. The black particles had gathered and settled in the ice to hide the greater part of the vision, and they were melting it very quickly.

Carefully the druidess brushed at the blemished surface of the ice, and she saw two broad paths through the mountains—one from Estwilde, the other from Gargath. Nothing else. And even that vision was fading, the ice now etched and buoyant.

He is nearby. He is almost here. I know it, she told herself. Ah. More than one of them, I think. L'Indasha's fingertips tingled and pricked. She drew up her shawl and bent lower over the bucket to see more clearly. Half a mile from the Nerakan road, wandering aimlessly north through the barren trees and the knee-deep snow, a man lurched into view.

Solamnic. She could tell by the insignia. Cloaked thinly against the terrible weather, dressed in useless armor. He was wandering, clearly lost, just far enough from the trail to be very near her cave.

The wind ripped through his robes. His beard, his gloves, and the leather lacings of his breastplate were crusted and stiff with ice, as though he had been carved from the mountain or born of the winter sky.

Solamnic, the druidess repeated to herself, lifting her eyes from the oracular ice. Probably searching for bandits. Following the sword and that pitiful code of his—bloody vows of honor and life. Let him go. She was no fool to meddle in the workings of pride and vainglory.

As she watched, the knight passed into shadow and cloud, lost at the edge of her auguries.

Let him go. Let him freeze in foolhardiness, along with his troops and followers. . . .

Followers. Almost at once, she dismissed her scorn and resentment. No matter his foolishness and Solamnic vanities, she thought, it is a merciless night for them.

Then, as though her compassion itself had summoned them, the other two staggered into her view. Two smaller forms desperately followed the knight, their gilded, embroidered clothing already tattered by the rending wind. Then the ice abruptly cleared, the cinders dropped to the bottom of the bucket, and the vision went black.

The druidess reached for her cloak and, with a brief pass of her hand and an ancient, dry mutter, deftly lighted a torch. The green light flashed and rose and steadied in her grasp. It was a dim fire, scarcely a guide on a night like this, but the magic would keep it aglow in the terrible wind.

* * * * *

Daeghrefn turned to see where they were. The wind struck him full in the face, stinging the back of his throat and leaving him breathless.

In the swirl of snow and shadow behind him, he could see his family barely outlined—woman and boy, shadows against the dark sky. Abelaard was struggling bravely, of course. He guided the woman, coaxing and urging her, but the stiff wind staggered them both, and the woman stumbled, pulling the lad backward into the snow. A strange, cold peace passed over Daeghrefn as the wind switched directions, as the stragglers labored to their feet.

The woman is weakening. Upright or fallen, she is nothing to me now. If the gods will that she survive the storm, she will do so. But my son walks beside her, and he will live through this night. By Oath and Measure, that much is true. I shall see to it with the last of my own strength.

Daeghrefn tried to double his fists, but his frozen gloves would not crease. The screaming wind switched direction again—this time from due east, lancing from the top of the range down mountainside and foothill, rattling branches in the desolate Nerakan Forest and plunging straight into the path of the dazed and snow-baffled knight. He gasped and cursed, staggered again in the snow.

And then the torchlit form was in front of him, a dark

outline of human or goblin or . . .

Clumsy as an old, besotted man, he groped with useless and disobedient fingers for his sword.

"No," said the voice at the heart of the shadow. "Come to shelter."

It was the voice of a woman, unfamiliar and young, strangely accented with the sharp, fluid music of Lemish.

"Begone!" the knight shouted.

"Don't be a fool!" the shadow urged, gesturing sweepingly in the blinding snow. Now she was motioning him somewhere . . . somewhere to the south . . . to shelter. . . .

"No!" Daeghrefn roared. "He'll not have this victory as well!"

"Don't be a fool," repeated the shadow.

She extended her hand toward the struggling knight.

Again, Daeghrefn's hand grappled for the ice-crusted hilt of his sword. "Begone!" he hissed, the exclamation lost in the roar of the wind. He grunted and shouted as he tried to draw the blade, but the sword hung frozen at his belt, sealed to the sheath by an absurdly thick layer of ice.

He would have struggled there forever, until the snow took him or the shadow descended, had not Abelaard called to him over the clamoring storm.

"May we stop, Father?" the lad shouted, his voice thin and uncertain. "May we stop? We're very tired and cold."

* * * * *

It was a druidess, of course, who led them out of the blinding snow and into the warmth and shadow and dodging light of a nearby cavern. The heat from the fire smarted on Daeghrefn's storm-burned skin. Blinking stupidly in the sudden brightness, he glanced from wall to cavern wall, where cascades of dried lavender and rosemary hung amid comfrey and foxglove, alongside mushrooms as gnarled and black as severed hands. Two cats, lean and ancient, wrestled solemnly in a shadowy corner. The place smelled of forest, of the deep glades of Lemish and elf country.

He should have known the woman was a druidess, Daeghrefn told himself. Celebrant of the dead gods and the dead year. Instantly his caution magnified. If druidess she was, there was danger in her. They were never what they seemed, with their woodsense and muttering and their irritating mysteries. He had heard they stole babies. Now *there* was a thought.

"Why?" asked the druidess L'Indasha Yman, shaking the snow from her robes. She was younger than he expected. Quite lovely, for that matter—auburn-haired and tall and dark-eyed as well. The cave light did not reveal the finer details of her face, and his eyes were too frost- and wind-burned to study her clearly.

He crouched by the fire and extended his hands, regarding the druidess warily. His eyes played over the soft, dark skin of her neck, the purple pendant at her throat that filtered the firelight as stained glass catches the sun. He would not trust beauty such as this. It was entangling, beguiling. . . .

L'Indasha noticed the stormcrow brooch, ice-encrusted, that held the man's cape uncertainly about his throat.

"You are Daeghrefn of Nidus," she noted, drawing a small iron kettle from a shadowy nook in the rocks. "The dayraven. The stormcrow. Your castle is not far from here. Why? Why do you travel on a night such as this? Where did you think you were?"

The woman cried out softly to Abelaard. The boy helped her closer to the fire.

Daeghrefn ignored them, his eyes fixed on the druidess. "You know already who and why and where," he muttered, "and you've augury enough to know more. Why ask?"

L'Indasha glared at him and stalked into the darkness, returning with the kettle brimful of water. "It would take more than augury to sound this foolishness," she said, soothing the man's wife with a soft brush of her hand. "Out in the Khalkists on the worst of winter nights, your wife and small son behind you like a straggling infantry. What could have . . . ?" Like the melting of ice or the settling of ashes, a slow awareness seeped into L'Indasha's mind. She tried to hide her face when the truth came to her, but Daeghrefn saw it.

"Ah," she breathed. "You've been cuckolded, haven't—" The druidess glanced down at the woman. The thin cloak had fallen and now revealed the source of the woman's crying. She was about to give birth.

L'Indasha didn't finish the sentence. Daeghrefn lurched up angrily with a clatter of breastplate and greaves.

"It is not your concern, druidess," he growled. He wished for a secret blade, for a sudden lapse of the Oath, and surprised himself with his own edged and ready anger. "Nose into your vegetation and your failed gods if you want," he murmured, his voice deep and menacing. "Pry into the heart of the oak and the phases of the moon, into whatever mysteries and omens you consult when your wits fail you. But keep out of my affairs."

The druidess stared at him darkly.

Brown, he thought absently as the wind outside whistled and eddied. Her eyes are brown . . .

His wife cried out again in Abelaard's small arms. "Too soon!" she wailed, her long scream rising in pitch and volume until it became deafening, as chilling as the wind in the mountain passes below.

Daeghrefn covered his ears as L'Indasha rushed to attend the woman. And then, as suddenly as it began, the scream cut off. One of the cats yawned in the cave's far corner.

L'Indasha's face was grim. The woman's pulse fluttered

and faded, then surged again as she cried out in agony. Reaching for the kettle, for soothing herbs—for anything—the druidess cast her eyes on the bucket by the mouth of the cave.

The last of the moonlight played almost cruelly over the ice. On the glazed surface of the water, the light took the form of thick stone, the snow like white robes swirling around a distant childbed. . . .

Another child. Another child was being born tonight. It was the other face, the brother to this bastard child. Somewhere, in some warm and nurturing country. But this poor woman lay moaning in an icy cavern, her first son young and helpless, her husband unbalanced and venomous. . . . L'Indasha Yman fought down her anger and bent to the work of the night.

Huma's kin were being born.

* * * * *

Somewhat later, in the uncanny silence, something in the depths of the cavern stirred from its hibernation with a stifled, painful cry. Daeghrefn strained to make out the distant sound as the creature scuttled deeper into the cave, where its cry echoed and redoubled back.

" . . . and you have all but killed her! The child was not ready. It is turned about wrong and cannot come forth!"

He startled. It was L'Indasha Yman shouting in his ear. How long had she been there railing at him—some gibberish about the woman, about the child she was bearing? Daeghrefn closed his ears to the wailing, to the druidess's words. He turned toward the mouth of the cave, put his back to his son and the two women, and reckoned out an old impartial calendar.

Too soon. The wretch had said *too soon*. Yes, it was. He had found her out much too soon. She had thought to fool him, but—

"I need your help!" the druidess shouted, penetrating his icy wall of silence, her voice colder still.

"Ask your gods," Daeghrefn insisted, his back to her.

The druidess sighed. Daeghrefn seated himself at the cave's entrance. Silent, unmoved by her incessant pleas for help in the lifting and pushing, by the rustle and clamor of Abelaard's clumsy assistance, the knight drew his sword and stared into the wheeling snow. The moonlight broke fitfully through the mountainous clouds, silver on red, and for a moment, he thought he saw the strange black magelight of Nuitari.

An hour passed, or more.

Finally the cry of the infant broke in the stormy air. It was muted, desperate, as though the newborn child had fallen into the depths of the cave.

"You have a son," the haggard druidess announced coldly, holding a swaddled thing toward the fire for warmth.

"I have a son?" Daeghrefn replied sardonically. "That is no news. He followed me to this cavern. He served you bravely, where even a midwife would have faltered."

There was a long silence.

"What will you name this child?" the druidess asked.

Daeghrefn stared more deeply, more intently, into the storm. Name the child? He turned the sword over in his palm. Why should he even keep it, let alone name it?

Triumphant, exhausted, Abelaard took the baby from L'Indasha and presented it to Daeghrefn. "He's beautiful, don't you think, Father? What will you call him?"

When he heard the boy's voice, Daeghrefn sheathed the sword. Abelaard was here. He could not kill the baby. But he would find a way to leave it with this sorceress—good payment for her trouble, he mused. So now was the time for omens, for auguries of his own, for the naming was Daeghrefn's by the Measure, no matter who was the child's father. Its mother was, still and all, his wife. And, more importantly, Abelaard's mother.

Daeghrefn set down the sword and steepled his hands, still stiff and red from the cold.

Yes, now was the time for names. A time to answer his wife in kind for her cruelty and betrayals. He thought of ice, of loneliness, of forbidding passage. . . .

Winterheart? Hiddukel?

He smiled spitefully at the second of the names. God of injustice. The broken balance.

But, no. There was a certain evil grandeur to the names of the dark gods. He would confer no grandeur on this child.

As if it had been summoned, a large tomcat, lean and ragged, slinked out of the inclement darkness, snow spangling its half-frozen fur. Daeghrefn regarded the creature in horrified fascination. This is the omen, he thought. The name is about to come to me. The cat carried something large and limp in its mouth—a dripping entanglement of matted fur and dirt and torn flesh.

A winter kill. A rat or a mole, perhaps. Something tunneling blindly beneath the snow, scratched from the hard earth, chittering and scrabbling in its dark nest.

Daeghrefn closed his eyes, warmed by his bloody imaginings. "Verminaard," he announced proudly. "The child's name is Verminaard. For he is vermin, dwelling in darkness and filth like his damned father."

L'Indasha's eyes widened in amazement. Quietly she moved to Abelaard's side. A shriek from Daeghrefn's wife pierced through the hush, through the knight's pronouncements and curses.

"Ah, no!" The druidess turned sharply, a new trouble in her voice.

Daeghrefn sat silently, his eyes closed. From the commotion, from the druidess's whispered instructions to the lad, the knight imagined the scene unfolding behind him.

The druidess knelt above the woman, her ministrations frantic and swift. But soon, inevitably, she sighed, her hands slowing, her touch more benediction than healing. Sorrowfully she pushed the boy and the baby away, gesturing toward a straw mattress in a candlelit alcove off the main cavern.

Abelaard lingered above his dying mother for a moment, his eyes dull and unreadable. A well-schooled Solamnic youth, he did as he was told, his emotions veiled behind the stern tutelage of his masters. And yet he was only a child, and for a moment, he bent low, his stubby fingers cradling the head of his newborn brother, and reached down to touch his mother's whitened cheek with the back of his hand. Then, with a soft and nonsensical whisper, he carried the baby to the alcove and settled onto the straw, wrapping a thin wool blanket about the both of them. Soon the infant nestled against his brother and slept deeply and silently.

*　*　*　*　*

"She's dead," L'Indasha announced scarcely an hour later. " 'Gone to Huma's breast,' as your Order says. What will you do now?"

Daeghrefn sniffed disgustedly, his eyes fixed on the wintry landscape beyond the cave entrance. The storm was swelling, the wind rising. The red moon Lunitari peeked from behind the racing clouds, flooding the snow with a staining crimson light.

The knight turned slowly, the side of his face bathed in the hovering torchlight. For a moment, he looked like a skeletal wraith, like the Death Knight of the old legends, through whose hands had slipped the power to turn back the Cataclysm.

"And who are you to question me, idolater?" he murmured, his voice low and menacing, like the humming of distant bees or the high whirring sound of the rocks over Godshome. "You have no claim on me or on my son." He gestured vaguely toward Abelaard, his sword waving grotesquely in the mingling light of the fire and the spinning moons. "You have no claim on any of us. Not even that dead harlot's get," he concluded venomously and stepped suddenly toward the fire, brushing the snow from his mantle.

L'Indasha inwardly shrank from the knight. Instinct told her to fly, to scatter elusive magic and escape in the confusion, to burrow into the sheltering dark. . . . But she squarely faced the knight and fought back with words calculated to wound.

"This child will eclipse your own darkness," she proclaimed, holding the baby above the firelight, holding him out to Daeghrefn. Her voice rang in the ancient inflections of druidic prophecy and sheer rage. "And his hand will strike your name. But I will not tell you the rest."

Daeghrefn laughed harshly. It was ridiculous druidic babble. Then her blazing eye caught his.

Her anger was real.

Daeghrefn held her gaze. Dire things passed briefly through his mind, and for a moment, the sword turned in his hand, the melted snow beading ominously on the sheath's carved raven. He would make her retract it. He would bury the blade in . . .

No. He would send Robert back here to . . . clean out this cave.

"So?" he said, shaking his head slowly, distractedly, his eye passing over the new child's fair hair and creamy skin. He beckoned for Abelaard. The boy approached him, stopping only to take the baby from the druidess and hold him cautiously in his shivering, thin arms.

"Druidic nonsense," the knight whispered. Then louder, his voice cold and assured, he added, "Put on your cloak, Abelaard, and leave the child." He stared balefully at the druidess. "We must be off for Nidus while there's aught of the night to travel. It's still a good walk home, by my reckoning."

The boy put on his garment, but he would not give the baby back to the druidess. "I've looked forward to a brother for so long, Father. Please. We must take care of him."

Daeghrefn could refuse Abelaard nothing short of this request. Nothing short, but not this.

"No," he replied.

The druidess stepped forward and placed her hand on Abelaard's shoulder, an idea forming as she spoke.

"No, Daeghrefn," she began, a dry warning in her voice. "You'll keep this child and keep him well. If you leave him—or worse—all those in your command will know of your cuckolding. And who would follow such a man? You cannot be undone before them, can you?"

Daeghrefn's dark eyes locked onto L'Indasha's, and she knew she had won his undying hatred.

And the baby's life.

"Nidus is ten miles from here," she urged, calmly holding his vacant stare. "You have seen our weather. You have challenged the storm enough for tonight."

Daeghrefn broke his gaze and removed his boots. For a moment, L'Indasha's hopes rose, until she realized he was only drying them by the fire, preparing for the long trek through the mountains.

"You have heard the stories," she began quietly, "about these mountains in the winter."

"I've no time for lore," Daeghrefn objected.

L'Indasha persisted. She told Daeghrefn about the frozen horses, the dozens of travelers irrecoverably lost. She told him of the bandits, sealed in ice like insects in a million years of amber. All the while her touch was light on the shoulder of the boy. Daeghrefn did not listen, but

Abelaard did.

As she knew he would.

And it was enough. When Daeghrefn drew on his boots and walked to the mouth of the cave, Abelaard remained by the fire. "Father?" he asked, his voice thin and uncertain.

Daeghrefn turned to him warily.

"Can't we just wait out the night here?" Abelaard pleaded. "We left Laca's castle ten days ago. We're away from the bad place now. Tomorrow we can all go home. The baby, too. Please, Father."

As he looked into Abelaard's hollow eyes, something in the knight seemed to turn and soften. It was sudden and unforeseen, as a line of troops will break in the midst of a pitched battle. Daeghrefn's shoulders slumped, and slowly he removed his sodden gloves.

"I suppose," he began, "that a night's stay could not altogether *harm* us, Abelaard. But just one night, mind you. We'll be home at Nidus on the morrow, regardless of storm or cold."

"One night is all you will need," the druidess said, for the lad's encouragement more than Daeghrefn's information. "Storms blow over quickly here, and there will be sun and a clear path come morning."

"We're off to Nidus regardless," the knight insisted, staring into the fire.

* * * * *

L'Indasha buried the dead woman at the far end of a side cavern, deep in the soft clay floor, while Daeghrefn huddled in blankets around the fire and Abelaard fed the newborn something the druidess had mixed and warmed for him.

When she finished singing the funeral prayers, they all

slept. Twice in the night L'Indasha stirred—once at the roar of wind across the high plateau, carrying the cry of a dozen lost travelers beyond her help in the hills of Estwilde, and once when the baby awoke and whimpered. It was the baby's cry that brought her to full waking. It began softly and rose steadily until she heard Abelaard's voice join with it awkwardly, singing a Solamnic lullaby. The child's voice was small and fragile amid the roar of wind tumbling through the surrounding hills.

May your gods keep you, L'Indasha thought, a modest spell shielding her ears against the plaintive sounds of the children in the center of the cave. If your gods can do anything, may they keep you in the days to come.

Chapter 2

The Bridge of Dreed arched narrowly over the canyon, a dark, knobby spine against the bright autumn sunset. It was the northernmost of three bridges across the gorge. The southern two were made of vallenwood and were old as the Cataclysm. But this structure was far older, a narrow stone footpath, one man's width, that had spanned the great chasm for as long as the histories recalled and the legends remembered. At its very top, a level, slightly wider area had provided this ceremony a perfect platform.

Barely twelve years old, Verminaard shifted nervously in the saddle. Of course, he had heard much about this place. Indeed, he had seen the Bridge of Dreed once before, from a distance, when he and his brother had been goat hunting in the high reaches above Daeghrefn's castle. It had seemed menacing even then—a black, crooked bow spanning the gorge from east to west. Abelaard had pointed it out to him, then steered him to lower ground as the younger lad glanced back at the ancient structure, his thoughts filled with legends of how the world was made.

The finger of Reorx, the forge god. A handle for the mountains he had raised in the Age of Dreams, as the stories told.

Two years after that hunt, and much closer now, the bridge looked no less grand and precarious. It arched from one side of the gorge to the other, and, below, there was a breathtaking drop of three hundred feet to the ragged igneous rocks on the chasm floor. The stones were littered with brush, dead wood, and old bones.

He would walk that narrow span of rock and exchange places with Laca's son. He would live in a foreign land and learn to be a knight, for his father said Laca still kept to the Order.

It was a place for solemn oaths indeed, the boy thought. And he closed his eyes amid the company, the armed men around him oblivious to his silent prayer.

He prayed that his knighthood would come in another way, that the two quarrelsome fathers—their rift as old as the night just before his birth, as wide as the spreading chasm before him—would knit their discord in the face of the coming war. That Daeghrefn would go back to the Order. Surely the organized Nerakan army, impelled from somewhere in the dark heart of the mountains, would persuade Laca of East Borders and Daeghrefn of Nidus to relent, to trust each other at last. Couldn't they join swords in good faith, without the approaching dance of deal and transaction? Couldn't they postpone the swapping of sons until the Nerakans were subdued?

He prayed he would do his father proud in this

exchange. But he knew his prayers tumbled like loose stones into the chasm below him, away from the starry hand of Paladine, from the eyes of Majere and Kiri-Jolith—far from the various gods Daeghrefn once revered and worshiped. . . .

Then renounced, when he left the Order.

Daeghrefn stood behind the boy, masking his smile due to the solemnity that would follow. It was perfect, this gebo-naud, a prime arrangement of fortune and war and politics. As the years had passed, the Lord of Nidus feared more and more that the secret of his cuckoldry would be guessed by the other knights. As Verminaard grew, the boy looked the very picture of Laca.

Who had played nicely into his hands with this treaty and exchange.

He would be rid of Verminaard, Daeghrefn thought with a grim contentment. And Laca would have his own bastard visited on him. It could not have been better arranged.

Verminaard started. *You will bid your brother farewell today*, the Voice told him. *Oh, yes, farewell, for you will not see him again, though good riddance will it be. And you will be the elder, the scion, your father's eventual heir.*

It always took him by surprise, that sinuous suggesting. The Voice had been with him for years—for as long as he could remember. Melodious and haunting, its tone neither masculine nor feminine, it would merge with his own thoughts and rise suddenly into hearing, its suggestions always a mixture of despair and grief and a strange, dark longing. He had never spoken to his father about it. Daeghrefn would not hold with voices.

What does this mean? Verminaard puzzled, wrestling as always with the Voice's dark prompting. It is an exchange of noble hostages, not a giving away!

And as always, the Voice was silent when he argued, slipping back into some dark recess, some alcove of memory, leaving him alone to bicker and wrestle with its insinuations. I will return! Verminaard assured himself. But the Voice was gone, leaving him to his rising dread and misgiving.

He opened his eyes and turned in the saddle. Abelaard, seated importantly amid the armed escort, winked at him solemnly.

Let it be over soon, the younger boy thought. If the exchange must take place, as the fathers have sworn on their swords and honors, let it take place quickly.

"You have your instructions?" the stern voice prodded behind them. Abelaard turned to Daeghrefn, murmuring something hasty and obedient.

Verminaard looked the other way—toward the chasm and the arching bridge and the impossible distance to the western side.

Daeghrefn moved between them, his dark horse snorting and capering in the brisk evening air.

"No one will attend you, Verminaard," the knight said. "Laca has not allowed as much."

Verminaard cast a sideward glance at the Lord of Nidus. Daeghrefn cut an imposing figure indeed: the chiseled nose, the dark thick brows above piercing eyes. The boy could understand why the soldiers feared him, why they had followed him out of the Order, become renegades along with their gloomy commander.

He looked closely at his father's face—a frightening, opaque mask of Solamnic instruction. Daeghrefn would show nothing of himself to Laca this evening. But the boy remembered Daeghrefn's smile two nights ago, when the last version of the treaty had reached him by the shaking hands of a Solamnic courier. Then Daeghrefn knew at last that the Lord of East Borders would accept Nidus's terms in the exchange. But now that triumph was contained behind a mask of cold composure.

"What is keeping them?" Daeghrefn muttered, shielding

his eyes and looking into the sunset, into the westernmost reaches of sight. "They ought to be here by now."

"You don't suppose that the Nerakans—" Verminaard began, a dark thought rising in his mind.

"Rest at ease, Brother," Abelaard whispered. "Laca will be as well armed as we are. The Nerakans would not dare cross swords or paths with a Solamnic company."

"'Tis heartening to hear that, Brother," Verminaard replied brightly, though his spirits sank at the words. Of course Laca's forces would be armed, and hundreds strong this far into the mountains. The Nerakans were moving in numbers and with tactics even the oldest men could not recall and had not expected.

Everywhere along the Khalkist Range, from Sanction to Gargath and still north, to where the mountains tumbled into the foothills of Estwilde, the Nerakans threatened the borders of more civilized country. Worse yet, the men of Estwilde and of Sanction had joined with them. The forces arrayed against the Solamnic Knights and their scattered allies were large enough and organized enough to pass for an army. Goblins and ogres even joined the bandit ranks, or so the scouts reported.

So all along the lofty spine of the Khalkists, the border lords were uniting in response, in mutual defense. Whether they were Solamnics or not, whether they were long-time friends or had feuded for years, commanders such as Daeghrefn and Laca formed alliances of blood or honor or urgency. Better to ally with a civilized foe than fall to the relentless, motley onslaught from the east.

It was why men always went heavily armed in the mountain passes. It was why, twelve years after the stormy night of Verminaard's birth, the last alliance would be sealed.

A month ago, after the Nerakans assaulted East Borders and pillaged the homesteads within a mile of Castle Nidus, Daeghrefn and Laca had communicated for the first time since that ill-omened night, exchanging information, then uncertain tokens, then veiled assurances . . . arguments. . . .

And now sons.

"There they are!" Abelaard exclaimed, pointing to the dark banners weaving through the western pass. The waning sunlight glittered red on their armor, and each crimson standard at the head of the column bore the silver kingfisher of the Order.

Daeghrefn rose in the stirrups, again shielding his eyes against the sunset. "It's Laca on the gray, I'm certain," he pronounced. "And the boy with him, on that horse's twin, must be his son."

He shot a curious glance at Verminaard, who met his gaze eagerly.

Daeghrefn turned away, speaking softly to Abelaard as the Solamnic column approached them in the distance. Verminaard strained to hear the conversation, but the words slid teasingly out of earshot.

Something about intelligence, it was. About couriers and signs.

Then his father sat back in the saddle, his veiled eyes red, as though he had looked too long into the westering sun.

"Where is the mage?" he asked the sergeant beside him, his voice troubled and hoarse. "We needn't linger over ceremony and drama."

Now Verminaard could see them, the two riders at the head of the column, framed by the kingfisher standards. A tall man, bareheaded amid a helmeted escort, his hair as white-blond as Verminaard's own. A small, lithe companion, dwarfed by his own horse. The boy was supposed to be twelve years old, born within minutes of Verminaard himself, in the warmth of the distant castle.

Abelaard had said they had much in common.

"Where is the mage?" Daeghrefn repeated, and the

sergeant wheeled his horse in search of the man in question.

Laca's party arrayed itself along the edge of the chasm, a formidable column of seasoned cavalry. Their commander leaned forward, awaiting some sign from the eastern edge of the gorge, and the slight rider beside him dismounted slowly.

Verminaard started at the touch of Abelaard's hand on his shoulder. His brother drew him close, embraced him. "Be strong," Abelaard whispered quickly, "and remember that whatever comes to pass, whatever befalls, I—"

"The boy is approaching, Abelaard," Daeghrefn interrupted. "There is no need to keep him waiting."

Abelaard nodded and gave his brother a long, encouraging glance. Verminaard leapt from the saddle.

Abelaard looked away, his eyes unreadable as he heard Verminaard's footsteps in the gravel at the bridge's edge. Abelaard had cared for his younger brother ever since his birth. And for Verminaard, it was as though his father had long ago handed him over to Abelaard, like a horse or a hunting dog.

I am going now, Verminaard thought. No matter what, I am going. Must gather myself . . . must stay under control. Father cannot see me shake . . . cannot see me . . .

"Where is the damned *mage?*" Daeghrefn thundered.

From behind him arose the sound of whispers, of urgings. Then the mage, Cerestes, brushed by, the hem of his dusty black robe grazing Daeghrefn's boot. He was young, dark-haired, handsome in a reptilian sort of way, his eyes golden and heavy-lidded.

"Where is Speratus?" Daeghrefn demanded. He little liked mages, keeping one at the castle only for defense. But this was not his archmage, only a mere pupil.

Cerestes presented his hasty services after a short explanation: The old mage, Speratus, had been found at the bottom of the chasm, no doubt besieged when he rode out alone to prepare the ceremony. His red robe had borne ragged evidence of the furtive, hooked daggers of Nerakan bandits.

One mage was the same as another, Daeghrefn told himself. This young Cerestes seemed confident, even wizardly. He would do. Anything to be rid of the boy. Solemnly the mage saluted his new employer and ushered Verminaard onto the spindly bridge.

"May the gods speed you, Verminaard," Daeghrefn breathed. He looked past the young wizard to the boy, who looked small and lonely as he neared the crown of the lofty arch. "At last you return to your father."

Abelaard looked up at him with a blank face, as unreadable as the soaring cliff, as the scattered rocks on the floor of the canyon.

The Bridge of Dreed was even more narrow than it appeared from the safety of the bordering cliffs. At the height of its arch, where the *gebo-naud*—the Solamnic rite of exchange—would take place, there was scarcely room for the two lads to stand side by side.

Verminaard moved steadily out toward the middle of the bridge. The Solamnic boy was less assured. He pulled on his hood and walked, heel cautiously in front of toe, weaving uncertainly, like an amateur ropewalker. As he approached from the west, the autumn winds ruffled his sleeves and the gossamer green of his family tabard.

Cerestes, as surefooted and sinuous as one of the huge panteras that were the bane of mountain herdsmen, followed Verminaard. At the last moment, the mage slipped impossibly past the lad and glided to the center of the bridge. There, standing between the two boys, he raised his hand to begin the incantations of the *gebo-naud*.

Suddenly there was an outcry from the platform.

Daeghrefn shifted uneasily, his eyes on the two boys.

"What's wrong, Father?" Abelaard asked. He asked again, and again, until Daeghrefn's seneschal, an older man named Robert, took pity on the lad's persistence.

"It'll be all right," Robert offered, leaning across his mare's neck toward the attentive boy.

"Hush, Robert," Daeghrefn ordered. "The ceremony begins."

But it did not begin. Cerestes strode westward from the center of the bridge and waved for one of Laca's retainers to meet him.

When the mage returned to the platform, he instructed the Solamnic boy to wait and brought Verminaard, bewildered, back to Daeghrefn's party.

"Lord Daeghrefn," he chimed, "the *gebo-naud* calls for the exchange of oldest for oldest. We will have your son Abelaard come forth."

A disembodied laugh echoed through the chasm as Laca received the same news. Daeghrefn clenched his teeth. Abelaard? he thought. This is ludicrous! I didn't agree to this.

Cerestes motioned for Abelaard to dismount and follow him.

"Hold!" Daeghrefn shouted. "There will be no exchange of oldest for oldest! Let Laca laugh, and let him die beneath Nerakan boots. It wasn't my castle that the hordes beseiged."

Cerestes turned. He spoke in hushed tones that melded with the tireless wind. "You cannot refuse now, Lord Daeghrefn. To end a *gebo-naud* once begun is an act of war."

Daeghrefn's face darkened, his eyes sparkling, inscrutable. He could defeat Laca in war, he was fairly certain of that—perhaps even hold at bay the Nerakan hordes while he did so.

As though listening to his lord's thoughts, the golden-eyed mage offered in conspiratory whispers, "You would more easily defeat Laca in alliance than in war, my Lord."

"You won't let Abelaard go!" Verminaard protested suddenly.

"Silence," the dark man growled, drawing tightly, reflexively, on his mount's reins. Daeghrefn lifted his head defiantly and whispered something through his bared teeth.

Only Robert heard him.

Flashing an iron-hard glare toward Abelaard, the Lord of Nidus spoke. "Go." He gestured broadly toward the awaiting mage, who extended a hand to the boy. With stone-hard features, the boy stepped from his mount and, sparing not a glance at his father, followed the mage.

In moments, the first words of the *gebo-naud* filtered to them in the midst of a shifting autumn breeze. The mage Cerestes lifted his hands, and a dark cloud pooled in the bottom of the gorge below. A hundred lights floated on its surface, until the cloud swirled and eddied and glittered like quicksilver.

"Let the mountains know," the mage began. "Let all assembled here—the garrisoned captains of East Borders and those of Castle Nidus—swear on their swords that they see what they see, and let them honor the change and surety of blood between these houses.

"Let the traded sons, Aglaca of East Borders and Abelaard of Nidus, find shelter and board, honor and comfort in their opposite homes.

"Let alliance rise from the commingling of houses.

"And if ill befall one lad, let the same ill befall the other.

"It is an oath secured by rock and air, by the bridge across the gap of the world."

Daeghrefn shifted in the saddle. These terms, at least, were the way he reckoned them.

Then the mage began the chant that would seal the bargain, would exchange one lad for the other in unsteady alliance.

> "Son to son and truce to truth,
> Peace for blood and youth for youth,
> In high passages of stone
> The heart returns to claim its own."

The Solamnic boy moved forward to exchange places with Abelaard. For a moment, he wavered in his balance and looked down, light hair and light robe caught in a sudden gust of wind. The black cloud Cerestes had summoned rose now beneath the bridge, and tendrils of vapor wrapped about the boy's ankles, threatening to pull him down into the abyss.

He is frozen up there, Verminaard thought. Perhaps he won't do it.

Then the boy gathered himself and continued, urged on by his father. Cerestes spoke the second verse as the lads joined hands over the swirling mist.

> "Let the words pass overhead,
> Heard by the memorious dead,
> Confirming what hearts have begun,
> Truce for truth and son for son."

Verminaard shuddered as the power of the words coursed over him, binding him as they did his father, his brother, and the pale Solamnics. This Aglaca was his brother now, his blood by oath until the Nerakans were subdued.

He was sure he would not like the boy.

Suddenly Verminaard felt dizzy. His sight flickered, failed him, and he weaved on his wobbly legs. In front of him, the bridge seemed to vanish, and with it the ceremony—the boys and the black-robed celebrant.

All Verminaard could see was darkness and a wavering point of light at the furthermost edge of the gloom. Slowly the light expanded, and he saw a blond youth on a dark, windy battlement, a lithe, blue-eyed, older image of himself.

Not me, he thought. A twin . . . my mirror image.

Not Abelaard, but still my brother.

The young man in the vision gestured toward him. His lips moved desperately in a soundless incantation, and Verminaard felt weaker, felt power drain from him. . . .

And then the vision ended in cold sunset and the high, thin air of the mountains. Cerestes lifted his hands from the lads at the center of the bridge, and black lightning danced across his arms.

What has happened? Verminaard asked himself, his thoughts a confusing swirl. Desperately he sought the Voice—its advice, its melodious assurances.

Only silence.

Shaken, Verminaard looked about. All eyes were trained on the arch of the bridge. He breathed another prayer to any listening god and turned back toward Cerestes.

From that point on, the ceremony was a ritual of its own silence. The boys turned, faced each other, and removed the ornamental tabards that covered their tunics. Solemnly they exchanged the thin garments, Aglaca wobbling again for a brief, nightmarish moment. Then slowly, almost reverently, each lad undertook to put on the other's tabard.

Verminaard smiled a bit then. Abelaard was at least four years older than the Solamnic boy and hardened by the hunt and the mountain climates. Aglaca's tabard was much too small for him, so after a brief, halfhearted attempt, he draped the garment over his shoulder and began to walk toward the Solamnic column on the western side of the gorge.

Laca's knights opened their ranks in a silent welcome.

It was now Aglaca's turn. Lost in the red folds of Abelaard's tabard, the boy waded carefully across the bridge, the garment trailing on the stones so that he looked like a gnomish enchanter, like an alchemist whose concoctions had backfired. A sharp wind buffeted him, and he drew his hood closer.

Steadily now, his steps gaining assurance the closer he came, Aglaca approached Daeghrefn on the narrow span. Behind him, Cerestes performed the last of the ceremonial rites. Breathing a prayer to Hiddukel, the old god of deals and transactions, the mage knelt and drew an obscure sign with his finger.

Verminaard peered from his place, straining to see. This mage had great power, he could tell. But Cerestes was too far from him, the gestures too veiled and intricate to see clearly. The clouds in the gorge rose to cover the mage, and for a moment, he seemed larger, darker in the thickening mist.

You could do such things as well, Lord Verminaard, the Voice soothed and tempted. *Raise clouds and magnify and bring down the bridling dark. You could rival the great spellmasters, Lord Verminaard, and write your name in the gray, metallic swirl of fog and dangerous rumor. . . .*

Verminaard listened and, bathed in dark suggestions, felt almost comforted, even though Abelaard was gone.

From out of the mist, Aglaca approached, the mage emerging from the cloud behind him, slender and stooped, diminished from the monstrous shadow he had cast at the end of the ceremony. But Cerestes was strangely unwearied, his gold eyes glittering like the metallic swirl he had conjured from the depths.

It was all Verminaard could do to draw his eyes away from the mage, to rest his gaze on the Solamnic hostage.

"M'Lord Aglaca," Cerestes announced. "May I present your . . . host, Lord Daeghrefn of Nidus."

The boy bowed politely, and Daeghrefn extended his hand.

"May your presence remind us . . . of one who is away,"

Lord Nidus announced, his voice thick with emotion, "and of the alliance his bravery affirms."

"I shall endeavor to be worthy of your honor and graciousness," Aglaca replied and turned to greet Verminaard.

"And you," he said, brushing back his hood, "will be my new brother in the war to come, alliance of my alliance."

Dumbstruck, Verminaard gazed into the face of the Solamnic boy. It was a revelation—the pale eyes, the thin nose, the white-blond hair and brow. It was his own face, his mirror image.

Somewhere deep in the mountains—whether from west or east, they could not tell for the echoes—the oracles of Godshome began to murmur and hum, and the druidess L'Indasha Yman looked up from her icy augury and nodded.

Chapter 3

"I shall . . . study your friendship as well, Master Verminaard," Aglaca declared politely, eyeing the other boy with cautious curiosity. He shifted from foot to foot, awaiting the courtly reply, the Solamnic greeting that traditionally followed an offer of service and goodwill.

Verminaard said nothing.

His young face was unreadable, like hard mountain stone obscured by mist and distance. Despite Robert's nudgings and coaxings, he refused to speak to the guest. He held his silence even as Daeghrefn's party returned on the high, snaking road east from the Jelek Pass, to where Castle Nidus awaited them.

Along the way, Aglaca reasoned with himself. Daeghrefn's family did not do things like his own. There was no Measure, little ceremony. Perhaps it was what his father had said—that the garrison of Nidus was half-barbaric, little better than the Nerakans. Or perhaps Verminaard mourned his brother. He could understand that. Aglaca wished he, too, were home again, with his friends and his dogs, wished that this new and forbidding duty had not befallen him.

Then there was the vision that had come to Aglaca on the Bridge of Dreed—the pale, muscular young man . . . the mace descending.

So it will be, unless you take this matter in your own hands, Aglaca Dragonbane, coaxed the Voice, low and seductive, neither man nor woman.

It came to him as always, with murky promises and dire threats. As always, he ignored its urgings.

But he did speculate until the last hour of the night, after the long dinner that was his uncomfortable welcome to the East, to the Khalkist Mountains, and to his new family.

* * * * *

Daeghrefn was the first to be seated, as was his custom. Ignoring his standing guests—the small party of family, servants, and courtiers—the knight slumped into the huge oaken chair at the head of the table. He was distracted by the flicker of the fire in the hearth, the rustle of pigeons in the cobwebbed rafters of the hall.

It was a shabby chamber indeed—dusty and disorderly, inclined toward ruin. The Lord of Nidus had only a small staff of servants, and attended more to his falcons and wine than he did to the upkeep of house and grounds.

The wine, poured by the steward into a faceted crystal goblet, was a vintage from a dozen summers past. The

goblet was the last of ten, a wedding gift to Daeghrefn
from Lord Gunthar Uth Wistan, its nine mates broken in
neglect over the twelve years since the death of Daeghrefn's wife. Last of a line it was, and when the knight
lifted it and the light glanced off its facets and sparkled
through the amber wine, Daeghrefn remembered a night
more than a dozen years earlier—a night of fires and wine
and a hundred reflecting facets. . . .

* * * * *

It was bad almost from the start. The smell of a blizzard in
the foothills, and cold daunting all but the hardiest travelers. Laca's wife, a bit further along than Daeghrefn's, was
in her quarters, attended by midwives and physicians as
the awaited day drew nigh. Daeghrefn had been glad of
the extended visit, of Laca's warm guest hall, of reunions
with his old friend after seven months' absence, and of the
eager anticipation with which both men awaited the
births of their children, most especially Laca's first.

Over dinner, with the wine abundant and the conversation ranging, Daeghrefn had almost forgotten the unsettling weather and wind and the strange disruptions
among the castle servants.

Four-year-old Abelaard was sprawled over the knee of
the man he called "Uncle Laca." Daeghrefn's wife was
reserved and quiet as usual around the outgoing Solamnics, and she was heavy with his own child—the second-
born, whom he intended to raise toward Paladine's
clergy. After a few cups, the words had come forth idly—
Laca's speculation that in some families hair and eyes
"turned sport," that despite Daeghrefn's dark coloring
and the night-black eyes of his wife, the child she was
carrying could be "as fair as . . . a thanoi hunter . . . a high
elf. . . .

"As fair as Laca himself."

Daeghrefn had laughed and pointed at Abelaard's dark hair and brown eyes. "I suppose that is 'turning sport,' " he joked, and Abelaard looked up at him curiously, his face a clear reflection of his father's.

But Laca kept with the issue, spoke of blondes and of fair eyes and of *sport* and *sport* until the wine and the turning of thoughts brought Daeghrefn to the one conclusion that the sly, teasing words could mask no longer.

"What are you saying, Laca?" he had asked finally, quietly, full knowing that the knight could give him no real answer.

"'Tis only a talk of generations," Laca murmured, his pale gaze and crooked smile flickering toward Daeghrefn's terrified wife.

Daeghrefn stood, overturning his chair, his wineglass. The golden wine spilled generously over the table, onto the woman and Laca, and a servant rushed for water and cloth. Laca stood as well, more slowly, his hands extended, a look of puzzlement on his face.

"What have you made of . . . my idle talk, Lord Daeghrefn?" Laca asked, but Daeghrefn listened to no denial, no reasoning, asking the question again and again as he drew sword.

"What are you saying, Laca?"

Laca's retainers then burst into the room—summoned, no doubt, by the retreating servant. A sea of unyielding Solamnic Knights stepped between the friends turned adversaries. Daeghrefn waved his sword helplessly over a burly fellow in full armor, as the tide of retainers pushed him farther and farther from the man who had wronged him, who had implied . . . no, who had *boasted* of his deed, now that he thought again of it.

Daeghrefn had looked to his wife then. Her head was bowed, and the pallor of her face told him that what Laca had admitted, had *proclaimed* to all present—including little Abelaard—was the truth.

The snow had been blinding, Daeghrefn remembered, and the guards at the gate of Laca's keep pleaded with him to stay, to take light and shelter. But he would accept no comfort from a false friend. After all, the infidelities of seven months past must have taken place at Nidus, in the heart of Daeghrefn's true hospitality. Under his protecting roof. Perhaps in his own chamber. He now remembered that Laca had declined the hunt one morning, saying he must be about his devotions.

Indeed.

In a frenzy of righteous anger, he herded his family from Laca's castle. It was the outcome of too much trust in friends, too much faith in the Oath.

Daeghrefn scorned the five days' path they had followed around the Khalkists. He chose instead a shortcut, which, even in clear weather, was a hard day's climb right through the mountains. But now it was obscured by snow and his own blinding rage. Gradually the steps of his wife grew slower, and she stumbled. Abelaard, only four, still duped by his mother's lies and wiles, stopped to help her. And the three of them straggled over the rocky road to Nidus into a new blizzard.

He would have guided them home that very last night. Perhaps the woman would have fallen in the mountains, even within sight of the castle walls, but she had been doomed anyway—doomed seven months before by the feverish promptings of her blood. Had the druidess not come, there would soon have been but two of them—Abelaard and himself—and there would have been no reminder of that betrayal.

None but this faceted glass he turned in his hand.

Daeghrefn shook his head, swallowed more wine, and plunged back into the memories.

Verminaard had always been underfoot, at the edge of sight, where his presence was a mocking reminder of that distant spring, the harsh revelations of that distant winter night. Only for Abelaard's sake had he tolerated the bastard at all. For Abelaard, and for a strange goading at the borders of his thought—some reason he could not put words around. But he knew that to injure the child or to abandon him would bring down fearful consequences.

Indeed, Verminaard had been such a thorn to Daeghrefn, such a torment and mockery. The *gebo-naud* seemed a just reprieve from his twelve years with the boy. With the Nerakans in the mountains forcing an alliance with his old enemy, he saw the *gebo-naud* as he wished to see it. *Son for son* meant he could give Verminaard to the Solamnics in exchange for Aglaca, sealing the alliance, ridding himself of Verminaard, and sending the boy back where he belonged, all in one thrifty gesture. And Abelaard would have understood. Eventually.

But the chance for that was past, the *gebo-naud* over and Daeghrefn's only son taken in the exchange. Daeghrefn's anger had not subsided. He thought of his own son, of Abelaard encamped somewhere in the western distances, and slammed the table with his fist. It shook the crystal and crockery; the faceted glass that had sparked his memory teetered precariously on the table's edge. Robert, rising from his venison long enough to notice, snatched the delicate object before it tumbled, then set it, almost reverently, beside his master's open hand.

"The druidess," Daeghrefn muttered absently, glaring at the flames. "What did she say? *What?*"

Robert blanched as he steadied the cup. He recalled the druidess as well—when the Lord of Nidus had returned with Abelaard and the infant, he sent Robert himself away into the mountains.

He could not do what Daeghrefn had asked. He found the druidess crouched among the evergreens, shaking the weight of snow from their branches. Her green robe and auburn hair shone against the faceless white of the drifts. She was lovely, a candle of warmth in the cold dusk.

He had slipped from behind the rock, sheathing his weapon even as he turned away. But she had seen him, had known he was there all along. She called him back, and they spoke briefly, their words falling amid wary silences. His heart had melted within him.

For the first time ever, Robert had disobeyed his lord. And though the druidess had promised her silence, had assured him that none other in Daeghrefn's service would see her again, he thought of her uneasily when the subject of druidry arose in the hall, or when the snow lay heavy on the juniper and blue aeterna.

Wide-eyed, pressing heavily against the back of his chair, Aglaca watched the pale seneschal steady the glass. It was like the jaws of Hiddukel, this dining hall—each man at the table doomed and damned, trapped in his own fears and gloomy thoughts. No one else seemed to notice Daeghrefn's outburst, and eyes and faces bent into the candlelight, to the bread and cheese and old venison, as fervently as if there were nothing else to eat in the castle.

His father had told him to be brave, that the war with Neraka would last but a matter of months. But he was only twelve, and the promised time in Nidus stretched before him like an eternal desert.

What would come of him here?

He whispered a prayer to Paladine over his untouched food. The childlike words were almost audible above the clatter of cutlery, the gurgle of pigeons in the eaves.

Cerestes did not hear the boy praying, but his fingers burned sharply at the words, and the knife shook in his long, pale hand.

Difficult. Aglaca would be difficult, with his Solamnic training and his mooning over Paladine and Huma and Kiri-Jolith.

The other one was a different matter. Verminaard had been lodged in these deep mountains, motherless and virtually tutorless, his father lapsed from the Order and no longer a believer in Oath and Measure—or even the gods themselves.

And yet the easy one was not always preferable. The Lady had taught him as much. Better to wait and watch and bide his time. Speratus's "unfortunate" fall and Aglaca's arrival had given Cerestes all the time he would need.

He leaned back in the chair, savoring the golden wine. Tilting the glass, he peered through the crystal toward the boy Verminaard, who stared back at him, his expression lost in the wavering candles and distortions of the wine.

But Verminaard, as he always did when someone new entered the fortress, was sizing the company, following the elaborate dance of eye and gesture with the hope that something would be revealed, some secret emerge from a sidelong glance, a subtle tilt of the hand.

He had learned this caution long ago in Daeghrefn's castle, where the violent, almost explosive moods of the knight were as unpredictable as the mountain weather. The angered Daeghrefn was a force to be skirted— avoided entirely, if he could manage it. There were alcoves in the halls where Verminaard could step aside from the dark processions of armor and torches and glowering stares; there was Robert's lodgings, as well, where a certain shelter could be found among the old seneschal's neatly arranged battle trophies, where the room smelled of oiled leather and fruity wine. But mostly the boy had learned the augury of instinct—that sometimes, in the instant before a voice rose or a hand descended, something undefinable in his father's face would either emerge or go away. It was his sense of this that had preserved him from Daeghrefn's enraged beatings and deprivations.

Verminaard had felt the outburst approach like the gathering of the mountains before an avalanche, when sound at the timberline rises beyond hearing until it is sensed only at the edge of the bones. When Daeghrefn had struck the table, Verminaard was already steeled, watching the others closely, learning the new terrain.

It was the boy, the Solamnic, who bore the most notice. Though the knightly training masked his fear, fear was there nevertheless. The pale eyes had widened just barely; the faint smell of salt sharpened the air.

Oh, yes, Aglaca was afraid. And Verminaard made note of that, for in a castle where uncertainty was the master, fear was the coin of the realm.

Verminaard glanced with great care at his father, and then at Aglaca again. From the slightest rise of the new boy's shoulder, Verminaard knew he still had not unclenched his right fist.

* * * * *

Dinner ended abruptly when Daeghrefn rose from the table and stalked to the hearth, empty wineglass clutched in his battle-scarred hand. He slumped into a low, straight-backed mahogany chair. The dogs skulked away, from him and the pigeons in the rafters fell quiet.

It was Robert's cue to stand up, to lead Aglaca up the stairs to his new lodgings. Verminaard's heart rose with them as the old man guided the noble hostage toward bed, for the stairway they chose led to only one suite of rooms, high in the western tower of the castle.

To Verminaard's room. If Father had decided to move Aglaca into Verminaard's quarters, Abelaard's rooms, now empty, would fall to Verminaard by right.

The room is yours! the Voice coaxed, singing in a dark minor melody, rising from nowhere, as though the table itself were talking. *Yours now by right as the eldest. Did I not tell you? Ask him; ask him. . . .*

It was a small triumph, Verminaard knew. He did not understand why he was so delighted, why his eyes blurred and brightened and his hand shook as he thought of the prospect.

He looked for the mage, but Cerestes was gone from the room—vanished suddenly, as though he had melted silently through a portal in the air. Only Verminaard and his father remained in the dining hall.

Daeghrefn stared into the dwindling fire.

For a moment, Verminaard hesitated, clutching the back of his chair unsteadily as he rose from the table. Slowly, more for delay than for tidiness, he straightened his plate and cutlery, then snuffed the pale candle that guttered beside his cup. The first step toward his father seemed as if he were wading through waist-deep snow, but the second was easier, and soon, almost suddenly, he stood beside the hearth.

"Father?" he asked, and slowly, with an old resentment, Daeghrefn's dark eyes rose from the fire to stare somewhere beyond Verminaard's face. Then, his gaze unwavering, the knight hurled the glittering, faceted goblet into the dying fire.

The rafters erupted with the rustle of wing beats, with the frightened cries of birds. Verminaard winced as slivers of glass knifed through his leggings into his ankles. He shifted in fright, in pain, blood pointing the tattered cloth on his shins.

"What?" Daeghrefn asked with quiet menace, and it seemed as though the fire in front of them gasped and guttered and dimmed further, until the room contracted to a wavering circle of light. For the first time in hours, Daeghrefn had spoken to his second son.

"Th—the room, sir," Verminaard began, and daunted by his own stuttering, fell into silence.

" 'Room'?" Daeghrefn's voice was flat and repellent.

Verminaard backed against the mantle, steadied himself. His ankles stung and nettled. He broke into a sudden, dizzying sweat, and his voice failed him once, twice, before he could summon the words.

"Abelaard's room, sir. I . . . I believe that since Aglaca . . . "

Daeghrefn loomed even taller in the chair, the dim light of the fire magnifying him, casting his gigantic shadow on the far wall.

"I know what you're after," the knight said. "And you will sleep and quarter where you have always slept and quartered. Abelaard is gone, and his rooms will await his return."

* * * * *

He took the steps two at a time, his ankles bloody and swelling, each stride a stinging rebuke to his courage. At his back, the Voice was chiding him, soft and insinuating, speaking from the terrible dark at the bottom of the stairwell.

So it is and will be in this devouring country, where the raptor dives and the panther stalks. . . . What did you expect from him, beyond this powerless mourning? Learn from me . . . from the panther and the raptor. . . .

He stopped on the stairs, his thoughts whirling. A great anger rose in him, and he struck the stone wall of the landing fiercely, methodically. His fist stung with the impacts, and he fought down a sudden rush of tears. He thought of Daeghrefn as he battered the wall. Of the cold dark eyes and the shattered cup.

It would not do. You could not feel that way about your father.

Slowly, almost staggering with his own uprooted anger, Verminaard mounted the last of the stairs, cursing the stones and the dark and the stars in the clerestory windows. He reached the landing and opened the door to his quarters.

Aglaca sat on the topmost bunk, leaning out the window. For a moment Verminaard's thoughts were violent, and the voice of his imaginings blurred with the voice on the stairs . . .

If something happened to Aglaca, his father would have no choice but to follow the rules of the gebo-naud. *So whatever happened to the boy . . . would happen to Abelaard. . . .*

And then Daeghrefn would mourn.

Verminaard caught himself, frightened by the largeness and power of his own speculations. He stared balefully at Aglaca, who looked back at him with curiosity and concern.

"Don't think that my possessions are yours as well," Verminaard menaced, rising to his full height, trying his best to obscure the doorway behind him. "You're an outsider here. Nobody wants you; you're here for the deal, and for that reason only. My brother is gone."

He took a long step toward Aglaca, who glanced out the window and then calmly returned a level stare to this new antagonist.

"If you remember one thing, Solamnic," Verminaard continued, standing in the center of the room now, clutching the back of his single chair as though Aglaca intended to take that from him as well, "remember this. You are a hostage in my presence. You are not my guest."

"He yelled at you, didn't he?" Aglaca asked, quietly and not without warmth. "I mean, Daeghrefn . . . "

"That is no concern of yours, Solamnic," Verminaard replied unsteadily, his stare wavering, his fingers nervously drumming the chair back. "I said you are a hostage. . . ."

"I know," Aglaca said. "I am an outsider here. So you've told me. I can't take Abelaard's place, Verminaard. But I can be your friend."

Verminaard stepped back to the door and closed it. Something was quenched in him by the boy's unexpected kindness. His hand smarted, and he turned uncertainly toward the bunk and the boy who sat atop it, regarding him curiously.

"Then . . . you won't take or touch anything that is mine?"

"I won't, Verminaard."

"Swear," Verminaard insisted, extending his hand and searching Aglaca's eyes.

Aglaca met both his grasp and his gaze. "I swear. We're bound together, Verminaard. The *gebo-naud* binds us as firmly as it binds our fathers. And we're bound by more, I believe. I know it, and you do, too."

Verminaard looked away in confusion, in irritation. He remembered the young man in the vision—the gesture, the soundless chant, the draining. . . .

He looked again at Aglaca in horror.

It's you! he thought.

But instead of visions and deceptive magic, the boy held forth a knife, hilt first, offering it to Verminaard. He took the jeweled hilt and examined the blade.

"It's yours," Aglaca declared. "As a sign of my trust."

"It's . . . it's *wonderful!*" Verminaard exclaimed. His eyes narrowed. "And what do you want?"

"It's yours," Aglaca declared. "I want nothing for it."

Verminaard danced gleefully across the floor of the chamber, waving the dagger like a sword, lunging at imagined enemies.

"It's not just a dagger, Verminaard!" the Solamnic boy protested. "It's a rune rister's knife. My father gave it to me. His mage said it would protect the wielder against all evil."

Verminaard lunged at the fireplace, whipped the blade through the chilly air. He wasn't listening.

"I know it isn't Huma's lance," Aglaca objected. "It's a small thing, and its magic is small as well. But it isn't a toy. It's . . . it's . . . "

"It's a fine knife," Verminaard said. He glanced at Aglaca cautiously. "Thank you," he said abruptly.

Aglaca smiled. "Now come over and look out the window. If you lean just a little and peer as far as you can down toward the west . . . what's that pass called?"

"Eira Goch. It means 'red snow' in the old tongue."

"Really?" Aglaca asked, extending his hand once more. "Well, if you look down to the mouth of that pass, you can see my father's campfires. Let me give you a hand up to the top bunk."

Verminaard regarded the other boy warily. It was the first time he remembered anyone except Abelaard reaching out to him. But, despite strong misgiving, he took the offered grasp. For a moment, before he hoisted himself onto the bunk, risking a fall and his dignity to the questionable intentions of this hostage, he tested the boy's strength, pulling Aglaca toward the edge of the bed.

Aglaca gritted his teeth and braced himself, recovering only when he dangled dangerously above the larger lad, who pushed him back onto the bed.

Good, Verminaard thought. I am stronger.

Then, with a deep breath, he climbed onto the top bunk, boosted by his new companion. Together they stared out the window into the uninterrupted darkness and saw the faraway gleam of torchlight. Verminaard did most of the talking, explaining to Aglaca the landmarks visible from the heights of Castle Nidus.

Fifty feet below and across the castle yard, in the shadows of the eastern battlements, the dark mage Cerestes leaned toward the ancient walls and placed his ear against the stones. There the words of the boys—innocent words, but words they believed to be unnoticed and unheard—tunneled through mortar, through rock, and by a devious magic, into the dark chambers of Cerestes' mind.

Chapter 4

It would be the first hunt of a cold, difficult spring, and the first centi-core hunt for either lad. Ancient custom had ordained, since both Verminaard and Aglaca had turned twenty in the snows of the previous winter, they must both hunt this spring. Yoked together by age, education, and rivalry, the two had passed from boyhood to the edge of manhood—to the time of testing in the wilds.

Since Aglaca's arrival at Castle Nidus, Verminaard felt he had come to know him well. Their eight years together had bound them, though the bonds were neither warm nor comfortable. Neither lad thought now of friendship: They had realized that possibility had come and gone even before they met. After all, Verminaard was too cautious and suspicious for friendship, especially with someone whose presence reminded him constantly of his absent brother Abelaard. And Aglaca was a hostage, all but imprisoned, quartered in Castle Nidus against his wishes. But the lads had become well acquainted, like weathered, familiar rivals in the shaky truce of the *gebonaud*, and with that acquaintance, outright hostility had become as difficult as friendship.

During long hours of instruction, when Verminaard sat on his stool in the northwest tower and nodded at Cerestes' lectures on spellcraft and alchemy, he had seen out the window where Aglaca wandered through the gardens north of the walls. The gardens were still immaculate despite the ten years' absence of Mort, the gardener who had left this spot when Daeghrefn's temper turned. In this sanctuary, Aglaca would stoop to examine a sprig of cedar, to smell a flower, then vanish altogether behind a blue stand of evergreens.

Why, the boy is only a gardener at heart, Verminaard thought scornfully. A floral fool.

And Verminaard would return to his lessons, delighted when the smoke rose from the palm of his hand, or when a brief, clumsy incantation drew water from the dark wall of the castle.

He did not realize that, from the gardens, Aglaca had also glimpsed his hulking shadow at the window of the tower. Nor did he suspect that Aglaca knew of his secret envy, the envy any prisoner of scholarship feels toward those who are free. Whenever Verminaard watched, Aglaca ducked behind the big stand of aeterna to practice his other studies. There he would mimic the movements of the mantis, standing with his arms poised above him in a grotesque, almost silly position, then bringing his hands down suddenly, repeatedly, tirelessly, in deadly accurate blows.

The months passed, and his reflexes quickened.

Once the mantis had taught him speed, he picked up

the sword he had hidden amid the blue-needled branches. And in what remained of Verminaard's mother's rose garden, he would wheel and dance, his feet stepping lightly and harmlessly between the roses, his deft hands whirling the sword above his head. Then suddenly, violently, as though taught by nature and blood for a thousand years, he would bring the blade whistling down to the tip of a rose petal. The metal edge would shear in precise halves an iridescent, predatory beetle, but leave the blossom intact, untouched even by the wind from the blade.

Verminaard never saw Aglaca's private schooling, but the Solamnic lad did not go unobserved. Under orders from Daeghrefn, the seneschal Robert would watch from behind a blue topiary, marveling as the youth grew in wisdom and stature and grace.

Nor did Aglaca always study alone. Since a month after he took up residence in Castle Nidus, a cloaked woman would meet him in the garden's seclusion. There she taught him herb lore, self-defense, and a muted, rudimentary magic. Robert would crane through the blue branches to overhear the both of them, and the woman's voice, tantalizing at the edge of hearing, charmed him with its music and lilt.

And its familiarity. The seneschal had heard that music before. On one sunlit day in midspring, the woman had turned toward him, looked right at him through the network of branches . . . Auburn-haired and tall and dark-eyed. He remembered the face at once.

L'Indasha Yman smiled and winked at Robert.

For a week afterward, the seneschal slept fitfully. The druidess was somehow spiriting herself onto castle grounds, and he wondered if she were treacherous enough to betray him or reckless enough to risk her life and his by these visits in broad daylight. Yet daily he saw her, and there was yet no alarm from the keep, no midnight summons from the Lord of Nidus.

Robert breathed more easily, until the day he saw Daeghrefn himself in the garden.

Aglaca and L'Indasha were bowed over a rose, and the druidess was lecturing the Solamnic youth about Mort the gardener. He was a sturdy, warmhearted man from Estwilde who had weathered the surliness of Daeghrefn while planting lilies and roses throughout the keep. But in Verminaard's second year, the patience of the gardener had vanished, and soon afterward Mort himself had disappeared.

But not before he had planted ten thousand sunflowers, which sprouted and bloomed both in and out of season, rising overnight everywhere from the bailey to the midden, taunting the brooding Daeghrefn with their bright, outrageous colors.

"He was a prankster, Mort the gardener," L'Indasha whispered with a chuckle. "Had some magic and a wondrous sense of humor. I miss him terribly."

Aglaca smiled, but at that moment, Daeghrefn walked into the garden. Robert had not seen him coming, and the seneschal held his breath as the Lord of Nidus halted beside the druidess and the lad.

"What are you laughing at, Aglaca?" Daeghrefn asked, and the boy looked up at him calmly. The druidess stood, brushed the dirt from her robes, and stepped back into the topiary.

It was then plain to Robert that L'Indasha was invisible to Daeghrefn. The druidess looked straight at the seneschal and winked and smiled in an odd conspiracy.

Robert's sleep was troubled no longer by fear of disclosure.

And so both lads received different instruction, different comings of age. Verminaard learned by the book, by mages, by laborious study. His companion—his hostage—learned by invisible druidry and a silent and natural grace. Their schoolings taught them of their many differences, but nothing of common ground.

* * * * *

On the morning of the hunt, at the windswept gate of Castle Nidus, Verminaard served in a place of honor. He assisted Cerestes the mage in the ritual. According to ancient tradition, the likeness of the centicore was drawn upon the thick wooden gate with madder root and woad, the red and blue lines swirling in an intricate pattern that drew and focused the gaze of the hunter into the painted image.

It was said that in the Age of Light, the artists drew the prey—centicore, wyvern, perhaps even dragons themselves—in a fashion so lifelike that the paintings had shrieked when the spears entered them.

Verminaard himself held the brushes for Cerestes as the mage painted the first and boldest designs. The young man chanted the old words along with his mentor. When the hunters lined up to cast spears at the effigy, the mage handed Verminaard the cherished third spear, which followed after Daeghrefn and Robert had cast their weapons.

It had been perfect—the ceremony, the intoned words from the black-robed mage, Verminaard's own spear finding the heart of the whirling red and blue. Verminaard stood back proudly, breathing a prayer to the Queen of Darkness, as Cerestes had taught him. Meanwhile, the rest of the hunters, fifty in all, each offered his spear to the image, each with a shout, a boast, a prayer, as the hunt assembled and the grooms readied the horses.

. . . all perfect until Aglaca refused to join.

The smug Solamnic had declined, claiming Paladine governed his spear, and Mishakal, and Branchala—the old gods of creation and reconciliation and inspiration. He would not do this, he said, and then said no more.

But Verminaard did not let this high-handedness spoil the day—*his* day. Had not his spear alone found the heart of the painted beast? One last confirmation of his trophy kill was all he needed.

Daeghrefn stood by his horse, preoccupied with saddle and gear, with securing the arsons that would brace him in the saddle if he used his lance. Lost in his own calculations, he was no more interested in Aglaca's refusal than he had been in the ritual itself. When the last man had hurled his spear, the Lord of Nidus was already mounted. He had ignored the painting, the incantation, the fellowship of the casting. He had fulfilled his own role in the ritual solely because the men expected it.

Verminaard knelt by the horses and cast the Amarach, the rune stones. The runes today were cloudy in the reading, as they often were. The Giant. The Chariot. Hail. Something about breaking resistance, the path of power, destruction . . . though he couldn't piece it together.

But the runes were prophetic surely, despite Cerestes' laughter when his promising student spoke of their power. For the stones were ancient and venerated, were they not? Only his skills were lacking. His father's words, soft at the edge of his revery, confirmed for Verminaard that all he believed of rune and augury was true.

"Verminaard will ride at the head of the hunt," Daeghrefn announced, rising in the stirrups and shielding his eyes as he gazed north across the plain. He scanned the horizon to the distant lift of the mountains, where the cloud descended and all paths led across Taman Busuk to the mystical, uncharted heart of the Khalkists. "He will ride at the point of Nidus's spear, and he will ride alone."

That was all. With a sullen silence, his gaze averted, the Lord of Nidus fell in beside Robert.

A fierce joy gripped Verminaard. Fumbling the runes to a pouch at his belt, he vaulted into the saddle. The boar lance shivered and vibrated in its rest beside his right knee, and he clutched it eagerly.

Daeghrefn had noticed! He was sure of it. This place at the vanguard was a sign of esteem, of Daeghrefn's respect for his bravery and wits.

Not a season past his twentieth birthday, and he would ride at the front of a veteran army.

* * * * *

Aglaca, on the other hand, had often heard his father's tales of the centicore hunt. The creature was deadly, surprisingly cunning. It led hunters an exhausting chase and then turned and charged when the lancers had outpaced the hunting party, when the odds were narrowed to one or two tired hunters against a huge, well-armored monster. At East Borders, whatever man rode in the vanguard on a centicore hunt did so only after bequeathing his belongings to family and friends, saying the Nine Prayers to Paladine and Mishakal and Kiri-Jolith of the hunt, and singing over himself the time-honored Solamnic funeral song.

Aglaca's eyes narrowed as he watched the jubilant Verminaard tying himself to the saddle, bracing his back, trying to hide a boyish grin beneath a mask of feigned calm. Daeghrefn knew better than this: He was a skilled huntsman and swordsman, and though a renegade, he had not forgotten his Solamnic training in strategy and field command.

Of all people, Daeghrefn would know . . .

And he did know. Of course he did.

"I beg your pardon, sir," the Solamnic youth ventured. He set his foot to the stirrup of a horse readied for him as Daeghrefn turned in the saddle to regard him distantly, indifferently. "I would that you might . . . let me ride with Verminaard."

Robert looked nervously at his lord.

It *had* to work, Aglaca thought. Regardless of this strange disregard for his son, Daeghrefn would not risk Aglaca in a foolish gamble. Were Laca to receive word that his son had fallen in the hunt, Abelaard's life would be forfeit to the *gebo-naud*.

Aglaca was the best protection Verminaard could have.

Daeghrefn did not flinch at the boy's request. Directly, his face unreadable, he regarded the upstart as though appraising terrain or a suit of tournament armor.

"Do not forget, Master Aglaca," the Lord of Nidus replied, his scolding mild and quiet, "that you are not as much a *guest* in our midst as you are . . . *captive* to an agreement between Nidus and East Borders. I cannot let you ride in the vanguard, for you might use the occasion to escape. Worse still, you might suffer an injury."

"I am twenty, sir," Aglaca persisted. "Twenty, and skilled with weaponry you, in your kindness, have allowed me to practice."

"True enough," Daeghrefn conceded. "Better than your burly lump of a companion, by all accounts."

Verminaard winced, but his face returned swiftly to its impassive, unreadable mask.

"As for your misgivings regarding escape, Lord Daeghrefn . . . " Aglaca continued. "If I gave you my word, sir? As the son of a Solamnic Knight?"

Daeghrefn sneered. "You could not imagine how little such promises mean to me, boy. But if you *must* ride at the point, Osman rides with you, and a squadron of twelve men. In case the call of East Borders becomes too strong."

Aglaca hid a satisfied smile. The game was his for now. Daeghrefn had conceded on the fear that spies, who he suspected were constantly in his garrison, might relay Aglaca's disappointment to his father. Had Verminaard alone been placed in the vanguard, no escort would accompany him. By riding at the front of the column,

Aglaca had assured Verminaard's protection: Osman was a veteran huntsman and a loyal sort, and his dozen troopers would protect them both.

* * * * *

As the young men and their escort rode forth at the head of the hunt, the castle and its settlement dwindled to a scattering of tents and standards in the southern fields. Cerestes raised his hands in the Litany of Farewells. Then a red mist rose about him, and he vanished in a flurry of faded banners and fragmented light. Back to Castle Nidus, they supposed.

Taciturn, windburnt Osman rode between the two young men, his face as dark as weathered oak. His eyes, black and brilliant, scanned the terrain for spoor and hoofprints.

Verminaard, at the huntsman's right, fumed and crouched in the saddle as though he rode into a powerful, icy head wind. He had been betrayed by this soft western lad who rode to Osman's left—faithless Aglaca, who had refused the comradeship of the casting, then demanded the glory of the hunt.

His hunt—his place of honor, his chance to be noble and courageous, to distinguish himself before Daeghrefn. Aglaca and these nursemaids! They didn't belong here beside him. For a moment, he wished that Aglaca alone accompanied him. The plateaus of Taman Busuk were treacherous country, filled with crevasses and cul-de-sacs, where a horse could stumble, a young man could fall. . . .

Verminaard pulled himself from the bloody revery. In the passing months, the murderous thoughts had come more often, more wildly. There were a thousand mishaps waiting for a Solamnic, a thousand deceptions and enemies. Verminaard dreamed of those awful moments, savored them until the dream dissolved before the cold truth of the *gebo-naud*—any misfortune that befell Aglaca could be visited on Abelaard in Solamnia.

And he would not let misfortune befall his brother.

In a heedless gloom, Verminaard kept his big black stallion in steady stride with Osman's roan. The landscape passed by him in a featureless, angry fog.

Aglaca, on the other side, prayed long and silently to Paladine, to Mishakal, and to Kiri-Jolith of the hunt, as his father Laca had taught him before he was old enough to hold a spear. Let the hunting be good, he beseeched the gods, and the kill clean and noble. And let each huntsman return to his hearth and his family, at the close of the day.

Smiling ruefully at the Solamnic, Verminaard eyed the massive company. They'll just be in my way, he thought, visions of the centicore entering his mind. The beast was slow-witted, ill-tempered, and nearsighted, but if it turned, grunting and lowering its tusks and gathering speed for a headlong and witless charge, the hunt changed radically. Then his companions would be a hindrance, his armor inadequate, his horse too slow, and all that remained between him and the gigantic, thick-skinned boar and its three-foot tusks was his couched lance, strong arm, and nerve.

It was an encounter Verminaard awaited eagerly. He spurred his horse to ride ahead of Aglaca, ahead of Osman. At twenty, Verminaard was burly and strong, and physical courage came easily for him. And, apparently recognizing it, his father had put him in a place of honor— in the vanguard of the hunt, where he would most likely see the first action.

An icy rain pummeled the column of horsemen as they rode north across the browned, awakening plains toward Taman Busuk. The tips of their long, barbed spears dipped and rose with the swell and fall of the trail. When they reached the high plains, the horsemen fanned out and rode four or five abreast, separating into squadrons carefully assigned by Lord Daeghrefn.

Riding in the foremost and smallest squadron, Verminaard leaned back on the iron arson of his saddle and inhaled the moist, chilly air. It was lowland breathing here—thicker, more nourishing than the air at the timberline where Castle Nidus kept its formidable watch. Aglaca, riding beside him, seemed suddenly more animate, suddenly more at home in the saddle and the journey.

They rested the horses in a narrow notch between two cliff faces—a glittering passage where the noonday sun flickered on black obsidian, porous volcanic rubble, and a little mountain pool still crusted with the winter's ice. Dismounting, Verminaard drank deeply of the drus flask at his belt—the visionary's potion that Cerestes said was the door to prophecy for servants of the Dragon Queen.

Then he drew forth again the bag of runes, rankling at the mage's insistence that auguring one's own future was impossible. He was sure self-augury could be done, some way, somehow. Especially now, vitalized by the drus potion: The carvings on the stones seemed to shimmer like veins of light.

"Osman," he called, and the huntsman, whetting his knife by a fallen log, looked up with a frown.

"Not the runes, if you please, young master. I don't take to auguries, nor to that mage of yours."

"They have nothing to do with him," Verminaard lied. The mage had given him the stones when he saw that the lad was curious. "They're fostered under the red moon— under Lunitari. All oracles are, because they're all neutral."

That much was true. Prophecy was a neutral thing. What you made of it was good or evil. And when you read the stones for someone else . . . well, sometimes you discovered the things that really concern you. The things that pertain directly to you.

Reluctantly Osman approached the young man. He mistrusted Verminaard's superstition, his preoccupation with dark ritual and ceremony. Being a bluff, commonsensical man, Osman had little love for the confusing auguries Verminaard constantly and eagerly placed in front of him.

Better the father, who believed in nothing, than this hex of a lad before him.

"Ask about the hunt, Osman," Verminaard urged. "Ask how your company will fare."

Osman cleared his throat, looking at Aglaca for rescue. The other lad knelt by his horse, smiled, and shook his head as he tightened the flank cinch of the saddle. He was not about to enter the fuss over symbol and omen.

"I expect we'll find out shortly enough, Master Verminaard," the huntsman replied, turning coolly back to the log.

Angrily Verminaard cast the runes himself. The flat, irregular stones scattered from his hands. It was an old Nerakan reading he tried—three stones in a sequence, determining the present, the immediate future, and the outcome of the event. The cryptic silver lines seemed to scatter, to flicker on the ground like edged fire.

Aglaca, meanwhile, rose and led one of the horses to the little pool. Leaning to break the ice so that the animal might drink, the youth was astonished to see another face, dark and serene, staring back at him from the glazed surface of the water.

"Great Paladine!" he breathed in astonishment.

It was the dark-eyed woman, regarding him serenely. Leaves hung in her auburn hair, and a curious amber light played over her forehead, as though she stared into the setting sun.

Her eyes widened. She smiled in brief recognition, then vanished into the smoky whirl of the ice. Now Aglaca saw an image of himself, sword drawn amid an alcove of granite and rubble. Verminaard stood behind him in the vision, his weapon sheathed and idle.

Aglaca stepped back and gasped, trying to make sense of the revelation.

It was then that the horses started and shied, their nostrils flaring at the whiff of something sharp and musty on the rising wind. Osman leapt to the saddle, followed instantly by Aglaca and the rest of the troopers. Standing in the stirrups, the huntsman scanned the featureless fields. Finally, like an old Plainsman visionary, Osman pointed to where the high grass thrashed and quivered, like the surface of a lake when something large and unfathomable rises from its depths and parts the shallow waters.

"There," Osman announced calmly, gesturing toward the moving furrow on the horizon. "A small one, but worthy of the hunt."

Verminaard scooped up the runes and pulled himself into the saddle. His companions already raced ahead of him, their horses spurred to a brisk trot toward the northern horizon, where his centicore rumbled and his glory would come thrashing through the high grass.

* * * * *

Their horses were good ones, swift and tireless. By midmorning, the centicore was clearly in sight, lumbering ahead of them, its stout legs churning with a slow and ceaseless power.

It was an ugly thing, Verminaard agreed, as he had been told it would be. Its thick skin was armored with dried mud and algae, its arm-length tail bulbous and spiked like a mace. As tall as a man at its shoulders, the centicore was a young one, no doubt, since its horns were smooth and unscarred. An old folktale said that to meet its stare was death, that the very rocks of the Khalkist foothills were the remains of hapless hunters who had been turned to stone by its gaze.

Of course, Daeghrefn maintained that the legends were nonsense. He had killed two centicores himself, and both times, he claimed, he had looked the thing full in the face as he took its life. There was no magic in the creature, Daeghrefn said, no power except the fear prompted by the wild imaginings of the mountain peoples.

Osman was one of those mountain folk, however, and as the horsemen closed on the centicore, he ordered the young men to each side of the plodding creature. With a grunt, the monster lurched into a small box canyon between two cliff faces. After all, Daeghrefn had appointed the huntsman as a guardian of sorts, and if the centicore turned to charge, the lads would be at its flanks, at a safe distance from its swiveling horns and its legendary gaze, and the shortsighted focus of its anger would fall on Osman and the troopers alone.

Circling to the right of the beast, his horse brushing against the rock face, Verminaard leveled his lance. The horse quivered nervously beneath him, the foul smell of the beast thick in the moist, windless air. Verminaard stood up in the stirrups, locked his legs at the knees, and leaned forward in the saddle.

To his left, skidding over the black volcanic rubble, the centicore reached the rocky cul-de-sac. Slowly and stupidly the beast turned, facing Verminaard. In that time—two seconds, perhaps three—their eyes locked in the shadow of the cliff walls, and the boy saw the dull, shallow stare of the beast, its eyes as drab as wet slate.

It barely knows I am here, he thought exultantly. And now as it turns, I shall charge it and . . .

Then something flickered deep in the eyes of the monster.

Verminaard weaved above the saddle. For a moment,

he believed he had imagined that strange, cold light that seemed to emerge from the heart of the beast, chilling yet beckoning him with some deeply malignant pressure. And yet it was not imagined, was not his own superstitious promptings, for how could his own mind freeze him, confuse him, and fascinate him so?

Verminaard blinked and fumbled his lance. The language of that light was something he almost knew, as though the thoughts of the beast had reached out across half the canyon and across a thousand years, embracing his thoughts and beginning a long and cold instruction. And yet he was not sure what it meant. The look had been cloudy, elusive, as indecipherable finally as the runes he tried vainly to read.

I shall charge it, he thought. I shall drive it into precious Aglaca.

His thoughts wrenched back to the moment, and he spurred his stallion. The beast turned and fled him, rumbling through the rough, gravelly stretch toward the other wall of the canyon where Aglaca waited, his lance leveled, his horse calm and steady.

Now! Verminaard thought, goading his horse after the barreling centicore. Now, while the thing is intent on Aglaca!

It would be a tough kill for an untried lad. The centicore lumbered toward Aglaca, its mouth agape, its horns swiveling like scythes. Aglaca blinked nervously and steadied his trembling lance, drawing again on his extraordinary courage as the monster closed the distance by half, the plodding strides gaining fluidity until the beast moved surprisingly fast over the gravelly edges of the cul-de-sac.

Then, unexpectedly, Osman rode between the lad and the charging animal. The older man had seen disaster unfolding from his post at the mouth of the cul-de-sac, and he realized at once that the post he had taken, chosen because it was the most likely place the beast would charge, was barely close enough to rescue the imperiled Solamnic youth. He spurred his horse over the gravel, shouting and whistling to distract the monster, and he reached Aglaca not a moment too soon, turning to face the centicore and raising his lance to receive its charge. The soft flesh at its breast lay exposed by the centicore's reckless assault, and all the veteran huntsman had to do was hold the lance as the creature drove itself upon the tapered shaft, then return with his seventh kill. His deeds would be sung in Castle Nidus, in the villages among the foothills, and by huntsmen as far away as Sanction and Zhakar.

So the hunt would have ended, had not Verminaard's pursuit distracted the beast.

Wheeling awkwardly on its forelegs, scattering gravel and earth as it turned, the centicore stumbled toward the charging youth. Alarmed, seeing the danger to his master's son, Osman spurred his horse forward, riding beside the centicore, seeking a soft spot, a vulnerable place in the filthy array of scales along the monster's back.

Suddenly the beast lashed out with its thick, macelike tail. The barb whistled through the air and crashed into the side of Osman's helmet with a ring that Robert's pursuing column heard a hundred yards from the mouth of the canyon.

Osman toppled from the saddle and fell heavily to the ground. For a moment, he tried to rise, his arms extended weakly above his lolling head, but then he shivered and lay still just as Verminaard's lance drove deeply, with a crackling of gristle and bone, into the breast of the centicore.

The impact of lance against the monster thrusted the young man back into the bracings of his saddle, and the breath fled from him as the air spangled with red light. He remembered only falling and being caught by the cords.

Then he remembered nothing at all.

Aglaca was kneeling beside him when Verminaard came to his senses. The huge hulk of the centicore lay not ten yards away, the broken lance embedded deep in its vitals. The shadows of horsemen surrounded him, and as he tried to stand, the seneschal Robert grabbed him under the arms, lifting him and bracing him.

"What happened here?" Daeghrefn's sharp voice asked, like a distant humming in his ears.

"The centicore is dead, sir," Aglaca volunteered. "And it was Verminaard's brave charge that killed it."

"And not only the centicore," Daeghrefn declared icily. "Osman has fallen to the same rash assault. Attend to his body and leave the centicore here for the ravens and kites. The beast is a shameful kill."

* * * * *

Verminaard could not believe his bad fortune.

He'd had scarcely a second's exulting, scarcely a moment to look across the churned and broken ground to the steamy, hulking body of the beast, to revel in his courageous act.

It was Aglaca's fault, the Voice soothed, gliding into his deepest thoughts as he sulked in the saddle. *He could have joined the ceremony, closed the circle of the hunt with a simple cast of the spear. He refused, out of a stupid and blind loyalty to a vanished god . . . and Osman died for Aglaca's pride and his helplessness. If he'd been man enough to kill the centicore . . .*

Verminaard rode home in the middle of the column, Aglaca beside him. Over the mile and a half from the box canyon to the edge of the plains, the smaller lad never spoke, but when they reached the foothills and the narrow pass that led through Taman Busuk and south toward Castle Nidus, Aglaca finally addressed him. The brisk wind that met them erased all memory of the grasslands, the rank smell of centicore, and the sweat of terror-stricken horses.

"Your father will come around, Verminaard," Aglaca soothed. "He's wounded over the loss of Osman, but he'll see soon enough that your act *was* courageous, that you were only trying to help me out."

Verminaard winced at this new needling but kept silent, his eyes fixed on the path in front of them. Once, maybe twice, Aglaca thought that his companion was ready to speak, but each time the other lad shook his head and sank back into a gloomy quiet.

They passed over a stone bridge, wider by far than Dreed, where the horses walked three abreast and the riders, forced to dismount and lead the animals, trudged over the causeway of rock and gravel, exchanging muted conversation and stories about Osman's bravery.

"What's this bridge called, Verminaard?" Aglaca asked.

"Bandit's Bone" came the answer, muttered and clipped.

"Is there some burial ground here?"

Verminaard was about to loose a tirade upon Aglaca, to berate him for his pride and smugness and self-righteous, bloody-minded ways, when suddenly the air bristled with arrows. Rising from the rocks on the far side of the bridge ahead, a dozen archers aimed, fired, and reloaded as the rider at the front of Daeghrefn's column toppled over the bridge and into the gorge, the black shaft of a Nerakan arrow run through his back.

"Nerakans!" Daeghrefn roared. "Ambush!"

Chapter 5

From the rocks behind them came a second group of bandits, also armed with bows, and instantly another deluge of arrows poured down on Daeghrefn's party. The relentless barrage eclipsed the midday sun, and the warriors on the rock bridge milled in confusion, while men before and behind Verminaard toppled into the gorge, some shot through several times.

Daeghrefn whirled in the saddle and shouted orders to his men. Verminaard strained to hear his father through the strange, aggressive yells of the Nerakan archers as they launched volley after volley upon the trapped hunters. But then the lad's eyes brought him the news as all the men turned their shields toward the far side of the bridge and, risking the arrows that whined and clattered on the stones behind them, lurched angrily toward the homeward side of the gorge like a long, armored serpent.

Slowly they moved toward the bandits, toward the ragged men who now discarded their bows and drew forth long knives and rusty maces. When Verminaard reached solid ground, there were ten of his party ahead, swords locked with their Nerakan adversaries, and the drift of battle was already shifting toward Daeghrefn, toward the commander of Castle Nidus.

Verminaard looked behind him. Aglaca leapt off the stone bridge and found safer footing, but past him lay a sprawl of bodies. A dozen of Daeghrefn's men slumped, dead or dying, on the stone bridge, and three more had fallen into the gorge. Fifteen in all, a dreadful blow to the castle garrison.

Ahead of the young men, the Nerakans made another vicious assault. Crouching and sidling like maniacal crabs, they would have been ludicrous if it hadn't been for their long knives, sharp and glittering. Daeghrefn's men backed unsteadily to the bridge, their shields raised again and their swords waving fruitlessly. Another man fell to Nerakan knives—Edred, it was, and he called out only once as the bandits swarmed over him. Soon the whole party, from Daeghrefn down to Verminaard and Aglaca, were huddled together behind their horses at the edge of the gorge, their feet slipping in rubble, their swords held narrowly before them. They braced themselves against the Nerakans, who regrouped not twenty feet from their makeshift lines, preparing for yet another charge.

Cramped against Aglaca on one side, with Robert on the other, Verminaard looked over his shoulder, past the huddle of horses to the bridge. There, amid the cluttered corpses, the first Nerakan archers had set foot on the rocky span.

Far behind them, on the other side of the chasm, a girl-ish form burst forth from the rocks, galloping on a roan mare, chased by two mounted bandits. Hooded and slight, her red robes kirtled around her thighs, she seemed diminished, almost elflike before her two hulking pursuers.

On her right leg was a prisoner's tattoo, the hand-sized silhouette of a dragon's black head.

The girl raised her hands toward the battle, and Verminaard noticed the ropes that bound her wrists together.

A captive, he thought. And a lovely one. She is blond and fair, I'm sure. . . .

What am I thinking of, here at sword's point? He shook his head to fling loose the distracting thoughts as the men around him stumbled forward. Overtaken by the bandits, the girl and her horse moved into the rocks. When Verminaard looked back, she was gone.

Finally the bandits had taken account of numbers. They were turning, retreating before Daeghrefn's superior forces, and the Lord of Nidus's troops were driving them, pressing in with their swords and shouting the names of the fallen.

Over the rocks and the gravel they chased the Nerakans, leaving the bridge, rushing up the mountain pass until the bandits vanished among the branching paths and the crags of the towering cliff face.

Just ahead of Verminaard and Aglaca, drawing his sword and casting his bulky shield aside, old Robert shouted and redoubled his pursuit of a scraggly, bearded Nerakan, who ducked into a tight passage and vanished.

"Follow me!" the seneschal cried, and when Aglaca hesitated, the veteran turned and scowled at him comically.

"After me, Lord Aglaca!" Robert rumbled. "Lest that

sword of yours is good only for slicing beetles in the garden!"

Recklessly the old man pivoted and lurched after the retreating Nerakan, and Verminaard and Aglaca, soon lost amid the maze of rock and rubble, followed.

Verminaard's thoughts outpaced his feet, and he fell behind. *The girl . . . I should have rescued her, burst back over the bridge like a questing knight. I could have found the way amid the archers and carried her off from her captors. She would have . . .*

He blinked stupidly. It was the Voice that spoke to him now, entirely enmeshed with his own thoughts. Ahead, Robert turned, slipped between two narrow rocks . . .

And immediately there came an outcry, the sound of too many voices. Instead of one Nerakan, there were three.

Bursting through the narrow passage after Aglaca, Verminaard saw the old seneschal hemmed in by a pair of bandits. One had forced him against a black rock face, while another, dagger in hand, had scrambled into the rocks above. He was coiled like an adder, waiting his chance to strike. The third, crouched not ten feet away, produced a poniard from a long sleeve and drew back to throw it.

With a ringing cry, Aglaca sprang toward the rocks, his feet and short sword whirling. The perched Nerakan started, lost his footing as he clutched vainly for the rock face, and fell, breaking his neck. Aglaca's small sword broke the arcing poniard in midair, and he was on its owner in an instant. Verminaard circled the struggling pair, sword at the ready but somehow locked out of the combat. Robert took the second man down with a neat cut to his hamstring.

Aglaca wrestled gamely with the bandit, who was far larger and stronger. The Solamnic couldn't get leverage to use his sword. All the while, the dark Voice continued to stir Verminaard's deepest imagining. . . .

Let them be. What if the bandit wins? Surely Laca would do nothing to Abelaard if his son met with . . . an accident of battle. And Aglaca brought it on himself with his arrogant refusal to cast the ceremonial spear. . . .

Verminaard stopped, the sword tilted uncertainly in his hand. The bandit rolled free, braced his back against the obsidian rock face, and, setting his feet to Aglaca's chest, launched the lad into the air with a compact, powerful push of his legs.

Aglaca rattled against the far wall of the passage, his sword loosed and clattering across the rock floor. Stunned by the blow, he groped vainly for the long knife at his belt. The bellowing Nerakan leapt to his feet, skidding crazily over gravel, and sprang toward the Solamnic lad, another glinting poniard seeking his throat.

Aglaca's senses cleared, and he found the hilt of his knife. In the split second after the bandit left his feet, the boy drew the weapon, raised it swiftly and certainly . . .

And met the bandit's last charge as he tumbled fiercely upon Aglaca's blade. The bandit's mouth went slack, and his eyes grew wide. Aglaca gazed up at him, coolly and straight on, until he slumped over in a heap.

Robert, meanwhile, had disposed of his hamstrung opponent. Dazed, kneeling in the rubble, he gathered himself and weaved dizzily to his feet, looking with amazement at the young man who had come to his rescue.

Verminaard, his weapon shamefully clean, shrank into the shadows, hoping somehow that the darkness would swallow him, hide him from blaming eyes. . . .

"You surely plucked those two off of me, Master Aglaca," the seneschal muttered.

Aglaca smiled and dusted off his breastplate and tunic. Dripping with sweat and scraped by his scuffle among the rocks, he leaned against a large stone until he had gathered balance and breath. "They weren't much different from any other kind of pest, Robert," he replied with a chuckle. Robert, too, broke into a laugh as he recalled his previous taunt. As the battle tension drained from them, they noticed Verminaard, who stood between the narrow rocks, drawn sword still frozen in his hand.

Say nothing, the Voice urged. *Whatever you do, do not say it.... They do not know you were here. He has no idea....*

Verminaard did as he was told.

The Solamnic lad looked Verminaard over carefully, then wiped his brow. "So at last you found us, Verminaard!" he said curiously. "'Twas tight quarters here. We could've used your arm."

"Indeed we could," Robert grumbled, eyeing him skeptically. He could have sworn he'd seen Verminaard earlier in the fray. Hobbling a bit from the basting he had suffered at the hands of the Nerakans, he limped past the young man back onto the mountain trail, headed toward the bridge and the rest of his companions.

"No matter," Aglaca quickly added, his voice cheerful and melodious. "No matter, because, as you see, there was no harm in your delay, no bruise in your waiting."

* * * * *

They found Daeghrefn not far from the bridge, gathering his men and reckoning his losses.

Of the forty retainers who had embarked on the morning's hunt with the Lord of Nidus, only two dozen remained. Osman, of course, had fallen in the encounter with the centicore. The Nerakan ambush had killed fifteen of Daeghrefn's finest troops.

When two of the retainers, rough farm boys from Kern, returned from the chase bearing two Nerakan heads on pikes, Daeghrefn turned away and said nothing, for he shared their bitterness and anger. Aside from that pair of especially unfortunate bandits and the three slain by Aglaca and Robert, the skirmish had brought no recompense for Daeghrefn's forces. The Nerakans had vanished into the rocks, leaving dead men and disarray on the paths behind them.

And the girl, Verminaard thought, standing in the background while Robert told Daeghrefn how Aglaca had shown mettle and speed in the struggle with the bandits. Whoever she was . . . bound and captive and . . . and in deep distress, I know.

Daeghrefn nodded brusquely at Robert's speech. Aglaca might be Laca's son, but despite the ancient quarrel, the boy had conducted himself with exceptional gallantry. He glanced from the disheveled, amiable Solamnic youth to the other, the darker, larger, and decidedly unfatigued presence, who sat atop his horse now, lost in a labyrinth of thought.

Verminaard didn't notice that Daeghrefn had looked at him, for his mind was elsewhere, high on the far and sunlit side of the stone bridge.

Had I but the chance to prove it, she . . . she would . . .

He couldn't imagine what would happen.

Trapped in his own reflections, communing with the dark Voice that arose from his thoughts and from somewhere deeper than his thoughts, he rode back to Castle Nidus, trailing the column.

* * * * *

From the battlements of Castle Nidus, sentries watched the approach of Daeghrefn's beaten line of riders. Almost at once, the sharper-eyed among them began to count, and counted again, as two dozen men rode in from the waning light of the foothills, torches already lifted against the oncoming evening.

Quickly, with rising apprehension, the sentries alerted the castle. Soon, with murmurings and rumor, everyone assembled in the bailey yard. There the kitchen sweep shifted from foot to foot next to the old astrologer from Estwilde, and the falconer leaned uneasily against the wall of the keep, exchanging hushed words with the cook. None had foreseen this grim news. Never had a routine hunt been so disastrous, and only twice before had the Nerakans attacked anyone this close to Nidus.

Aglaca turned over the day's unhappy events in his mind and knew that it would be a long time before he could go home to East Borders. Eight long years past . . . how many more to go until some sort of peace would release him from Nidus? His youth was being poured out in the *gebo-naud*, and by now he should have attained his knighthood. Or maybe even his most secret desire—to serve Paladine with all his being.

Perhaps Daeghrefn had been right about his needing a guard to keep him from answering the call of East Borders. Like the dead of the day, Aglaca had not chosen his fate nor his company.

* * * * *

Perched at the mouth of a high cave, almost a mile above the three lofty turrets of the castle, there was one who understood more clearly. Cerestes shielded his golden eyes against the red slant of sun and counted the approaching troops. Then his gaze narrowed and focused, and the birds around the mouth of the cavern hushed in a sort of fearful expectancy.

This time he could count the holes in the tattered foremost banner. Eagerly his sight raced down the column.

Good. Aglaca and Verminaard both were there.

Satisfied, he stalked into the growing darkness, into an enormous circular chamber, void of light and wind and silent except for the perpetual dripping of water somewhere even farther back in the cave.

It was the appointed spot. She had told him in a dream, when he had begged her again to reveal his purpose in this place. Though the years in Daeghrefn's service were not long as his kind measured time, she had kept him beyond his patience.

Softly at first, insinuating her voice with the slow, rhythmic music of the water, she came to him, the Dark Queen Takhisis, foremost in the evil pantheon, her voice as intimate as his own thoughts.

So this is how it is for them, Cerestes mused. For Aglaca and Verminaard, to whom she has spoken since childhood. How they hear her voice in their own imaginings.

This is no game, the goddess reminded him, her voice louder now, sweet and low-pitched like the distant murmur of bees, like the sound of the night over Godshome. *What care you for their hearing, for the soft persuasions that bring them to me? Those are mine and theirs. Are they aught of your concern?*

"Of course not," Cerestes replied, knowing her question was no question, but a grim reminder of his boundaries.

Deep in the recesses of the cavern, the sound of the water ceased. He was alone now, with his thoughts and her quiet and sinuous voice.

Become yourself, cleric, Takhisis urged. *Reveal your true self before your queen.*

Cerestes coughed and glanced nervously toward the faint sliver of light behind him.

Oh, we are alone, she soothed. *Those below are far too concerned with ambush and accident, rapt in the counting of their little deaths. None have followed you here.*

"Are you sure?" he asked, and regretted his words at once.

In the depths of the cavern, the darkness roiled and swirled.

This is no time for questions, the Lady said, and her darkness surged to surround Cerestes. The void tugged at him, molding him, drawing him from his body into an older, more familiar shape, forsaken for years. A green half-light sweated from the walls, and he saw the floor of the chamber, the rows of stalagmites like jagged teeth, the litter of broken bones and charcoal.

He saw his hands, as well, as they began the painful metamorphosis that the Lady commanded, as the red webbing sprouted between his fingers and the fingers themselves grew into long claws with a crackling of bone and tendon. Once he cried out, as always he did when the Change first swept over him, but the cry had already passed beyond human, into a terrible shriek, like the tearing of metal. The muscles of his legs bunched and doubled, his ribs buckled and tugged as wings burst forth from his back, and he was growing now, yes, Cerestes was growing, into what he had always been, would always be. The red of his scales blackened in the green light of the chamber, in the familiar blood and the burning that marked this metamorphosis. And the laughter of Takhisis rang so loudly in his mind that he covered his receded ears, imagining that the noise had burst out of his thoughts and rung the cavern walls.

As the noise subsided, Cerestes slowly curled in the middle of the chamber. He began to enlarge, his dorsal bones scraping, pressing against the far wall of the cavern. Soon the light from the entrance was blocked out entirely by his huge, bulking body.

Sternly, as the pain settled in his wings, in his enormous haunches, in the long tail that had burst from the base of his spine, the voice of the Lady echoed all around him. On the chamber ceiling, reflecting among legions of startled bats, amid the shimmering droop of stalactites, a single golden eye stared mercilessly down upon the coiled red dragon that was Cerestes.

You are no longer Cerestes, the Lady soothed, *but you are once again Ember, and entirely my creature. . . .*

"'Tis a painful Change, Majesty," Ember protested, his voice dry and grating, speaking now in a draconic language of hisses and hard consonants. His voice was like the rattle of the bats' wings.

'Painful.' The voice of the Dragonqueen was icy, mocking. *How painful do you think it was for Speratus, the Red Robe, when I arranged your . . . promotion to Daeghrefn's wizard? If you're squeamish when it comes to the pain, Ember, and the Change itself is painful, then perhaps you should never change again.*

Ember squirmed uneasily. The form of Cerestes was his veil, his protective guise in a world in which the dragons could not yet force their presence. For eight years, he had walked in human form.

Oh, yes, Takhisis continued, smelling his thoughts as if they were a faint whiff of blood. *Imagine being always yourself, coiled here like a giant serpent, like the dale worm of centuries past, unable to escape. Prey to your own hungers, perhaps, or to the lances of name-eager knights.*

"Do with me what you will, m'Lady," the dragon rumbled, shutting his thoughts to her with a brief, powerful spell of masking. He stirred on the chamber floor, his confined movements dislodging rocks and old guano, startling the bats, who launched into the darkness with piping cries, their leathery wings brushing against Ember in their whirling flight.

Very well. Keep your thoughts from me. Let it not be said that the Dark Queen . . . intrudes, Takhisis conceded ironically. *I shall pry no further, though if I willed it so, that spell of yours would be thin as as . . . as . . .*

"Gossamer?" Ember asked, with a dark, toothsome smile. It was good that she stopped at the masking spell. He could feel no encroachments, no attempts by her sharp, mysterious sight to pierce the veils of his own magic.

Perhaps she could not even do it. Not while she hovered in the abyss, awaiting a chance at entry to this plane.

Yes. Until they found the green gemstone, the goddess waited behind the portal, a poor version of what she was yet to be.

You have asked again why I sent you here. Well, I have fires for you to start, she said. *And all the fires begin with those two.*

"Verminaard and Aglaca?" Ember asked, his cloaked thoughts racing. "What would you have me do?"

Continue in your role as mage. Reveal to none that you are my cleric—not yet, at least. Continue to tutor Aglaca and Verminaard; nurture them. But become more than their teacher. Be now their confidant, the eyes that shape their world.

One will be your companion in the years to come, when we are stronger and more numerous in this hostile country.

One will be your companion.

Ember opened a golden eye, regarding the light at the ceiling of the chamber with curiosity and dread.

"Which one, Your Highness?" he asked, his rough voice laced with suspicion.

They will choose. Aglaca and Verminaard. In this world, there is room for only one of them.

And they might have already chosen. The larger is the more pliable, the smaller more spirited. Verminaard will be the easier won, Aglaca the prouder trophy. But they will choose. I shall provide the occasion.

"Why these two?" Ember asked, and in the long silence that followed, he heard the air buzz and crackle, like the sound in the sky at the beginning of lightning. He feared he had angered her, insulted her, and yet, after a long pause, she chose to tell him.

Laca. I've a long grudge against Laca. How better to pay him back, and the cursed Order . . .

"And if the other one is chosen," Ember added slyly, "what greater blow to the Order than to have your servant fathered by the great rebel Daeghrefn!"

Takhisis was silent. In the depths of the cavern, Ember heard his last words echoing, the echo circling and catching itself until echo flowed over echo and the dark recesses of the mountain bristled with tangling voices and words: *other one . . . chosen . . . father . . .*

I shall provide the occasion, Takhisis said, breaking the settling silence. *First the girl. Then the other . . . circumstances.*

"What girl?" Ember asked eagerly, his long, branched tongue flickering excitedly, hotly into the darkness. "You told me of no girl, m'Lady."

Why, the one that Paladine has chosen. The one he sends to the druidess regarding the runes. Or so I believe.

"The runes?" Ember asked, closing his eyes, struggling for a note of idleness, of indifference. "I thought they were only a game. Indeed, I've kept Verminaard busy with them when his questions annoyed me."

And indeed they are but a game, Takhisis answered. *For now, that is. Until the blank rune is sounded.*

Ember opened the other double-lidded eye. In the slanted light of the chamber, his gaze was golden and scheming.

"The blank rune?" he asked. "So the old legend is true?"

Paladine has hidden it too long. Since the time of . . . Huma.

Ember masked a smile. The Lady still stumbled on the name of the Solamnic hero whose lance had driven her back into the Abyss.

He has hidden it so long, Takhisis continued, *that they teach the mages that the blank stone is a substitute, a replacement in case another stone is lost or damaged.*

"Indeed," Cerestes conceded. "So I have told Verminaard, who rummages in rune lore constantly."

So I have seen, Takhisis said. *Perhaps the time will come when all the runes will lie before him, the blank rune adorned with its symbols. . . .*

"What then?" The dragon was eager, hungry for the forbidden knowledge. "What then, Lady?"

Then we shall wield the greatest of oracles, Takhisis purred. *The augury that has lain silent and broken because the rune was blank, its symbol forgotten.*

All of this time, it seems, L'Indasha Yman has kept the secret.

L'Indasha Yman? Of the druids? Ember thought. And she has not used this power? Takhisis is lying. Or she is holding something back.

The girl, Takhisis said, her deep voice lazing over the words. *She's something to do with the runes . . . with the sounding. I know it.*

Ember shifted uneasily in the cramped chamber, awaiting the connection between the girl and the runes that Takhisis seemed about to make.

When I . . . came here, there were things forbidden me. Things he hid from me in my banishment. Things I have forgotten as well. So you must continue to learn for me, to do for me . . . for now.

That ice in her voice, Ember thought. She knows more, and she is not telling. But with these runes . . .

The Nerakans have her now, Takhisis informed him. *They intend her for my temple's first sacrifice, because of her lavender eyes. But they will not destroy her, nor will they keep her forever.*

"Suppose they find her secrets before . . . before *we* do, m'Lady? Nerakans have a way of gathering secrets."

The voice of the goddess rose softly after another long, uncomfortable silence. *The Nerakans are my servants. They will not rebel. But if they do, and if they dare to sound the rune . . .*

All of the gods will know it at once. And whom, my dear Cerestes, do the hundred clerics worship? Who controls armies in Sanction and Estwilde? All that the Nerakans would augur in the runes are their own deaths.

"This . . . quarrel with Laca," the dragon offered, shifting the ground of the talk.

Will cost him a son, Takhisis interrupted. *Of that I am certain.*

"But what of the other? This Verminaard—"

Is no less the son of Laca Dragonbane, fool! the Dark Queen announced sharply. The cavern walls seemed to recede, and the dragon began the slow transformation back to his human form, back to the dark mage Cerestes.

He should have known. The silence as to Verminaard's birth. Daeghrefn's cruelty and marked prejudice against the boy. The lack of physical resemblance between father and son.

Astonished at the Lady's tidings, Cerestes suddenly felt frail, baffled and cold, as a whole cloudy history of deceit and betrayals formed at the edge of his understanding, something he needed to know, needed to use.

I will use one, Takhisis said and chuckled. *The other is . . . dispensable. Lord Laca has left me an abundance of sons, and I shall need only one of them. For the blood of Huma runs through Laca Dragonbane, and Huma's line is tied with the sounding of the rune. I need just one of Huma's line. He will be the last survivor.*

"B-But how, Highness? How do the young ones fit?" Cerestes asked. But the goddess was not telling. The dark eye above him faded, and the exhausted mage lay at the center of the chamber, his black robes, tattered and split by the Change, scattered to the far corners of the cavern. Again the uncovered slant of light glowed silver and gray from the mouth of the cave, and the mage rose blearily and crouched at the edge of light, stitching his robes back together with spells.

I shall win, Takhisis prophesied, her voice no more than a whisper of thought or memory, *no matter what anyone chooses, I shall be triumphant. Go now and do my bidding, Cerestes. . . .*

Chapter 6

Verminaard could not forget the girl.

At night, in the midst of his meditations, her hooded form and the black tattoo on her leg haunted him, as did his fleeting view of her as her horse turned on the far side of the stone bridge and she rode away, bound to the saddle and guarded by bandits. When Aglaca bent to his devotions, Verminaard would draw forth the Amarach runes, turning them intently in his hand as if some new symbol on the ancient stones would appear to give him a clue as to her name, her origins. . . .

Why the bandits held her as captive.

He had no idea why she drew him so, but he thought of her all his waking hours, and especially when he was supposed to be at his studies.

Not long after the hunt, through Cerestes' suggestive power, Daeghrefn appointed the mage official tutor to the boys. It was an acknowledgement rather than a promotion, but now Cerestes began their instruction in earnest, with rigorous classes in higher astronomy, mathematics, and ceremony. As Verminaard scratched on parchment the phases of the black moon and learned more powerful dark spells, Cerestes quarreled with Aglaca, who was now forced to attend the lectures but sat stubbornly in the corner, still refusing to give himself to the new mysteries.

In the midst of this new academic pressure, Verminaard found his mind wandering, wool-gathering in long, adventurous fantasies in which he rescued the girl from dragons, from ogres, from other dangers.

The mage would rap the table, and Verminaard's thoughts would return grudgingly to the castle's solar, to the sunlit classroom made suddenly strange by his own imagination and consuming dreams. Aglaca, poring over his botanicals rather than the books of spellcraft, would regard him with concern, and Cerestes would scowl and point to the text. Verminaard would renew his attention with energy, with promises. . . .

And in a matter of minutes, he would be lost once more in thoughts of the girl.

Once, in high summer, when the images of her were still unmanageably strong, he boasted to Aglaca all he had imagined.

It was late evening, one of those summer nights when the darkness itself delays and the world seems to hover in a half-light until nigh onto midnight, an evening when nightingales keep awake the restless. After a few minutes of practicing a slow, graceful fighting kick, Aglaca had stretched against the battlement and asked him unsettling questions.

Had he seen her eyes?

The expression on her face? What color was her hair?

He smiled at Verminaard's stammer, his dodging answers.

"I suppose *you* could draw her portrait, then?" Verminaard retorted coldly.

Not ten yards away, three ravens settled ominously on the crenels, and Aglaca shivered and turned away. "I saw little more than you, Verminaard, though I'd wager I could pick her out by the way she sits a horse."

He looked out over the battlements toward the reddening west as the sun settled on the Solamnic foothills.

"'Tis summer again, Verminaard," he continued, his voice distant and softer still, scarcely audible over the boding and rustling of the roosting birds. "And when the summer comes, dreams spill over into waking hours. My father told me to beware that time. 'High summer smoke and deception, light sickness,' he called it."

"A right poet, your father is," Verminaard grumbled, catching only the final phrase. "But I've enough of his verse and your cautions for this long season."

Aglaca lifted an eyebrow. When Verminaard began to grumble and declare, it was always a sign of recklessness and challenge—a ride on a hunt, perhaps, or a climb up a sheer rock face. He was predictable, and though the shape of the deed might change, Aglaca knew a deed was coming, that Verminaard was sick of shadows, eager for the tumult of chase and discovery.

Aglaca smiled to himself and shielded his eyes against the last reddening flood of sunlight.

The deed was coming, and he did not mind at all.

For the druidess had withdrawn since his battle with the Nerakans; she said she had taught him all she could. And now what had he at Nidus but this long captivity and the dark lessons he refused to learn? And unsettled thoughts of his own.

"And therefore the poetry shall be set aside,"

Verminaard declared, his voice hushed to a whisper, drawing Aglaca toward him by the collar, his grip firm and commanding. "When the season turns and the night isn't so blasted short, I'm off to Neraka to find her."

Aglaca smiled calmly into a face the very image of his own.

* * * * *

Verminaard consulted the runes for a plan and an auspicious night. In the solitude of his quarters, crouched over a table in the dim candlelight, he pondered the Circle of Life—the six irregular rune stones set in a sanctioned pattern centuries old, reflecting the energies of the past and indicating the challenges ahead.

Let the others laugh at him. Let Robert and Daeghrefn and even Aglaca call the runes childishness and nonsense.

The laughter would change when he found the key to prophecy.

Solemnly Verminaard set the stones before him, and gazed long and deeply at the scarred lines along their faces, banishing thoughts of the girl, of his father's anger, of the perils of Neraka.

Yet again the stones were silent. The old proverb held, he thought sourly, that a man cannot read his own future in the runes.

It was that proverb, that surrounding silence, that brought Verminaard to Cerestes.

The mage reclined on a soft chair, his feet propped on the windowsill and his gaze fixed on the constellation Hiddukel, which tilted in the black sky out his window.

Verminaard held his breath as he entered the room. Cerestes' presence always daunted him, and the gap in the upper sky once filled by the stars of Takhisis, three thousand years vanished, seemed to beckon him as he inched to the center of the room. Now that he was there, asking the mage to read the runes for him seemed forward and disrespectful, and the young man shifted from foot to foot, glancing awkwardly back toward the door.

The mage sighed, tilting an astrolabe toward the constellation. "What's your pleasure, young master?" he asked, his voice sinuous and low and echoing unexpectedly in the small and cluttered room, as though Verminaard remembered it less from the classroom than from somewhere in a half-forgotten dream.

He did not know, nor could he figure how the mage had climbed to this place of power. Long years back, an eleventh-hour substitute in a hurried ritual, Cerestes was now one of Daeghrefn's chief advisors, trusted as much as the Lord of Nidus trusted anyone.

He was also the one man in all the castle Verminaard could trust with the plan he had hatched with Aglaca earlier that month.

"I would have you read me the runes, sir," he replied, glancing one last wistful time toward the door behind him, closing slowly of its own volition.

"The Amarach again?" the mage asked, his hidden eyes narrowing, and Verminaard steeled himself for the lecture—how the stones were a child's toy and the desperate preoccupation of the old, who read them fearfully, imagining they could augur their own dates of death.

"It will be your undoing, Master Verminaard," the mage had always told him. "Forgo this clerical nonsense and attend to the hunt and the castle and your studies."

But not this time. For some reason, the mage's reply floated away from lectures. Lazily, with a slow, almost reptilian movement, he rose from the chair.

"And what might the runes tell you that good common sense would not?" he asked as Verminaard reached to his belt for the pouch that contained the carved stones.

"Common sense tells me to consult the runes, sir."

The mage smiled wearily. Verminaard opened the bag and poured the runestones into the mage's cupped hands.

"Think of the question, Master Verminaard," Cerestes said, lifting the stones over the lad's head.

Verminaard nodded solemnly and then, with his eyes closed, reached up and drew three stones. He dropped them to the floor, one after the other, in a coarse, almost careless manner.

Cerestes crouched over the stones and stared at the lad. "What is the question?" he asked again into the silence, as Verminaard fidgeted and looked to the window, where the stars seemed to weave and fade.

The lad inhaled and confessed his plan.

"There's a girl . . . "

"At twenty-one, there generally is," Cerestes observed dryly, and then remembered Takhisis's words. "Go on."

"I—I saw her at the edge of the stone bridge. On the day of the hunt and the ambush."

Cerestes nodded, his golden eyes suddenly fixed and intent. Heartened, Verminaard burst forth with the rest of his secret.

"She's been in my thoughts for a season, sir. She's the bandits' prisoner, for no man binds his ally."

"Aglaca might tell you otherwise," the mage observed sardonically, his intensity vanished and his eyes hooded and vague. "Or Abelaard. But you want to rescue this girl?"

"Read the runes, sir. Please?"

The mage turned to the stones at his feet, touching each with the tip of a bony finger as his hand moved slowly from left to right. "Birch. Thunder. The Hammer," he murmured, and glanced up at the lad. "If there were anything to this musty augury, Verminaard, I would take this as pleasant prospects indeed. Inspired by the woman, you make a journey of beginnings. At the final aspect is the Hammer—symbol both of the power of giants and the source of that power."

Verminaard's eyes widened. "It is as I imagined, then. I am *destined* to find her!"

Cerestes shook his head. "Caution, young master, caution. Remember the placement of the stones."

His hand repeated the pattern, moving slowly left to right, touching each stone in turn.

"That which was. That which is. That which is yet to be—*not* 'that which is sure to happen.' "

"I won't tell Father that you read the runes for me," Verminaard said, with a wide, wolfish smile.

Cerestes turned toward the window, hiding a similar smile of his own. The skull of Chemosh was brilliantly visible now, framed by stone and darkness and the deep purple western sky. It could not have been easier.

* * * * *

So it was that Verminaard of Nidus received the blessing of the mage and the veiled direction of the rune stones. He did not linger in Cerestes' chambers, for the hour was late and he had much to do on the morrow. Gathering the stones, he bowed respectfully and backed out the door as it closed softly.

The mage remained at the window, pondering the shifting stars and the cool eddies of night wind on the keep below him as it scattered straw and pale leaves. Cerestes' smile widened.

The game was beginning, and he did so relish a game. Already Takhisis had set her plans in motion, obscure to the mage for now, but he did not need the details yet.

The mysterious girl was on her way, and it was enough. From a distance, the unwitting lad was being drawn toward her, toward a shadowy form he had seen, or rather glimpsed, months ago on a cloudy mountain afternoon.

They would bring this woman to Castle Nidus, and with her safely beneath his roof, Cerestes was sure that it would take little time to uncover her secret.

But the road to Neraka was long and menacing. It crossed the high and desolate grasslands south of the castle, bending east through a narrow pass between foothills surrounding Mount Berkanth and the infamous Nerakan Forest. And even then, after perilous miles of travel, the journey was not over. A southward path took the traveler on between two volcanoes now smoldering and seething with new life. Only then would Verminaard reach the encampments that surrounded the city, and only then would his search for the girl begin in earnest.

In the heart of Neraka, where the Dark Queen was raising a hidden temple.

The mage backed away from the window and settled into his soft chair. The night had turned, and the stars seemed to tilt and beckon as the first birds of the morning awakened and the servants rose as well. The silence was broken by a tentative song from an aderyn perched somewhere on the battlements, followed by the lonely footsteps of a groom as he shuffled across the bailey to the stables.

Cerestes closed his eyes for a moment, drifting on the soft fading of the night. The runes had encouraged the lad, as Cerestes knew they would. It was why he had invented the obscure and hopeful reading, spinning a story out of the flat and meaningless stones.

He laughed scornfully at human foolishness. Until the blank rune was sounded, its symbol recovered, a man might as well read his fingernails for augury.

Cerestes rose from the chair and glided to the center of the room.

It might be as Takhisis claimed, he thought, casting a spell to mask his thoughts in case others—perhaps even the Dark Queen herself—used the night and his dream state to pry into his thought. Perhaps the girl *had* been chosen by Paladine to carry, somehow, the secret of the vanished rune. If that were true, then she carried a powerful knowledge, the key to an omniscient oracle. Armed with that oracle, Takhisis could find the green gemstone, the last component to the portal she was building in Neraka. It was the cornerstone to her temple, and once it was in place, she could return to the world of Krynn, to the bright and agreeable world she had once poisoned and sullied, that she would again cover with her own abiding darkness.

But the same oracle in another's hand could stop her entry entirely.

And establish a darkness of his own.

And what, indeed, might be accomplished with *both* of Huma's kin?

Cerestes smiled and knelt by the hearth, idly tracing the patterns of the runes in the ashes of the hearthstone.

Birch. Thunder. Hammer. They could apply to him as well—better, in fact, than to a lad's moonstruck plans of rescue.

He stilled his rising excitement, gathering his robes and curling up on the hearth. He lay there like a sleeping cat, like a coiled serpent.

Once again, he told himself, the blank rune's faces were still missing. And until they were restored, all auguries were in vain. And yet the stark symbols of Verminaard's reading occupied his thoughts when he closed his eyes. . . .

Birch. Thunder. Hammer.

He drifted off to a deep dragon's sleep that would rest him well by the afternoon. He would awaken by the hearth, his black robes chalked and smeared with ashes, his heart resolved to follow Verminaard to Neraka.

For after all, Verminaard and Aglaca must be protected, since Daeghrefn paid Cerestes' wages. Surely Takhisis would agree.

And since *She* seemed resolved to test the youths by allowing them this adventure, Cerestes could not seize the girl himself. . . .

And since one of the lads, no doubt, would be the Dark Lady's cleric, and the dragon queen paid him in a harder currency. . .

And there was the matter of the missing rune. And finally of a temple in Neraka.

He would see that temple, he resolved, but not for Takhisis's sake. In the temple's obsidian stones lay secrets as mysterious as those housed in the sixteenth and hidden rune. But these were different secrets—of worldly architecture, of politics and power and the strategies of a hundred dark clerics who awaited the arrival of their mistress.

A dragon's eye could translate those secrets—the simple intrigues of humans to whom the goddess had not yet come.

And then, with Takhisis safely imprisoned behind the portal, he would sound the runes, find the green gemstone, and remove it from her grasp forever. Perhaps he would have it made into a ring of power, a symbol of his own new order.

Cerestes murmured in obscure anticipation, a veil of spells like smoke enshrouding his face. He was a rune himself, a blank rune, he thought, his imagination more fanciful as he crossed over, at last, into sleep.

He was, after all, a dragon. A superior being. He could fashion a prophecy of his own, and what he desired would come to pass.

* * * * *

Verminaard checked his plan again.

The groom's son was bribed, as well as the sentries at the east gate.

Two horses would await him in the stable—one for himself, and one for the returning girl—and the east gate of the castle would remain mysteriously open and unguarded for an hour after midnight.

It was orchestrated completely and carefully, and yet Verminaard fidgeted through the sparse meal in the early evening at the silent, somber table with Daeghrefn and Aglaca, Robert and the mage. He hovered nervously above the cold food, certain that all eyes were upon him, all thoughts uncovering his secret quest.

He cursed himself for having been foolish enough to confide in others. Left to his own, Daeghrefn could spend days, weeks without even once speaking to him. Verminaard could travel all the way to the Icewall and back, a journey of some nine hundred miles coming and going, and be assured that Daeghrefn would not notice.

But perhaps the mage had warned the Lord of Nidus. Or Aglaca had told, naturally, in some meddlesome concern for his safety. Though Verminaard had clued neither of them that this was the appointed night, he feared they might know, for the insinuating Voice, silent for so long as he had arranged his adventure, had begun to goad him late last evening that *this* night—with the banked clouds and the summer winds dying—would be ideal for unseen travel.

Perhaps someone else heard the same Voice, the same goading?

And yet they seemed unperturbed, seated in their high-backed chairs, the yellow light from the hearth dancing over Cerestes' wine cup, over Aglaca's glittering knife as he set it to the venison and carved gracefully, deftly, with the Solamnic manners that nine years at Castle Nidus had not shaken from him.

The mage and Aglaca finished their meals and excused themselves. Verminaard pushed back his chair as well, intent on following Aglaca, but a cold stare from

Daeghrefn stopped him before he completely stood, and it was a long moment until Robert rose, muttered something to Lord Nidus about "tallage" and "archer's pay," and the two older men retired to the fireside, a ledger and another bottle of wine set between them.

Backing at last from the chamber, Verminaard glanced one more time at the grayed heads bowed over the castle records. The tilting light magnified his father's shadow until Daeghrefn seemed to fill the hall with a thin, indefinite darkness, through which the lean hounds stalked, scavenging under the table. It was a shadow that seemed to follow the lad down the corridor and up the stairs to his quarters, where a huddled shape under the blankets told him that Aglaca had already fallen off to sleep.

Quietly he draped his heavy cloak over his shoulder, slowly buckled on his sword and knife, and took up his bow. Then there was the little jeweled risting dagger Aglaca had given him after the *gebo-naud*. It was two days' ride to Neraka, and he had thought it better to forage for food along the way than to risk calling attention to himself by taking provisions from Robert's closely monitored larders. He withdrew the sack of runes from beneath his mattress, holding his breath as the stones clicked together loudly in the leather bag.

Aglaca did not stir, but lay in a leaden silence—a thick, invulnerable sleep.

Verminaard leaned over the edge of Aglaca's bed and stared perplexedly at the draped form, heavily covered and blanketed on a night unseasonably warm. He and the Solamnic youth had spent most of their time together in silence or argument and rivalry, in the long foraging hunts through the highlands and mock combat of Robert's demanding lists. Verminaard, much the larger and stronger of the two, managed to baste Aglaca thoroughly in tests of strength, and Aglaca still refused outright to compete in Cerestes' classroom, stoically scorning the instructions of the dark mage.

"There is no defeat in you," Verminaard whispered, then caught himself, surprised at the respect in his voice. Quietly, angrily, he unsheathed and tossed Aglaca's small gift dagger onto the foot of the bed.

In the eight years Verminaard had held it, the magic Aglaca had claimed for the weapon had yet to show itself. Protection against evil indeed! He had never seen the blade do its work, never seen it glow with the fierce and arcane light of real enchanted weaponry. If it hadn't protected him against the lesser evils of Castle Nidus, what good would it be on the dark roads through the mountains?

After all, it was only a small knife, a child's gaudy toy. And he was about a man's business, traveling south to Neraka in the dead of night.

Verminaard stood uncomfortably and strode to the door. The corridor was dark and damp, and he removed his boots to take the stairs silently, attentive to every sound in the castle—the resettling of beams, the murmur of deep voices from downstairs, and the rustle and growl of the dogs in the great hall. Twice he had to wait, holding his breath in the dark recesses of the corridors as sentries passed by. It seemed like hours until he stepped into the night air, into the bailey, and raced across the castle courtyard to the stables against the east wall.

He would bid it all good-bye gladly—castle and garrison and especially Daeghrefn. A new freedom lay before him, frightening him and inspiring him at the same time, and Verminaard longed to embrace it as he moved toward a solitary light waving in the shadows of the east tower.

The stable door was open and the stalls lit dimly by that lonely lantern, just as the bribed boy had promised. Verminaard slipped through the door and closed it behind him, starting for a moment at the hooded form that stood between the stalls, tightening the cinch on a black mare's saddle.

Young Frith, it seemed, was intent on earning his illicit pay. In the adjoining stall, Verminaard's black stallion Orlog stood saddled and set for the coming journey.

Verminaard inspected the boy's work.

"Good," he breathed. "Very good. Frith, you saddle a horse for a knight. When I return, I'll see to it that your lot rises with my father."

"See to your own lot," the hood replied, and turned to face him with a crooked smile and dancing eyes.

"Aglaca!" Verminaard exclaimed much too loudly. Then, angrily clutching the youth by the hood, he threw him roughly to the floor of the stall.

Chapter 7

"What are you doing here?" Verminaard hissed, his fist hovering an inch from Aglaca's face.

"I'm going with you," the lad whispered, his pale eyes intent and dauntless. He had not flinched once, not when Verminaard had pulled him down, kicked him, nor even now, when Verminaard's big knuckles promised a broken nose.

Slowly Verminaard drew back his hand. The horses, confounded by the struggle at their feet, whickered nervously and kicked against their stalls, and the dogs began to bark in the keep.

"Go back to bed," Verminaard urged, opening the stable door and looking nervously out toward the keep.

The windows were dark. Good. Daeghrefn must be abed. There was time yet.

But that time had narrowed sharply.

Breathing an old calming spell Cerestes had taught him for the occasions when he had to speak with Daeghrefn, Verminaard led the horses into the bailey. The sky had cleared suddenly, disturbingly, and the grounds were starlit and silver.

"I'm going with you," Aglaca said again, dusting the straw from his hair. "You need me."

"Never! Just hand up my pack."

Aglaca grunted as he hoisted the bundle onto the stallion. The barking from the keep became louder, more insistent, and the first light—from Robert's lodgings, it seemed—flickered to life from the other side of the courtyard.

"Now you help me," Aglaca urged as Verminaard turned away. "Hold this. They'll be here any moment."

Verminaard started to spur the stallion toward the east gate, risking the noise and the commotion, the attentions of a dozen guards. Better to be stopped now, to answer to Daeghrefn for a midnight disturbance, than to ride over the Khalkist mountains with this . . . this *child* in tow. It was *his* adventure, planned and dreamt of and augured for half a year, and Aglaca would be . . .

"Could you even pick her out, Verminaard?"

"What?" he shouted, spinning in the saddle, losing his balance, clutching frantically at the reins and the saddle horn as he leaned, rocked . . .

. . . and steadied, gasping in fright and anger, glaring coldly at Aglaca, who had somehow managed to hoist both himself and his pack onto the other horse.

"Would you know this girl if they set ten Nerakan women before you?"

"Of course! Now let me—"

"What color are her eyes?" Aglaca was persistent, intent on an embarrassing truth.

"Go back to bed!"

"What color are her eyes, Verminaard?"

"Well, I know they'll be the color of sea or sky—but I suppose you've *seen* them?" Verminaard spat, his horse prancing, turning in tight circles. He wanted to strike the lad, knock him from the saddle and be on his way, but already the doubts were rising, the great misgiving he had tried to hide from himself. . . .

It had been misty that day. He had seen her from a great distance.

"What color *are* her eyes, damn it?" Verminaard roared, and the keep erupted in a flurry of lights and shouts and barking.

"Make for the gate!" Aglaca cried.

* * * * *

They were out into the night before the bleary garrison had mustered to find them. Galloping swiftly over the rocky trail, stone and gravel flying from the horses' hooves, they kept a reckless pace. Finally, in a stretch of country where the trail opened into the grassy flatland, Aglaca overtook Verminaard, who gradually, reluctantly, slowed Orlog to a trot, then a walk.

Behind them, the towers of Castle Nidus were lost in the distance and in a strange dark wall of clouds that had descended—or must have descended—from somewhere in the clear night sky. Peering back over his shoulder, Aglaca gave a low whistle.

"We've come far in a short spell, Master Verminaard," he observed wryly, giving the mare's flank a soft, reassuring pat.

Verminaard regarded his companion coldly. "How did you know, Aglaca?" he asked.

"Know?"

"That I was leaving for Neraka tonight? I told no one of the time."

"That you did not." Aglaca guided his mare to a high green patch of harrowgrass, where she bent amiably and began to graze. "But by your deeds I knew. Cleaned boots, for the first time in a month. Two capes draped over the foot of the bed, and your old gloves for travel. If anyone ever prepared for the road, and prepared obviously and visibly, it was you, Verminaard of Nidus."

His face burning, Verminaard followed Aglaca, guiding his stallion slowly over the dry ground. The beast snatched at the nourishing harrowgrass eagerly as Aglaca recounted the events of the day—how Verminaard had sharpened his blades and restrung his bow, how he had passed by the stable twice, looking in on the well-being of the horses.

"And finally," the lad continued, dismounting from the mare and drawing forth a strip of *quith-pa*, the dried fruit of elven travelers, "you steered even farther away from Robert and Daeghrefn than usual, as if Daeghrefn would actually attend to anything you'd a mind to do."

Verminaard nodded, eyeing the *quith-pa* wistfully. Already the romance of foraging had passed away, and the real hunger of the trail had set in.

He was soft, he knew—scarcely two hours from Castle Nidus, but he would gladly trade his sword for some dried fruit.

"Where's your dagger?"

Aglaca's question shocked him.

Wordlessly he dismounted, letting the moment pass. He muttered something about "forgotten," about "hurried departures" and "I prefer my sword, for that matter". Aglaca said nothing, but regarded him quietly.

"I hope your 'hurried departure' didn't keep you from bringing that second cloak," he observed, nodding toward the cloud bank to the north, rising out of the country they had left behind. "There's a storm following us. North to south, fast, with sheets of water and a day-long dark. Should be here about midmorning, by the way those nightbirds flew over."

Verminaard frowned. How did Aglaca know all this weather lore and counsel?

Aglaca smiled and vaulted into the saddle as though he had left some mysterious heaviness at the gates of Castle Nidus. "So you'd best have a rain-fast cloak on your person, Verminaard, or the two of us should find a cave or a copse very soon—a dry place to wait out the wind."

Verminaard lifted himself back onto Orlog and led the way toward the foothills and the rocky ground above the great Nerakan forest. Aglaca paused for a moment, watching his companion ride ahead.

"Where is your dagger indeed?" he whispered. Sadly, he brought the small glittering blade from beneath his cloak and held it aloft in the pale light of Solinari.

"It *will* protect you from evil, brother Verminaard," the Solamnic youth declared. "Even if *I* have to wield it."

* * * * *

The promised storm never reached them, but the dark clouds did.

For an hour or so, the lads rode at the head of a cold, moist wind as tendrils of ashen fog reached out and passed over them. The temperature dropped rapidly, and soon their breath misted and the flanks of the trotting horses steamed in the brisk new weather.

But there was still no rain, and a shadowy midday passed as Verminaard and Aglaca kept moving south, where the forest abutted a steep ridge of mountains, on the other side of which, Aglaca promised, lay the Plains of Neraka and the settlement itself.

All around them, the clouds thickened, covering the rock face, descending in a thick fog that blotted the sun entirely. They rode through a swimming grayness, the trail ahead lost, until Verminaard surrendered guidance to Orlog, letting the reins go slack as the stallion waded his way through the narrow passage. Aglaca followed closely, his mare's nose inches from Orlog's switching tail.

There were tales about the mountain bandits, how they bred for keen eyesight and could follow unwary travelers through storm and fog. How they called to their intended victims from the sides of the road. Hidden in mist and obscurity, they would cry out deceptively, like wounded men or lost babies.

Verminaard rose in the saddle, his hand resting uneasily on his sword. Twice he started at noises in the mist, at the sudden, flurried wingbeat of rooks and then at something large crashing blindly through the high aeterna foliage in the foothills. He had assured himself that the sounds meant nothing—were nothing, indeed, beyond the weavings of his own fears and imaginations—when the Voice came to him again, as though it rose to greet him out of the chill and the fog . . .

. . . or the fog itself was speaking.

Excellent, Lord Verminaard, it said, the old familiar accents sugary with praise. Verminaard glanced quickly behind him, but Aglaca's head was turned, his shoulders relaxed.

He did not hear the Voice. Good.

Of course he does not hear, Lord Verminaard, the Voice broke in, low and musical and neither masculine nor feminine, as usual. *Why should I let him hear what passes between us? He could not . . . understand. He is different, but it is much more than that. You understand, don't you? How singling you out was . . . all I could do?*

Verminaard nodded dimly, then looked back uneasily through the mist at his companion.

Just look at him, coaxed the Voice, and the fog seemed to play with Aglaca's angular features, molding his face to the soft roundness of a child's. *He hasn't an inkling. Nor does he have the instruments. The faculties.*

Verminaard blinked. Aglaca had always seemed clever enough to him. There was a certain blessing on the boy, a certain art like that of the runemaster's risting, where a humble stone is transformed to something magical with a quick stroke of the carving knife. And Aglaca could take a defeat—in the lists, in the hunt, wherever defeat was handed him—and turn it toward graciousness, to where defeat was no longer humiliating, and the victory no longer mattered as much, either.

But these are new circumstances, the Voice insisted, rising in pitch, in volume, drowning out his charitable thoughts. *And this time the victory matters—matters more than anything and anyone, yes, because it is this victory that can make your name.*

"Verminaard? Slow your horse," Aglaca urged. "This little mare's not used to following the likes of Orlog."

All of your mistakes and misdeeds, the Voice persisted, higher in pitch and more penetrating, *will be set right if you bring back the girl. Your father's favor is won, yes, and the esteem of the garrison—of Robert and the mage and the rest of them. What need will you have of runestones then, with your future assured and seamless and joyous?*

The reins shook in Verminaard's hands. It was too good, this prophecy, too good. . . .

Too good if you fail to do this alone, the Voice continued, a faint hum at the edge of hearing, *for if the child helps you, whom will your father credit for the rescue? And whom the mage?*

And whom the girl, for that matter?

"Wait!" Aglaca shouted as Verminaard urged Orlog to sudden speed on the trail ahead, vanishing into the gray fog.

* * * * *

Aglaca's voice faded behind him, the strained shouts of "Verminaard!" echoing in the maze of rock and cliff and entangled forest. At times, it seemed as though there were two or three voices clamoring in the mist.

Good, Verminaard thought, steering Orlog through the precarious fog. Let him find his own way back to Nidus. Or let him find worse, for all I care. Neraka is mine, and the girl. I don't need him to find the way.

Was it his own thought, or was it the Voice, returned to him and muffled by murk and distance until he could no longer distinguish it from his own musings?

He reached for the pouch of runes at his belt. They rattled reassuringly as Orlog passed through a passage of rubble and pine, and the trail narrowed and sloped southeast, weaving into the foothills, shadowed by the black looming form of Mount Berkanth.

Instinctively Verminaard touched the hilt of his sword. He could see better now. He was in the heart of bandit country, in the rocky highlands where the crack Nerakan cavalry patroled—worse by far than the bandits, and the horror of huntsman and horseman from Nidus all the way to the grasslands of Estwilde and Throt. Once no more than competent brigands, they were disciplined now and far more deadly, their numbers increasing as a great and unfathomable power pushed them to raids more and more daring, more and more successful.

He coughed nervously. It was a time that he wished for company. The Voice was utterly gone.

Steering the stallion over the sloping ground, he traveled by instinct, offering prayers to the gods of darkness. Takhisis he asked for safe passage, and Sargonnas the Consort, Hiddukel and Chemosh and Zeboim and the others until the names failed him. Then, with a deeper and more basic instinct, he drew his sword, resting the blade across the swell of the saddle.

Instantly, almost as a perverse answer to his prayers, shadows flitted through the mist around him, dark horsemen at the edge of his sight—some scarcely ten yards from where he trembled atop Orlog. Verminaard heard the snort and whinny of horses, a hushed flurry of what seemed to be command and instruction in a cant of Common speech and a language he did not understand—a rocky tongue, full of hard consonants and gutturals.

The shapes milled about at a threatening distance. Had they carried torches, as regular cavalry often did in a fog, he would have been discovered at once.

Bandits again. For surely they were the ones encircling him, lightless in the way of brigand riders, their destination west—through the forest, no doubt, then north to the high plains of Taman Busuk beyond. Soon their paths would cross his, and no fog would conceal that he was a stranger, and alone, and bearing the emblems of Castle Nidus.

For a moment, he froze in the saddle, paralyzed by fear and indecision. They would raise his head on a pike; they would torture him and leave him for dead on the high plains.

Where was Aglaca when you needed his wits?

Desperately Verminaard reversed his path. If he doubled back and rode among them, veiled by murk and distance, the bandits might assume he was one of them. They would be less likely to investigate, and the fog might give him enough time to figure an escape.

* * * * *

The bandits ambled into the forest, the sheer vallenwoods and tall evergreens black against the fog. Riding among them, Verminaard crouched in the saddle, his hood drawn over his eyes.

Was the fog dwindling again? He saw a dark shape to his left. A rider had stopped, waiting for him. He gripped his sword more tightly.

The moment was on him. Would he fight like his father, like Robert—like Aglaca, for that matter? Or would he back away as he had done at the stone bridge two seasons ago, when bravery and skill might have brought him the girl to begin with?

Grimly he resolved to fight through the lot of them or to die in the attempt. His hand shook on the pommel of the sword as he prepared to engage the man.

It was then that the fog dissolved around the shape, and Verminaard saw that it was no rider but a high outcropping of rock—a stone dolmen set five thousand years ago by the original inhabitants of the high Nerakan plains. He shook with relief.

Past the rock and into the thickening maze of the forest the bandits continued. Their voices swirled around Verminaard in a navigator's nightmare as sound dropped into confusion and the lad moved blindly, fearfully, his only guidance his fast-fading hope of escape.

It is like the Abyss, he thought, *where the soul is unraveled and eaten.*

Nonsense, the Voice comforted, rising from the black rocks and bathing him in a cold and soothing flow of words. *For there is no Abyss beyond the black recesses of the self, none but in your own imagining. Be a man! Be your father and steel yourself against these few! For the time will come. . . .*

"Where are you?" someone cried in front of him. The horses stopped around him.

See? I have already sent your help . . . your salvation. . . .

"Where *are* you, Verminaard?" came the cry again.

Aglaca. Lost and wandering.

A bandit twenty feet in front of him rose in the saddle and sniffed the air. Breathing a low, harsh curse in Nerakan, he tugged at the man nearest him.

"Straight on the Jelek trail, I'll wager," the bandit hissed, gesturing dramatically at the wide path branching west through the trees ahead. "Whoever it is, the fog has turned the poor fool about, and he's set for the worst we can give."

His companion laughed wickedly, and from all points behind Verminaard, horses seemed to emerge from the labyrinth of fog and shadow, moving west toward the end of the pass and the desperate, vulnerable voice that drew them like hunting wolves.

Verminaard brought Orlog to a halt as the last of the bandits passed scarcely a dozen feet to his right. Breathing a prayer to Hiddukel and Sargonnas, the young man sat motionless until the horseman passed into the mist and vanished.

The Voice had brought Aglaca back to him. Verminaard was sure of that. And the cry of the Solamnic youth had drawn the bandits away, into the fog and forest.

Perhaps they would overtake Aglaca. Perhaps he would escape them. Well, Aglaca was clever, resourceful. Maybe he would survive.

Verminaard suppressed a malicious smile. And then, for a moment, Abelaard crossed his mind—his father's pact with Laca and the reprisals that would come if Aglaca did not return.

He tried not to think of those.

The horse-sized obsidian rock that had startled him so loomed close again on his left. Verminaard smiled again. Another hundred yards and he would be clear of the woods, back on the open foothills.

Suddenly what he had thought was the rock moved forward, lifted its gloved hand. Verminaard gasped, fumbled for his sword, and . . .

"Thank the gods it's you, Verminaard!" Aglaca exclaimed.

"Aglaca! What . . . how . . ."

The Solamnic lad laughed merrily, slapping Verminaard on the shoulder affectionately.

"When Orlog started and carried you off, I thought it might be days until we found each other. And then . . . by Paladine! The bandits! I guided the mare behind a stone about a hundred yards east of here and quieted her. She's a good horse—calm and amiable, with scarcely a sniff or a snort as the whole column passed within a stone's throw of me.

"I saw you in front of them, and it looked as if you needed some help. So when they all had gone by, I shouted for you into the forest, and . . . well, the peculiar echoes in there must have done even better than I'd hoped, because here you are, and they're—well, they're somewhere else."

He sat back in the saddle and beamed.

Wordlessly, his mind a jumble of guilt and anger and simple perplexity, Verminaard sniffed and nodded. Things were back as they had been before the fog, before the Voice's prophecy, before his attempt to leave Aglaca in the dark isolation of the Khalkists.

He was stuck with him, stuck with the annoying cheer and the even more annoying cleverness—and the road to Neraka was clearing before him.

At least for the time being.

Slowly the horses moved east up the rise, and a wind rose from the south, scattering the fog from their path.

"Look at the sky!" Aglaca noted, pointing to a gray gap in the clouds. "Here I thought it was only fog. But it's gloaming as well. We've passed a day back and forth, you and I. Thanks be to Paladine that we found one another by nightfall!"

Chapter 8

"What color *are* her eyes?" Verminaard pressed as he and Aglaca steered the horses up a narrow path along the rock face, searching for high shelter away from the night and its predators, animal and human.

"It's hard to explain, Verminaard," the boy replied. "Oh, look—it's a cave of some sort. I figured as much. There's drasil trees aplenty sprouted on the plateau up there, and I've never known a cut path to lead to outright *nowhere*."

"A cave, you say?" Verminaard forgot all eyes and colors in the prospect. "What kind of—"

"Bats for certain," Aglaca interrupted. "Spiders near the mouth, and those strange blind crickets in the darkness, if it goes back far enough past the entrance. Perhaps a bear." He stared at Verminaard in mock fear. "Though that's unlikely, with all the maneuvering he'd have to do in the rootmaze. But if a bear sets upon us, at least there are two of us this time."

This time? Verminaard thought, his mind racing guiltily back to the fight with the bandits on the bridge. What does he know? What does he suspect?

Were it not for the bats fluttering into the mountain evening, the cave would have seemed comfortable, even pleasant. Rushes were strewn at its mouth, and its occupant had left not long ago at all and intended to return, judging from the lack of dust and cobweb, the fresh, fragrant straw, and the brooms neatly stacked outside the opening.

"Let's go in," Verminaard urged, stepping toward the overhanging rock.

"It's someone's dwelling," Aglaca objected, squinting into the darkness.

"Then you can sleep outside," Verminaard replied coldly. He stepped inside and foraged for serviceable kindling. Aglaca stood hesitantly at the cave mouth, then climbed the rock face to higher ground and a lookout point.

As Verminaard rummaged through straw and stacked crockery, he picked up a pitcher and examined it with a growing, uneasy sense that he had been here, or had at least seen these very things before.

"Look, Verminaard!" Aglaca exclaimed from the cave mouth. "Carrots and radishes! There's a little garden just above here. Not a sunlit acre, what with the shade from the drasil trees, but surprisingly good soil for this rocky country! I don't know how they did it, not at this height. There are late tomatoes as well, and the whole plot is bordered in daylilies! Some of them are blooming! You really should come and see! One has a face in it—"

110

"Did you find anything to use for a fire?" Verminaard asked curtly, his attention drawn back to the rubble on the floor of the cave. Aglaca vexed him with all this knowledge of plants and weeds and flowers. It was unseemly, irregular to him. Gruffly he waved his companion away. Better to burn what wood he could find in the cavern—chairs, perhaps, or the oaken bucket—than to wait while Aglaca dawdled, his nose again in the lilies.

His gaze returned to the bucket again. It was somehow the center of the cave, the focal point of the strange familiarity that seemed to inhabit the place. He approached it cautiously. A wizard might live here, and wizards were known to charge an item with fire, with venom, with destructive spells, so that when the unwary hand touched it, flame would course through the bones and poison through the veins. A thousand years after a wizard's departure or death, the spell could arise to ignite or corrupt.

This bucket had all the signs. A line of ragged marks along the rim—not weathering or chipping, but the intentional carvings of a knowing hand.

Verminaard listened for the Voice. Whatever it was that spoke to him no doubt had a storehouse of lore and magic.

But again the Voice was silent.

Verminaard swore softly and looked into the bottom of the pail. He blinked and looked again.

There was something about the swirl of the damp wood grain in the bottom of the bucket that seemed to shimmer and change. For a moment, it was a spiral, a swirl, then it seemed like the dark matrix at the hub of a spider's web, like the *hagall* rune, which promised misfortune and crisis.

And then, as though he gazed into the proverbial crystals and orbs at the Tower of High Sorcery, he thought he saw a rocky landscape, like the Khalkists but even darker, more severe, a hand reaching out to him from the depths of the swirling wood, reaching, grasping, failing. . . .

Verminaard shook his head and looked again. The hand and the webbing, the rocks and the rune had all passed from sight, merely a trick of light on the water-stained wood of the bucket. Aglaca called again from outside, something about columbines.

But the back of the cave drew Verminaard now. A small mound in a shadowy corner, more humble and less mysterious than the bucket, but very compelling. Quietly, with a single glance over his shoulder, he crept toward the shadows and the strange construction.

Dirt and stones. Someone was buried here.

An unfathomable sadness passed over the young man as he knelt beside the gravesite. Something just below his memory stirred, a warmth and a faint, fragile peace. . . .

"Verminaard!" Aglaca shouted a third time, and the thoughts fled suddenly. With a growl of impatience, Verminaard started off to find him.

As he moved toward the mouth of the cave, a glitter in the straw caught his eye. He knelt and picked up a small pendant, the silver chain broken, the thumb-sized gemstone sparkling. Rubbing the stone with the hem of his tunic, Verminaard marveled at the midnight purple of the thing, a color halfway between violet and blue. There was no feel of magic or omen about the pendant, but it might turn a pretty penny from some courtier at Nidus.

Or make a gift for a mysterious young woman.

He thought little more of it, dropping it in the bag with the rune stones. It clicked and rolled against them softly, the sound as if someone deep in the cavern had opened a hidden door. Verminaard shrugged and hastened up the trail to the garden, where Aglaca crouched above a fan-shaped plant, his gaze intent on the solitary flower that bloomed from its solitary scape.

"See?" Aglaca said, beaming, cupping the unplucked

blossom delicately in his hand. He motioned Verminaard closer.

"Delightful," the larger youth declared flatly, his eyes elsewhere, alert to danger from predator or bandit.

"It's a beautiful peach color, and its eye zone is an odd sort of purple . . . and this marking—the face, or maybe it looks more like a mask. And the flower is a perfect triangle," Aglaca insisted, but Verminaard wasn't listening.

"There must be a better place to stay the night, Aglaca. We should move on before the darkness overtakes us."

"I don't understand, Verminaard."

There's a haunt to the cave, he wanted to say. Some . . . presence. I don't know if it's friendly or hostile, but that bucket in there . . .

Don't tell him, the Voice urged, rising from the cave's mouth, as if the black, glinting mountain itself was speaking. *You know how the ignorant laugh at your lore and runes and signs. Speak of defense. Of the depth of the cave . . .*

"The cave goes back forever," Verminaard said dutifully. "It burrows through the mountain, I'd wager, and with no telling how many branches and chambers and passages. Dangerous things could hide in those depths, and I'm not going to risk your safety again."

He forced a grimaced smile at his irritating companion, who smiled in response.

"The danger of that's a slim one, Verminaard. The roots of the drasil tree go down a hundred feet, maybe more. They grow over caves to . . . well, I suppose it's to feed the roots or something—some kind of nourishment they need in the cavern air. They know enough to grow through the rock, but not enough to stop growing. The back of that cave is probably atangle with 'em, like a cage or a baffle. Nothing bigger than a man could navigate it, and a small man indeed, no match for you."

"But there could be something else," Verminaard

murmured. "Something unreckoned in your botany. Scorpions, maybe. Some kind of cave viper."

Aglaca frowned. "It's getting dark. And there's—"

Verminaard did not wait. "We'll go at once. You are my responsibility, after all."

He had almost convinced himself with his own excuses.

But still the cave and the little garden haunted him as he and Aglaca saddled and rode south, and the dark vanished over his shoulder in the unsettling red of a Khalkist sunset. The place haunted him still as he warmed himself at the night's campfire, the light muffled deftly by Aglaca against the eyes of beasts and bandits and worse.

It would haunt him through the morning as they passed the south edge of the Nerakan Forest—the Blood Grove, where it was said that the victims of banditry hung, dried and blackened like unpicked grapes, and wild cats scuttled along the woodland trails in even more unspeakable foraging.

Dark and deep, serenaded the Voice, which seemed to beckon from the shadowy woods. *Dark and deep, and the desolate secrets hanging in decay, in decay and forgetfulness. . . .*

Is it not an ending place for enemies? For unloving and unlovely fathers?

Verminaard hearkened to the Voice, to its bottomless seduction. He vividly imagined Daeghrefn swinging slowly from the black branches of a drooping, rotting aeterna tree, the air aswarm with kites, with raptors. . . .

"No!" he exclaimed, wrenching his thoughts back to sunlight, to breathing, to the cool Nerakan plains and the spreading grasslands.

To Aglaca, riding beside him on the mare, who regarded him with alarm and concern, he muttered, "It's nothing. I must have . . . must have fallen asleep. Don't bother yourself."

"It's a voice, isn't it?" Aglaca asked quietly, leaning across the saddle.

"A voice? Don't be foolish." His own reply sounded shrill, frightened.

Aglaca slowed the mare, brought her to a halt. Verminaard swore softly, reined in the stallion, and guided him gently back to the spot where Aglaca waited, his face cloudy and solemn.

"Foolish it may be to you, Verminaard," Aglaca said, his words still unnaturally hushed, "but I've heard a voice myself sometimes, and maybe I'm gone a bit to the wayside from staring at the red moon for too long, but that voice has told me things best never spoken. And best never listened to."

"Then don't listen," Verminaard blurted. Then quietly, more cautiously, "What does it tell you?"

"That I'm *exceptional*," Aglaca replied, with a strange half-smile, "and in a way that no one else is exceptional. It's a heady wine that voice pours, telling me that it talks to me alone, and that some arrangement in time and space has brought me, and me alone, to high degree and to great position. It tells me darker things, too—that my father has abandoned me, that he and your father consider me only a pawn in some long, political game, but it does not matter what the voice says, because I choose not to believe it. I believe what my father said before I left: that he loved me no matter what."

Verminaard sniffed, goading Orlog to a trot, heading south over the Nerakan plains. But his thoughts wandered back down a blind tunnel, at the end of which the Voice lay coiled in the depths of his memory, and the coveted words of the Voice were deeper, more sweet than Aglaca's thickheaded skepticism.

He would choose not to believe as well. But he would choose not to believe Aglaca. And so he changed the line of talk altogether. "What color are her eyes, for the last time?"

Aglaca fumbled for an image, for words of hue and

light, and then he had it. "They are exactly the color of that lily's eye," he said gleefully.

Verminaard ground his teeth and swore Aglaca's doom, silently, on all the dark gods. Savagely he spurred Orlog forward.

"Wait for me!" Aglaca shouted, urging the mare to a gallop. "Wait for me, Verminaard!"

Already Verminaard was racing into the flatlands of the Nerakan plateau.

* * * * *

The town of Neraka was a vagabond place, makeshift and dirty.

The decent mountain folk who had peopled it first, goatherds and humble, ingenious farmers, had been forced out over the years by a constant flow of brigands and highwaymen, cutthroats and ne'er-do-wells of all countries and races. There it would have ended, the village dying out on its own when plunder grew scarce, were it not for the building that sprouted in its midst.

For Takhisis had chosen the place, in the way that she always chose—quietly and secretly, in a place where the black obsidian foundations of the temple would raise no alarm. For when she returned to the world and restored her dominion, Neraka was to be the heart of her empire.

And already that heart was beginning to beat.

As Aglaca and Verminaard approached from the north over the flat volcanic plain, the spire of the temple was the first thing they saw. Gnarled like an ancient oak in the heart of the town, it twisted amid half-finished city walls, clouding the southern sky with its bulk and with the strange, shimmering aura of darkness that surrounded it.

Outside the temple walls, the builders' scaffolding, and the ramshackle guardhouses, a hundred fires littered the surrounding village, the black smoke of smithy and kitchen and shrine intermingling with the foul smell of tannery and slaughterhouse. Beyond the village itself, in the outlying plains, scores of squat black tents lay scattered almost randomly, above them an array of pennants and banners—white and black closest to Verminaard, but blue and yellow, red and green in the distance, each adorned with the scowling face of a dragon, each waving in the shifting mountain winds.

The two young men crouched not fifty yards from the northernmost encampment. There, shielded by the tall grass, they ate sparingly from the raw vegetables Aglaca had sensibly gathered from the garden above the cave.

"I feel like a rabbit," Verminaard muttered. "Hidden in the grass eating radishes."

Aglaca snickered and shook his head. Then, rising until he could see over the top of the grass, he peered solemnly toward the army of banners.

"I had no idea the bandits were so plentiful," he declared. "It's no wonder Daeghrefn hasn't killed them all yet."

"Enough of the bandits. Where now?" Verminaard asked. "Where is *she*?"

Aglaca looked at him curiously. "I can't tell amid all these flags and commotions. We'll have to scout it out, keeping our distances and wits about us and our ears open as well as our eyes. Not even bandits can hide her from us forever."

* * * * *

But it seemed long indeed, as the lads skirted the outlying camps.

No sooner had they started to move west, in a wide counterclockwise circle about the village, than their presence was masked by yet another thick mist. Out of nowhere it rose again, rolling over the city until only the towers of the temple were visible through the dense fog, and the colors of the banners were muted, lost in a dozen layers of gray.

It was no ragtag group of bandits that they circled, no disorganized band of cutthroats. Around Neraka was assembling the makings of an army, and judging from the languages and accents and dialects that carried to them through the fog, it was an army gathered from far and exotic places—from Sanction and Estwilde, but also from Kern and from other places where the accents were even stranger. They were far from alert, and far from ready, but the numbers were great and growing.

"See? Aglaca whispered. "Some of them are only now pitching tents. This is a time of arrivals, but what they're arriving *for* is a mystery."

"Whatever it is," Verminaard observed, "my father should know. He'll not take to a huge Nerakan army at his doorstep."

"Nor will they take to him, I'd reckon," Aglaca agreed. "Perhaps the girl can tell us."

"If I ever *find* her," Verminaard muttered gloomily. "Perhaps this whole business has been unwise."

Then the Voice came to him, its inflections as soft and mysterious as the fog, its tones more melodious, more feminine than ever before.

Unwise? Of course not. You have traveled this far this well, and the prison is at hand. The Pen, they call it, on the western grounds, in the midst of the green encampment.

Be ruled by me. Despite the fog and the sentries and the perils ahead of you, I am here to guide you.

"But there are so many of them," Verminaard protested aloud, his voice shrill and thin in the foggy air. Aglaca looked back at him in alarm and signaled for silence.

The day will come, the Voice continued, quietly and

alluringly, *when you will be thankful for their numbers. You will come back here, Verminaard of Nidus, and all this power I will give you, and the glory of it, for it is given to me of old, and in my power to give it to whomever I please. . . .*

"Stay behind me," Aglaca whispered sharply. "And stay down where you belong!"

Verminaard blinked stupidly, his thoughts drawn from the maze of the Voice by his companion's warning. He found himself standing full upright in the waist-high grass, an easy target had the fog been thinner and the sentries more alert.

Instantly he crouched, but the Voice was not through with him.

Be ruled by me, it intoned. *These things are mine to give, for the smallest of favors. I shall show you this as the hours unfold.*

"No," Aglaca said flatly, to nothing and no one, his back to Verminaard. The older lad turned toward him in astonishment, and looking over his shoulder, Aglaca grinned sheepishly.

"Just that voice again, Verminaard," he admitted. "Come to me with another set of lies. Guess I forgot myself in the quarrel."

"Enough of voices," Verminaard declared. "We need to find the girl. This fog can't last forever."

* * * * *

It can if a dragon wields it, Ember thought, coiled not a hundred yards from the young men, his thoughts masked against intrusion and his wings moving slowly, cyclically, fanning the fog he had summoned magically as it spread through the landscape, darkening and thickening.

Takhisis's commands were convenient, the dragon mused. How better to take the girl than to have Verminaard and Aglaca do it for him?

119

He smiled, baring his many rows of long teeth. His golden eyes glittered as he searched the mist, then found Verminaard and Aglaca again as they stooped in the grass and waited. It would not be long before they found the Pen.

His scales rippled red and gold and red with a fierce anticipation. It was all falling into place.

Only this *voice* troubled him. Aglaca spoke of it now freely and often, and to hear him tell it, you would think he argued with it daily. It might be hallucination, born of his loneliness at Castle Nidus, but the dragon suspected otherwise.

It might be what prompted Aglaca when, in the guise of the mage Cerestes, Ember had offered the young man magic. Perhaps this voice had urged Aglaca to refuse those studies.

The other one seemed oblivious to the coaxing of this voice—of any voice. Then again, he was dense and stubborn, not the kind to be won by words and argument. Aglaca was the brains and Verminaard the muscle of this quest, and, masked by this magical fog, it would not be long until the girl was in their hands. Then, in the safety of Nidus, in the trust of her rescuers, her lips would open to a kindly dark mage named Cerestes. She would tell him of druids and runes and magnificent strategies, never knowing she spoke those words into the ears of a dragon.

He would know before all of them. Before Verminaard and Daeghrefn, to be sure, but before Aglaca as well. And therefore, before Laca's spies and Laca himself. . . .

And before Takhisis. Before the Dark Queen knew, and found the missing rune, and the stone, and the key to her worldly kingdom.

He would sound the girl and the rune, the lads and the grounds of the temple he faced, dark in the midst of the fog he had engendered. He would sound them all, and when the Dragon Queen's mission failed at the gates of her own temple, he would be the lord of the mountains and the lands that lay beyond them. The clerics would answer to him, and it would be his governing voice in the ears of the rich and powerful, not some thin, insinuating babble in the mind of a lone Solamnic boy.

The dragon purred, a low, rumbling sound that the lads and the sentries beyond mistook for thunder, for a rising storm out of the north.

* * * * *

This is a comedy of mirrors, the goddess thought, reclining in the warm, swirling night winds of the Abyss.

Around her lay darkness on darkness, darkness layering darkness until those places where light had fled entirely seemed hazy, almost luminous, compared to places darker still that surrounded them — a gloom not only of shadows but of spirit.

But Takhisis was laughing now, her low, melodious laugh echoing in the great surrounding void. A comedy of mirrors, when one character watches another, who in turn watches a third watching a fourth, and all of this observed by the audience itself, watching from beyond the play's little world of spies and intruders.

Ember certainly did not know she watched him as he crouched, flightless and stupid, in the high, foggy grasslands. Let him approach her temple; let him see what he would see.

She would win, regardless of what he discovered.

As for the lads, they knew her only fleetingly, when what they called "the Voice" came to them, and she told them dark, unimaginable things. One would be hers, twisted from his high bloodline to her desire and design.

There would be no room for the other.

Turning in the perpetual blackness, fluttering her

pennons, she dropped straight down ten thousand fathoms, plummeting, falling, dreaming, until at length she floated amid a wild, universal hubbub of stunning sounds, of disembodied voices all confused, borne through the hollow dark. She laughed amidst the chaos of noise, and she thought of Laca.

His pedigreed line, aflourish since the Age of Light, would end in a traitorous son.

It would be the last drop of Huma's blood, she thought. With one of the two—whether Verminaard or Aglaca, she cared not which, though she had begun to suspect which one it would be—the line would end.

She thought of Huma and shivered. Thought of the bright lance exploding in her chest, the incandescent swirl of darkness and the crackle of the firmament as the lance thrust her into the negative plane of dark and chaos, of the night winds that whirled about her, buoying and buffeting her, and of the continual whining and whirring of these voices at the edge of nothingness, the hysterical gnatsong of the damned.

She had destroyed him in their battle, but at the great cost of three thousand years of banishment. She had destroyed him, brotherless and heirless, and for centuries, she had dreamt, believing that his line had died against her in that final battle, there at the end of the Second Dragon War.

But there were the cousins, and the cousins had sons. Laca had been the last. Distant in descent and in blood, but Huma's kin nonetheless. And then there was Aglaca.

And along with Aglaca, there was the visit of Laca to Nidus, beneath the roof of his old friend Daeghrefn, with whose comely wife he forgot all loyalty, all honor and Oath and Measure, if for only a bright morning. . . .

So with Aglaca, there was the child Verminaard, fair of hair and blue-eyed, the opposite of Daeghrefn, but the image of his real father.

So Huma's line had branched again. Almost as though it had scattered to elude her, to distract her from her three-millennia search. But she had located them both—both of Laca's sons—and time, circumstance, and her own devices had brought them together at last.

And before she chose between them—or rather, before one of them chose *her*—there was the matter of the girl.

For a while, Takhisis had let the Nerakans hold the girl. Surely that softhearted wretch L'Indasha would reveal herself and come to the rescue—in a hostile country where the veils Paladine had cast over her whereabouts would no longer protect her.

But weeks had passed, and there had been no sign of the druidess. So she had turned to Laca's sons: They would bring her the girl—they and that scheming subordinate of hers, who fanned the fog unwittingly, veiling their movements to the Nerakan guards.

Once they had brought the girl to Nidus, the sounding would begin. Something in the girl's thoughts resisted all probing, and her dreams were opaque and unfathomable.

No doubt Paladine had veiled her as well.

But the girl would leave Nidus eventually, and her path would lead to L'Indasha Yman, to the secret of the blank rune. Then all the ingredients would fall into place—the mysterious Judyth of Solamnia, the immortal druidess, and the last of Huma's line.

The last of Huma's line. In whatever role he would play. She would sound him soon, try him in the darkness of her own choosing. Oh, yes. The ingredients were all there. It would all make sense when Takhisis gathered them. Of that she was sure.

The voices wailed and gibbered around her in a chaos of laments. The Queen of the Dragons extended her sable wings.

The time would come when the rune was blank no longer, but inscribed with its long-lost opposing symbols, and when the last rune was added to the others, their prophetic powers would be perfect. She would find the green keystone to the Temple then, for the restored runes would see through all—through centuries of stone and through the clouded chaos of history. The runes were knowledge, and with that knowledge, Takhisis could open the portals to the world. And return to govern it.

She spread her wings and turned in a hot, dry wind, rising to the lip of the Abyss, to the glazed and dividing firmament beyond which she could not travel. It looked forbidding, mysterious, like thick ice on a bottomless pool. There, in the heart of nothing, Takhisis banked and glided, aloft on the wafting current and her own dark strategies.

Chapter 9

As the Voice had told Verminaard, the Pen lay to the west, in an encampment amid a forest of green banners.

He crept closer, almost to the banners themselves, where he could hear the sniffling and coughing of a rheumy sentry. Aglaca followed gamely, crouching in the shadow of a large green pavilion, peering across the campground at the Nerakan stockade.

"I've never seen anything of this sort," Aglaca marveled. "The stockade is a living thing."

Verminaard gave the stockade a second look.

Sure enough, the Pen was alive and growing—a tight circle of small-boled trees, so close together that a mouse could barely pass between the trunks. Their branches spread and intertwined, forming a netted canopy that kept out the rain, no doubt, and most of the sunlight. Near the Pen's narrow entrance, the sentries paced, and the air seemed to bristle and crackle before them.

Aglaca smiled. "It's easier than I thought."

Verminaard shot him a puzzled look.

"Those are drasil trees," the young Solamnic explained. "Remember the ones above the cave in the mountains?"

Verminaard did not.

With a sigh, Aglaca continued, leaning back into the darkness. "Once again, they grow over caves. That's the point. This whole area must sit atop a cavern—perhaps a system of caverns. When we find an entrance, it will be simple. We'll come up under the Pen and burrow her out."

"Won't that be hard to do? To break through all that cavern rock?" Verminaard still did not understand.

"The trees have already done that for us," Aglaca replied delightedly. "The system of roots has broken it to gravelly soil, I'd wager. The two of us, at work for a couple of hours with sword and knife, could hack a hole big enough to draw out the girl—to draw out her entourage, if need be. Then it's back to where we left the horses, and on to Nidus before the Nerakans know they've been . . . *undermined*."

* * * * *

The caves were easy enough to find.

And Aglaca was right: The whole plateau was riddled with tunnels and fissures. The tunnels branched and burgeoned, forming an intricate network that spread roughly westward, toward the Nerakan walls, the center of town, and the temple itself.

Aglaca led the way. It seemed that he had a dwarf's

underground sense, weaving through the dark, perplexing tunnel system, his hands extended before him. Rejecting blind passages almost by instinct, he would feel at an opening, shake his head and pass by.

Deep within the tunnels, Aglaca withdrew a tinderbox and a small lamp from a pouch at his belt. Crouching quietly and suddenly, so that Verminaard almost stumbled over him in the gloom, the Solamnic youth lit the lamp deftly and held it aloft.

The darkness dispelled a little. Amid confusion and discord, rubble and guano, strange, translucent crickets whirred and stalked blindly over the glistening stone walls and the ancient cobwebbed beams that supported the tunnels ahead.

"I had no idea they were . . ." Verminaard began. But the depth and extent of the caverns baffled him.

Another sound, high and melodious, filtered to the young men like a chorus of a thousand distant voices, the harmonies so intricate that the music itself teetered on the edge of chaos. Beautiful though it was, the sound was distracting, and Verminaard shielded his ears.

"What is it?" he whispered, but Aglaca only shook his head.

"You should know. It's the sound of spellcraft," the smaller youth explained. "Something surrounds the Pen—a shell of energy or light. Since we can't pass around it or through it, we're on our way under it and up to the girl."

"How do you know, Aglaca?" Verminaard slipped narrowly through a latticework of thick roots. "You don't listen when it comes to magic."

"I don't listen to *Cerestes*," Aglaca corrected mysteriously and handed the lamp to his companion.

Though he was thoroughly lost by now, turned about in the tunnels, and though each passage was indistinguishable from the last, Verminaard could tell that, slowly but directly, Aglaca was guiding them *somewhere*. Resentfully he held the lamp aloft, giving the smaller lad the light to see by.

The rescue had been Verminaard's idea, after all, planned over runes and misgivings in the dark nights of Castle Nidus, and now this interloper—this *hostage*—had seized command with his cleverness and know-how.

I am no oracle, he thought. And yet I see the lay of this tunnel—how this venture will be reported to the ears of those at home, and who will receive the glory for the rescue.

He glared at Aglaca, who bent down a tunnel, nodded, and motioned to Verminaard excitedly, urgently.

"Here it is!" he whispered. His blue eyes caught for a moment in the torchlight, flickering a bright, unexplainable red. "Drasil roots. Looks to be a circle of 'em, like a ring of mushrooms. We're directly under the Pen, I'll wager. It's all digging and a straight climb from here, Verminaard. Set the lamp where it gives the most light."

Verminaard's enmity vanished with the news. Thoughts of the girl returned like a fresh wind in the damp and musty cavern. Verminaard wedged the lamp into a crack in the tunnel wall, split by one of the drasil roots in its blind plummet through both ceiling and floor of the cave. Taking up his sword, he sprang compliantly to Aglaca's side, ready to hack and dig and fight anything that stood between him and the captured girl.

He was so close now to realizing his daydreams. She would be a beauty of unparalleled fairness. Verminaard had had his share of serving girls and milkmaids, but none of them would be like this creature. Her eyes would be pale blue stars and her silky hair the color of flax. She would know him immediately for the one who'd planned and propelled her rescue, and she would be forever grateful—so grateful that she would never wish to speak to another man. The way she would say his name would—

"Verminaard! I said you can start anytime! Where have you been?"

"You wouldn't understand. And don't get pushy with me."

It was only a matter of minutes before the roots knotted above them, as thick as cords, as fingers, tendrils snagging their weapons, dulling them in a maddening, fibrous web. Verminaard thrashed vainly at the snarl of root and dirt and rock that seemed to open for him and engulf him as he climbed past the more slender roots to ankle-thick, leg-thick monstrosities that broke through the rock above and below, searching blindly for air and water and sustenance.

Slowly the network of roots surrounded them. It seemed like an underground stockade, a mirror image of the Pen that stood directly above.

"We could work like loggers for a week down here," Aglaca muttered, "and still be no closer to squeezing those shoulders of yours through this tangle."

Verminaard gasped for breath and wiped his dirty brow. Between the dust and his exertion, the air in the cavern was slowly becoming unbreathable.

"We'll go back to the surface. Fight our way in," said Verminaard, moving back the way he'd come.

"Nonsense," Aglaca replied. "You saw their numbers. And there are ogres as well—I could smell them through the fog. I'll bet they're penned up nearby, no doubt enchanted into service to build the wall around the temple. Prisoners or not, they'll fight for the bandits rather than help us out. No, between the brigands and their servants, this is still the best of entries."

Verminaard winced and twisted his foot out of a long tendril.

Aglaca grinned slyly. "Listen. I spoke only of loggers," he said. "Not of burglars."

Verminaard scowled. He was doing it again. A plan was hatching in that ever so clever Solamnic brain—something complicated and intricate, no doubt, rife with twists and illusions, masks and double-talk. Sheathing his sword, his hands still numb from hacking at the roots, he sat on the cavern floor, awaiting a long explanation.

He was surprised at how simple it was.

But he did not like it one whit.

And his thoughts dwelt on the woman pent above them, and the charms and imagined deceits of Aglaca Dragonbane.

*   *   *   *   *

Hagalaz and Isa, two young bandit sentries, stood watch at the narrow opening to the Pen. It was no more than a small gap in the drasil trees, curtained of late by their courtly sergeant, who respected the captive's dignity and modesty.

Now was the time when the curtain most availed the girl, as the servingwomen brought in the pitchers of warm water, poured it into the hostage's tub, then backed courteously from the living enclosure, their heads bowed and the pitchers empty. Shortly, the men could hear the girl moving behind the thick canvas. She muttered to herself, and it sounded like two voices in the Pen, like a hushed conversation, but that was nothing new. Judyth of Solanthus always talked to herself, or murmured incantation, or prayed to her foreign gods.

The thoughts of the guards were scarcely on her prayers. Instead, they were concluding a long speculation as to what the Lady Judyth wore beneath that purple cloak and riding tunic, each sentry goading the other to inch aside the curtain and peer in on the girl as she undressed for her bath.

The speculation was merely cultural, they told themselves. It could be of interest to the Nerakan wives and mothers as to how a wealthy Solamnic girl might dress, especially since she hailed from one of the more ancient and honored cities of that western country.

The interest was academic, they told themselves, at least for now, while the sergeant's orders were strict. The temple clerics had told him not to lay a hostile hand on the girl. Not until Takhisis had given them a sign as to her fate.

So for now, the interest *was* academic, and their attentions as well. They winked in a most scholarly fashion, holding their breath as they quietly peeked through the curtain. It was a far better job than guarding a foul-smelling band of fifty ogres.

* * * * *

Aglaca climbed higher through the tough entanglements, hands clutching at coarse, sandy root, the leavings of guano, and silt and gravelly dust. Finally, balanced a dozen feet above Verminaard, he could reach no farther. The crumbling ceiling of the cave dipped directly above, and the sound of the girl's muffled words reached him through the thin layer of dirt and rock.

He gritted his teeth and began to dig—slowly and cautiously at first, but with rising urgency as he heard the murmuring cease, heard the girl's voice clearly for the first time: *"What in the name of Branchala . . . "*

Then there was light, and the torn edge of a wooden tub hovering over him. The water swirled and trickled above him, yet he remained dry.

"By Paladine!" he breathed.

The water pooled and was caught on some strange shimmering tension in the air. It was like looking at a rainstorm through glass or ice, and for a moment, Aglaca thought that indeed it was glass above him. He weaved a moment on his ladder of rough roots, clutching for purchase in the fractured dark.

"Who—who *are* you?" the girl whispered, peering through the puddle. He recognized the face, the lavender gown she clutched to her breast, the brilliant blue-lavender eyes.

"Y-Your rescuer, by Paladine's grace! We are two. The other waits below," he muttered triumphantly and vaulted toward the light.

It was then that he discovered the magical shell that lay between him and the astonished girl. The spell-charged air snared him, pushed him back. He fell back into the roots with a crash and an oath, staring stupidly up at her. His hands crackled with sparks as he clutched for balance, and his hair stood on end.

"Do you think a simple line of trees could keep me in?" the girl hissed to Aglaca. "Or keep the guardsmen out, if they fancied to trouble me? The priests in that temple have magicked the Pen with a glyph of warding."

"Glyph of warding?"

"An old sign, it is. Charged with shamanic conjury when the black moon rises."

Aglaca swallowed. This hostage girl knew magic beyond his wildest dreams. "How do we . . ." he began, but a quick wave of her hand urged him to silence.

"I know the countercharm," she whispered. "I didn't go guileless into the mountains, but I need another voice for the casting."

"Another voice? Why?"

"No time. Speak after me. Then stand back. There's a big leak in this bathtub. You're partway under it."

Blushing, his eyes averted and his legs lodged in a chaos of roots, the lad waited for Judyth to dress, then repeated the spinning, incomprehensible Elvish that she spoke to him. It was a brief verse, its vowels dancing in subtle arrangements, and twice the girl had to stop him, correct him, and start him again in the strange incantation.

But the third time it worked.

In triumph and relief, Aglaca repeated the last line, and the air above him stirred and snapped. A deluge of soapy water tumbled from the broken tub, and Judyth, now fully dressed in the lavender robe, slipped through the wet hole and clutched her rescuer about the waist.

"Hurry!" she ordered through clenched teeth, untangling her sleeve from a stray root tendril. "You've freed more than a damsel in distress."

* * * * *

Verminaard had waited sullenly in the cavern, clutching an oozing shoulder wound he had received from backing into a sharp broken root. Then he heard her voice—hushed and melodious and low, not the high-stringed harp music he had imagined—and it was suddenly drowned by a rumble overhead, a tumult of shouting and screaming and the crashing sound of buildings and lean-tos shaking and toppling.

Judyth quickly descended into the torchlight, Aglaca leading her carefully over and around the latticework of roots. They were both wet, dripping with soapy water, and it would be much later before Verminaard discovered the reason.

Verminaard stepped back indignantly.

It was your *plan,* the Voice insinuated. *Your plan, and a good one, conceived in a noble spirit . . . the stuff of heroism, all—* For a moment, the Voice paused and garbled, as though at the edge of an unpronounceable word. Then it continued. *All Huma and lances and glorious victory. It was*

*your idea and your doing, and who leads the girl forth? And
why does he lead her?*

The Voice repeated the questions again and again, each
time more softly until they merged entirely with Verminaard's thoughts, and the lad forgot the Voice altogether, asking the questions himself as he reached out to
help the girl through the last of the knotted entanglements.

"Thank you," she breathed, and brushed back her
hood.

Behind her, a stalactite crashed to the cavern floor.

For the first time, Verminaard looked into the face of the
girl he had dreamt of and pursued through two seasons.
Her dark hair shone like obsidian in the guttering lamp-
light; it was not the spun gold he had imagined. And
though her skin was flawless, the touch of her hand like
fine silk or velvet, that hand was dark, not porcelain or
alabaster as the poems had told him it would be, should
be.

And the eyes. Deep and lavender, a strange blue, bright
and fathomless. Like the eye of that daylily.

She was not the girl he had imagined at all.

Behind her, a rockslide opened the cavern to a shifting,
misty light from above. She shoved Verminaard toward
the cave entrance and shouted as he staggered back in
amazement.

"Don't stand there gawking or we'll all be crushed! Get
us out of here!"

* * * * *

They emerged from the cavern just as it collapsed behind
them. Verminaard wheeled about, open-mouthed, as the
passage behind him caved in with a dusty crash, the
plateau collapsing, concentrically spreading all the way to

the base of the Nerakan walls, toppling tents and lean-tos and makeshift cottages in a matter of seconds.

He could barely speak. His order that they move quickly to retrieve the horses came as a dry, croaking sound in a landscape of deafening noise. They hurried toward the wooded rise where Orlog and the mare nervously waited, and did not look behind again as the tower itself quaked and the first fires sparked in the town of Neraka.

* * * * *

They did not look back, but not far from the green encampment, another pen—this one fashioned of stone and timber—toppled when the ogres pushed against it. There were two dozen of them, freed from ensorcellment by the chanting of Judyth and Aglaca, and they were joined by thirty others whose chains had burst on the scaffolding near the walls. Drowsily, stupidly, as though they had freshly awakened, the monsters tramped through the fallen tents, gathering torches as they wandered, weaving in dangerous circles and rapidly igniting more thatch and wood. They were dark and hulking in the torchlight, draped in skins and furs, their own sallow hides and blue-black hair glistening in the rising flames as the fires spread through the settlement.

By dark instinct, the ogres moved to the spot of the chanting, where the spell that had contained them was first broken. They reached the Pen and milled together, gaping at one another, uprooting tent posts and wattled walls in their dull uncertainty.

Then one of them—grizzled and small for his race—lifted his face and smelled the switching wind.

"Horse!" he cried out, his broken mouth salivating at the prospect of food. "Horse . . . and young humans!"

With an exultant, rumbling cry, the ancient ogre rushed toward the green flags, and the rest of the monsters followed.

* * * * *

Ember heard the outcry of the sentries—the name "Judyth" rising like an alarm out of the smoke—and fanned his wings contentedly as the magical fog redoubled over the city and the plains, mingling with the smoke and casting the town into a thick and abiding darkness.

They had her now. Ember was certain. And they would need cover of shadow and cloud to mask their path west through the mountains.

The dragon stirred and rumbled. He had done all he could. He would return to Castle Nidus and await their arrival. There he would be Cerestes again, handsome and witty and learned for the benefit of the captive girl. He would charm the rune-wielder, and he would sound her like the lost rune, rist her in his intricate thoughts and plans until she told him everything she had learned at the feet of the druids.

He would steal her out from the watch of the young humans.

And when he had learned her heart, he would also learn the heart of all the runes.

* * * * *

The dragon lumbered into the sky, rose above the maze of fog into the clear mountain air, and turned his golden eyes to the northwest and to Castle Nidus, abuzz with rumors and vanishments of its own.

Two days into the lads' journey, their absence had

become unbearable to the seneschal Robert. He had coaxed, wheedled, and finally berated the master of the castle. Lord Daeghrefn, lost in memories of betrayal and winter, finally stirred at the harsh words of his retainer and noticed that the young men were indeed missing.

"Where would they take those horses for this long, Robert?" he bellowed, stalking down the halls of the castle toward the entrance, the bailey, and the stable beyond them. With a growl, he swept a torch from its sconce on the wall. The brand struck the floor, sputtered, and went out, and Robert coughed behind him.

"Two days is a long time in the saddle if you're hunting, sir. I fear the worst: that they've decided to be heroes, as young men are prone to decide, and that they've taken off toward Neraka with some quest a-brewing."

"Then it's Verminaard's fault!" Daeghrefn stormed, wheeling to face Robert at the sunlit door to the bailey. "What if something happens to Aglaca?"

"Sir?"

"If Aglaca falls in some harebrained escapade, then Abelaard's life is forfeit!"

Robert hesitated. "I reckon that's the rules of the *gebonaud*, but I don't think—"

"Where's the fool who helped them with the horses?" Daeghrefn shouted, and made for the distant stable.

* * * * *

Frith was long gone by the time Daeghrefn burst through the stable doors.

He had seen it coming for an hour or two. The young masters were not yet back, though Master Verminaard had sworn they would need the horses only for a night. There was tumult in the keep, and the loudest voice belonged to old Daeghrefn—Lord Stormcrow himself.

Finally Frith's father had been summoned to the council hall. It could mean only one thing.

"They don't summon a groom for matters of state," Frith mumbled to himself, wrapping a cheese and a loaf of bread in his other clean pair of stockings. "It's punishments they're after, punishments and blame, and they'll know before they ask him that Pa don't know a thing.

"But I do." He tucked the woolen package under his arm. The cheese had already begun to smell.

"Whoof!" Frith exclaimed, shifting his burden at once. "Great Reorx forbid 'em to think of the hounds!"

Silently he slipped from the stable atop a swift little gray, figuring that Daeghrefn couldn't kill him but once. Passing through the gate, he coaxed the horse north, toward the shelter of the mountain passes in the long direction of Gargath. The castle dwindled behind him, and he would never return to it, never know that the lads would come home safely, with a mysterious girl in tow, and that Daeghrefn's anger would blow over within a week.

Nor would young Frith discover, until he was much older and the passage of twelve winters had softened the distant news, that his father would be put to death by a furious Daeghrefn for the high crime of not keeping track of his son.

* * * * *

But at the moment Aglaca declared his plan to Verminaard, before the Nerakan guards discovered the missing girl and Ember rose above the fog, almost at the same moment that the groom's son Frith decided to flee Castle Nidus, the largest of all the plans was evolving in the depths of the Abyss.

Takhisis watched everything, even forseeing some of it,

her golden eye lazing from guard to dragon, from questing lad to stable groom, and her thoughts raced over actions and words to make sense of what would come next.

They are like runes, she decided—Aglaca, Verminaard, the captive girl, Daeghrefn, and the dragon. Somehow they had converged, had all come together in this little rescue story.

Takhisis smiled. It was her task to read convergences. That which was. That which is. That which might become.

Daeghrefn was simple. The wild, immutable force of anger. Whenever he showed in the arrangement, it became volatile . . . explosive.

The dragon was Daeghrefn's opposite. Ever calm and outwardly serene, laborate and involved, Ember's thoughts turned in on themselves, knotting and entangling until he suspected his own suspicions, deceived himself with his own lies.

The boys were opposites as well. When they glared at one another—in anger, in rivalry, or even in rare agreement—it was as though they looked into a mirror, each the image of the other. Such are brothers, she thought affectionately. But when Verminaard's left hand raised, Aglaca's right hand countered, so that each was the other reversed.

And in rune lore, the Dark Lady remembered, the sign reversed is its opposite as well: The Sun rune reversed foretold darkness, the reversed Harvest rune foretold famine.

Balances. It was all balances. So she had known for ten thousand years, and the little commotions of mortals followed the same vast pattern.

But the girl was different. Unmatched, unpaired, and so far unreadable, she had come from the west, urged on by Paladine's guiding hand. Takhisis could not read her, could not yet discover her mystery or her opposite.

Perhaps she was the blank rune.

The shaman's magic that encircled the Pen had been a test for the girl: a primitive spell, easily broken by mage and by cleric as well, if there were clerics left to break it, but since the girl had done it, she was even more than Takhisis had figured.

For the time being, Takhisis would watch. The girl was more useful alive and free. If she *was* the blank rune—and when before had the Dark Lady been mistaken?—Judyth would lead Takhisis to L'Indasha Yman, to the secret of the augury.

The girl was the lapwing, the lure that would draw the druidess from hiding.

It would have to be done carefully, this strategy. As soon as Judyth reached Castle Nidus, Takhisis would have the mage cast a warding spell far stronger than the one encircling the Pen in Neraka. She would aid him in the casting, breathe power into his paltry skills so that no enchanter—not even the skillful L'Indasha Yman—could pass through the warding undetected.

No, the druidess would not disrupt these plans. Eventually Judyth would go to her, and when that time came, Takhisis's spies would follow. She would find the druidess, sound the rune, and through the restored prophecies, Takhisis would discover yet another stone—green and priceless and hidden for a century—that would complete the circle of her temple, would bring into being the promised towers in the depth of her dreams.

She turned again on the hot darkwind, watching and waiting.

Chapter 10

Verminaard could not believe, as the three of them retrieved the horses and rode west in the lifting fog, that he and Aglaca had rescued the right girl.

He looked back at this Judyth twice. She was seated behind Aglaca on the mare. Dark hair, dark skin, the fiery blue-lavender eyes Aglaca had promised.

And the black tattoo, the dragon's head, he had seen on her right leg that day at the bridge.

And yet she was not at all the girl he had expected. Again he asked himself, Where is the blonde hair, the pale eyes, the temperament mild and grateful? She should have been near death—defenseless.

But Judyth was lovely and tall and pleasant, with a

sharp mind and an assurance that had guided the three of them through even the thickest fog. She had steered them by scattered memories, recalling blasted trees and clusters of rocks she had seen but once or twice, and from those paltry landmarks, she directed them generally toward the Nerakan Forest and the Jelek Path.

Verminaard had doubted her at first, but then, when the mist subsided, he looked back. Dwindling into the distance was the village of Neraka, the afternoon sun blazing clearly on the right side of Takhisis's dark tower.

A hundred small fires burned on the battlements and walls, spreading rapidly through the outlying encampments.

"There's a fire spreading through the town!" he called to his companions, and Aglaca wheeled the mare about. Standing in the stirrups, Judyth gazed over Aglalca's head into the distance, her gemstone eyes bright and sharp.

"Ogres," she declared, her voice calm and strangely musical. "It's as I reckoned. Our incantation freed them as well. Best keep at the path we've chosen. That should be the Nerakan forest, far ahead and to our right."

Verminaard followed her gesture and saw a gray-green mass on the far horizon. The girl was right after all. They were northward bound indeed.

He glanced once again at her leg. Yes, it was the same leg, all right.

For the last mile or so, even before the fog had cleared entirely, Judyth and Aglaca had engaged in quiet conversation. Verminaard had caught bits of it from his seat atop Orlog. Judyth prattled contentedly about things remote and Solamnic, and Aglaca joined in with a flurry of questions, his voice rising dangerously above a whisper, cracking with excitement in the thin, crisp air.

"Around the Great Library of Palanthas," Judyth explained as Aglaca guided the mare through a heap of fallen rock, "there are over a hundred kinds of roses planted. Some never cease to bloom."

"Are there blue daisies? The medicinal ones?" Aglaca asked eagerly. "How about nard and black iris?"

Verminaard muttered something hot, indecipherable.

Judyth turned and looked at the hulking figure on the black stallion. Her face set in a cold frown, she clutched the front of her robe tightly against the cool mountain winds. This Verminaard is handsome, she thought. Those blue eyes, and those shoulders, and arms like drasil trees. Though he's cut badly on the right arm—probably in the tunnel. I'll see to it later if he'll let me. There's something about him that's so stormy and melancholy, though. It makes you . . .

Verminaard rumbled through his clenched teeth. "Perhaps if the two of you could cease this talk of libraries and roses long enough to spot high ground," he said, "you could make yourselves useful on the long road home."

Judyth looked away. Amazing blue eyes, yes, but a voice sharp and critical.

"That's easy enough, Verminaard," Aglaca answered cheerily. "And with a hard ride behind us and the good mare double-burdened, you're wise to be looking for rest this early in the evening."

They rode on in a stunted silence for an hour or so, with only the lofty cry of raptors as accompaniment, and then, as the sun started to set and the sky to darken, the muffled, distant hoot of an owl sounded in the bordering trees of the Nerakan Forest. And a new rumbling, deep and even more distant, arose on the plains behind them. In the last of the gloaming, they reached a rise and looked back to the south, where a dozen torches spread over the wide plains, moving steadily and tirelessly north.

"Cavalry," Verminaard observed.

Judyth shook her head. "Ogres. Your idea of high ground looks better and better. Traveling over the rocks

will cover our tracks better than traveling through grass-
land."

"D'you think—" Aglaca began.

"No. They're probably *not* after us," Judyth explained.
"Or if they were, they've been distracted by other sounds
and smells by now. Ogres are notoriously stupid, and I
saw enough of them in Neraka to know their reputation's
earned. It's a hunt, surely, but a random and disorganized
one. We're safe if we're out of their way. Besides," she concluded, drawing a pouch from her belt, "your arm needs
mending, Verminaard."

The riders took to a high, rocky path veering toward the
stark, obsidian cliffs that lined the western border of the
Nerakan plains. They rode a mile more in the diminishing
light, until Aglaca reined the mare to a halt at the mouth
of a little box canyon, an inlet in the rocks not thirty feet
across, bordered by scrub plants and rubble and a solitary
high trail that meandered up the cliffside.

"Look ahead of us!" Aglaca exclaimed, pointing toward
a spot in the shadow of the rock face. "*That's* out of the
way, I'd reckon. It's a campsite ready made—an abandoned bed of rushes and a smothered fire not two days
old."

He leaned forward and peered at the ground. "And
some sort of stone arrangement. I'm not sure what it's
here for, but it's as fresh as the fire by the markings
around it."

Judyth studied it as well, her gaze following Aglaca's
pointing finger. "Stones? Oh. 'Tis a pair of warding
signs—no more. Logr and Yr. Water and yew bow, journey and protection. Quite common around here. Travelers
and bandits set 'em alike, though I cannot remember seeing the two of these ever placed together."

"I saw two placed side by side at the edge of the garden
at Nidus," Aglaca observed. "Kaun and Kaun. Sore and
sore. Made Lord Daeghrefn break out in hives when he

passed between 'em. I took it as the old gardener's work."

"But these runes mark a serious business," Judyth said.

Aglaca nodded, his eyes on the lush greenery around the warding. Roses and comfrey, rosemary and marrow—the red symbol of love amid herbs of healing, memory, and the banishment of melancholy. "'Tis a blessed place indeed," he whispered.

Unconcerned with the vegetation, Verminaard craned toward the stones, marveling at the rune signs.

"What was a good campsite so recently is probably still a good place to stay the night," Judyth observed cautiously, scanning the horizon for any sign of bandits, of pursuit.

"That's not always the case, girl," Verminaard said testily. "Why do you think the site was abandoned?"

"No dramatic reason," Judyth declared, regarding the big lad calmly. "Someone moved on. D'you plan to stay here two nights? Or are we bound elsewhere on the morrow?"

Aglaca hid a smile and slipped from the mare. Approaching the campsite, he crouched before the extinguished fire and whistled appreciatively.

"Somebody knows the full particulars of camping," he observed, looking up wide-eyed at his two companions. "No more than a handful of wood, and this fire burned through the night!"

"How do you know?" Verminaard asked sullenly, dismounting from the weary stallion.

"Didn't go to get more wood," Aglaca replied solemnly, pointing at the tracks around the fire. "So it's my guess that this was enough."

"We can't have a fire, you know," said Judyth. "The ogres will see it."

"Trust me," Aglaca said. "I can kindle a fire that an eagle couldn't spot."

Verminaard glared at the young Solamnic. Preening for

the girl, he was, and charming her with his glib, western airs.

Sullenly he stepped aside. The time would come when strength would avail. Then those lavender eyes would turn to him, and the story would be different.

There was something about the campsite, a smell of flowers and aeterna and some strange and exotic attar that hinted at a deep, cryptic wisdom. Verminaard fidgeted, shifting from foot to foot as he stood watch, and Aglaca kindled the fire with a quiet, almost secretive reverence. Only Judyth seemed unaffected, merrily mixing an herb tea made from some nearby berries and leaves. "A bracer," she claimed, "after a long journey." All the while, and even as she cleaned and stitched Verminaard's wounded shoulder, she continued to regale Aglaca with quiet stories of fabled Palanthas—of the High Clerist's Tower, of the Tower of High Sorcery, and the winding streets that linked district after district of Solamnia's aristocracy as the thin spirals of a spider's web link its anchoring spokes and radials.

"I wouldn't want to go west," Verminaard offered, rubbing at his newly stitched shoulder despite Judyth's advice, as the darkness deepened. "Too much pomp and Solamnic ceremony."

"You lie. It's because Daeghrefn no longer believes in the Order," Aglaca declared flatly.

"And what of that?" Verminaard asked defensively, turning toward his companion, who knelt by Judyth as the tea steeped, their faces radiant, bathed in the last rays of the westering sun.

"Nothing, Verminaard. Sorry. It's been a long time, and I'm missing the Order a bit myself . . . and my father, and home on the East Borders."

"Well, gather yourself, Aglaca," Verminaard said coldly. "You're not the first to be exiled, you know. And all this talk of Solamnia and Palanthas and Oath and Measure is more than annoying after a while."

"Then don't listen," Judyth declared calmly, smiling, her gaze fastened defiantly on this big, boorish blond oaf who seemed to rankle at the joy of others. "Simply stand there and look out for ogres."

Flushed and silent, Verminaard backed away. Then he turned with a contemptuous smile, intent again on a man's business. He *would* stand watch. They were not fit for it.

It was then he began to hear Solamnic.

"*Est othas calathansas bara . . .*" Judyth began, and off raced a new and alien conversation, the pair of Solamnics by the fire masked in the old language, its liquid sounds and its musical, sudden vowels. Judyth's stifled laughter rang in the outpouring of words, and Aglaca, delighted to hear once again the sounds of his home, of the Order, of his father's tongue, laughed with her. It was the happiest he had been in nearly ten years.

Verminaard tried to listen, and recognized a word now and then. But it felt as if the fog had returned, as if his senses were muffled and shut. From the time when Daeghrefn had left the Solamnic Order, that language had been forbidden in Castle Nidus, and the few simple verbs he had learned from Aglaca's attendants and from a rare Solamnic emissary served him ill in the swift conversation.

It was all he could take. Muttering, he stuffed his belongings in the saddlebag—the Amarach runes, the *quith-pa*, the purple pendant—and took off on foot toward high ground.

Let them band together to shut him out, in the affected, gossipy fashion of courtier or knave. He had better things to do! Adventures to seek on the harsh Nerakan plains, where a stout arm availed more than some urbane knowledge of manners and far-flung places and pretty words!

There were better women elsewhere—more agreeable and compliant.

He could scarcely believe it when he looked back and saw how far he was from the camp. The little canyon below shielded them from the plains in the rising Nerakan night. The sun was well gone and the afterglow fading fast. He had traveled a good two hundred feet or so up the sheer mountain trail, amid scrubby aeterna and the little deciduous plants the mountain folk called *broucherei*. . . .

"Damn it!" he exclaimed. "They have *me* studying foliage now!" His gaze shot up the rock face to a plateau, void of the lush, surrounding vegetation, where four drasil trees stood in a circle, stark and black against the last of the light, like a sign from the gods.

* * * * *

"There's the entrance," Verminaard said to himself, stooping to enter the mouth of the cave. A quartet of bats flashed by his ears, chattering, and he shivered as one touched his face.

He had made up his mind when he recognized the trees and finally remembered that they always grew above caverns. He would go into the cave—go there alone—and find his way past the thick arrangement of roots and tendrils, exploring the dark as far as his courage would take him.

"Which is much farther than Aglaca would go," he muttered, and he crouched in the palpable gloom, moving slowly into the depths of the cave.

It wasn't long before the Voice reached him, familiar and embracing, as it had always been, but there was something new in its suggestion, some haunting note of urgency that Verminaard had never heard before. For the first time, he paused and wondered whether he should go on.

Enough of the day, the low, feminine voice intoned, almost singing, as Verminaard caught his breath and sank to his knees, leaning against the moist wall of the cavern. *Enough of the treachery of sun, the little deceits of the stars in their courses. Leave them behind, Prince Verminaard, lord of a thousand leagues and the scion of dragons. . . .*

Undefined shapes flitted through the shadows ahead, spectral, robed figures mingling with the darkness, their voices mixing with the low insect drone of sound he had first heard in the depths of the Nerakan caverns, a sound like the high-pitched humming from the ruins about God-shome. He stood, his knees shaking, and breathed a prayer to Hiddukel, to Zeboim, to Takhisis.

And at the finish of the third prayer, it was as though the Lady herself had reached forth and embraced him. In the warm darkness, he traveled deeper into the cave, past the insubstantial shapes.

He gathered strength and courage with each stride.

One voice rose above all the babble, the bewitching Voice of his childhood, of a thousand thoughts that had passed through his beleaguered mind. *In voluptuous darkness lies the truth,* it urged, and then, as the cloaked shapes wavered and danced at the edge of Verminaard's sight, the urging intensified, growing more rhythmic, more melodious, until the cavern echoed with a cold and melancholy song.

> *Set aside the buried light*
> *Of candle, torch, and rotting wood,*
> *And listen to the turn of night*
> *Caught in your rising blood.*
>
> *How quiet is the midnight, love,*
> *How warm the winds where ravens fly,*
> *Where all the changing moonlight, love,*
> *Pales in your fading eye.*

How loud your heart is calling, love,
How close the darkness at your breast,
How hectic are the rivers, love,
Drawn through your dying wrist.

And, love, what heat your frail skin hides,
As pure as salt, as sweet as death,
And in the dark the red moon rides
The foxfire of your breath.

He followed the song in a daze, as newly visible stalactites strangely dripped and melted around him and the
cavern rippled and eddied like the heart of a whirlpool.
Voices called to him from the center of the walls; pale
hands seemed to reach from the stone, grasping at his
tunic, his hair, coldly fingering the wound in his arm until
his hand tingled, his fingers numbed about the hilt of his
drawn sword. Before him, the shadows twitched and
cavorted, chittering like bats, and time and again bright
shocks of color flashed behind them in the darkness—pale
purple, deep red, occasional green.

Then all shadow and the odd light descended to a single slim corridor, a green-white sickly glow emanating
from it like a dying phosfire, like the damaged soul of a
marshland. Verminaard followed mindlessly, shuffling in
the dried clay of the corridor, the trail behind him a fading
stream of light.

* * * * *

Aglaca looked up and noticed that Verminaard had vanished.

Waving his hand, the Solamnic lad stilled Judyth's
florid description of the purple clematis that scaled the
western walls of Dargaard Keep.

"Verminaard!" he said, a low note of concern in his voice. Quickly he leapt from the fireside and raced toward the mouth of the little box canyon, where the plains spread before him ten miles to the darkened east.

No sign of him. Aglaca stared disconsolately across the low expanse to the black edge of the Nerakan Forest, where the torches of the ogres danced in the distance, moving steadily north and away.

They were safe from the monsters, but there was no sign of Verminaard. If he had stomped off in anger, he could be a mile away by now. A mile in any direction . . .

Aglaca brightened, wheeled suddenly, and raced toward the cliffside trail. Sure enough, there were footprints in the dust. He knelt, recognized the outline of Verminaard's enormous boot . . .

And started when Judyth's hand clasped him on the shoulder.

"If you're bent on finding him, don't go alone," she urged.

Aglaca smiled, but the smile faded when the tracks led into a cave—a low, bramble-covered burrow in the rock face, framed by hardy juniper and a blue mask of aeterna. Carefully, with Judyth still clutching his arm for balance, safety, and support, the lad leaned into the darkness, following the footprints until his sight failed and he lost them in a strange, pale green light.

"Judyth! Look here!" Aglaca urged. "What's this?"

"I don't know exactly," the girl declared. "Nor do I like my first sight of it."

"Nonetheless," Aglaca insisted, "Verminaard is nearly family—kind of like a brother. Well, *exactly* like a brother. And he's always doing things like this. I wouldn't blame you one whit for waiting right here. I'd do it, if I had a choice. But by my honor, I have to continue and see what's befallen him."

Gently the lad freed himself from Judyth's grip and

stepped toward the heart of the cave. The girl followed him at once, and together they moved toward the odd, disturbing glow.

They had not traveled a dozen steps when a Voice rose out of the light, musical and seductive and venomous.

Not yet, it said. *Wait . . . not yet.*

"What's that?" Judyth asked. "Who is it?"

Aglaca shivered and tugged at her hand.

"Hurry," he whispered.

*   *   *   *   *

They found him at the enlarged end of the passage, at the source of the light.

Verminaard stood rapt before a green, glowing stalactite. The ancient stone formation shimmered, shifted, and boiled with a cold, morbid light, and before the astonished eyes of the trespassers, it assumed the shape of a mace, long and narrow, ending in a terrible spiked head that glowed like some unearthly gemstone.

When Aglaca and Judyth stepped into the final chamber and Verminaard wheeled to face them, the Voice spoke again instantly. It spoke as always, low and dangerous, rising melodically from some great depth in the earth, echoing from the moist and glittering walls of the cavern, but for the first time, it addressed both Verminaard and Aglaca at once.

From the Age of Light, I have chosen you both, it proclaimed, and Judyth, knowing the words were not for her, inched cautiously back toward the mouth of the cavern.

But she stopped when the Voice continued.

I have known you since then, known you by the promise of your blood, by your blood's fulfillment in three thousand years of waiting in the darkness.

Aglaca frowned. It was prattle as usual, the same

deceptive poetry he had ignored for a dozen years. And yet this time . . .

He glanced at Verminaard, who swayed again in a rapturous ecstasy before the glowing stone, his eyes half-lidded, an empty smile on his lips.

I have chosen you among thousands, the Voice continued, honeyed and insistent. *You for your strength and physical courage, Lord Verminaard, and you, Lord Aglaca, for your inventiveness and grace.*

The mace deepened in color and intensity of light until its green darkened to blood purple, to black, then to a color beyond black itself, until all that seemed to remain was its outline, its shadow against the dark of the cave walls a silhouette darker still.

And though both of you are worthy indeed . . . oh, indeed worthy, the Voice continued, *and though I could offer both of you the lineaments of your fondest desire . . .*

As the words tumbled forth from the light and embraced them, Aglaca saw the walls of Castle East Borders in the glowing head of the mace. For a moment, it seemed that the great eastern gate of the castle, in one corner of which he had carved his name when he first learned to write, was opening slowly, and someone, his craggy, thin face bathed in a pure and simple light, stood open-armed in the gateway.

Aglaca blinked. His eyes smarted, and for a moment, tears blurred his sight.

But Verminaard saw clearly, coldly, a different vision—a castle, its battlements ablaze, its towers crumbling. Above it, he flew on the back of . . . he could not tell what it was, but it was enormous, its broad shoulders thick and striated with powerful muscles. All around him, the sky was darkened by the sweep of black wings. The sunlight dimmed, and he knew that the destruction below him, the crushed and defenseless fortress, was the work of his own hand and heart and will, and he delighted in its fierce, magnificent ruin.

I ask for only one of you. Which of you has the courage to seize the night? the voice prodded, taunted.

Verminaard smiled triumphantly. He had seen enough. He looked over his shoulder at Aglaca, who stood protectively between Judyth and the glowing rocks.

"Don't do it, Verminaard," Aglaca urged, painfully fighting his own temptations. "If you choose this, you'll forget that you can ever choose again."

For you there is power, Lord Verminaard, and rule to be wrested in strength and violence. And there is the bridal of blood and night, the nuptials of your willing soul.

If you choose this, you will not need to choose again, for men will fall before you, and the fortresses of men.

"There are snares in that voice," Aglaca cautioned.

"So be it," Verminaard declared, lunging assuredly for the mace. "My power will free me from all snares."

"No!" Aglaca cried.

"Go home, little boy," Verminaard hissed, and grasped the handle of the mace.

Its dark fire coursed up Verminaard's clutching hand, raced through his wrist and forearm in rivulets of purple flame. Judyth's careful stitching burst apart on his arm, and the blood trickled forth, steaming and boiling on the charged surface of his skin. Verminaard writhed in the pulsing flames, his grimace turning slowly to a dark, unholy leer as he broke the mace free.

Aglaca shouted and sprang toward Verminaard, but Judyth's strong grip held him back.

"There's nothing you can do," she urged. "He's in the hands of a goddess."

Slowly, reluctantly, the two backtracked to the mouth of the cave, where they stood shaking in the hushed night air, listening helplessly to the cries and shouts of the young man who tangled in the depths of the earth with stone and fire and absolute shadow.

Alone with the goddess, Verminaard gritted his teeth, exulting in the pain. His whole body bristled with glittering fire, and sparks scattered from his hair and fingers. The Voice returned, soothing and soft, motherly and yet uncomfortably seductive and strange, singing to him the last verse of the song that had drawn him here, the love song and dirge and lullaby wrapped in an intricate bewildering melody:

> *And, love, what heat your frail skin hides,*
> *As pure as salt, as sweet as death,*
> *And in the dark the red moon rides*
> *The foxfire of your breath.*

And still Verminaard held on, marshaling the sum of his despair and his anger to cling to the weapon as it jolted and blistered him, as it staggered him until he grasped it mainly to keep his balance, to keep from falling to where he would never, never rise again.

Then at last it was over.

You will do, the Voice breathed, all seduction gone, after a long, abiding silence, answered only by the dying sputters of the stone mace and the sobs of the youth who had wrested it from the living stone. *Yes, you will do. . . .*

All other covenants are broken, soothed the Voice. *Bonds of family, blood, friendship, or oath . . . all of your bonds.*

Save for those with me.

"Aglaca," Verminaard whispered. "What of Aglaca?"

You must use him. Then you can destroy him. I shall reveal to you how and when.

Oh, you will do, the Voice repeated, again hypnotic and soft.

Oh, I will do, Verminaard's thoughts sang in response. I will more than do. . . .

For I choose you as well, Takhisis.

* * * * *

"Let's go from here now, Aglaca," Judyth urged. "Leave him be."

The young Solamnic shook his head.

They stood together at the bottom of the mountain trail, glancing nervously up into the rocks, where the shouting and rumbling had died into a menacing silence.

"Come away," Judyth whispered. "There are trails enough through the mountains. We can skirt Jelek and Daeghrefn's pursuit, ride through a little pass south of the ruins at Godshome, and be back in East Borders before the morrow. *Home*, Aglaca! I can guide you *home!*"

Aglaca glanced curiously at his new companion. "You know the passes well, Judyth," he observed, "and the way to East Borders. For a western lass, you have a very eastern geography."

Judyth flushed and looked away. "Question your own bearings, Aglaca Dragonbane, for you're on the road to the Abyss itself if you keep *that* one company."

She gestured disgustedly at the cave, and for a moment, an uncomfortable silence rose between them. The first cool winds of night passed over them, carrying the smell of smoke and the faint sound of shouting from the plains.

"I can't leave him, Judyth," Aglaca explained. "There's still the *gebo-naud* that binds us, and just because he'll break his part now doesn't mean that I can break my own—mine and my father's."

"Silly Solamnic Measure-wrangling," the girl muttered. "You'll honor yourself to death, Aglaca."

"Oh, I know exactly what will come to pass now," Aglaca replied. "He'll be changed . . . changed for good. We both heard the Voice when Verminaard took the mace. He's with *her* now, whoever *she* is, and I've more than a suspicion she'll swallow him whole and try to kill me in the bargain."

"Then go west," Judyth insisted.

"It isn't that easy. There's blood between us. Verminaard is my brother."

"Your *brother!*" Judyth exlaimed. "But he *couldn't* be! You *couldn't* . . . though you *do* have the same features . . . but, no, Laca . . ."

Aglaca's eyes narrowed. What did she know of his father?

"B-Besides," Judyth stammered quickly, "how can you be sure?"

"My surety is that I know it," Aglaca declared. "As well as I know he has taken the Dark Gods to him and that I shall never hear that Voice again. Perhaps he's taken the Dark Queen herself, but he can still choose to . . . to set her aside."

Judyth glanced at Aglaca skeptically.

"He's my brother, Judyth," Aglaca insisted. "And I am all he has, though he doesn't know it."

"Not anymore," the girl whispered, and pointed toward the mouth of the cave, where a dark, hulking shape emerged into the night air.

* * * * *

Verminaard shielded his eyes against the moonlight. The entrance of the cave seemed unbearably bright, as though he had walked from midnight into the fullness of noonday.

Hand in hand, Judyth and Aglaca stood waiting, their faces turned toward him, eyes wide in consternation and dread. For a moment, he thought that he was taller, older . . . somehow terrifying with the dark weapon in his seared hand, the blood dripping from his reopened shoulder.

He smiled scornfully down at them and started to speak. . . .

Then, with a cry of dismay, Aglaca pointed beyond him toward the plains.

Verminaard turned, slipping on the narrow footpath, and fell to his knees facing north, his eyes toward the plains.

In a swath five miles from west to east, the summer-dry grasslands were burning in a mad and relentless blaze.

Chapter 11

High up the slanting hills, where prickly gorse grew into thick mats that shepherds sometimes skirted for miles, L'Indasha Yman moved deftly through the tangles of thorn and yellow bloom toward Mount Berkanth, where the ice never thawed.

Of late, the ice of her augury, still holding through careful attention and the deepness of her cave well, had shown a black tower growing, almost as if it were alive, attended by scores of chained ogres. And this morning she had discovered someone near that tower, barely visible and only for an instant, shielded from view by some kind of warding.

The one Paladine had sent.

In L'Indasha's excitement, she had looked too long at the vision, and her chances of exactly locating the girl had melted away. Emptying the bucket and taking up a light oaken bowl instead, she had raced from her cave toward the permanent frost of arid Berkanth to try to catch another ice-augured vision and find the violet-eyed helper.

Fatigued from the intense concentration and speed the trek required, the precarious footing and the high switching winds, the druidess stopped to rest and check her progress. She was now just above the timberline, where the forest gave way to rugged, short alpine vegetation. While the climb was steeper, the view was at last unhindered. Her breath steamed in the cool, thin air. It was a long, precipitous way down the side of this nameless rise, the highest of the Nerakan foothills. The plains spread out and away in voluptuous green waves below the trees. Several miles to the south, smoke danced over tents and banners. L'Indasha stared in shocked wonder when the cloud feathered away and revealed the twisted, spiring shape of the black tower of her vision, in the midst of the huts, barracks, and pigpens.

The druidess wrapped her green robes closer and stared out at the smoke and flames rising from the village. The sky was nearly dark. That tower was no Nerakan invention, if she knew Nerakans, but the construction of darker and more powerful forces. She made a quick decision. She must get there somehow, in secret, and bring out the girl. A warding would no doubt surround the captive, but breaking it would be no hindrance once she deciphered its pattern. The journey would take some thought and planning—and nourishment; it had already been a very long day.

Digging through her pockets for a bit of food, she found only the last of the daylilies from yesterday's dividing and replanting. It was an undersized fan, with only a couple of decent leaves, but the vigor of the little plant had kept it firm and healthy despite its sojourn in her pocket. She marveled at the strength of life in its greener forms and started to return the lily to her robes; there would be time to plant it later. But as she closed her hand over the sprig, a remembrance of Paladine's words came to her: *Plant against famine and fire.*

She dropped to the ground and quickly began to sing the sowing prayer over the plant and its lofty new home. Only a moment later, she was dusting off the mountain soil from her hands and knees, and the runtish daylily was settled within a protective circle of stones.

As L'Indasha turned to mark the place in her mind, she froze at what she now saw out on the dark plains. The tiny puff of smoke had become a huge billowing thundercloud, and bright fire lashed at the edge of the grasslands. Two horses raced down from higher ground southeast, galloping obliquely along the edge of the fire, their riders low in the saddle. Behind them, swarming like queenless bees, a great many ogres lumbered in pursuit. From the North—Nidus?—through the smoke to the edge of her sight, the druidess could see a small party riding toward the forest. Two dozen men or so, their torchmen wearing red standards, all no doubt unaware of what ill wind blew before them.

She felt for the purple pendant around her neck, but it wasn't there. She vaguely remembered tearing the clasp in her recent haste, somewhere in the cave. There was no help for it now. She would have to brave the flames without Paladine's protective gift.

L'Indasha slung her skirts up over her arm and raced down the hillside, this time catching her bare legs and feet on every thornbush she ran through. Another fire. Another burning. Another darkness.

* * * * *

Daeghrefn wheeled in the saddle, shouting vain orders to his confused search party.

The fire storm had surged all around him, rushing over the plains and into the forest like a devouring wind. The plume of his helmet was charred and smoking, and the mane of his stallion brittle and tipped with ash. He had called to Reginn, to Asa, called desperately to his captain Kenaz, but they had vanished behind a wall of smoke. Beside him, five young guardsmen sat their horses unsteadily, their eyes fixed on the commander, awaiting orders, strength, assurance. Robert, mounted on a skittish roan mare, watched the thickest part of the smoke, the column to their south, in which dark, hulking shapes turned and doubled and danced amid the burning trees.

What had begun as a simple search for Aglaca and Verminaard had come to disaster just as they emerged from the Nerakan Forest, intending to follow the foothills south to the borders of the settlement.

Then the fire had rushed on them like something out of the Rending, like the images in a shaman's vision. Daeghrefn's column had scattered, a dozen crack soldiers bolting from heat and curling flame, and he had led them back through the forest, groping toward open country and the castle beyond, toward thinning smoke and clear skies and unimpeded breathing. . . .

And then, surging through the flame, their filthy hides blackened and smoldering, the ogres rushed at the soldiers through the trees and drove them toward the plains. Thunar fell at once, Nidus's best swordsman pulled from his horse, and a breath later Ullr fell, torn in the terrible hands of monsters. Daeghrefn himself had lurched in the saddle, clinging desperately to his stallion's brittle mane, one foot precariously in the stirrup, as a huge ogre, crashing through smoke and undergrowth, scored his leg with its filthy, ragged claws.

It was fear that had righted him atop the horse, a desperate scrabbling animal fear that had surged from somewhere beneath his skin, rushing over him like the fire storm, rushing over his shouts and tears and finally his screams as he kicked the horrible, drooling thing away, as the ogre's fingers clutched and loosened on his ankle, and the horse quickened under him and suddenly, mercifully, he was clear of the monster and regained the saddle in the heaving smoke.

Before the fire and in the heart of the flames, the ogres danced ecstatically, their madness propelled by the fury they had ignited.

Now Daeghrefn's men regrouped on a rocky rise on the plains to the north of the forest's edge. The hard flatlands stretched around them, ending in smoke, in flame, in a border of ignited trees. As the flames approached through the crackling and toppling conifers—and with the flames, the ogres—the Lord of Nidus counted his losses.

Five men. One of them Kenaz, his captain, lost somewhere near the center of the woods where the trails branched. And with all those dead or vanished men, Daeghrefn's own courage.

For Daeghrefn was afraid. For the first time in his adult life, his legs trembled as he stood in the stirrups, the hair still bristling on the back of his neck. The fear was a kind of fire, too, spreading and expanding the longer he allowed it to dwell within him.

Scarcely a moment ago, when the monster had tried to pull him from the horse, he had felt its grasp, smelled its hot, feral stink. It was no soldier, no swordsman meeting him blade to blade in the battle he knew and trusted. It was a monster, but more monstrous was the fear that had unmanned him.

Galloping and screaming at the head of his squadron, he had ridden until the panic had ebbed, until his senses had left him and the hands of his men had steadied him in the saddle. Now, though the ogres were distant and the flames behind him, a new fear rose to undo him.

The reins shook in his hand. For a moment, Daeghrefn longed for the Solamnic Order he had abandoned, for its rule of honor and courage, for Oath and Measure to compel him and uphold his collapsing spirit.

But when he had banished knighthood, he had banished the shape of his courage.

His men stared at him, eagerly awaiting his orders, but through the glass of his despair and terror, their features were distorted, and Daeghrefn looked on them as enemies, as usurpers.

Now they are contemptuous, he thought. Now they are judging me. They will seek a new leader.

"Enough waiting," he rasped, desperately trying to mask the rising panic in his voice. "The forest will go up like tinder before this fire." Daeghrefn nodded toward the approaching wall of flame. "So we had best get farther north, in sight of the castle. There the garrison can come to our aid."

There. He had spoken like a commander, though his voice shook and his heart rattled. Steadied, Daeghrefn stared back toward the woods, his eyes smarting with smoke, and signaled to the men to move north, back to Nidus, across the smoky plains.

The remaining men, five wide-eyed young archers from Estwilde, followed their commander toward a rise in the grasslands circled by a thin outcropping of evergreen. There, in the shade of fir and cedar, they dismounted, nervously readying their bows to cover the withdrawal of the rear guard.

Robert alone was that rear guard.

As the fire surged relentlessly toward him, the weathered seneschal remained at the edge of the woods. The red mare pawed and snorted nervously beneath his calming hand, but she stayed her ground amid harsh smoke and the harsher cries of the ogres.

Robert counted two heartbeats until Daeghrefn had reached the rise. Then, just as the flames touched the borders of the forest, he wheeled his horse and galloped across the plains, headed for the line of archers with a hot wind coursing at his back.

He saw the ogres then, the flanking column that waded through the rising smoke in a swift, hungry arch toward Daeghrefn's rear.

Robert cried out, pointing and waving wildly, tottering in the saddle with the strength of his own gestures. Daeghrefn shielded his eyes and craned to hear.

Then he understood.

With a shout, the Lord of Nidus alerted his men, who scrambled awkwardly to their horses, dropping their weapons in panic. They were off in a gallop, a scant ten yards ahead of him, as Robert reached the rise and spurred his horse to catch up.

At the sharp dig of spurs, the little roan mare bolted and bucked with a shrieking whinny. Clinging for a last desperate moment to the reins, Robert felt himself lifted from the saddle. The ground spun and tumbled and rushed toward him, and then the hard earth of the plains drove the breath from him.

The mare caught up with the other horses and kept running.

Dazed, Robert tried to rise and felt his leg buckle. Struggling painfully to his knees, he looked desperately north toward the retreating column of horsemen.

"Daeghrefn!" he cried, and the foremost rider turned as the soldiers rode on past out of the smoke. "Daeghrefn! Help!"

He could see the man dimly, standing in the stirrups. Then the ogres lumbered out of the vapor, and the Lord of Nidus wheeled and galloped away, shouting over his shoulder, "I'm sorry, Robert! I cannot help you where you are going."

Robert fell to the hard earth. For a moment, lying on his back, he glimpsed the evening stars through the swirling smoke. The broken scale of Hiddukel reeled over him in the northern sky, the stars in the constellation painfully bright.

So this is the end of service, Robert thought grimly, drawing his sword. But better this than to end as the lackey of a cowardly, heartless bastard.

He glared toward the dwindling form of the rider, watched it vanish in the lower hills.

The rumble and call of the ogres was closer now, and a dreadful sniffing rose from the lip of the haze, where two black, shapeless forms shifted and bent like vallenwoods in a high wind.

Robert willed himself not to think of the stories. The ravaged caravans in the Throtl Gap, the children plucked from wagon beds, the village of two hundred in Taman Busuk, the gnawed, scattered bones found in the wreckage each time.

If it is the end, it's best to go out fighting. I have nothing to lose. And perhaps I will be fortunate. Perhaps the fire will reach me before the ogres do.

The smoke to the east glowed orange and red, and sharp tongues of flame shot through the blackness, making bizarre daylight of this frightful, burning evening. Robert lay back on the ground, clenching his teeth against the hammering pain in his leg.

Suddenly all sight vanished into a purple, obliterating fog. It covered the rise where the seneschal lay, muffling all sound as well, so that the crackle of flames and the cry of the ogres reached him only as vibrations through the ground.

Robert breathed deeply. No coughing, no sting to the eye.

"Damned if it . . ." he began, then lost the words at the

sight of the bare-footed, green-robed woman weaving through the smoke. Slowly, with the trust that arises only when one has seen a dozen battles, a thousand enemies, and has learned thereby to distinguish friends, the old veteran sheathed his sword and waited.

In the swirling silence, the woman approached.

* * * * *

As Verminaard, Aglaca, and Judyth skirted the eastern edge of the forest, keeping to the high ground of the foothills, they saw the ogres rushing down from the mountains after them.

The monsters trailed fire and ash, shed sparks as they lumbered west through the burning woods and onto the devastated plains. They hastened toward the level country north of the Nerakan Forest, where a dark gap lay in the fire and smoke.

Even from the heights, from the rocky highlands and from the back of his stallion, Verminaard couldn't discern what was happening down on the burning steppe. He reined Orlog to an uneasy halt and waited for the durable little mare to catch up, Judyth and Aglaca bent with weariness in the saddle.

"There," the bigger lad pronounced, his hand sweeping the landscape around them—the bunched fires, the ogres, the smoke covering the country for miles. "If it were daylight and clear, I could see our way home."

"But since it is as it is," Aglaca pondered cautiously, "where do we go from here?" He didn't trust his transformed companion, but the fire and assaulting ogres were a more obvious danger.

And even after the worst had happened in the cave, there would still be a way to rescue his companion. There had to be.

"We'll ride down into the midst of it," Verminaard said. A strange confidence had risen in him. In Takhisis's cavern, his uncertainties and pain had vanished. A black-hot bolt had shot through his hand, blistering him from fingertips to elbow, welding his fingers to the handle of the captured mace for a time.

But that was nothing before the older injuries of lifelong fear, all the more terrible because they had continued to cripple and humiliate him. Strangely, his new wound did not hurt at all.

In the short ride through the foothills, the Voice had traveled beside him, coaxing, flattering, promising. *The weapon that can harm you*, it said, *has not been forged by dwarf or ogre. It is far from you now, but your power is near.*

And then, when the northern grasslands opened for him, veiled and misted by smoke but stretching toward the old Battle Plain, toward Castle Nidus, the Voice returned again, and with it the greatest of its hushed and seductive vows.

This smoke will spread, Lord Verminaard, and cover all kingdoms of the world . . . all kingdoms in a moment of time. And even the farthest ground that the smoke will cover can belong to you, for I can deliver that country and power and glory to those who worship me. . . .

He breathed in the acrid smoke exultantly. It was a heady promise, and the prospect of such dominion was sweet. Beneath him, the broad back of Orlog felt more powerful still.

Could it be that the vision that had arrayed itself before him in the depths of the cave was already coming to pass?

". . . to pass through the fire."

Verminaard started. Judyth and Aglaca sat beside him on the mare, and the girl was saying something, something he had lost in his revery.

He turned to her politely, attentively, brushing the drooping hair from his eyes. She was not the girl he had imagined, and that really didn't matter anymore. None of his previous disappointments did. But she was lovely and dark, and she would do.

"I beg your pardon, Lady Judyth," he replied, his voice husky and low.

"The fire," Aglaca said impatiently. "It's a blazing wall between us and Nidus, and the ogres are stalking along it like wolves. If we expect to see your castle again, we'll have to pass *through* the fire."

"Then that is just what we shall do," Verminaard said calmly, pointing toward the gap in the flame. "Follow me, and ask no questions."

"But Verminaard . . ." Aglaca began.

Verminaard glared at him. "Be ruled by me, Aglaca. Be ruled by me or be damned where you stand."

* * * * *

Verminaard's confident words died swiftly when they reached the plain.

From above, the fire had seemed navigable to him. There was an end to it, and borders, and the ogres that moved around it and through it were scattered and few in number.

But now, the horses picked uncertainly around the southern edge of the rolling flames, and the path through the blaze seemed to have vanished in the short journey to the edge of the fire wall. The scorched ground smoldered beneath Orlog's hooves as the big stallion stepped gingerly from patch to patch of remaining green. The evening sky was smoke black and unreadable.

As he rode down the spreading wave of flame, Judyth and Aglaca close behind, Verminaard's assurance continued to wither like the blackened grass in the fire wall's wake. At this distance, the choices were quick and baffling. The shouts of ogres came to him from the smoke, from the flames, from the charred woods behind, and he moved through a country of doubling echoes. Dodging through the black grass, foxes and rabbits, pheasant and squirrel, all panic-stricken, were driven by an instinct to flee, to burrow, to vanish, and the horses leapt and shied as the wild things scurried beneath them. Orlog leapt over fire-felled oak and aeterna, and for the first time since he had broken the beast in the high meadows north of Nidus, Verminaard could not control the black stallion beneath him. Twice Orlog veered dangerously north, until the flames rose like a battlement above them, and twice the big horse shied away, whinnying wildly and sidling through the seared undergrowth as the blazes broke around them, leaving them astoundingly untouched.

Where is the Voice now? Verminaard thought, clinging frantically to the reins. This is my country, my power and glory. It told me so.

He looked back. Astride the mare, at the smoke's edge, Judyth peered calmly into the roiling fire. Aglaca sat behind her in the saddle, his wiry arms wrapped gently about her waist, but there was no gentleness in his eyes. Instead, he stared at Verminaard coldly, accusingly.

Suddenly Judyth called out, pointing toward a gap in the flames. There, where the fire wavered and lapsed over a little rise, a cloud of purple smoke hovered and swirled.

"Through that!" Judyth shouted. "Make haste!"

With a shrill whistle, she snapped the reins against the mare's neck. The tough little beast snorted, wheeled, and raced toward the heart of the cloud, scattering sparks and fire-blackened clods in her wake.

Verminaard gasped and started to call out, to stop her, but the mare flashed by before he could speak, could reach out, and he had to follow because Orlog had already made his own choice.

* * * * *

The smoke rushed over them like water.

For a moment, Aglaca held his breath, and then, as Judyth steered the mare through the whirling obscurity, he leaned back, opened his eyes, and breathed carefully.

The air was bracing and moist, awash in an odor of lilac.

"Where . . ." he whispered, but Judyth reached back and motioned to him for quiet.

"Hush," she murmured over her shoulder. "There is danger in words. Someone ahead beckons us through the smoke."

* * * * *

Verminaard strained to follow his companions, craning over Orlog's neck at the distant, dark shape of Aglaca's back, which vanished and reappeared, then vanished again in the thick, rolling smoke.

It's stifling here, he thought. Blind and stifling, and smelling of ash. How can I follow when . . . when Judyth . . .

Where is the Voice *now?*

* * * * *

The smoke parted instantly around a green-robed woman.

Instinctively Judyth tugged at the reins.

But the woman was farther away than she had imagined, standing over a fallen man in a circle of foliage. Around her, the bright grass spread and waved, and a dozen violet flowers, various and tall, blossomed strangely on the scorched plain.

The woman motioned gracefully, waving them on. Judyth felt that she knew the woman in green, that she *should* know her, but the smoke was rising again, and the face was fading, fading into the purple mist until all that remained was a pale arm gesturing, motioning, waving. . . .

"Go on," the woman called. "Follow."

"How?" Judyth asked. "Where?"

"You knew before. You'll know again."

The pale hand swirled a shape from the smoke: a passage, whirling and doubling on itself like a folding tunnel, dwindling and fading slowly.

Instinctively again, Judyth guided the mare through the passage, through a flurry of shape and image, out into starlight and air, Aglaca clinging desperately to her waist and Verminaard sputtering on his stallion as it burst through the smoke behind her.

Still coughing, Verminaard rode on ahead, reoriented now, assured by faint stars and familiar terrain.

With a deep breath, Judyth guided the mare onto the open plains. Aglaca shifted in the saddle, and Judyth felt suddenly safer.

But she marveled as white Solinari peeked through the scattering smoke, marveled at what she had seen in the quiet, purple mists of the strange enchantress.

A flower, she had seen. Or the shape of a flower.

And within it, the shape of a mask.

Chapter 12

Cerestes watched from a high grove overlooking the castle as the fire raged toward Nidus.

Again in human form and wearied from flight and the Change, he knelt amid cedar and taxus, his black robes wrapped closely about his shoulders. In cold, unblinking curiosity, he gazed out at the riders bursting through the edge of the flame, the standard of Nidus—black storm-crow on a red field—tattered and burning in the diminishing light.

There were five of them left. Daeghrefn and four others. No sign of Robert.

And the ogres were closing from west and east and north.

Covered in mud and moss and dung from a long, oblivious sleep, a harsh battle cry now on their lips, yet another band of the monsters swarmed out of the foothills below him. They crashed down the hillside, skidding through rocks, uprooting small trees in their descent. They stopped only to gather weapons—huge felled branches, stones for slinging and hurling. A dozen of them lumbered onto the plain to join their advancing brothers.

Cerestes chuckled, brushing the ash from his hair. The creatures were considerably far from him now, but moving resolutely onto the plains, and the dark was coming. The dark, where human eyes would fail and falter, where the fire would cast long, deceptive shadows, in which an ogre could hide or the road itself could vanish.

Night was the ally of monsters.

"And night is lovely, and *my* friend as well," he murmured ecstatically as the red moon and the silver tilted over the smoke-blurred landscape, and black Nuitari rose between them. Cerestes stood in the copse of evergreens and breathed a low prayer to the black moon and Hiddukel, to Zeboim and Chemosh and Sargonnas—to all the dark gods, even to the Lady herself.

He had seen Takhisis's tower in far Neraka, the black stone and scaffolding heaped at the foot of its surrounding walls when the enchantments broke and the ogres fled. It was a setback, a slowing of her plans, but only a brief one. The tower was almost complete—grown out of rock, out of earth, out of nothing. The walls were an afterthought, scarcely necessary when strong magic ruled in Neraka.

Cerestes had seen enough to know. The devices of the Dark Queen were well under way, but they could still be disrupted with a clever mind and a subtle tongue. His own safety lay in continuing to serve her for now, to seem strong and resolute as her captain in the waking world. The time would come, and the secret of the runes would come to him—but not now, not yet. Open rebellion seemed thin and futile, like the hopes of these horsemen on the darkening plain.

He laughed again at *that* prospect. It looked as though Daeghrefn had found disaster within sight of his own fortress. But there was always the garrison—a hundred stout men in Nidus's walls, who, on seeing the danger to their lord and master, would . . .

What *would* they do? What indeed?

The world was filled with unfaithful servants, he mused ironically. And sometimes it seemed that they were the safe ones, huddling and skulking behind the walls while their masters stood in the open and braved the approaching peril.

Braved the fires and the ogres.

But if the fire raged further and the ogres ran riot, Daeghrefn would not fall alone. Somewhere behind the flames wandered the mace-wielder, and the druidess's girl was with him, and the other lad.

Softly, insistently, the Voice spoke to him now, low and melodious and achingly feminine. *Those three cannot perish on the plains*, it said. *They must not fall into the clutches of the ogres.*

"I know," he replied, whispering a quick spell of veiling. Then he stood in the midst of the evergreen grove, his face shadowed by the crisp-smelling darkness, his deepest thoughts concealed in a layer of spellcraft. "What would you have me do, Lady?" he asked aloud to the wind and the night.

It is time, the Voice proclaimed as the branches rustled with a warm breeze, upon it the smell of lilac. But beneath that sweet and lulling smell lay the sharp, disturbing odor of fire and carrion, so that Cerestes reeled for a moment, wondering if the smoke had risen from the plains or if he had imagined the gruesome smell on the air.

Or if, on the wings of the night, the breath of the goddess had passed over him.

It is time, she repeated, and he knew what she meant. *Time to show yourself.*

"But they will fear me as well," he protested. "The mace-wielder. His companions."

The mace-wielder understands me, Takhisis explained. *And I am the Queen of Dragons.*

Mystified, Cerestes nodded. And though he was weary of changing and longed for a form that was ever the same, he answered her call. He focused his will past pain and fear, past the barriers that the mind sets for the body's limits and boundaries, and his thoughts rocked in a white-hot ecstasy. His bones stretched and thickened. Scales erupted on his blistering arms, and he groaned with the fresh pain of metamorphosis, with the remembered pain of a thousand years of waiting for this moment.

All who wandered the plains would look upon the dragon, and the will of the Dark Queen would be done.

* * * * *

Daeghrefn shielded his eyes against the heat and the rush of smoke. One of the men—Mozer, he believed—tugged at his cape, shouted something loud and urgent and indecipherable, but it was lost in the roar of the flames, the whinny of horses, the fierce war cries of the ogres.

A half-mile's ride north toward Nidus had brought them up against yet another wall of fire. Yet another band of ogres had arranged themselves in the flatlands south of the castle, so that Daeghrefn and his men were caught between two converging parties of the enemy.

"Lord Daeghrefn!" Mozer shouted insistently, tugging again.

With the back of his hand, the Lord of Nidus slapped away the sniveling wretch, then guided his horse to yet another rise in the midst of the plains—a small, bare moraine glittering with black obsidian.

The men followed him numbly onto the rise. Graaf, Mozer, Tangaard, and Gundling—they were the survivors, all who remained of the proud dozen who had set off for Neraka.

"What now, sir?" Graaf shouted above the din.

He was the sensible one. The veteran.

"The north is thick with ogres," Graaf continued. "There's a score of 'em between us and the castle, and a brace of 'em alone would be a handful for five tired men."

"I am aware of the tactics, Sergeant," Daeghrefn answered hotly, his mind on the fire coursing relentlessly over the plains behind them. They had passed through it twice, and the second time Aschraf had fallen from the saddle. As the flames engulfed him, the soldier had tried to rise. But he stumbled, and the blood burst from his face, and he stretched his dying hand pitifully toward his commander, a flame on the tip of each finger.

Daeghrefn shook his head and banished the thought.

Gundling spoke now, a rough voice to his left, his Estwilde accent still thick after a dozen years at Nidus. Something about "more" and "last hopes."

Daeghrefn looked to Gundling. For a brief, nightmarish moment, he saw Aschraf's face, mottled and fire-sheared. Then he blinked, and Gundling stared at him, his beard singed and blackened.

Gundling was pointing to Castle Nidus, where twenty more of the monsters were circling and menacing, hurling rocks wildly at the old black battlements.

Daeghrefn looked toward the eastern foothills. Perhaps there was still a way to get to the highlands, circle the castle, and approach from the northern side. There was a rise he remembered . . . a copse of evergreen . . .

As he looked toward the jagged silhouettes of the trees framed against the white of Solinari, Daeghrefn saw the dragon's dark wings rise above the black aeterna, and the hillside shook, and the tall pines snapped like kindling.

"Lord Daeghrefn, what do we do?" Gundling shouted, his eyes on his commander. "Lord Daeghrefn? Lord Daeghrefn!"

When Daeghrefn froze in the saddle on the fiery plain, it was not from fear of ogre or flame, but from a darker cause. He would never remember the dragon itself—the dark web of wings passing over the moon—but he would remember the fear always.

And he would think, as a man who believes in neither monsters nor gods, that the fear was again of his own making.

* * * * *

Verminaard galloped over the blackened plain, moonlight glimmering on his uplifted mace.

At a distance, he saw the ogres, milling around a small group of soldiers atop South Moraine. It was defensible ground, and the men had bows, but the ogres were closing on them slowly, batting at the arrows. The men were few and the weapons paltry against such monsters. The soldiers wouldn't hold out much longer.

"Verminaard!" Aglaca shouted. "It's your father's squadron!"

Verminaard looked more closely at the stone-tattered standard nodding above the horse soldiers, a black raven on a red field.

The black mace whistled and droned in his scorched hand, and he was suddenly filled with surety and power. Here was an enemy he could fight!

With a shout, he turned Orlog toward the milling ogres and lifted the mace above his head. Exuberant and wild, he swung the weapon in a wide arc. Black fire flashed before the mace head, and its wake painted a wide stream of darkness, a blackness against which the depths of a starless night sky seemed afire.

Two hulking ogres, bound for the battle at the moraine, turned at the sound of Orlog's hoofbeats. Verminaard galloped toward them, mace uplifted, and before the first of them could raise its club, he brought the weapon flashing down upon the monster's shoulder.

"Midnight!" he cried, as the Voice in the cave had instructed.

The air rained blood and black fire. The ogre shrieked, its skin curling and blackening, and it fell to its scabious knees in the high grass. Its eyes, suddenly and strangely blinded, rolled white and terrified toward the slate-gray sky, where the stars of Morgion shone coldly above the fiery bloodbath.

The second ogre leapt away with a shout, crossing swiftly before Judyth's charging mare and stumbling and sliding through the rock-littered grass on its way back to the smoke and safety. Verminaard veered to follow it, spurring Orlog swiftly across the field in pursuit. The ogre reeled and tried to bring up its weapon, but the mace descended again with a crash, and the monster bellowed as the darkness encircled it.

Verminaard shouted again, held the dripping mace aloft, then steered the black stallion toward the rise, toward the ogres, and toward his father. Caught up in the blind rush, the roaring swirl of the mace, and the chaos of fire and noise, Judyth whistled shrilly, and the mare followed Orlog, picking her way over the few remaining spots of unburned ground.

Now the ogres loomed before them, hulking, ash-covered shapes lurching from the smoke, their weapons raised as they charged toward the rattled party. Judyth had heard the stories the knights told back in Solamnia—how the monsters strayed out of the mountains, ravaging livestock, caravans, occasional drowsy villages. One of them, it was said, was a fighting match for five men, ten of them for a whole company of knights.

But here on the plain there were twenty . . . thirty . . . *forty* against a mere eight men.

She looked toward the castle, where yet another score advanced, beating their breasts and roaring, pummeling the ground with stone, axe, and club.

There were far and away too many. It was a massacre in the making.

Judyth brought the mare to a struggling halt twenty yards from the gathering monsters as two ogres, rushing out from the smoke, closed ground rapidly, their stony teeth chattering in fury. Aglaca leapt from the saddle as the girl grabbed vainly for his arm. He twisted through the air like a cyclone, shouting and kicking out at the nearest ogre, who toppled forward, choking from a crushing blow to its windpipe. Aglaca hurdled onto the shoulders of the other ogre, a big fellow with a club the size of a fence rail, who swatted at him vainly, like a bear fending off a darting wasp. And then Aglaca slammed an elbow to the side of the monster's baffled face and sprang back for the saddle while the ogre staggered and dropped to its knees, its head and shoulder in a new and grotesque arrangement.

"Judyth! Ride toward those three!" Aglaca shouted, pointing toward a trio of ogres in the gathering smoke.

Judyth did not stop to question. With a shrill whistle and a slap of the reins against the mare's withers, she goaded the willing little beast to a gallop.

The ogres were caught unaware. The smallest raised its club and bellowed, but Aglaca was plunging from the saddle before the weapon descended, his sinewy arms wrapped about the creature's wrist, his weight pulling the thing over backward. The ogre reeled, teetered, then suddenly, surprisingly, flew through the air, as the young

Solamnic tossed it over his shoulder with a levering move he had learned from L'Indasha Yman. Crashing into its two oncoming companions, who fell dazed to the hard, fire-blackened earth, the monster roared, grunted, and lay still.

"Take the horse, Judyth!" Aglaca shouted. "Ride for the castle! They're bound for Daeghrefn. Perhaps we can hold them off until—"

"It'll be too late!" she protested.

Aglaca nodded. "All the more reason to stand with the soldiers," he declared calmly.

She stared down at him, reached for him, tried to speak.

Then overhead, a dark shape eclipsed the white moon, and the plains themselves shadowed for a breath. Judyth paled.

"Don't look up!" she shouted at Aglaca, shielding his eyes with her hand. In front of them, Verminaard, the ogres, and the horsemen from Nidus stared into the night sky, where the dragon swooped and vanished in smoke and cloud. A long moment passed.

"Wh-what was that?" Aglaca asked, still holding her gaze.

"I'm not sure," Judyth replied, "but I know we shouldn't look on it directly."

"But look *now*," Aglaca said. "What, in the name of Paladine . . ."

Most of the ogres were scattering in panic, lumbering toward the foothills or toward the fire itself, covering their heads, grunting and shrieking. The others stood still in fear, like a circle of stones around the frozen riders of Nidus.

All were still except Verminaard. He reeled for a moment with Dragonawe, then righted himself in the saddle, clutching Orlog's mane until the dizziness passed. Then he raised his mace and brought it thundering down onto the head of a panic-stricken ogre, and a black wind muffled the screams of the dying monster.

Verminaard swung again, shouting wildly, as a passing ogre, a large one, ducked, dodging the blow. The creature lunged at the mace-wielding rider and passed through the whirl of darkness that followed the weapon's arc through the air. At once, the ogre fell to its knees, clutching its eyes, then groped and gibbered as it crawled toward the fire wall and vanished into the white-hot flames.

Slapping the mace excitedly against his broad thigh, Verminaard guided his horse through the dazed monsters and rode to the side of the Lord of Nidus.

"Lord Daeghrefn?" he called, tugging on the scorched sleeve. "Father?"

Daeghrefn stared blankly at the northern sky.

* * * * *

Propped against a sturdy young vallenwood in the foothills, Robert had watched the plains below through the swirl of smoke and moonlight. By the red light of Lunitari, his eyes had followed Verminaard's path through the ogres to Daeghrefn, the mace-wielder untouched by the scattering ogres. And as the druidess set and splinted Robert's shattered leg, the seneschal had seen the new battle begin, the moon darken and the deepest of shadows pass over the battlefield.

She had told him to close his eyes then, and he had done so. But still he felt a breathless, sweating dizziness, overwhelming nausea, and the sudden, brief impulse to run.

Indeed, he *would* have run, had his leg allowed it, the rough old seneschal thought bitterly.

"What *was* that shadow, Lady?" he muttered, but the druidess shook her head. Her auburn hair shimmered in the faint moonlight, and for a moment, Robert was again breathless.

"Not yet," she cautioned. "The world is not yet ready to see it, nor even to hear again the stories and rumors."

"But it . . .it laid out half of 'em!" the seneschal protested. "Put most of the ogres to flight! What in the—"

"'Tis the Awe, if my guess is right," L'Indasha Yman explained cryptically. "The creature inspires the Awe in most mortals. They break, panic-stricken, for safety, or else they are frozen dead."

"Then Daeghrefn's boy must be a god," Robert replied in perplexity. "Not that I ever fancied him one. But did you see how he didn't run? Didn't freeze? Why, he stood alone against it!"

"He's no god," L'Indasha replied with an ironic smile, "but that mace he carries will give him illusions of it."

Robert lowered himself painfully to the ground, lifting his battered leg onto the litter the druidess had fashioned of vines and fallen limbs. "He had illusions to begin with, Lady. Right curious ones, of runes and hocus-pocus."

The druidess laughed softly, musically. "Rest now, loyal Robert. You have earned this brief holiday."

* * * * *

"We need help here, Verminaard," Aglaca insisted. Come down from your horse and help us lift Tangaard."

Judyth and Aglaca struggled with the dazed cavalryman, a man noted in his company for strength and bulk. Between the two of them, they had scarcely the strength to lift the enormous soldier to his feet, much less to hoist him over a horse's back.

The others, however, were ready to be carried into Nidus. Daeghrefn and his surviving soldiers lay draped across the saddles of their horses, and Aglaca's wondrous little mare, still shaking from the shadows across Solinari, was pawing the earth, ready to guide the lot of them into Nidus.

"Verminaard?" Aglaca called again, but the lad sat astride Orlog, staring out at the fading fire as though he, too, had been paralyzed by something in its depths. "Verminaard!"

Verminaard turned, regarding Aglaca with a wild, exuberant stare.

"Help?" he asked, his strong hands shaking on the stallion's reins. "Oh, rest assured I'll help, Aglaca. While you take them into the castle, I shall cover our escape."

"Cover our . . . I don't understand."

"Quickly, Aglaca," Judyth urged. "Before the ogres waken."

She glanced nervously at the circle of monsters. Nine ogres remained after the darkening of the moon and the panic and flight of their comrades. Stunned by the Dragonawe, they lay stiff and scattered like tomb effigies in the forsaken field.

"Carry our comrades in, Lady Judyth," Verminaard commanded, a strange note of hilarity in his voice, "and let the banquet be called to celebrate our victory over the assembled ogres and the powers of the enemy."

Aglaca and Judyth glanced nervously at one another.

"As you say, Verminaard," Aglaca murmured. "For now."

Verminaard lifted the mace again, holding it delicately, almost lovingly, fitting its handle in the scar-notched groove of his palm. "Do so, and I shall attend to the rear guard action, to the last despicable attempt to spoil our victory."

Aglaca shook his head and started to speak, but Judyth set her hand on his shoulder. Wordlessly she nodded toward the unconscious soldiers tied carefully to the horses they were leading, and Aglaca understood. Swiftly, almost shamefully, with scarcely a look behind them, they mounted the horses, Judyth atop the mare and Aglaca on

Daeghrefn's stallion, steadying the petrified Lord of Nidus across the horse's rump.

It was a strange caravan that made for the gates of the castle. Traveling in darkness, the dying fires behind them, the party of seven approached the battlements, where, at their posts, the sentries began to waken and stir.

Gundling was the first to sit up in the saddle. Blearily he looked toward the battlements. The sentries waved and the gates opened.

"By the gods!" he cried ecstatically. "By the Book of Gilean, by Zivilyn and by great Kiri-Jolith, we have weathered the lot of it!"

He looked beside him, where the dark girl, her hands gently on the reins of his horse, led them toward safety, toward a good meal, no doubt, and a warm bath.

With a sooty hand, Gundling rubbed his head. His hair was a little singed, his right ear bloodied. Otherwise, he thought, he was unbroken and sound. And yet he felt he had seen . . . no doubt had imagined . . .

What was it? He couldn't remember, and the opaque, troubled stare of the girl riding beside him told him nothing.

With a groan, Graaf sat up on the other side of the girl, weaving atop his horse, almost falling, until Aglaca rode up and caught him.

"Be calm," the Solamnic was saying with a thin, unassuring smile. "Rest and try not to stir. You nearly fell from your horse there, Sergeant Graaf, and it'd be a shame to weather threescore ogres only to break your crown in a riding accident."

The ogres. Where were the ogres? Gundling steadied himself, turned painfully in the saddle.

Behind him, dark in the light of the waning fire, Master Verminaard stood on the plains. He was shouting—riotous words, incomprehensible—and lifting a black mace to the night sky. A dozen ogres lay lifeless around him, and he stood over the last one shouting, the mace rising, wheeling, and falling in a lethal, silent rhythm.

Twelve of them, Gundling marveled, a strange and numbing awe spreading over him. Twelve of them, by the gods, and if he's been unsung before, he will be unsung no longer.

Not if I have breath and voice to sing.

Chapter 13

It was a custom in the mountains, a custom honored since the Age of Might, that victory in battle was followed by a night of banquet and celebration, but also of the Minding, when the story of the victory was told, the fallen mourned, the brave honored, and the history of the battle enrolled in the thoughts and memories of those who had not been present. Regardless of rank or station, everyone was permitted to speak.

So was it done in other castles throughout Taman Busuk, in Jelek and Estwilde, through the Kalkhists, into the Doom Range, and down into Neraka.

Not so, however, in Castle Nidus. It had been Daeghrefn's custom to conduct the Minding all by himself.

Instead of allowing the men to tell their version of the day's events on the battlefield, the Lord of Nidus would assemble the troops and speak briefly of the deaths that had befallen his house that day, of its heroism and tragedy. Then the ceremony was over—observed, so as not to arouse the traditionalists, but bleak and quiet and altogether joyless, the words floating aimlessly into the dark rafters of the great hall.

After the surprising, near-disastrous battle with the ogres on the plains near Nidus, many of the men wondered if the Minding were in order at all, if what had taken place that night, within sight of the battlements, could have been more defeat than victory.

And yet on the next evening, after wounds had been stitched and bruises salved, the boards of the tables bent low with fowl and venison. The wine swirled and spilled, the servants busied themselves with pouring and porting and setting salt, bread, and water by each place, and the music began at sunset, a thin and graceful trumpet signaling that the Lord of Nidus requested the pleasure of his soldiers at the meal.

In preparation and prologue, the Minding began like the dozen or so that had taken place at Nidus since the Nerakan Wars had resumed. And yet, almost before the sound of the trumpet died, all who were summoned—from the family of the lord to his noble hostage, to the veteran cavalrymen who returned with him yesterday, all the way down to the youngest of the servants—knew that this night would be different, would be like no other.

As usual, Daeghrefn was the last to arrive at the Minding. Flanked by two cavalrymen, he made for the long table, for his customary seat in the high-backed chair adorned with the arms of Nidus: *Raven Displayed on a Field Gules*, the stormcrow of ancient lineage, sign of the house, perpetually and unchangingly honored.

And yet something *had* changed in the climate of the

hall. The dozen chairs by the lord's seat, by the gift throne, were empty tonight—empty of petitioners, courtiers, sycophants. The knights and retainers who usually sat at the master's table had moved elsewhere, to the opposite end of the chamber. To the table by the fire, the far hearth which now blossomed with laughter and the first of the songs, for the men in the great hall had gathered around Lord Verminaard.

Daeghrefn scowled from his distant vantage. He struck the boards once, twice, but only Juventus and Onnozel, two of the younger troopers, untested in battle, even looked in his direction.

Gracefully, confidently, Verminaard held forth in the midst of the men. Raising a black mace, a weapon that seemed to catch the firelight and set it astir and spinning, Verminaard began the festivities, as the hero should—or in the absence of a single hero, the lord of the castle— with the formal, warlike speech of the mountain mead-hall.

> "Say to me, soldiers, soul-mated in battle,
> stones and mountain, sea and river,
> before whom the fire has broke, is breaking,
> will break in the final hours of fire.
> Say to me, soldiers, the afternoon's story
> of what came to pass in the country of ogres,
> to honor the Nine in the Regions of Night,
> a dirge for the Lady dwelling in darkness,
> a song for Takhisis, a song for the queen. . . ."

Daeghrefn leaned back in astonishment. Where had Verminaard learned the songs of the mead hall? This kind of foolishness had never gained ear in Castle Nidus—too sloppy and eastern, it was, smacking of Nerakan dives and the dockside bars of Sanction. This was a *solemn* hall, after a solemn battle. Men had been slain. Men had not returned. And this . . . this cursed *usurper* . . .

Daeghrefn had heard enough. With a shout, he rose and stalked to the center of the hall, hiding the limp from the wound suffered at the ogre's hand. The long scoring lacerations had been stitched neatly by the girl Judyth, the very one whose rescue had prompted all the disastrous, harebrained journeys of the last several days. Stiff and aching, Daeghrefn stood before the entire garrison, folded his arms, and glared balefully at the young man who would commandeer his place at table, who would turn the solemn occasion into a pulpit for vulgar legend and drunken boast.

All eyes turned to the lord of the castle, and for a moment the hall fell hush. A pigeon flapped in the eaves, and a solitary dog padded across the flagstone floor on its way to the safer darkness.

Old Graaf stood first to tell the first story, as was his place by age and honor.

Daeghrefn smiled. A loyal retainer. A man who knew his benefit and safety in the ranks of Nidus.

Slowly, with a strong voice unshaken by time and wounds in the service of his lord, Graaf turned to the young man standing at the head of the new table.

"Master Verminaard," he began, humbly but assuredly, "I haven't the high lord's poetry, nor the song of the olden times, when men such as my grandsire spoke in verses themselves, a song to the gift throne."

Daeghrefn glanced angrily at Verminaard, who met his gaze directly. The first of the speakers had broken protocol, had addressed this supplanter rather than the rightful Lord of Nidus.

The pale eyes of the young man met the dark eyes of the older. Daeghrefn felt a chill pass down his back, and he shivered involuntarily. He might as well be staring at his old friend—his old enemy—Laca Dragonbane.

Graaf continued, his voice acquiring resonance and

strength. "And indeed there is no song of the harp this evening, gold string and sound of heaven, to gladden even the harshest voice with song. No song of the harp, for Robert the seneschal did not return from Neraka Forest."

Daeghrefn winced. Robert had always been the harper at the Minding—a surprising talent, for the rough old soldier had played like a bard.

"But here is the way your servant remembers," Graaf announced, his voice gaining power and confidence as he stepped away from the table. "To the best of his saying, these things he remembers."

"We had searched for Verminaard, Son of the Stormcrow," the grizzled sergeant began, raising his cup in the ceremonial stance of the scop, the teller, the rememberer. "We had searched for Aglaca, Son of the West. We had searched for them south of the forest where the victims of banditry hang dried and blackened like unpicked grapes, where wild cats roam in the bleeding woodland, where the trees scream of murder and conspiracies."

He took a deep breath and handed the cup to Tangaard. The burly young cavalryman drank fully, with a defiant glare at Lord Daeghrefn, then stood, raised the cup, and continued the story.

"It was then that the fire from the south overtook us," Tangaard began. "It caught us like beasts at the edge of the forest, at the forest's edge where Fittela fell. Then came the ogres, mark-steppers, man-eaters, falling on Thunar, finest of swordsmen, then upon Ullr, wielder of hammers, dear to Majere and fierce Kiri-Jolith."

Tangaard could no longer speak. The men kept respectful silence. It was well known that Tangaard and Ullr were the oldest and best of friends.

Mutely, glaring with rage at Daeghrefn, the young man handed the cup to Mozer.

Where Mozer had found the courage to join in the Minding, none could say. He was the softest of the men who had traveled with Daeghrefn—an aristocrat's son from Sanction, and he had gibbered and wept in the midst of the burning forest. Yet something had happened to him on the fire-struck plains. His eyes were deeper now, strangely fathomless, and he drank from the cup wearily and reverently, as a pilgrim might at the altar of some ancient shrine.

"Asa the Bright One, Longbow of Lemish, fell to the fire in a cauldron of cedar. . . ."

Aglaca, standing in a shadowy corner of the hall, dropped his head. He had almost forgotten Asa's love of the bow—the big, gap-toothed westerner, ready with laughter and arrows.

"Asa the Bright One," Mozer continued, "and after him Reginn, Son of the Smith and the Hammer of Reorx. None can remember a stronger hand, the foe of rock, the destroyer of ramparts. Fallen to fire, to the leveling blazes, and abandoned deep in Neraka's forest."

Furtively, without looking at the Lord of Nidus, Mozer extended the cup toward Aglaca, beckoning him toward the hearth and the table.

Aglaca shook his head, waving away the invitation. He could not speak of what he had seen.

Aglaca had looked away, or tried to look away, on the fire-torn fields south of Nidus when Verminaard offered to cover their retreat. He had known well what would happen, but the men in his charge were stunned and weakened, and if the dazed ogres had come to themselves before he and Judyth could get the men into the castle . . .

So he had left Verminaard to cover their retreat. He was not proud of it.

His back to the battlefield, Aglaca had heard the sound of the mace as it whirled and roared, had heard it descend on the stunned, defenseless ogres, the wet, breaking sound of metal against powerless bone, Verminaard's exultant cries as again and again he brought down the black, shimmering weapon.

Aglaca shuddered and clenched his fists. He had secreted Judyth in the elaborate garden, far from the notice of Verminaard, Daeghrefn, Cerestes—the whole evil lot of them. She was hidden for a while, but she was hardly safe. And if anything happened to him, she would be as good as dead in the viper's pit that Nidus had become.

And yet he would not leave, would not return to Solamnia. The *gebo-naud* was deeply binding, and his father's words returned to him over the miles and years: *No son of mine is an oath-breaker, Aglaca. Remember that in the halls of Nidus.*

And, after all, the man at that table was his brother.

The cup had passed on now, into the hands of Gundling. Perhaps the best of Daeghrefn's soldiers, this man had been a bandit himself, and a good one, but had balked at the raising of the dark temple in the midst of his village and at the ogres brought in to construct the walls around the Dark Queen's stronghold.

Gundling was a man of few illusions and fewer sympathies. And yet he was honorable, and he lifted the cup and drank from it, his eyes never leaving Lord Daeghrefn. Then slowly, sonorously, he began the end of the story.

"Out of the forest on the northern plains, where the fire had taken the last of the woodland, there we lost Aschraf, who was not yet himself in the lists of battle. Bold as a wolf, the bearer of promises, he fell to the fire, and the fire found him worthy. Robert the Seneschal, Robert the Harper, the last of our number to fall in the battle, left in the midst of fire and ogres, loyal to Nidus in the rear guard of armies. While the gates of the castle, the gates of the ear, were closed to his cries, Robert the Seneschal drew the last sword in the burning of memories."

All of the men kept the silence. Gundling held forth the

cup, for any taker, any man who could complete the story. Aglaca looked wonderingly at the assembled soldiers: None of them remembered the dark wings over the moon, the welling, paralyzing fear that had passed across the high prairie and then vanished, leaving them scattered and dazed and forlorn.

None, that is, except Aglaca himself.

And Verminaard, of course, who now sat on a stool by the fire, his gaze fixed on the guttering flames and his hands folded softly, almost prayerfully under his chin. He would not take the cup to end the story; traditionally, that was the duty of the lord of the castle.

When Daeghrefn moved toward the cup, there was a sharp intake of breath from one of the men—Mozer, perhaps, or Tangaard. Slowly the Lord of Nidus extended his hand, grasped the jeweled goblet, drank the dregs of the wine . . .

And spoke, his words halting and listless.

They all knew he spoke from hearsay, from the words that had passed through the castle the night before, this morning, and into the waning hours of the afternoon. But it was his task to complete the story, to end the Minding with all the dead reckoned and the heroes acclaimed.

"Let not the night pass," Daeghrefn said resentfully, sarcastically, with the eyes of the men fixed upon him, "without the remembrance of Verminaard of Nidus, black mace-wielder, slayer of ogres, scourge of the flame, defender of battlements, right arm of the castle."

He coughed and set the cup on the table.

Verminaard rose from his seat by the fire. Coldly and balefully, the mace swinging menacingly in his gloved hand, he stared after Daeghrefn, who averted his eyes.

"Had I heard such a speech years ago," he began flatly, "and had you meant it . . . had I heard its beginning, its ending . . . *one word* of it, even last week, it might have moved me."

He stalked from the fire to the great hall's entrance, past the astounded sentries and out the door of the keep.

Daeghrefn stood by the table, staring into the wine-stained bowl of the cup. The men began to eat, in silence at first, but then amid muffled and uncertain conversation. He looked up once, met Tangaard's resentful stare, and lowered his gaze again.

Until the ogres and the fires, Daeghrefn had not remembered fear. It had come from the shadows like a thief, rising from the smoke to steal his nerve and his warrior's heart, and the castle walls were narrow and dark, the corners menacing and comfortless. He had gazed in the basin this morning as he washed his face, and for a moment—a dark, horrific moment—he thought he saw something standing over him, waiting. . . .

A thing with pale eyes and pale hair, blocking out the sunlight.

And again he was afraid. Of the fires and the ogres, of the men in his garrison.

Of Verminaard. And of something else he could not remember.

* * * * *

Verminaard burst into the moonlight of the bailey, a bitter oath on his lips. He fought his way through the ipomoea, the perennial morning glory whose vines plagued the castle and garrison in a spreading, entangling joke. Wrestling himself free of the tenacious plant, the young man looked up to curse the moons and the constellations.

He let the words die in his throat when he saw Cerestes on the battlements, gazing south over the plains.

In that moment and from that vantage, there in the tangling light of Solinari and Lunitari, the twining moons, silver and red, it seemed to Verminaard that the mage's skin was almost insubstantial. It shimmered and glowed with a strange translucence, shifting in a luminous cloud until Cerestes seemed a cloud himself, then a shadow, then a dwindling black light on the crenels, like the light Verminaard had seen in the cave where he found the mace.

Then suddenly Cerestes emerged, and thin ebony lightning danced over his sleeves, on his hands, on his fingers . . .

And the shadow he cast on the tower walls was reptilian, enormous, disproportionate even for moon-crazed battlements.

Verminaard gasped, recalling the shadow on the moon.

And then Cerestes looked like himself once more, the black robe shimmering faintly, almost shabby now in the clouded moonlight.

Only strange light, Verminaard thought. Or weariness from my battle yesterday. Or a simple magic on a cloud-struck night—a spell for sleep, perhaps, or to augur the fitful stars. The young man climbed the ladder to stand by his tutor.

"Out at the edge of sight," Cerestes said, forgoing greeting as though he had known Verminaard was there all along, "there's still a fire. See? If you look long enough toward the South Moraine . . ."

Verminaard stared across the darkening plain. He could see no fire from where he stood, but then Cerestes' eyesight had always been better than his.

Expressionlessly the mage turned to his pupil.

"The real courage came when you trusted Night-bringer," he explained quietly.

Verminaard frowned. "Nightbringer?"

Cerestes nodded. "The mace. 'Nightbringer' is the name it went by in Godshome. Powerful it is, but how would you know? How would you believe in it without courage?"

The lad smiled wider.

"I know what you mean, Cerestes," he said. "When Father left the Order . . . stopped believing in it . . . they say he changed. I don't remember the time, but Abelaard said that a sort of *daring* left him when Daeghrefn left the old gods, and that in its place was something . . . small. Something not at all, perhaps.

"But 'Nightbringer,' you say? The name of the mace is 'Nightbringer'?"

Cerestes nodded. "We had heard of it for years, knew it would be found by a chosen one, by a special one . . ."

Verminaard's ears felt hot. He looked to the sky, where the last vestiges of smoke had faded and dispersed, and the clouds parted over the red moon Lunitari. There was something Aglaca had told him long ago, something about the Voice, about why he refused to believe it.

Verminaard could not remember.

"And that's me, I suppose?" he asked. "The chosen one?"

"They spoke of you in Godshome," Cerestes replied, and something had deepened in his voice, choiring and resonating, until Verminaard realized there were two voices speaking: the old familiar voice he had heard in the classroom, at table, and on the battlements until this night, this moment, and another voice below that—a Voice even more familiar, more intimate, low and musical and feminine—and together the voices praised him, reassured him.

"You are the mace-wielder, the chosen one. Unto you will fall this castle, this country, and the mountains from the foothills of Estwilde to the peaks of the Doom Range and the breathless heights of Berkanth."

Cerestes shimmered as he spoke, and his skin seemed to ripple and change. And then he was strangely diminished in the cloud and spell light.

"Your rule," he said, his voice as dry and thin as the

scorched grass at the foot of the castle wall, "begins tonight. Your father is no father, but weak and distracted and lost."

And Cerestes told him the story of that night years ago. Of Laca's transgressions with Daeghrefn's wife . . . and that Verminaard's true father was Laca Dragonbane, Lord of East Borders.

"I knew it all along," Verminaard replied, masking his astonishment, averting his eyes. "Not—not that my father was Laca. I didn't know *that*. But that he was not, *could not* be Daeghrefn."

It was Cerestes' turn to smile.

"Then there's prophecy in you as well, Lord Verminaard. Father or no father, Nidus is yours—not by blood, but by virtue and might. Soon there will be worlds elsewhere to conquer. But now, in the wake of your victory, there are smaller and sweeter conquests as well."

Verminaard glanced at him curiously.

Cerestes returned the look as his smile broadened to a leer. "When you took up the mace, you traded one girl for another. But the first one is still there—the first fruits of your power, if you'd have her. Go to her, lad. If you are not too late with your caution and false kindness, there is still a chance that she will be yours, and yours tonight. After all, she saw Nightbringer in your victorious hand."

It was something Verminaard had not considered. He had been too busy with rescues, with caverns and ogres and fires. But now the girl seemed like the first and best prospect. Verminaard's eyes grew bright, and he threw back his head and laughed harshly.

Cerestes had seen the look before on the face of young men—not courting swains bearing sonnets and flowers, but the young raiders at the borders of the enemy, bearing arms into unprotected country.

* * * * *

As the first of Daeghrefn's soldiers nodded with wine and the late hour, Aglaca pushed away from the table.

He had eaten little, drunk less. The events of the last nights and days had been unsettling. Now was a time for moonlight and fresh air. A walk in the bailey would clear his senses and leave behind the smoke and noise.

Silently he crossed the dark courtyard. The silver harp of Branchala, a score of white stars, shone in the cloud-crossed sky, and he passed by the dimly lit stable, where the new groom struggled with the uneasy horses.

In the shadow of the southern wall, something turned slowly, a pale garment catching the edge of the moonlight. Instinctively Aglaca reached for his dagger. Then Judyth stepped from the shadows and stared calmly at him, her remarkable eyes charged with reflected starlight. Gazing into them for a brief, breathless moment, Aglaca saw the blue in the depths of lavender.

"What should we do about Verminaard?" she began. "I—I saw him storm up to the battlements. He'll kill Daeghrefn, if not now, eventually. And then what shall we—"

Aglaca stepped forward and gently placed a finger to her lips. He pulled her back into the shadows, out of the sight of sentries and dangerous rivals.

"Nothing," he whispered. "For we *can* do nothing. 'Tis a struggle between son and father. It began long before I came. Who knows when and how it will end?"

"But you saw what Verminaard did."

"That and worse," Aglaca conceded. "But we can do nothing yet, except ward against a growing evil."

He handed Judyth the little dagger.

"I think of Verminaard getting the hero's portion," Judyth muttered hotly, slipping the weapon up her sleeve, "then I think of you, going about acts of kindness instead of *butchery*. How you helped those helpless men to horse, risking yourself at each moment. An ogre could have wakened, could have risen up and—"

"You did the same, Lady Judyth," Aglaca said, brushing her hair from her eyes. "Entirely the same, in the prospect of the same fire and ogres."

"But you were the one in the tunnels."

"And you showed me how to master the warding."

They laughed, and Aglaca thought it was good that there were shadows here, that Judyth could not see his face grow red.

"I suppose we both have earned the true hero's portion," he murmured. Slowly he wrapped his arms about her waist and drew her closer.

Her eyes closed in the dark, and her lips parted.

* * * * *

Descending from the battlements, Verminaard heard muffled laughter from the shadows below.

He stopped on the ladder, caution giving way to curiosity. After all, sounds such as these promised no ambush, no escaping hostage or prisoner. Quietly, holding his breath, he leaned forward on the ladder . . .

And saw the couple kissing, embracing, the girl's dark hair caught in a thin shaft of moonlight.

Dark hair, dark skin . . .

He imagined the lavender eyes, the tattoo, and he knew who it was that stood with her in the dark beneath the walls. For a moment, he reeled on the ladder, and the thoughts of murder that rose through the heart of his anger were murky and monstrous, as deep as the caverns that spawned them.

I shall not forget this, Aglaca, he thought. And he

perched there, huddled in blackness like a roosting raven, until the couple walked across the bailey back toward the lamplit keep.

Chapter 14

In the hands of the druidess, the seneschal recovered miraculously.

Robert had expected the mending to take weeks, perhaps months, given his age and the severity of the broken bone. But within two days, the bones had knitted, and in a week's time he was walking—warily, unsteadily, and with a hardwood cane, but walking nonetheless.

L'Indasha had carried and dragged him above the worst of the fire, to a small cave in the foothills due east of the Neraka Forest. The cave itself was pleasant enough, bright and neat and well settled. In its recesses, surrounded by a cage of drasil roots, a fresh underground spring bubbled and spouted, and the druidess's stores—barrels of dried fruit and waybread wrapped in moist, preservative vallenwood leaves—had escaped the burning when the ogres' fires razed the countryside. The stores served L'Indasha and her guest as their sole source of food while Robert was immobilized and the forest began to heal.

In that same week, as Robert grew stronger, L'Indasha had grown increasingly distressed. Robert had watched as the woman's bright auburn hair became muted and brown, as though she were enduring a kind of gloomy autumn of the heart. Her once-bright eyes grew dull and lifeless, and her skin seemed to tighten, to become almost transparent, until one afternoon, three days after the fire, the seneschal believed she would just dwindle away. He feared that the next morning would find him disabled and alone on the hilltop, his only companion and guardian fallen like a dried leaf.

That had been a week ago. There were signs of late that L'Indasha was now recovering, but from what ailment, what mishap, Robert could only guess.

At first he had thought it was the strange and lingering discomforts of an unknown intrusion, for when L'Indasha had brought him back to the cave, she discovered that someone else had been there. While she tended to Robert's leg, the druidess had fretted over the disarray that someone had wrought amid the kindling and stores, and—oddly enough, the seneschal thought—seemed even more concerned about a wooden bucket that had been moved. Finally, and as the last insult, she had discovered that some prized piece of jewelry, a pendant with a purple stone, was missing.

It was a day or two before Robert gently inquired and found that her anger and sorrow had more to do with the fire in the forest and foothills than with burglary or trespass.

"It makes sense now," he said to her. "After all, don't you druids worship trees?"

"Of course not," she said. "We love them and tend

them, but they are only our responsibility, not our gods. They and all the other life of the land. My gardens. The flowers. You see, when a tree dies, it takes a while—several days, even when the damage is severe and sudden. The agony is constant until the roots go. And what fell to the fire a week ago was the show of my life's work. How would you feel?"

Robert thought of South Moraine and of the departing horsemen. "I see," he murmured.

And he did.

On the eighth day, she examined his leg, her strong, gentle fingers coursing from ankle to knee, and her own hollow countenance showed a little color and life once more as she pronounced him mended.

"Mended, that is. Not healed," she insisted. "You'll do the healing yourself—with walk and exercise and a change in heart from fear to certainty."

"Will you walk with me, Lady?" the seneschal asked with a grin. "I mean . . . seeing as it's medicinal and all? Perhaps I could be of some use to you as well."

So they began their walks as the seneschal's leg grew stronger and the spirit of the druidess was restored in the soft rains and new undergrowth of the repairing land.

But little was left of the grove-covered foothills to the east. The fire had climbed practically to the height of the mountains, and except for the steepest peaks—Berkanth, for example, and Minith Luc—the foliage was blasted to the timberline, and the big trees would take years to recover or return.

Perhaps he had never understood the druids before now, Robert thought, glancing often at the woman who walked beside him, turning away as her intent brown eyes locked with his. All the talk he had heard in Nidus—of tree worship, of entombing enemies in hollow logs, of stealing babies—seemed like rumor and foolishness now. For what he saw in this woman was none of the mystical, green treachery against which a generation of mages had warned him. She was instead a keeper of life, a seneschal of the land.

He thought again of Daeghrefn, of the riders vanishing into the smoke, of the words hurled coldly at him from horseback: *I'm sorry, Robert! I cannot help you where you are going.*

"Are you alone?" he continued to ask, and asked again one day as they stood on a bare obsidian rise overlooking the plains. There, scarce a fortnight before, he had been left for dead by his commander. "Are you alone, L'Indasha Yman?"

Her hair—bright auburn again, as though the last days had been but a fitful, nightmarish dream—was bound with dried holly. She looked up at him, her dark eyes hooded and elusive. She thought of the promise the god had made her twenty years before. "Not for long," she murmured. "Or so says Paladine."

Robert nodded. He leaned against his cane and climbed a step along the rising trail.

"And when does your . . . visitor arrive?"

"I had been told," the druidess replied, "to expect her any day."

"Her?"

"Yes. I believe my visitor is a woman, sent to help me with a wearisome task," L'Indasha said mysteriously. Then, turning toward Robert, she regarded him with a level, disarming directness.

"Do you remember the young woman who passed through the smoke that afternoon on the South Moraine, when you lay on the field of battle? She is the one. At least, I *think* she is. But I found her only to lose her, it seems."

"I remember little of her, m'Lady," the seneschal replied with an ironic smile. He bent and rubbed his leg. "I must allow that my thoughts were elsewhere at the time—on fire and ogres and what in the devouring name of Hiddukel was happening in that purple smoke. But I am certain of the young men who rode with her. If they were homeward bound, they're no doubt in Castle Nidus."

* * * * *

"I believe I am healed now," Robert said the next morning.

The druidess glanced up alertly from a caldron.

"Healed, not merely mended," the seneschal continued with a smile. "I expect I've imposed on your hospitality too long."

"Where will you go?" L'Indasha asked.

"I'm not sure. Not back to Nidus." He rose carefully and walked without aid to the mouth of the cavern. Below, at the edge of the forest, there was more green than blackness and ruin, and to the south, the faint song of a larkenvale. L'Indasha's work had not been in vain, he noted, and more than ever he longed to stay with her, to see through the greening of a thousand things.

"You offered to be of service not long ago," L'Indasha said, seeming to read his thoughts. "And there's a journey I must make—not an easy one, but you say you're healed now."

Robert leaned against the stone and smiled. "Nidus?"

L'Indasha shook her head from side to side. "From here, I can feel the power of Cerestes' warding spell about the castle. If I were to go to Nidus, the Lady would know at once of my presence. She would have me, and the girl's life would be forfeit."

Robert nodded. "Nidus or Neraka or the ends of the earth, my offer of service stands. Where might we be heading?"

"North . . . then up," the druidess announced, standing and dusting off her green robes. In the new light of the morning, she looked even younger, as though over the last week she had shed twenty years. "To the slopes of Berkanth, that mountain sacred to Paladine. Then a rocky climb to ice."

L'Indasha picked up the wooden bucket. "I can take this along now that I've your arm to aid with the carrying."

Robert's face reddened, and he looked away.

"Wherever my helper is," L'Indasha declared, "in Nidus or Neraka or at the edges of the earth, it is on Berkanth I shall find that help. Take the provisions, if you would. They're in the linen sack near the back of the cave. And the blankets beside them as well. It will be cold traveling."

Robert obeyed compliantly as the druidess brushed by him and up the narrow trail above the cavern. With a shrug, lifting the belongings to his shoulder, he followed, crossing the charred garden as the druidess took to the rocky path between obsidian cliffs, on her way to Berkanth, toward the highlands and the longer view.

* * * * *

To the north, in the hills above Nidus, Cerestes as well was upward bound.

Takhisis had summoned him as he lay drowsing in his study. She appeared as a dark presence at the edge of his dream, her voice, low and melodious, twined with his breathing until the mage thought she had called from his heart.

He awoke in a sweat, sprawled across the sunlit table amid papers and vials.

Come to the grotto, the Lady had commanded. *I have need of you.*

And so, in the hours before sunset, he had wakened and slipped into the foothills, to the same small grotto that had marked their place of communion in an earlier time. There, in the bare circular chamber, in a silence broken only by the distant dripping of water and the rustle of the returning bats, the mage knelt on the stone floor, awaiting the Change and the goddess.

Above all, stay calm, he told himself, casting forth the flurry of spells to mask his thoughts from the prying goddess.

What have I thought ill of her? She does not know . . . not yet. I did her bidding. I saved Verminaard and his companions from the ogres.

How could she know?

My loyalties will give me time with this Judyth. The girl will trust herself to me, and Takhisis will approve it all. Who better to discover what knowledge Judyth hides—a goddess who veils herself in blackness and golden eyes and sinister voices in the night? Or a kindly mage, a scholar, a tutor to the young of the castle?

Why, eventually, I shall be the only one Judyth *can* trust.

And I will use her trust for myself alone.

Cerestes smiled as his thoughts dipped and vanished behind a dozen intricate veils of magic.

* * * * *

It began as it always had, with Takhisis's voice low and resonant in the dark reaches of the cave and with the single glowing eye in the midst of the darkness.

Become yourself, Ember, she commanded again. *Show yourself before your queen.*

What followed was the old tugging of air, the first moldings of the spell soft and electric against his legs and shoulders. He felt, as always, the pain, and he cried out as always, but it would be over soon, he would be Ember again. And then he began to grow, to push against the walls of the cavern, to fill the chamber with his scales and wings and enormity, blocking the light from the passage to the cavern entrance. . . .

Suddenly he realized something was wrong. He continued to grow, or the walls were closer, or . . .

He felt the crackle of tendon and bone as his spine twisted in the cold grip of the rock. Frightened, smothering, the dragon struggled against tons of stone, against the layers and pressures of the planet itself, which descended on him, tightening, grinding.

Now! the goddess proclaimed, all softness gone from her voice. The rumble of the earth took on her words, and the words passed suddenly from the congested rock around him to a place inside him, and she spoke from the depths of his thoughts and heart.

All this time, my Ember, you have fancied to mask your thoughts of rebellion.

No, he thought. That's not it. That's not . . .

The rocks shoved in on him, and he gasped for breath.

Silence! the goddess commanded. *You who followed them to Neraka to spy on my tower. You who have plotted from rune stone to gemstone, from druidess to Solamnic hostage to whosoever serves your purpose . . .*

This is what it was like, the dragon thought hysterically, absently. This is how they felt when she entered their minds, when she . . .

Attend to me, Ember! Takhisis commanded, and the dragon's scales glazed and blistered. Ember shrieked aloud, and the sound shook the mountain, but the rocks rested firmly upon him.

Do you believe you are the only one of your kind?

Ember could not reply. His forelegs bunched against his heaving chest, the air in the chamber dwindling . . . dwindling. . . .

Could you imagine, even for a moment, that I could not summon a dozen of your kind to replace you?

He shrieked again, but the sound was lost in the rock and the spiraling echo of the goddess's voice.

I could crush you now. A thousand years from this day, when my followers excavate these hills, they will find your skeleton and speculate . . . and marvel. . . .

And you will float in a windless abyss of your own, eaten daily by the jaws of Hiddukel and burned endlessly by the terrible judgments of Sargonnas and Morgion. . . .

No! the dragon thought. Please, no! What would you have me—

Simply obey, the goddess urged, her voice sinking back into a muffled music. *'Tis all I've ever asked—simple obedience. In exchange for which my boundless favor is yours.*

Oh, yes. Oh, yes, immortal Lady, mistress of my thoughts and my heart and my every immutable action. I shall obey until the last. Your devoted servant I will be now and in times to come, and . . . and . . .

And in return receive my favor, which is more generous than you can imagine.

Ember held his breath. Had the rock around him suddenly begun to shift, to loosen?

For if you follow my commands, and if you accompany Lord Verminaard in the perilous path from novice to Dragonlord . . .

Yes? Yes? Your wish, Your Infinite Majesty . . .

Silence. If you follow my commands, I shall let you govern the man.

Govern?

He must not know it. As Dragonlord, he will think he commands you. But let it not be said that your cleverness went unnoticed because of your treachery. I am no fool, my Ember, and I see that under the guise of servitude, of servility, you intended to rule me. So you intended once. So you will no longer intend.

And yet 'tis not a foolish ambition when it comes to the gov-

ernance of men. I can use it . . . can use you, my darling. Under the mask of Verminaard's servant, you will answer only to me.

Yes. Yes. The idea delights me. Should I bind him more closely to your service?

I speak to him through Nightbringer. He is mine. But, yes, you may bind him further. Further, irrevocably, beyond all choice, so that he will never return to uncertainty but will stay fully, completely mine.

Yes. I will do that. Teach me the spells. I will do your bidding.

I shall speak those spells through your voice when the time comes. All you will have to do is relax, blank your mind, and give yourself over to me.

But there is also the matter of the girl. When the time is right, I shall tell you what to do. She is the candle that will guide me to L'Indasha Yman. And in return for your obedience, Verminaard shall follow your veiled commands and do your will. For from this time on, your will is my will, your desire my own. . . .

The rocks were definitely looser now. Slowly, painfully, the dragon slipped from his rough entombment, breathing hysterical prayers of gratitude to the goddess, to her six cohorts in the Dark Pantheon, and to forgotten gods, stone deities that ruled the madness of men and beasts while the true gods had vanished from the face of the planet. But always to Takhisis his gibbering words returned, and the cool air rushed into his throat, and he slept from the pain and exhaustion, forgetting all his plans and rebellions.

He was her creature again.

Cerestes awoke at midday to the sound of thunder. Furtively, shamefully, but grateful for his life, he gathered his tattered robes together, stitched them together with spells, and slipped from the cavern, wading down the rock trails in an icy net of autumn rain. At the gates, the sentries barely recognized him, for his hair had whitened, and the gold of his eyes had been swallowed by a dull and featureless gray—the color of bedrock and abiding fear.

And in the cavern above him, the goddess laughed.

Servitude and servility. It was a phrase she relished and a strategy she loved—as one minion kept watch on another.

She had told Ember the truth—that though he would deal with Verminaard, he would answer only to her.

And now it was the young man's turn, the Dragonlord apparent, who would hear the same story.

* * * * *

In the chill of the early evening, the druidess found the place. The entrance was little more than a large hole in the side of an old igneous rock formation, but it was large enough for L'Indasha to crawl through and retrieve a bucket full of ice. She had broken off a good, clean hunk that almost filled the oaken vessel, and Robert helped her to the outside and the moonlight and air.

"What will you do with this?" he asked.

"The ice offers a certain reflection of reality. Sometimes it's cloudy, and always it's skewed, but this kind of augury is helpful for searching, for seeing . . . possibilities," the druidess replied. "Watch now, and think of Castle Nidus. My helper must surely be there, as you have said."

As Robert bent to the spangled surface of the ice block, he felt L'Indasha take his hand. Deep in the frozen currents, a slow movement began, and he could see the outline of towers and walls, of flying standards and parapets.

"Try for the inside." L'Indasha smiled.

He grinned, too, and the inner garden of Nidus took shape in the swirl of an ice cloud. At last he saw the girl, and with her, one of the young men.

"That's Aglaca!" crowed Robert, nearly dumping the bucket down the hillside. "Look at him; he's romancing her."

In the vision, Aglaca was clearly holding the girl in his arms, preparing to kiss her. L'Indasha glanced quickly up at Robert, not wishing to invade the couple's privacy. He, too, broke his gaze from the bucket and found L'Indasha's face not three inches from his own. His chest pounding and his hand still in hers, he suddenly spoke his heart to her.

"L'Indasha—I would that I were by your side, to share your life for all time," he whispered. "You are the keeper of the land, but I would keep you—love you, care for you, and give my life to you, now that I have it to give. What say you to this?"

She looked long and deeply into his blue eyes. There was no guile there, no deception, no hidden purpose. Robert held her gaze until she began to speak. She fumbled at the phrases, knowing all the while that every moment she delayed broke his heart a little more. For three thousand years, she had wanted this kind of companionship, this honesty and love. And Robert was watching all three thousand of those years, their memories of loneliness and hope, pass by in the space of a few moments.

But what of her promise to Paladine? She was more than any keeper that Robert knew of. She was the sole keeper of the missing rune, and immortal until she lay that promise down or Paladine relieved her of it. Robert did not know what he asked her, and she needed time to think.

"I say that I may not say," she finally replied. "But go from me a little way and let me consider. For I love you, too, Robert."

He was not disheartened. As he rose to leave her, he lifted her up to her feet and kissed her hand. "I have waited a very long time for you, druidess—since that snowy night in the mountains. I will wait a bit longer."

* * * * *

The clear autumn sky of the day slowly turned purple in the chill gloaming, and the first of the stars winked back at L'Indasha as she stared up at them. The loneliness she had complained to Paladine about years ago in the spring garden had utterly vanished at the sound of Robert's words. How long had she loved him? she wondered. Maybe from that first day, the day he had spoken of, when he lowered his sword and told her he could not do the bidding of the Lord of Nidus—that he could not kill her. That his honor recoiled at such monstrosities.

He had asked her, in a hope and faith beyond reason, to keep his honor secret on that account. It had made her laugh then.

And he made her laugh now. Even as they had walked in the worst of the damage from the fire, he had made her remember life in spite of the ashes, renewal despite the charred forest. He joked about how nothing could kill aeterna, and how the first name of evergreen was *ever*.

She smiled at the thought of him, at his foolish jests. She smiled as well at the line of greenery, miraculously untouched by the fire, that another hand had warded with the ancient runic signs. Mort had been here—of that she was certain, and Nidus's former gardener had diverted a greater disaster with his foresight and his skillful spells. The flames had stopped short at the edge of the magic, and whatever plants lay above it were subject only to the autumn weather.

Logr and Yr. Water and yew bow. Journey and protection. The runes were wisely used, and she had seen them before, twice on the plains. Within the shelter of the sign,

214

every plant seemed eternal.

Eternal. What would it be like without Robert? He was perhaps fifty; she had seen thirty centuries pass. If they went their own ways, time would treat them differently. When he was old, she would be unchanged by the years, scarcely a breath older by his reckoning; when he died, she would be worse off than to have never known him.

Just then a hand touched her shoulder, and she whirled to face not Robert, whom she had supposed it to be, but an old man in a shabby hat, the silver triangle on it gleaming in the brightening starlight.

"My Lord Pal—"

"Hush, girl. Remember who's always listening. Something on your mind?"

"Oh, yes. And you know what it is."

"You have the same choice as always, my dear. You know I will not demand of my friends what they do not will to give. And if you believe that for three thousand years you have not changed, reconsider, for you are still alive. And living things always change and grow. He will abide until you choose again.

"Take heed now to your helper's fate. For her protection, she has no idea of my purpose and her calling. I want Robert to bring her to you, and for you all to meet me here again when that is done."

Chapter 15

In the weeks that followed the Minding, the struggle for Castle Nidus grew treacherous and tangled. From the moment when Daeghrefn entered the chamber to sullen looks and shaken allegiances, Nidus had been a vast and intricate web, with Verminaard the spider at its center.

Cerestes lurked in the background of all the intrigues. Immediately after he had returned from the grotto, the mage had breathed the first of the incantations—the one the Queen of Darkness had designed to draw the loyalty of the garrison from Daeghrefn to Verminaard.

The mage was surprised that he knew the spell. After all, he had never heard it spoken, never read it. The words felt alien in his mouth as he chanted them, and it was only after the spell was spoken that Cerestes knew that his voice was no longer his own, that Takhisis herself spoke his words for him.

That his breath was the breath of the goddess.

He leaned against the battlements, shaking with confusion and anger. Slowly he calmed himself, staring at the tilted stars of Hiddukel, the bright scales in the southern sky.

It was just as well. His thoughts and words were no longer his own, but the end of the journey would have its rewards. Takhisis had promised. She had promised him Verminaard to govern and control.

Staring silently into the darkening night, Cerestes wondered for a moment if the prize was worth what the Lady took in return.

He would think on that matter deeply when the time was right. *When the moon is hollow*, she had told him.

Wait until the moon is hollow.

* * * * *

Having lamely sidestepped the open rebellion he saw brewing in the eyes of his garrison, Daeghrefn roamed the strangely deserted castle halls, accompanied only by the ever-present Cerestes, who urged him to calm all misgivings, to return to business as usual. There were the fire-damaged castle grounds to mend and preparations to be made in case of Nerakan attack. The enemy would know, Cerestes urged, that defenses here would be meager.

It seemed like good advice, and Daeghrefn plunged into the work of regrouping and repair. Then he saw that the mead hall insurrection was not over, that his orders were followed sullenly, halfheartedly, or, on most occasions, ignored altogether.

But the men jumped at even the smallest requests of

Verminaard, sat by him at table, and vied for his attentions. And the young man listened to them, laughed at their jests, and lent a hand himself in lifting rocks and raising scaffolding, his broad shoulders rippling under twice the weight the others lifted.

Here is a man that soldiers follow, Daeghrefn told himself.

And not only soldiers.

For perched on the battlements of the east wall was the mage Cerestes, his black robes billowing like enormous wings. He looked down upon Verminaard and laughed and cheered as well, joining the chorus of soldiers and workers as this strange young man gathered his admirers.

Here is a man they all will follow. And what do I command, then? Daeghrefn wondered. Where are my troops? My retainers? My holdings? He will have them all, and soon. Why have I suffered him? Why did I let him live when he was but a new trouble in the world?

And the words of the druidess—so long ago, on that blindingly cold night on the way home from the treacherous Laca's castle—came back to Daeghrefn in a memory as cloudy and cracked as ice.

This child will eclipse your own darkness. And his hand will strike your name.

At long last, Daeghrefn believed her.

* * * * *

Daeghrefn couldn't remember how he heard about the rebellion.

He knew he should recall it clearly, that the moment should be engraved in all his waking hours—the first news of the first betrayals. But he could not remember. At night, he would stand in the balcony window, ransacking his thoughts for the names of forgotten constellations, and on the fourth evening after the Minding, preoccupied with the aloofness of his men, he had forgotten entirely the way back to his quarters and wandered the halls in aimless embarrassment for an hour until he had gathered himself enough to collar a wayward page and have the boy "help carry this torch to my chambers."

It had been desperate and no doubt obvious, but the lad had been taught not to question. Daeghrefn had followed the nodding light down the corridor, and when the child had opened the door and handed him the torch, Daeghrefn had dismissed the lad abruptly and sat on the bed, the burning torch in his hands filling the room with a fitful, evasive light.

He had forgotten the way to his own chambers.

That was not important now. All that mattered was the rising rebellion. Why couldn't he remember its source? Its birth?

Perhaps it had been a slipped word between the guards at the gate that night he crept along the battlements, cloaked and masked and listening to the conversations of sentries, the passing words of soldiers and servants. Perhaps it was something in the comings and goings from Verminaard's new quarters in Robert's old rooms at the edge of the bailey.

Perhaps he had even dreamt it. Before the fires and the Minding, he had never remembered his dreams. But they came to him regularly nowadays, filling his thoughts in the morning with images vivid and violent.

By whatever means the knowledge of rebellion had reached him, he was sure the news was true.

So sure was Daeghrefn that he summoned three of the veteran soldiers—Sergeant Graaf, Tangaard, and the archer Gundling—and spent a long afternoon in the vaulted council hall, interrogating and menacing and bullying as the autumn sun sank over the spine of the Doom Range. The garrison waited for supper in the hall outside the bolted doors, the muffled shouts of Lord Daeghrefn reaching them even through the thick oak.

The three men had listened politely, impassively to a string of bizarre tirades. When Daeghrefn had threatened them with a dozen deaths and a score of tortures, the Lord of Nidus ran out of breath and imagination and glowered at them from his seat by the fireside. The soldiers nodded politely, turned, and filed out the doorway, out of the keep, and across the bailey, directly to young Verminaard.

"Since he knows of it, your Lordship," Graaf proposed, leaning against a narrow fireplace, once Robert's, as a dozen soldiers gathered around their newly chosen commander, "and since there's no need for secrecy, seein' as not one man sides with him, why not now? Why don't we move you into the lord's chamber and set the old storm-crow to flight?"

His companions murmured in agreement, each offering more elaborate, more gruesome suggestions of what to do with the deposed lord. Verminaard raised his hand, enjoining their silence.

"Though I can appreciate your fervor, Sergeant Graaf, for now, we shall put no man to flight. The old dayraven knows this castle is mine, and that is enough. Let him keep his quarters. Post guards outside them to assure he will spend his time in his luxurious surroundings . . . and nowhere else. I am the Lord of Nidus now, and he is my prisoner. Let him learn what it is like to dangle upon the barbed whim of the powerful."

* * * * *

As Cerestes had advised that night on the battlements, there was much to do between the desire for power and the taking of the power in hand.

Verminaard had to set Castle Nidus in order.

It was not only the east wall that was shaky and vulnerable. The strange series of alliances as well, the treaties and pacts that Daeghrefn had made to bolster his little mountain fief, needed reconsideration and change.

Compelled by that need, Verminaard summoned Aglaca to the old seneschal's quarters at the edge of the bailey. There would be long words, he promised, and offers befitting the scion of a noble house.

There would be the accord of companions, he claimed. The agreement of brothers.

Inside the seneschal's quarters, Verminaard waited, his fingers drumming against the scarred wooden table, his eyes fixed on the closed door. What Cerestes had told him was true: He sensed it thoroughly in his bones and fingertips, in the unsteady tingling of his scarred hand.

It was his brother, his only kin in Castle Nidus, who approached from the beleaguered keep. But Aglaca was more than that, more than just complicated blood kin. He was the one ungovernable soul, the man untouched by Verminaard's force and threats and manipulations.

He is like me, Verminaard thought, staring into the guttering fire. I remember the day on the Bridge of Dreed, how his face even then resembled my own. The feeling, even then, that I was bound to him forever.

And now, as we have grown together and endured that monster in the keep, I am sure that his face is my face, his eyes my eyes.

Slowly his scarred fingers encircled the handle of the mace, and he lifted the weapon, its black head glittering in the deceptive firelight.

He is like me in his will and courage as well. When the dark passed over the moon and the ogres fled and the soldiers froze, he was the only other man who could yet move, who could yet act.

Nightbringer glowed evilly in his hand. Verminaard turned the weapon adoringly.

And this mace, he thought. Though it offered him praise and the prospect of home, something contrary in him kept him from taking it.

I cannot mold him nor twist him nor force him to my liking. But there is always the girl. She is nothing to me now that sweet Nightbringer rides in my hand, but she is important to Aglaca. Yes, a bauble my brother fancies. A suitable pawn for my proposal.

He clenched his fist and breathed slowly, his eyes narrowing like an archer's gazing down the long shaft of the arrow.

So I shall offer him a choice. Yes, a prospect that a man of his cunning—and he is cunning, for we both inherited that from our true father—a prospect that will delight him past all refusals.

* * * * *

Cautiously Aglaca waded through guards outside the former seneschal's quarters. The garrison whose discipline had been Daeghrefn's pride, drilled according to a kind of measure even when the Lord of Nidus had left the Order himself, had now set aside all its regimen and polish in a mere five days since the Minding. These men were on the edge of banditry themselves—dirty and stubbled, all insignia effaced from their dull armor. Under their new commander, they had traded their broadswords and bows for less noble, more cruel weapons: the long scimitars of Neraka and the barbed spears of Estwilde.

When Aglaca opened the door, the smell of woodsmoke and wine rushed from the mottled darkness, and before his eyes closed from the strong fumes, he saw Verminaard seated in front of a thick, scarred table.

"Aglaca. Do come in," Verminaard urged, a strange, sugary politeness in his voice.

The younger man paused reluctantly at the threshold of the building, but Verminaard beckoned him, and eventually, taking a last deep breath of the fresh outside air, Aglaca stepped into the shadowy chambers.

"I'm glad you came," Verminaard said, "for I feel that you, of all people, have been party to my innermost thoughts over the terrible years. Since things are about to change, good Aglaca, I thought you should know. So that you might . . . share in the good fortune."

Aglaca's face was unreadable, as blank as the mythical rune.

Verminaard cleared his throat and continued. "Within a fortnight, I plan a journey to the village of Neraka. There I shall meet with Hugin, captain of the bandits, and I shall demand his obeisance, his service under the red banner of Nidus."

"What makes you think that this Hugin is going to delight in your offer?" Aglaca asked uneasily. "After all, he's scarcely been agreeable in the past."

"Sneer if you will, Aglaca," Verminaard said, a note of coldness creeping into his voice, "but you know that when I speak, I do not speak alone." He held the mace to the light and made a show of examining it. "You were in the cave with me. You heard the Voice when Nightbringer passed to my hand."

"Nightbringer?"

Verminaard nodded. "'Tis the name that comes to me. Therefore, 'tis the name of the mace. But you heard the Voice. You know that I've been chosen." He paused, glared at Aglaca. "I'd like it if you sat down."

Reluctantly Aglaca seated himself on a bare stool. "It's treason you're talking, Verminaard. You know that the Nerakans have been our foes for—"

"Nine years. It's why you're here, Aglaca, in case *you've* forgotten. But I shall sue for peace in Neraka, and Hugin and his lot will march with me."

"March?" Aglaca shifted uncomfortably. "Where?"

"Why, west, of course," Verminaard replied, his sound hand stroking the mace head lazily. "Which brings me to more delicate matters. I have canceled the *gebo-naud*. The Nerakans are no longer a threat to Nidus. You are free."

Aglaca stared at the floor, his thoughts racing. "Free to go home, then?"

"Aglaca, it hurts me that you *still* do not consider Nidus your home. I think of this castle as your home as well as mine. I think of you as a brother."

Aglaca glanced at him curiously. How much did Verminaard know? "But my father is in East Borders, Verminaard," he said.

Verminaard snorted and waved his left hand as though brushing away a fly. His right hand clutched the mace more tightly, his scarred knuckles white against the black stone.

"Why serve at a small holding when you could be my captain?"

Aglaca frowned. "I don't understand."

Verminaard rose from the table. "When Hugin's troops join my own, there will need to be one man beneath me to yoke my unlikely forces together and be answerable for the lot of them. I'll need someone I can trust. You're my only true friend—the only soul in whom I can confide, because we are so alike in honor and loneliness and . . . in other things."

"But my home is East Borders, Verminaard. That was the idea long ago. That's why I am here and . . . and your brother far away."

Verminaard nodded, his eyes fixed on the heart of the mace. "I want you to be my captain."

"I'm not sure I was clear, Verminaard, but—"

"It's quite simple." Verminaard stood over him now, the broad shoulders blocking the firelight so that Aglaca looked up into a thick, impermeable darkness. "If you are my captain, you may keep the girl. To do with as you wish."

"I *may keep the girl?*" Aglaca asked incredulously. "And what . . . what do you have in mind if . . ."

"If you refuse, Judyth is mine—to do with as *I* wish." He paused to let the enormity of the possibility build in Aglaca. "You cannot hide her in your quarters forever. If I demand the girl, she is mine. And I *will* demand her when the red moon is full. Until then, neither of you is free to leave the castle. But you, Aglaca, *are* free to choose. And there's no hard feelings, whatever you decide. After all, what's a slip of a purple-eyed girl between brothers?"

"Your brother is at East Borders, Verminaard," Aglaca insisted, "where I should be now instead."

"My brother is with me now as well, Aglaca," Verminaard hissed. "You know it as well as I do. But perhaps you haven't imagined the particulars. Let me tell you of a night long ago, when a traveling knight named Daeghrefn stopped in East Borders to lodge with . . . *a friend.*"

* * * * *

Aglaca went to the garden as the shadow of the western walls lengthened over the taxus and the blue aeterna. Politely, the soldier assigned to guard him stayed at the garden gate, allowing the youth to wander in the midst of the rich evergreens where he had sought refuge as a small child. Then he had been uprooted by an alliance he did not understand. It was much the same now, Aglaca thought—the green smell and the dense, wiry foliage soothing but finally comfortless, more a place to hide than a place to recover.

Aglaca traced over that evening in the former seneschal's cottage—the grotesque offers, the badgering, and the threats. He looked in horror at Verminaard now, at the rising evil and the fierce obsession with fire and violence. He remembered the horror on the plains, with Nightbringer rising and falling in the smoky moonlight, its obsidian head slick with the blood of ogres.

And now this offer. To be his second in such outrage.

He is my brother, Aglaca thought. *He has changed beyond belief or desire, but Verminaard is still my brother.*

He stared bleakly at the red sliver of Lunitari as the moon began its slow passage toward the appointed time.

* * * * *

Daeghrefn sat and stared into the fire, an uncorked bottle of wine on the table beside him. He was gaunt, pale, almost cadaverous—a far cry from the robust man who had stood on the Bridge of Dreed nine years ago awaiting the arrival of his Solamnic hostage. His eyes red-rimmed and his hair matted, he stared wretchedly into the fire, turning a stemmed glass slowly in his hand.

The door to the hall opened abruptly, and it was a moment before Daeghrefn heard the footsteps approaching, loud and heedless, over the ancient stone floor.

"You wanted to see me, *Father*?" Verminaard asked icily, and the Lord of Nidus turned to face him. "Very well. I'll grant you audience. After all, these chambers are mine. You are here through my generosity only."

A wide and witless grin spread over Daeghrefn's face. Vainly he tried to stand, then weaved over the chair and thought better of it. Seated once more, addled by the wine and breathing roughly, raspily, he glared at the monstrous young man who stood above him, blocking the torchlight.

"Audience?" Daeghrefn asked. "Did you say . . . " His voice dwindled into the vaulted hall. "Well. We can talk of that later, Verminaard. As for now, my mind is on another thing."

He rose, braced himself against the back of the chair, and balanced before the reeling fireplace. Verminaard's face seemed veiled from him in the deceptive firelight. Clearing his throat, Daeghrefn continued.

"I am thinking that I do not know you all that well. That I haven't been . . . good to you. And now . . . well, now you intend to take all Nidus away from me." Daeghrefn sighed. "I expect your bitterness and anger are justified and that I have no choice but to make a good end of it."

The Lord of Nidus poured wine into a glittering metal cup and offered it to Verminaard. The young man took it and stared into the ambered bowl of the vessel while Daeghrefn talked on idly.

"This has been a long estrangement, and little has been your doing. If you would agree to a way that we might coexist, I'd . . ."

Verminaard ignored the prattle, his senses drawn by the strange fragrance of the wine. As he lifted the cup toward his lips, the new scars on his hand began to twitch and tingle.

He had come to know this as a warning.

Warily Verminaard peered over the rim of the cup, then handed the wine to Daeghrefn. "If we are to make accord, *Father*," he said with a sneer, "we should drink from the same cup."

Slowly, his hand shaking, Daeghrefn lifted the vessel. Verminaard stared at him frostily as the firelight seemed to tilt and shudder. Quietly, with a scarcely detectable movement of his fingers, the Lord of Nidus let the cup drop clattering to the floor, spilling its contents in a steaming, corrosive mist over the stones.

Verminaard seized the older man, hurling him against the stones of the fireplace. Then, lifting him by the front of his tunic, he pinned Daeghrefn against the wall and snarled at him.

"You *adder!*" he shouted. "Your fangs are devious and veiled, even when the venom is dry! At last I have you where I have wanted you for twenty years—backed against a wall, your power and poison useless!" He raised Nightbringer, its black handle quivering and droning in his hand.

"I let you live," Daeghrefn gasped. "I let you live, when I could have killed you merely by walking away!"

The grip about his neck slackened.

"You're mad!" Verminaard muttered. "*You* let me *live?* And what was that in the cup? I owe you nothing, old man—not even the chance to bargain!"

Daeghrefn watched in terror as the mace wheeled over the young man's head, then lowered slowly, quietly to his side.

"But look at you. You're already dead," Verminaard observed, his voice thick with scorn. "A mere husk of a man, the skin of a locust in a blighted year. You haven't even the decency to lie down."

Daeghrefn quivered and whimpered. He closed his eyes, and when he looked again, Verminaard was halfway across the room, headed for the doors to the chamber.

"I could have killed you once," he whispered. "In the snow . . . in a lost time . . . before . . . before all of this. . . . "

The words were lost in the crackle of the fire, the slam of the oaken doors.

Chapter 16

Safely in the garden, hidden amid the evergreens and the bare fruit trees, Aglaca knelt and began the Seven Prayers of Conscience, calling upon the gods to aid him in the approaching hard decisions. They were long prayers, and the young man struggled to remember them, for he was shaken by Verminaard's news and by a choice in which both options were impossible.

He had been told long ago that the Prayers of Conscience were always answered, that if he placed a question before Paladine and his glittering family, the answer would rise in the words of the prayer itself, or on the wind or in the harmonies of birdsong. Or perhaps it would come as a quiet, still voice in the hollow of his heart, when the words and the wind and the music had died away.

So faithfully he began the prayers, asking Kiri-Jolith for courage, Mishakal for compassion, Habbakuk for justice, Majere for insight, Branchala for faith, Solinari for grace, and Paladine for wisdom. The words rose readily from his lips, as though they had been planted for years, awaiting the chance to blossom.

He sang the hymn that marked the end of the ritual, the old Solamnic song of benediction. At the end of the hymn, the garden lay hush. The autumn birds—the jays and the lingering dove—were silent, almost as though they were startled by the song. Aglaca breathed deeply and started to rise from his knees.

The gray branches of a young vallenwood, scarcely ten feet away from him, shone with a strange silver light, which moved from branch to branch like a white flame.

Suddenly the light fractured into a million reflectant shards, spangling the trees at the edge of the grove until all of them—taxus and juniper and blue aeterna, bare oak and vallenwood—shimmered like a forest after an ice storm, and music rose out of the wind in the branches.

Aglaca bowed his head reverently. He closed his eyes and waited until a voice, high and thin and immoderately ancient, ended the silence.

"Well, don't just sit there. You've said the Seven Prayers, and you sang the hymn. I expect there's a question in this as well."

The old man clambered from the branches of the vallenwood, brushing the light like dust from his shoulders. With a crack and creak of aged bone and tendon, he scurried from the bole of the tree toward Aglaca like some ruined, white-haired spider, his thin robes bunched and knotted above his knees.

The old man dusted the bark and moss from his threadbare clothes, sat unceremoniously on the ground before Aglaca, and, removing his hat, batted it against his knee as a servant would beat a rug. The garden filled with floating dust as the two of them—the young Solamnic and his surprising visitor—appraised one another amid a flurry of sneezes.

"Who *are* you?" Aglaca asked.

The old man waved his long, bony fingers. "Only the gardener. You were praying for something?"

Aglaca remembered that the real gardener, an ingenious and honest man named Mort, had left Nidus long ago, in exasperation at the constant intrigues of the castle after Daeghrefn's wife had died. Suddenly Aglaca's eye found the silver triangle pinned to the old man's hat. "Wisdom," he murmured reverently. "The right decision. That light when you were in the tree—"

"Just a bit of pageantry for an entrance," the old fellow announced proudly. "Works wonders with the pharus plants. One flash and they blossom on overcast days—at night, too, for that matter." He coughed. "Looks like the dust is clearing at last."

Aglaca regarded the intruder. A graybeard, gangling and thin, stooped at the shoulders like a benign praying mantis. "You are no gardener," he said, a half-smile on his lips.

"But I am," the old man said suddenly. "Appointed to tend this spot since before you were born. You didn't think the taxus trimmed itself, now, did you?"

Aglaca started. The old fellow could read his thoughts. Despite himself, the young man warmed to the bearded, stooped oddity seated before him. He extended a hand and helped the ancient intruder to his feet.

"It's a hard decision I'm after, sir," Aglaca began, astounded at his own rashness. "The lord of this castle—not the old lord, mind you, but the young man who rules in everything but name—wants me to become his captain. Time was when I would have done so gladly, but Verminaard has changed. He has undergone a dealing with darkness in the caverns south of this castle, and what he has become . . . I am not sure. I suspect the worst."

The old fellow regarded him seriously, listening and nodding. "No hard decision. Seems like you'd refuse such an offer, then."

Aglaca cleared his throat. "If that was the lot of it, deciding would be simple enough. But Verminaard has been my companion for many years at Nidus, as close to a friend as I figure I've had. It's been lonely here, sir, when all the talents you have—every interest and delight and gift you would bring to a household or a family or a friendship—are the things that they never cared about. Not that Verminaard was much better. But then there's also this—he's my half-brother as well."

"Verminaard is your brother." The old man nodded. "And what he asks of you is treasonous, against both your country and your spirit. Then either of the choices—"

"And it doesn't stop there, sir," Aglaca interrupted, his politeness giving way to a troubled eagerness. "Verminaard has *threatened* me. If I refuse his offer, he'll seize my friend Judyth."

The old man leaned against the gray trunk of a vallenwood. A strange silver radiance danced over his shaggy hair, and the triangle on the crown of his hat caught the light and glinted. "Judyth," he repeated. "I see. I almost forgot that when young men tug and wrangle, there's generally a young woman to tug and wrangle over."

Aglaca shrugged. "That, sir, is the long and short of it. It's wrong to choose for Verminaard, and it's disaster to choose against him. I suspect it's a test of sorts, imposed to try my spirit and wisdom."

He looked intently at the old man.

"I see." The old gentleman smiled. "I, on the other hand, suspect that *you* are making this a test. You just haven't yet found the other choice."

"The other choice? I don't understand, Old One."

The gray fellow shook his head. "It must be there some-place. There's never only one pass through the mountains. With every confrontation, there comes an escape route, so that you may be able to bear all temptations."

"Where is my other choice, sir?"

"Somewhere . . . *between* the two of you," the old man replied mysteriously.

"Between?"

"Ages ago, the power behind the mace, behind the Voice, walked the face of the earth."

"What does that have to do—" Aglaca began, but the gray fellow waved his hand for silence.

"I listened to *you* for a spell, Aglaca Dragonbane. Now it's your turn."

Chastened, the young man nodded politely, and the old illusionist continued.

"In the Age of Light, the dark dragons ruled the sky, and their queen—whose name I shall not say, even though I am safe from her power—claimed all Ansalon as her own."

"Huma Dragonbane defeated her," Aglaca said. "Drove her away."

The old man regarded him with a thin smile.

"He was my ancestor," Aglaca muttered, and sank into embarrassed silence.

"I know that well," the illusionist replied, "which is why you figure into this elaborate mess. At the time Huma banished the Dragon Queen, banished as well was the secret of the Amarach runes."

Aglaca started to speak, but the old man stared him to silence.

"Yes, Aglaca. The very runes your brother Verminaard employs in a silly fortune-telling game. The Amarach is not silly, though, just incomplete. He's one stone away from immeasurable power."

The illusionist stood and paced around the clearing, the

branches in his wake sparkling with a strange, silver light. "And the Dragon Queen is looking for the secret of that stone now. To sound the runes. To find the key to enter the world, to seize power before the forces arrayed against her are strong enough to stop her."

He paused. The clearing was completely silent.

"But once again," the illusionist continued, "Huma's blood stands against her. The two of you are needed—Verminaard and Aglaca—dark strength and bright wisdom. Your compassion balances his force, his judgment your mercy.

"You two are the opposite sides of the rune, Aglaca. When the symbol of the stone is revealed to you, and that time will be soon, then the two of you can use the power of the rune—"

"To stop her before she comes into the world!" Aglaca cried.

A larkenvale fluttered in the branches of the glowing vallenwood. The garden settled again into silence as the young man took in the gravity of what had been entrusted him.

"How—how do we use it?" he asked meekly. "How do we use the rune?"

"You will know when the symbol is revealed," the old gentleman told him. "Each of you carries half the story in his heart."

"Verminaard's heart is changed," Aglaca argued. "But I will stay by him. I will seek to help him change it back. But I cannot do it alone."

The illusionist nodded. "I know. I have something that will be quite useful. It is dangerous, and for you, more dangerous still after you use it. For then you must trust in Verminaard's decision, and the choice will be his, finally. Your choice comes now, Aglaca. You can risk your life, or the life of the world."

Aglaca took a deep breath. "Then the choice is simple.

234

For the sake of all I hold dear—for the sake of *everything*—
I'll stay in Nidus. I'll use whatever you want me to use.
Verminaard will change. I know he will."

With a kindly smile, the old man beckoned Aglaca
closer. "Then these may help you. I will tell you things
about Cerestes, and things about binding and loosing.
Volatile words, these are," he cautioned, "and you may
use them but once. Then you will forget them—forget
them forever—and your chance to help Verminaard will
be over."

Aglaca took a deep breath. "I am ready to hear."

And there in the garden, the old man whispered them
in the young man's waiting ear.

Aglaca didn't know when the gardener left. He was
staring into the old man's kindly eyes, his mind filled
with the verses of the two powerful songs he had just
learned, then suddenly the ancient was gone. In his wake
shone a last shimmer of light in the lowest branch of the
vallenwood.

"Thank you," Aglaca breathed. "My thanks for the
words and the wind and the birdsong. And for revealing
the hidden passage in the mountains, dangerous though it
may be."

* * * * *

Robert stood at the edge of the garden, watching the boy
babble and gesture.

It was the oddest thing, with young Aglaca standing in
the midst of the evergreens, holding forth on something
or other to the airy nothing of the garden. Robert always
reckoned that when a man talked to himself, it was time
for the surgeons.

And yet this one had saved his life not two years ago.
Aglaca was a cool and level lad, not one for fancy or lunacy.

Perhaps *he* was the lunatic for coming back to the traitor's castle, simply because the druidess had asked him to help search for the girl. A victim of brown eyes and auburn hair, he was, his soldier's resolution melting before the wishes of L'Indasha Yman.

He had passed easily through the south gates, where the sentries, two lads he himself had trained, had squinted suspiciously as the swirling leaves skittered under the arch and into the castle, borne aloft by a brisk wind. For a moment, the leaf storm seemed to take the shape of a man, but when the sentries blinked, the image had vanished, as L'Indasha had told Robert it would. When he had reached the garden, he had taken his own shape again and, hidden behind living leaves in a decidedly unmagical fashion, had set up a watch on Castle Nidus.

Daeghrefn would be enraged to find him here, Robert thought gleefully. But he was not here for revenge. He was here to find the druidess's helper and take her back to the mountains.

Now, at least, he had found Aglaca. He figured the girl was not far away. After all, L'Indasha had seen her with the wiry Solamnic lad.

And yet, standing in the garden, talking to the taxus, Aglaca seemed to have lost a little of his graceful balance in the last month or so.

Robert rubbed at his eyes and peered through the bushes. Perhaps it was best that L'Indasha wanted him to bring back the girl. Perhaps it was a rescue of sorts.

The crack of a dried twig sent him burrowing deep in the aeterna. Cautiously, as if he were scouting an enemy camp, he parted the blue branches.

The girl. He had not needed to wait long.

* * * * *

"We can't leave," Aglaca maintained. "Even if we could elude the guards, I will not leave."

Judyth regarded him skeptically.

"It's odd to keep honor with Daeghrefn and Verminaard, since neither knows the word," she declared fiercely, and Aglaca started at the heat of her reply.

The two of them sat quietly in the garden as the evening stars emerged in the autumn sky. His head in Judyth's lap, Aglaca looked up into the turning constellations and watched Solinari rising in the eastern sky.

The silver moon was in High Sanction, in the phase of fullness and power. Whatever magic rode upon the night was good now, was auspicious.

"It's not Daeghrefn and Verminaard. It's . . . something else," Aglaca said. "Something I learned this afternoon."

But he remained silent about what he had learned.

"I see," Judyth said after a long silence, resting her hand on Aglaca's shoulder. "But brother or friend or . . . whatever, I think it would be foolhardy to believe that Verminaard will protect you. He's going to join with the Nerakans, Aglaca. Do you think his other treaties will fare any better? When the bargains are his alone to strike or break?"

"Yes. Hmmm. I don't know."

Judyth leaned back against the wall and closed her eyes. "He's come to find me. He's trying to court me, Aglaca."

"To *court* you?" Aglaca shot to his feet.

"For a week now," Judyth explained. "At first it was confusing. He stood at the door to your quarters and boasted of his deeds against the ogres, as if I hadn't the eyes nor the sense to know *that* for the lie it was. The number of monsters he had killed multiplied with each telling, and each time he stepped farther into the room."

"'Farther into the room'? You let him in?" Aglaca asked icily, jumping up from the bench.

"No farther when I told him to stop," Judyth replied hastily, her eyes averted. "And then it was gifts. Always jewelry: bracelets, a ring, cloisonne—"

"What's a cloisonne?"

Ignoring his question, Judyth reached for something around her neck. "And then it was this."

"Bring it to the light, Judyth. I can't see it."

She stepped away from the shadows and, standing in the cool light of Solinari, displayed the jewel. The moonlight shone on a single triangular lavender-blue stone, fixed in the heart of six silver flower petals.

"What is it?" Aglaca asked. "And why—"

"I *had* to take it," Judyth explained. "It wasn't his to give."

"How do you know?"

"I don't," she confessed, hiding away the pendant. "At least, I'm not sure how I do. But the moment I saw it . . . well, something told me I must take it, must return it to its proper owner."

"And now he thinks you've received gifts from him," Aglaca said. "And he'll take that to mean . . . *That's* why he thinks . . . ." He caught himself, averting his gaze from Judyth's.

"Are you taking your *brother's* part?" the girl snapped, and the couple fumed in the shadows as an owl soared over the walls with the faintest whisper of wings.

Judyth almost told Aglaca then—almost told him of the orders that had urged her to leave the safety of her home two years ago, the command that had led her wandering over the plains of Solamnia into the dangerous East, through Throt and Estwilde until she reached the foothills of the Khalkists, where the bandits . . .

She rubbed at the hated tattoo on her leg. They had not been gentle.

She almost told him, but she wasn't sure he would understand. It sounded foolish, she admitted: that his father, her commander, would send a lone girl traveling through bandit and goblin country, armed with only a dagger and led . . .

Led by old intelligence. By the ancient rules of Solamnic espionage. But led by more, as well, in ways that Laca hadn't reckoned. By instinct. By intuition and dream.

How else could she explain consenting to a dangerous and reckless undertaking—going forth with few guide-posts beyond her bookish knowledge of the mountains and a strange, secret sense that whatever it was she pursued was still just ahead of her, or passing somewhere nearby, in the cloaked and mysterious night?

It sounded too flighty and foolish for words. But by indirection, she had come to the place she was sent, to the duties with which she had been charged years back by Aglaca's father.

Sound the situation at Nidus, Laca Dragonbane had charged her. *And send me word of my son.* But something had sent her long before the Solamnic orders, and when he had commanded, she had sensed then and there that her journey east was the beginning of what she had lived to do.

It was all too veiled and mysterious. She was relieved beyond measure when Aglaca finally spoke.

"Judyth, we shouldn't argue," he said, touching her shoulder softly. "We shouldn't *begin* to argue, with the castle around us filled with conspiracy and scheme."

Slipping her arm about his neck, the girl nodded. "You have your honor, I suppose. And whatever mystery you've discovered. And I . . . well, I believe that I am bound for something important and good and needful. It's . . . it's only Castle Nidus that makes those things seem foolish."

"You're right, Judyth," Aglaca conceded. "Which is why I shall have to find a way to get us free of this dilemma. Verminaard is not in control of himself. I'll wager my life on it. And of late, I have found something that may help in the wager."

"Something?" her forehead rested against the back of his neck. He felt her skin, cool and soft against his skin.

"Another choice," he replied softly. "Another pass through the mountains. For instead of following one of Verminaard's proffered choices and betraying you, my father, and even him in the process, I shall choose a third path."

"A third path?"

"I shall turn him from this romance with Nightbringer, this marriage to darkness. But there are forces against me—forces at work in this castle, Judyth, that seek to bind him to a bitter pact. He has taken instruction from the worst of teachers."

"The mage!" Judyth exclaimed. "All along I've known! There's something at the core of Cerestes that is bleak and inhumane."

"And *inhuman* as well," Aglaca added. "For human is not his natural form. Though it may be hard to believe, Cerestes the mage—"

"Is the dragon!" Judyth hissed, grabbing Aglaca's arm. "Oh, Aglaca, the night of the fire, when those dark wings passed over the face of the moon, I *knew* that the dragons had returned, that the legends and rumors were true. But what hope do we have against a dragon?"

Aglaca smiled. "There is a passage through those mountains as well. And I've been given the password."

Leaning close to Judyth, he told her of the old man in the garden and the songs he had learned from him—magical songs of binding and loosening, composed years ago in the Age of Light to unravel the cords of spellcraft. The first would bind Cerestes in a human form, restraining him from his draconic powers, and the second would loosen Nightbringer's power over Verminaard, if he wished it to be loosened.

"'Tis a tall order, that wish," Judyth observed, looking long into Aglaca's eyes.

"And a greater risk as well," Aglaca replied. "I can use the songs but once. The breath of Paladine will pass through me, and my lips will shape the words. I must remember them all, must sing them in their proper rhythm and tone, just as the old man sang them to me. And that still is not enough. After the singing, I must trust that something of light and good remains in Verminaard, and that, released from the powers of mage and mace, he will turn from the darkness."

He smiled at Judyth, and a great foreboding rose in her heart.

"Verminaard told me once that he trusted me," Aglaca said, "and I must show him my trust so that he might act on his."

❧ ❧ ❧ ❧ ❧

Robert crouched silently in the midst of the evergreens as the young couple stood, kissed softly, and parted. Then he rose and walked into the heart of the garden, into concentric circles of taxus and aeterna, the maze of cedar and juniper and sleeping fruit trees. On the soft earth, his steps were muffled, and the only other sound was the high silver song of one unseasonably late nightingale.

It changed everything, Robert thought, this meeting, this romance. He had seen the pendant in the girl's hand, and he knew it was the one L'Indasha had lost, that it had returned by fortune and circumstance—perhaps even by destiny—to the woman who had been sent to help her. For a moment, when the light of Solinari glinted on the pendant's silver flower, he had almost risen from his hiding place, almost called to the both of them, explained his mission, and taken the girl then and there.

She would be safe in the mountains, far from the corrupting hand of Verminaard.

And yet he knew how this Judyth must feel, knew that the ties that bound her to the Solamnic lad were stronger than duty—stronger, perhaps, than any destiny that oracle or prophecy might imagine. He knew what it was like, knew how the boy felt as well, how his difficult tangle of honor and duty would seem impossible without Judyth nearby to strengthen him.

"May the gods and L'Indasha forgive me," he whispered quietly, "but she should stay the course until her own choosing." He slipped from the garden into the shadows along the west wall of Nidus, where the nightingale sang a final note before it flew north on the morrow—north to safer, more clement weather.

KGW

Chapter 17

On the third night following Verminaard's meeting with Aglaca, the noises began from the top of the keep. Strange shouts and calls tumbled to the bailey onto the dumbstruck sentries, who glanced nervously at one another from their posts. Daeghrefn called out "betrayal" and "murder," "abandoned" and "fire," and "Laca" and "dark dark wings," and throughout the long wail into the morning watch, the shouted name of "Abelaard" tolled the hours regularly, like a ship's bell.

Verminaard stirred on his cot in the seneschal's quarters, unable to sleep in the shrill, pathetic din. Finally, just before dawn, he arose and stepped into the bailey, wrapping Cerestes' black cloak about his shoulders against the crisp autumn morning. The grass crackled with frost as he walked to the foot of the keep and glanced up into the vaulted darkness, the cloudy night sky where Solinari had waned to a sliver.

On the battlements, Daeghrefn had lit a single candle. It glowed bravely, forlornly in the windless morning. It seemed as though the fire itself were calling as the flame waved and beckoned, as Daeghrefn's wail slipped suddenly beneath words and was now a simple, terrifying bleating.

On the next night, a second candle stood by the first, like a pair of glowing eyes, and one of the younger sentries, a boy from Estwilde named Phillip, had begged off duty, maintaining that the tower had come alive and was watching him.

Verminaard had laughed at the boy, had told him the dungeon had far more dangerous eyes, and offered to show him where to look for them. Reluctantly Phillip returned to his post and shivered for three nights through a tense and tedious watch.

On the fifth night since Daeghrefn's confinement, young Phillip came breathlessly to the seneschal's quarters with the news that the whole battlement was ablaze.

Indeed, it was so. The topmost walls of the keep blazed with candle and torch and lantern. It was a beacon visible for miles, and Verminaard's cavalry, patrolling the South Moraine on a watch for Hugin's arrival, steered their horses by its light.

Then, at midnight, a breeze lifted from the south—a cold wind diving down from the Doom Range, and the array of lights began to waver and sputter. And then young Phillip, the impressionable lad who saw eyes in the clouds and fire on the battlements, looked up . . .

And saw the black shape dancing on the tower ramparts.

The long black cape spread behind it like tattered wings

as it leapt from merlon to merlon like a large demented bird. Twice it teetered dangerously above a fifty-foot drop, and the second time it whooped and called over the rapt bailey—a shrill, mournful cry that chilled Phillip, Tangaard, and the others.

For the cry was completely wordless now, a long, cascading howl that startled the horses in the stables and raised the hackles of the dogs.

And the veterans of the garrison—even Gundling, who feared nothing—felt their blood twitch and their hands shake.

For the cry was a raven's, a carrion bird's, but the voice was Daeghrefn's own.

* * * * *

Verminaard leaned over the seneschal's stained table and examined the runes.

Estate. Chariot. Earth.

Idly, with his scarred hand, he stirred the Amarach stones and cast them again.

Estate. Birch. Hail.

He had waited a week in Castle Nidus—seven days since the offer to Aglaca, since Daeghrefn's retreat. And in that time, Aglaca had avoided him, and the old man in the keep was mad and useless. Even Hugin, the captain of the Nerakan bandits, had the audacity to promise and promise and fail to arrive.

The waiting had begun to ravel at Verminaard's patience.

For a third time, he gathered the rune stones. They were becoming but a parlor game—the constant casting and reading, the passion of fools and fortune-tellers. In disgust, Verminaard pushed them carelessly off the table, and they clicked and clattered on the hard stone floor.

It was then that the mace spoke to him.

He had known it was *going* to speak from the first time he touched it in the cave above the Nerakan plains. When the dark fire raced over him and his hand burned with the transforming pain and his heart with the vision and insight, he had known it was only a matter of time until the Voice itself would return, transformed as well by the dark fire.

For after what had happened deep in the haunted recesses of the cavern, how could the Voice ever be the same?

So when it spoke—when the head of the mace glistened with an ebony fire and the room around him lapsed into absolute darkness and silence, so that he saw nothing but the weapon, heard nothing but the soft insinuations of the Voice—he was frightened and awestruck but not surprised.

Never surprised. It was no longer his way.

Throw not away your auguries, child, it said, the low, feminine Voice rushing down on him like a hot, fragrant rain. Verminaard's fear melted at once to a rich and forbidden delight, and he leaned back in his chair, closing his eyes in relief and release.

He had not known how much he had missed her.

Throw them not away, for though they speak to few in this profane and uneventful time, they speak with clarity to you— with clarity and with wisdom, if you but listen to what they say.

"Estate. Chariot. Earth," he murmured. "Estate. Birch. Hail."

You look too closely—too much at the depth of things, Lord Verminaard, the weapon coaxed.

Verminaard opened his eyes. The room had folded in on itself, the far walls at arm's length, strangely illumined by the pulsating black light. Once propped by the fireplace, the mace now lay within his grasp.

He blinked and murmured the names of the runes once

more. "Estate. Twice the rune of Estate."

The Voice did not reply, but the air crackled. The hair on the young man's arm rose and swayed in a warm wind, and he gasped as he took the mace in his scarred hand.

What does it mean? the Voice asked—or he thought it was asking, for he could no longer tell whether the words rose from the room or the weapon or his own racing heart.

"Estate. Ancestral inheritance. Old spirituality," he replied haltingly.

A low laughter filled the borrowed chamber, and the rune stones clacked together on the floor. *Foolishness. Double-talk. Where is your estate, Lord Verminaard?*

"Castle Nidus," Verminaard replied confidently. "Mine by right and might and the show of weapon."

Nidus is yours indeed, the Voice granted, *but not by inheritance. Where is your estate?*

An obscure smile spread over the young man's face. "East Borders," he replied. "Castle East Borders. I am the son of Laca Dragonbane, Solamnic Knight of the Sword."

Go alone, the Voice urged. *Take no escort, no companion. I shall be with you, and Nightbringer will rest in the dark moorings of your hand.*

* * * * *

Verminaard rode alone, as the Voice had told him. He did not look back as he rode, cloaked and hooded, through the secret gate near the back of Daeghrefn's tower, riding quietly into the cover of the mountain night. Is it not foolish? he asked himself. Will I lose Nidus by neglect, when my ambitions draw me to East Borders? What will Daeghrefn do in my absence? And what about Aglaca? Where is Cerestes?

Be still, the Voice urged him. *Still your thoughts and steady your ride, Lord Verminaard. Nidus is yours, whether far or near, for I have eyes in Daeghrefn's castle, and naught can be done to harm or hinder you without my knowing.*

I believe you, Verminaard thought. We are bound by the strongest of covenants, the vows we made to one another in the cave of Takhisis. But show me a sign. Give me the vision that ends my questioning.

A long silence filled the night air, then the mace whined and sputtered in his hand.

You still do not trust me. But very well. Look to the battlements.

Verminaard pivoted in the saddle and looked back toward Castle Nidus. He saw a dark form trooping on the moonlit wall, in the blood-red glow of Lunitari.

Who is it? he asked. Who is it, Lady?

Why, 'tis you, my dear, the Voice exulted. *'Tis you, to all mortal eyes. For whoever told you that Cerestes had but one form, one countenance? He rules with your face and voice, and with my magic. It is a pattern of things to come.*

Verminaard smiled malevolently.

I am confirmed, Lady. I am assured past disbelief.

Good, the Voice prompted as Castle Nidus vanished into the swiftly falling darkness. *This is no time for questions and fears. Depart like a man to arrive like a man.*

* * * * *

West from Nidus, a single night's ride on the well-traveled Jelek Road took Verminaard to Jelek itself. He skirted the town to the south, then veered west over the farthest stretch of Taman Busuk, toward Estwilde and the easternmost Solamnic outposts. Armed only with his mace, guided by the stars and the Voice and the scattered auguries of the rune stones, he carried but seven days' worth of waybread, certain that the week's end would find him in East Borders, safe in the house of his father.

And when he arrived there . . .

Well, the Voice would tell him what to do, what to say. And how to demand his rights from the father he had seen only once, gray and distant beyond an arching bridge.

Verminaard traveled by night, hooded and cloaked against the wind and masked from curious eyes. He traveled swiftly as well. Orlog was tireless and fluid beneath him, erasing the miles as though he were winged. Those who met them on the road—the caravans to Sanction and the pilgrims to Gargath and Godshome, the patrols and the solitary travelers bound for more private destinations—all wondered whether someone had passed their camps indeed, dark and flying toward the western horizon, or whether the night and the wind and the shifting clouds had conspired to form a dream of a rider, cloaked in black, astride an enormous black stallion.

Through five long nights, Verminaard spoke only to himself and to the Voice arising from the mace. He muttered in the saddle as Orlog rushed past the outskirts of Jelek and into the gray foothills north of the ruins of Godshome, then north again through the narrow, rubble-strewn pass of Chaktamir, site of a Solamnic victory a full century ago, and down to the rocky, forbidding borders of Estwilde.

Estwilde was a stark country, a place of vast and desolate stretches, seldom touched by rain and even less frequently by mild and temperate winds. Verminaard rode on tirelessly, and his vision in the cave of the gods returned to him as he rode—how he flew on the proud, enormous beast, its broad back thick and striated with powerful muscles. . . .

And he was sure that this was the moment that the vision had foretold, the tale of the young man returning to claim his inheritance.

* * * * *

Early the sixth morning, horse and rider rested on a rocky rise overlooking East Borders. Orlog grazed wearily while Verminaard stretched in the short, crisp grass and peered down at the distant castle.

The castle was where the Voice had told him, set on a knoll in the midst of a wide and barren plain, prime country for the huntsmen and a good vantage against approaching armies.

And yet East Borders itself was a simple motte and bailey that looked modest, almost meager compared to the lofty battlements and the four towers of Castle Nidus. Verminaard had hoped for something more grand and daunting, and for a moment, he suspected he had lost his way, only to stumble on the moat house of some petty noble or bandit chieftain, misplaced and forgotten in the middle of Estwilde.

But it was Laca's castle, all right. He could tell by the insignia on the banners: the silver kingfisher of the Solamnic Order, fluttering side by side with the black dragon and white lance of Family Dragonbane.

"This is my home," he whispered uncertainly.

This is your possession, the Voice corrected, its inflections soft and urgent and musical. *Ride down and claim it.*

The mace quivered in his hand, and a strange, unbidden confidence surged through him.

"So be it," he whispered. "East Borders is mine."

Verminaard wrapped the cloak about him tightly as he rode toward the castle. The old black garment was showing its inadequacy from the hard and inclement ride. Frayed and tattered, it offered little protection from the cold southern breezes, and the young rider shivered in the saddle.

He had never thought they would come to meet him.

The gate of Laca's castle opened in the morning grayness, and five men rode forth beneath the standard of Dragonbane. Crossing the drawbridge and the outer ditch, they spread out on the plain and approached, each of them armed with the short cavalry spears favored by the mountain armies. Helmets and aventails masked their faces, and they were bundled against the cold wind as well, but from the silver kingfishers on their breastplates, Verminaard could tell that they were members of the Solamnic Order and therefore splendid fighters.

Well, I shall speak with them, he thought. Tell them who I am and demand escort to Lord Laca himself.

Speak? the Voice taunted. *Do you think they have come to speak? They stand between you and your inheritance!*

The mace lurched in his hand, flickering with a sudden ebony glow. Before he could protest or speak or even think otherwise, Verminaard found himself pulled by the weapon toward the standard-bearer, the centermost man in the rank. It was as though Nightbringer called him to battle, and he was impelled to answer.

He remembered Aglaca's words in the deepest chambers of Nightbringer's cave: *If you choose this, you'll forget that you can ever choose again.*

The standard-bearer reined in his horse and stopped on the level plain, his banner uplifted in the time-honored Solamnic sign of truce and parley. Verminaard rode to meet him, Nightbringer lowered and set across the front of the saddle, so that none of the Solamnics could see how tightly he gripped the weapon. He guided Orlog to the side of the standard-bearer, a green-eyed, freckled youth with red hair. The lad stared at Verminaard nervously, intently, and his fingers twitched on the banner pole.

Nightbringer made the decision. Heedlessly, so quickly that Verminaard thought it was his own arm, his own doing, the mace flashed in the air and shrieked into the side of the man's head.

In a crash of bone and metal, the standard-bearer hurtled from his horse. The other knights wheeled and galloped toward the black-robed invader.

Verminaard glanced about. He was encircled—trapped in the midst of four charging knights. Orlog whinnied nervously and bucked, but the Voice in the mace soothed horse and rider.

What if there are four? Would four men have daunted Lord Soth? My champions of a thousand, two thousand years ago? Fret not, Lord Verminaard, for I am with you, and your mace is the comfort I send.

Verminaard smiled and faced the first of the oncoming enemy.

The knight bent low in the saddle, couching the short spear in a jouster's attack. He charged, and Verminaard twisted as the spear tore through the folds of his black cape. Spinning with a raw, awkward power, Verminaard brought the mace thundering down upon the back of the passing knight, who slumped over his horse in a flood of black light and fell soundlessly to the dry plain.

Three left, the Voice proclaimed. *They'll come at you one by one, for honor's sake. Three, and the castle is yours.*

The next knight approached, circling and menacing like a Nerakan cavalryman, the short spear jabbing the air, waiting for an opening. The other two hung back, veiled spectators at the edge of sight. With a roar, Verminaard spurred Orlog toward the defiant man, who raised the spear and hurled it.

Verminaard blocked the weapon with the mace, and black fire raced over his arm and shoulder as the spear splintered in the air. *Steady,* the Voice urged. *Steady. Oh, is this not a lovely thing?*

Then Verminaard closed with the knight, who lifted his shield as he groped for the hilt of his sword. Verminaard rose in the saddle and brought down the mace with all of his weight and strength. The ornate silver kingfisher exploded in the heart of the shield, and the man rocked violently in the saddle. With a cry of triumph, Verminaard raised the weapon to strike again, but the knight's head lolled and his hand fell slack on the hilt of his half-drawn sword. The ropes that held him in the saddle snapped with his full weight, and he toppled from the horse, slain by the sheer force of the blow.

Two remaining, the Voice coaxed, high and thin with excitement and delight. *And you are coming to love this, my love, my love. . . .*

And he was. Exultantly Verminaard galloped toward the last surviving Solamnics. One of them—the larger one—dismounted, suddenly and surprisingly, and motioned for Verminaard to do the same.

"He wants it hand to hand and man to man!" Verminaard muttered, pulling up Orlog not a spear's cast from the valiant, honorable knight. "And if he is brave enough to offer the challenge, then so be it!"

As he moved to dismount, the Voice resounded from the mace, dazing him, banishing his thoughts. *You fool! There are two of them. When he has you afoot, then the other—*

But they don't fight that way, Verminaard thought. They're Solamnics! They don't . . .

Unless things have changed.

He leaned forward in the saddle, peering mistrustfully at the masked knight who awaited him. It would be just like the deceptive Solamnic Order to call him forth on a pretext of honor, then ambush him when he had given up the advantage. And yet something about this man . . .

The Voice returned immediately, taking away the thought before it formed. *Now!* it urged. *The sun is behind you! Now!*

Verminaard looked over his shoulder into the blinding, blood-red sunrise.

Now!

With a shout, he launched the stallion toward the

knight, who blinked, dazzled by the sun, then leapt away just as Verminaard drove the mace by his head.

"Midnight!" cried Verminaard, and the black light in Nightbringer's wake engulfed the man. He cried out once, struggled to his knees, and clutched his face.

"I can't see!" he shouted, groping through the dry grass for his dropped weapon.

Now! the Voice urged again. *The mace has blinded him. Now!*

Chapter 18

As he steered the horse toward the helpless man, his mace raised high for the killing blow, Verminaard saw something flash in the corner of his eye.

The last of the knights swooped by, a silver blur as rider and horse crossed in front of him. With a shrill whistle, the man leaned out of the saddle, stretching his sinewy arm toward his blinded companion. In one graceful, incredibly powerful movement, he caught up the injured man, lifting him onto the horse, and together they rode toward the open castle gates. Verminaard, astonished, pressed his horse hard behind them.

The Solamnic horse was now overburdened, but in the mile's gallop across the flatlands, Orlog's weariness made it hard for Verminaard to make up the distance. At last, sweeping wide around the hapless riders, Verminaard cut off the path to the castle bridge, and the Solamnic was forced to rein in his horse scarcely a hundred yards from the bailey walls. Resolutely the rider lowered his wounded companion and, rising in the saddle, faced Verminaard fearlessly.

"Good adversary," the Knight called out, raising his sword in the traditional Solamnic salute, "you have shown yourself strong in arms and enduring in battle. I give you the chance to show honor as well."

Listen to him! the Voice whispered as Nightbringer pulsed in Verminaard's hand. *The Solamnic prattle of honor and code and oath is about to begin. Beware, my child: He will entangle you in honor.*

Verminaard nodded. The Voice was right. He had seen the honor-mongers before, and he knew that their words carried poison and knives.

"My friend is injured," the knight continued. "He is blind and helpless. Allow him to pass over the drawbridge and into the bailey. Whatever quarrels you have with our country, our lord, and our Order, you and I can settle here on the plains, in full sight of my countrymen."

"Damn your country! Your lord and your Order be damned!" Verminaard roared, whirling the mace above his head until a dark spiral formed in the morning air, widening and widening until it covered the horses and riders, veiling the view of the garrison on the bailey walls like a thick, gloomy cloud. "As I see it, you've no grounds to bargain. Your companion stays where he is."

"So be it," the knight replied tersely. "Before these walls and the men assembled there, I say that you are a base, ignoble coward, and should the gods grant me the power to defeat you, you will be shown no mercy."

Verminaard sneered. "Oh, but I'll show mercy to *you*, Sir Knight. I shall prolong your miserable time of breath until the lord of the castle himself begs that I finish the job."

"Villain!" someone shouted from the castle walls, and from farther away, the shout was answered by another, the words indistinguishable, muffled by distance.

The raised hand of the knight stilled further outcry. "The lord of the castle begs to no brigand. If it must come again to sword and mace, then let it come, by Paladine and by Huma!"

"And let it come on foot," Verminaard declared, dismounting in a rustle of robes and a creak of black leather armor. "For I yearn to face you man to man and arm to arm, so that none will credit my victory to the stallion beneath me, nor your defeat to poor horse-mastery."

The knight dismounted as well, removing his shield from the back of the saddle and uncovering it so that the risen sun danced fitfully on the embossed white lance and black dragon that adorned its polished center.

Nightbringer shivered and hummed in Verminaard's hand.

Do not spare him, the Voice murmured with a new, frenzied urgency. *Oh, do not spare him, Lord Verminaard, for he is the worst of our enemies and the fount of our suffering. Because of his line, we lie in darkness, and at the end of his descendants, we will breathe again!*

"He will not be spared," Verminaard muttered, "for he stands between me and the lord of the castle."

As he approached the veiled knight, Verminaard knew that he faced the strongest fighter yet.

The man dropped into a swordsman's crouch, sidling gracefully to high ground, away from his wounded companion. Verminard lumbered after him, noisy and awkward afoot, but confident in his strength and his weapon and in the mysterious power that ran through the pulsing mace.

Their paths met on a little rise not fifty yards from the

castle bridge. There, under the sight of Laca's archers, they circled each other twice and closed for the first attack.

The knight struck first, his saber switching and flashing like the tail of a snake. A quick backhand slash brought the blade across Verminaard's chest, furrowing effortlessly through the leather armor. Had the larger man not stepped back quickly, he would have been slain before the fight had really begun.

Backing away, gasping, Verminaard staggered down the rise, the knight in calm, relentless pursuit. The blade whistled by his ear once, twice, and he could barely stifle a whimper as he blocked a thrust with the handle of Nightbringer.

It was then, at the bottom of the rise, that sword locked with mace, steel with ancient stone. The knight pushed against Verminaard, his mailed face only inches from Verminaard's own, so that the young man could see the color of his enemy's eyes.

Blue. Pale like his own. Like Aglaca's.

Something in those eyes softened. Verminaard dug his heels in the dry, cracked earth and pushed, and the knight tumbled backward, landing with a rough clatter on the hard ground.

He was back to his feet at once, but the tide of the battle had changed. Verminaard knew now that he was stronger than the man before him, that for this time, at least, the quickness and skill of Solamnic swordsmanship fell short against the sheer brute power of muscle and rock.

With a jubilant shout, Verminaard brought the mace shrieking down at his pressed opponent, who scrambled free of the blow at the cost of a shattered shield. Reeling, his left arm limp and useless, the swordsman backed from the violet darkness and staggered up the rise once more, seeking the vantage of higher ground.

Now! the Voice urged again as the spiked head of

Nightbringer swirled, its stone surface roiling like black lava. *He's yours if you strike now!*

"Who are you?" the wounded knight rasped, weaving from pain and exertion.

Don't tell . . . don't tell. He will entangle you in honor. . . .

"Verminaard of Nidus," the young man announced proudly. "I have come far to meet the lord of this castle and demand from him what is rightly mine."

The knight dropped his sword and fell to his knees. With his one good arm, he removed the helm and aventail. His blond hair was streaked with first gray, but his eyes were brilliant and young, as resolute as they had appeared nine years ago across the Bridge of Dreed.

Verminaard gasped. It was his own face, thirty years older.

"You!" he cried. "Laca Dragonbane!"

The man met his stare serenely. "What would you have from *the lord of the castle*, Verminaard of Nidus?"

Verminaard took a tentative step toward his blood father, then another. Laca rose slowly to his feet, turned his back on the approaching warrior, and walked calmly, almost casually to the side of the wounded knight.

"I would have the castle." Verminaard replied. "I would have the rest of my inheritance, Laca. And I would have vengeance on you for your years of silence, for my years of suffering at the hand of Daeghrefn for your deed."

Laca knelt silently by the blinded man, cradling the fellow's head in his lean, long-fingered hands. He glared up at the monstrous young man before him and spoke to him coldly, as though across a great chasm.

"You're a creature apart now, Verminaard of Nidus," he pronounced. "And you have made your choices." He lifted the helm from the face of the injured man. The clouded eyes rolled back in the head of the hapless man, who lay stunned and moaning in Laca's arms.

"Abelaard!" Verminaard roared. "No! *No!*"

The wounded man blinked pathetically at the sound of the voice, raising his bruised arm vaguely.

"No!" Verminaard shouted again, and fell to his knees, Nightbringer black and glittering in his hand.

He would strike something. Rock and wind . . . Laca . . . himself. He would end everything, here at the borders of Estwilde, and there would be nothing but night, and night upon night. . . .

And a darkness rushed over him, and he saw and remembered nothing.

* * * * *

Laca watched the young man vanish in a swirl of black, engulfing fire. Clouds broke over the landscape, and for the first time in hours, sunlight spread over the bailey walls of Castle East Borders. Wearily the Lord of East Borders took the reins of the shivering Orlog and led the stallion back toward the injured Abelaard.

"Who . . . who was it, Uncle Laca?" the young man asked, rubbing his vacant and useless eyes.

"I don't know," Laca replied.

* * * * *

In the Khalkist Mountains, overlooking the Nerakan plains, overlooking Nidus and the razed forest to its south, Verminaard received a new and stern discipline at the hands of nature.

He awoke in a sunlit grotto high above Castle Nidus. The shriek of a raptor wakened him, and he sprawled blearily, painfully on the stone floor of the little cavern, breathing in the moist air, the odor of guano and mildew, and a dark, alien stench that underlay all these—something profound and fierce and reptilian.

He could not figure how he had come there, but he knew he was far from East Borders and close to home.

Nightbringer lay beside him, glowing with a cold, ebony fire. He shuddered at the memory of those flames on his arm, of the black oblivion, and most of all at the prospect of wielding the weapon again.

"No more," he whispered, his voice as dry and desolate as the vanished plains of Estwilde. "I shall bear you no more, fight no more."

And yet as he said the words, his hand reached for the handle of the mace and closed about it.

He did not know how he had come to that spot. He had knelt in Estwilde, raging and mourning, and the darkness had swept him away. And now he was miles from the fields of East Borders, where he could see the smoke rising from the hearth fires of his childhood home.

Though Nidus was in full view below him, it was a week before he considered returning there. He stayed in the grotto, in its deepest recesses, faring to the mouth of the cavern only at night, and then only when the hunger became overwhelming. Though the sun would not harm him, daylight was strange to him now—alien and unnerving, like darkness to a child.

Far better to stay in the dark awhile, he told himself as the red moon passed sullenly overhead on his second night in the cave. Better to abide here and mend and recover strength.

He ate what bitter roots he could forage from the spare highland terrain: knol and dioscor and the foul-tasting purple betys—chastise root, old Speratus had called it. And by night, the brown madfall beetles were sluggish and unaware. Their flesh was cold and slippery, but it was nutrient enough as long as he did not eat the poisonous tail.

Once he stood at the edge of a precipice, bathed eerily

in the red glow of Lunitari, and tried to drop Nightbringer into the obscure and rocky darkness. It seemed fitting, as though dropping it into the darkness would make retrieval impossible if he was weak and returned for the mace. But the weapon fastened itself to his hand, glowing and droning, twisting like some monstrous black leech, and he told himself, Not yet. I can rid myself of it anytime, once my strength is returned. But not yet.

Yet he mistrusted his own thoughts, and so he tried once more. A shadowy pool lay in the nethermost reach of the cavern, so far from light that only the green glow of the vespertile bats lightened its black waters. The madfall beetles who dwelt by its banks had evolved for generations in the near-total darkness, eyeless now, their shells a pale, translucent pink. It seemed like the spot to leave Nightbringer, and for a moment, his heart leaped. There would be rest from all of this—from hunger and cold and from the consuming presence of the mace. He would find peace in the depths of this darkness.

But though Verminaard plunged his hand in the icy water and tried to release the weapon into the calm, deep pool, still the mace adhered to the skin of his hand. It glowed beneath the water, if *glowed* was the word, a deep, velvety blackness within the abject shadows of the pool.

He tried more drastic methods after that, but fire failed to damage the weapon, and his own paltry spellcraft was powerless against it. It could not be lost, nor could it be destroyed, it seemed, but the deeper truth came to him as the fruitless days passed.

It was a week before he admitted that he *could not* deliver himself from Nightbringer because he *would not* be delivered.

But by then he had other concerns, other callings. For Castle Nidus was drawing him as well, and he knew his long night of solitude was almost over. Soon the gates of the castle would open for him, and he would enter as a man utterly changed, brought into total compliance with the Lady's will.

He was the Arm of Takhisis, her champion in the black and flowing light.

* * * * *

Verminaard had found the drus berries earlier that morning. Crushed into a potion, they were the stuff of visionaries, carried in flasks by shaman and druid, by the scattered dark clerics of the Dragon Queen. Growing in the wild, untempered by waters of the alchemist's art, the raw berries offered wilder, more erratic visions. Sometimes more profound.

Or so Cerestes had told him in the long, magical studies of his childhood.

Now, following a long afternoon's meditation at the edge of the daylight, he ate a handful of the violet berries and crept back into the grotto. There he crouched on his massive haunches and waited for the visions and auguries to begin.

He drew forth the rune stones. He would know what She willed. The runes would tell him.

In the days of his solitude, the stones had been as constant a companion as Nightbringer. He felt their strong assurance in the pouch at his belt, and in the day, when he longed for the darkness and the serenity it brought, he would retire into the depths of the cave. There, in the protective shadows, he would clutch the stones like totems. But he had not cast them, had not even looked at them.

But now it was different. Now, in the red moonlight, where their edges glimmered like veins of gold, he called on the Amarach to bode and prophesy.

"Say me the truth, stones," he whispered. "No matter the laughter of soldiers, the scorn of the mages." Closing his eyes, he breathed a brief prayer to the Seven Dark Gods, to the Lady, and to the spirit of the runes, and cast three stones before him.

"That which was," he muttered. "That which is. That which is yet to be."

He opened his eyes and gaped in astonishment.

Blank. Blank. Blank. The same rune in all three positions.

Verminaard rubbed his eyes and looked again. He had not imagined it. The stark nothingness of the blank rune stared at him from past, present, and future.

"Blank," he muttered. "The absence of dark and light."

But there was only one blank rune in the set of stones! How could . . .

Quickly he rummaged through the discarded runes. Blank . . . blank . . . blank. The smooth face of each stone stared at him mockingly.

* * * * *

That night, in the rubble below the cavern, Verminaard danced beneath the full red moon, his tattered black robes brilliant in a bloody light.

The effect of the drus would not wear off until the next morning, and so the young man had set aside the runes and offered worship to the shapes of the dark gods in the stars overhead. He held up the mace to the tilting constellations, and he called for the old powers to course through the weapon and into his willing blood.

Let the covenant be renewed, he told himself, as it was in the cave of the Lady, when I took this mace. Then tomorrow night I shall return to Nidus. Aglaca and I have business to contract. For Lunitari is full, and he will be my general. Or I shall take the girl and destroy them both.

Verminaard blinked drunkenly and watched the stars pass over.

Hiddukel the Scales tilted angrily overhead, a memory of the old injustices, of the betrayals that had brought him to Nidus in infancy and his cold, neglected boyhood. Chemosh of the Yellow Robes brought the dead from the plains and the mountains, and Verminaard exulted at the battered ogres who trooped before his sight, at the knights, clad still in their dented and bloodied armor, who stared at him with milky, vacant eyes.

He laughed as well at the Hood of Morgion, the great mask of disease and decay, for he knew firsthand the deception of masks, and the eyes of his brother Abelaard were blind and vacant as well.

He exulted in the terrible red condor, Sargonnas of the Fires, and he remembered the fires in the forest and on the plains south of Nidus.

But finally the queen emerged in the black sky—the Lady of the Dragons, She of the Many Faces. He knelt and adored her, the black mace quivering in his hand, pulsing and burning. And in her presence, Verminaard of Nidus rose and began to dance.

Or perhaps Nightbringer drew him to his feet and turned him in a quickening spiral, there amid the black rubble and the burned country and the mouth of the grotto. He did not know whether his thoughts or those of the weapon ruled his body and heart.

But in the swirling moonlight, there on the hills that someday men would call the Dragon's Overlook, the Voice spoke again to him out of the heart of the mace.

Dance, my love, it urged him. *Dance, my Lord Verminaard, ruler of armies . . . my love.*

Chapter 19

From the top of the tower, he could see the faces of the gods.

Daeghrefn knew that they all were watching—twenty sets of eyes in the blackness of the firmament, all eternally fixed upon this castle, this tower, this circle of candle and torch.

How foolish he had been not to believe in them!

For they sang in the stars and rustled in the stones of the tower. And none of them forgave him, for Verminaard had told them terrible things.

Daeghrefn had covered the mirror in his chambers, draping the polished glass with black cloth, as though the castle were in mourning. It was a precaution, he told himself. He had set the mirror by the window years ago, to illumine the bare interiors of his bedroom with reflected moonlight, but his invention had now turned dangerous. Now the gods could watch him in it, mark his reflection always in the mirror as he passed by, and his presence anywhere in the deep interiors of the tower.

Daeghrefn shivered and looked over the pass at Eira Goch, west into the black face of the Khalkists. Estwilde was miles away, on the other side of the range—or so his men insisted. But Daeghrefn knew otherwise. At night, when the black moon shone on the slopes of the mountains, the entire country crept eastward, its boundaries swelling over Jelek, over the forgotten ruins of Godshome. . . .

The dry steppes of Estwilde were moving at night, and Laca was at the head of the armies—pale-eyed Laca, traitor for these twenty years.

Laca was not content to steal sons. He would steal Abelaard's inheritance as well.

Daeghrefn leaned against the tower walls, turning south now toward the fire-blackened forest. Holding aloft a sputtering torch, he peered into the shadowy, moonlit wasteland. There would be no aid from that direction, nor from beyond. What help could he expect from a band of Nerakans he had fought for nine years? Their leader—a cutthroat named Hugin—had vowed to "skewer the Stormcrow on a pike and carry him like a flapping standard through his own gates."

He had overheard that vow in a dream. So it had to be true. And Verminaard planned to join with the bandits.

Daeghrefn covered his ears. The incessant whine from the mountains—shrill and maddening, like a choir of gnats—had begun again. The gods were mocking him, he was sure. Soon Nidus would be alone on the plains of Neraka, crushed between two armies and sapped from within by an ungrateful boy.

There was no escape to the north, where Gargath lay,

sacred to the dwarves and gnomes. He would find no refuge among the worshipers of Reorx, for none of the gods forgave him.

But there was always the east. The high peaks of Berkanth and Minith Luc, and beyond a high green plain, no doubt untouched by the ogres' fire, where a man could lose himself for years, could vanish until the gods themselves could not find him. He looked hopefully toward the eastern foothills, where Solinari was on the rise in the autumn sky.

Someone was dancing on the rocky cliffs above the castle, framed by the silver light of the moon. He held something aloft—something glittering and black.

Daeghrefn leaned over the parapet, craning for a better look. For a moment, he thought it was Kiri-Jolith himself, the ancient god of battles, or perhaps black Nuitari rising out of the silver heart of his sister.

Then he saw that the figure held up a mace, and he knew who it was, dancing alone in the eastern mountains.

"Verminaard!" he spat. "May the Dark Seven devour you!"

Frightened, fascinated, Daeghrefn leaned out even farther, until the bailey seemed to spin below him. He strained beyond the torchlight into the chilling dark, and he watched as the shadow rose to cover the moon, to block out the light with its black, leathery wings. . . .

Then he remembered the druidess's prophecy: *This child will eclipse your own darkness.*

And the moon was engulfed in Verminaard's shadow.

Alone on the parapet, awash in the thin light of torches and candles, the Lord of Nidus shrank against the stone walls, his hands shaking. In the firelight, he cast no shadow, and it occurred to him that his shadow would not return, that he had no substance left to summon it.

I am becoming transparent, he thought, a wild laugh rising to his lips. Transparent, like madfall beetles in the cavern depths. He held up his hands, examining them closely. They were blue and cadaverous, blanching as he watched.

Daeghrefn staggered into his chambers, crying aloud as he jostled the mirror. He wheeled, tore the cloth from the glass, and glared at his own reflection.

His hair was straw-pale, and his eyes were light blue—the color of vacant skies.

*　*　*　*　*

"It is my pleasure to come at the bidding of the Lord of Nidus," Judyth began formally, and the haunted eyes pivoted toward her. "And to offer him tonic and balm for his malady."

"Then Verminaard sent you? And you treat with him? For *he* is the Lord of Nidus. Or so they are all saying."

Judyth did not answer. Nervously she fingered the pendant at her throat.

Daeghrefn cleared his throat and rose painfully from his chair. He was hooded, and he shied away from the light as he spoke. Judyth felt as if she were talking to a wraith, to a walking dead man.

"You're with Verminaard often," Daeghrefn said. "You were there at his birth."

"Sir?" Judyth asked, immediately confused. But she answered cautiously, "I see him little of late."

That much was true. Twice she had seen Verminaard from the window of Aglaca's quarters as he paced over the battlements in the moonlight—a cloaked shadow gripping that black, infernal mace. He kept his distance now, Aglaca said—from the castle garrison, from the soldiers, from all his old companions—and Judyth had begun to wonder if the new Lord of Nidus wasn't as mad as the old one who stood before her, muttering of fire and snow and conspiracy.

"Even so," Daeghrefn replied oddly, as though he had read her thoughts. He turned toward the fire and braced himself against the back of the chair, which creaked and teetered beneath him. "What does he want, druidess?"

"I . . . I don't understand, sir. And my name is Judyth."

"It's a simple question, really. What does Verminaard want?"

Judyth shifted uncomfortably on her stool. "I don't know, sir."

"Are you *with* him?"

"I beg your pardon?" Daeghrefn's questions were vague and needling. Judyth felt suddenly hot and itchy, as though she were dressed in wool under high summer sunlight.

"Are you part of the mutiny, damn it!"

He was much too loud. The voices in the hallway stopped abruptly, and Judyth imagined the soldiers who had escorted her to Daeghrefn's chambers now crouched at the door outside, listening as their commander further unraveled.

"No, sir. I would not conspire against you."

"So there *is* a conspiracy. I knew it! What have you heard, then?"

I must leave his presence, Judyth thought. I must get word to the west, regardless of soldiers and mages and dragons. Nidus is fast becoming a madhouse.

She started to stand, but Daeghrefn's menacing stare fixed her to her seat. He slipped into the shadows, crouching behind a statue of great Zivilyn, a spreading vallenwood carved from veined marble.

"I have heard little, sir," Judyth replied uneasily. "Bits and snatches, but no more than that. Actually, I'm not certain. I have only just met him."

"You met him on a snowy night twenty years ago, in a cave south of here. Do not lie to me. And you said then, druidess, you said *then*, that his darkness would eclipse my own. Look upon your curse, woman!" He emerged from behind the marble tree, and he threw back his hood.

Judith quietly gazed upon the dark skin, though somewhat paler for his confinement in the tower, the dark hair, and the wild, dark eyes.

"Don't you see what he's done?" Daeghrefn insisted. "What *you've* done? I should have killed you both that night. Had it not been for Abelaard . . ."

Daeghrefn snorted and turned back toward the fire. Quietly, after a long, uncomfortable silence, Judyth rose

"I shall be leaving now, sir. That is, if you have no more questions."

"You know much more than you are saying," the Lord of Nidus declared calmly, solemnly. "Do you remember how cold it was?"

" 'How cold', sir?"

"The night of his birth. In the mountains south of here. Before the fire."

Judith glanced nervously toward the door. Daeghrefn was shifting from time to time, place to place. For a brief, nightmarish moment, Judyth lost sight of him in the shadows. Then suddenly he was standing before the little chapel altar, a candle in his hand. His eyes gleamed brilliantly, like twin flames.

"Oh, I know who you are. This innocence and *Lord Daeghrefn, sir* serves you ill, druidess. I thought you were long dead, but, no, Robert failed me. He was worthless, and it is good that I left him on the plains. Though perhaps you fooled him as well. I know that your kind can change shape, altering like the seasons or like clouds in the summer sky, though I recognized you at once by the pendant around your neck."

"I still do not understand, sir." Judyth covered the purple stone at her throat.

"The old stories are right," Daeghrefn pronounced,

turning to face the altar. "The druids *do* steal babies."

"Steal babies, sir?"

"They take the promised son, the second child whose birth you await with joy for seven long months, and in its stead they leave . . . a *night-grown changeling*." He laughed bitterly.

"I do not—"

"So you have said!" Daeghrefn roared. Then softly, almost wonderingly, he continued. "I saw him dancing last night in the eastern hills, where the little copse of evergreen . . . where, on the night of the fire . . . "

He fell silent. Judyth cleared her throat and waited for words that did not come as a minute passed, then another. Finally she backed from the room, leaving the Lord of Nidus staring into the fire.

As he looked at the flickering flames, Daeghrefn remembered another fire, another burning. Suddenly, as though the Abyss had opened to receive him, his thoughts were consumed again with a vision of dark, spreading wings.

* * * * *

Two figures walked the walls of Castle Nidus that night.

On the southwest corner of the battlements, Aglaca kept a lonely vigil, watching the walls, the towers, and the bailey for a sign of his old companion. He had slipped his guards by the stables, but it was nothing new. A lazy pair, they would no doubt wait for him to return, knowing he was going nowhere without Judyth, without all his belongings, left in the room he had stayed in since he was twelve years old.

Resting for a moment against the stone crenelations, the Solamnic youth gazed toward Eira Goch, veiled in a deep western darkness, and smiled as he remembered how he had pointed out the pass to Verminaard from their bedroom window ten years ago, on the night after the *gebo-naud*.

Verminaard had known the name of the place and its history, but he could not locate it in the dark. Aglaca had given Verminaard the dagger then, and though the little weapon lay polished and well kept in the room upstairs, the promise of their friendship had suffered far worse over the years.

It seemed somehow fitting. Fitting and circular. Aglaca would have to find the pass for Verminaard again—another kind of pass, through another kind of darkness.

For the last three weeks, Verminaard had kept to himself. No one knew where he was quartered, nor had any in the garrison—from aged Graaf down to Tangaard and young Phillip—spoken with the new Lord of Nidus. All of them, however, had glimpsed him at twilight, walking these very battlements.

Pacing in the moonlight. Clutching the mace.

The men were afraid to approach him.

Aglaca was not afraid, but he waited as well, as the dark form stalked the battlements. For Aglaca did not relish new meetings with Verminaard, nor the prospects of being asked again to become the new Marshal of Nidus, second-in-command of a bleak legion of bandits and mercenaries.

No. His part of the story did not lie in war and conquest.

That evening, standing on the cold battlements of Nidus, Aglaca had at last understood that the story he was in was not really his own. It was not an easy thing to admit, even for a gentle and generous soul such as Aglaca, but after he had spoken with the old man in the garden, it came to him quietly that his was only a small part in a great unfolding tale. While he had spent his time in Nidus, hostage in a pact of lesser nobles, large, ungovernable forces had wrestled and warred in the mountains, over the entire continent of Ansalon—throughout all Krynn, for that matter. At stake in their vast contest was history itself, for whichever side in the struggle emerged victorious, the world Aglaca had known would all be changed in a moment.

He knew as well, and with a strange serenity and relief, that his role in the coming history, one way or another, would be over soon. Soon the songs that the old man had taught him would come of age. They were dangerous and volatile words, a god's magic to distract the mage and save his friend. After the magic was spent, Aglaca could never use it again. Then he would walk a path even more dangerous and volatile as Verminaard made a choice of his own.

But Aglaca would try the spell and brave the danger to free Verminaard from his own *gebo-naud* with Nightbringer and the goddess who gave the weapon life.

"So be it," Aglaca whispered, and a warm, unseasonable wind rose from the western slopes. "I am almost eager for it to begin."

But where was the mage? And where was Verminaard?

A strange shadow over his shoulder caused the young man to turn toward the western tower. There, atop the battlements, a cloaked figure stepped into the moonlight. He recognized the strides at once—the broad shoulders and the hair as fair as his own.

Aglaca crouched at once, hiding in the shadows of the crenelations.

At the moment the moonbeam touched his robes, Verminaard began to shimmer with an eerie black light. The robes seemed to expand, to double in on one another, folding and boiling like a distant stormy ocean. For a moment, his face seemed to lengthen, his skin to dapple and scale.

Then, in a dizzying swirl of color and light, he became the mage Cerestes. He lifted his hands to the east, to the foothills above the castle, where the old copse of evergreens had risen before the fire.

Aglaca shook his head. He had been watching the change with fascination, as a small defenseless animal watches the hypnotic nod and weave of the neidr snake. So the man he had seen on the battlements was not Verminaard at all but the dark mage in disguise.

Then where was Verminaard?

Low in the eastern sky, a black shadow crossed over the face of Lunitari. "The hollow moon," Cerestes said, his voice carrying eerily in the night air. The mage began to chant, his hands weaving gracefully, gesturing toward the foothills, toward a patch of darkness gliding there in the moonlight, moving swiftly toward the castle.

Slipping along the shadows of the battlements, Aglaca drew nearer and nearer the black-clad mage. He stopped in astonishment at the tower walls as a new voice rose out of the chanting, low and feminine, familiar from the days of his childhood, when he had fought its soft insinuations.

It was the Voice in the cave, the taunting voice of the goddess. Cerestes mouthed the words, but it was the Voice who spoke through him.

And out on the foothills, the approaching darkness took solid form—the broad shoulders . . . the fair hair. Verminaard was approaching, and a dark magic was ready to meet him.

Aglaca took a deep breath. Best to bind Cerestes now, while his thoughts were elsewhere and his energies linked to the dark and distant hill. Best do it quickly as well, for his own chant was a long one, one verse for each of the moons. He breathed a quick prayer to Paladine that the saying of these words would not consume him, for had not the old man spoken of their dangerous and volatile power?

He was no enchanter. But for this one time, the words

were his to speak.

" 'By the lights of Paladine,' " he began,

> *"And Solinari's silver glow,*
> *Let the words unite and bind*
> *Light above to light below;*
> *Let candle, torch, and lantern shine,*
> *By the lights of Paladine."*

* * * * *

Cerestes stood upright, his long meditation on the Lady—on the chants that would bind the returning Verminaard—brought to a sudden halt.

The tips of his fingers burned, as they always did when the Light Gods threatened, and Cerestes knew the disturbance for what it was.

Swiftly, urgently, he wheeled and sniffed the air, his heightened senses tasting the mustiness of the tower, the smoky, autumnal bailey, the sharp animal stench of the stables.

Where was the chanter?

His keen ears gathered the whir of a cricket near the seneschal's quarters, the call of an owl in the garden, something scuttling in the battlements of the western tower.

Where? *Where?*

Already his senses were fading, binding to human limits, the keen draconic eyesight dwindling into blurs of distant shadow as the far walls seemed to vanish before his straining gaze.

Then, from the wall below, at last he heard the voice. He heard the second verse begin.

> *"In Gilean's red and balanced light,*
> *Let light before match light behind,*

And Lunitari charge the night
With shadows human and confined.
Let eyes define the edge of sight
In Gilean's red and balanced light."

Something moved in the shadow of the western wall.

Cerestes shielded his eyes and looked down, but the dark had encroached, and he could not see the chanter. His fingers burned horribly, and he rushed for the stairwell, cold panic propelling his steps onto the battlements.

Quickly. Before the third verse.

He teetered precariously on the narrow ramparts, stumbling and clutching the walls as he raced toward the chanter.

He was too late. The verse had already begun.

"Back into Nuitari's gloom,
Let all rough magic now depart . . ."

Cerestes breathed an old, evil incantation, and black fire settled in his hand. With a muted outcry, he hurled the fireball at the sound of the voice and staggered on when the chant continued . . .

* * * * *

Aglaca felt the hot wind brush by his face, heard the wall shatter behind him. Still he continued, his memory holding the last words of the song, untouched by the heat and burning as a dark fire encircled him, rose, then suddenly began to fade.

"Let centuries of night entomb
The dark maneuverings of the heart . . ."

The ramparts beneath him rumbled and shook. Aglaca leapt to the tower, clutching the mortared stone, scrambling up the face of the wall. The mage leaned over the battlement, and red fire flashed from his hands.

Aglaca clutched the base of a tower window, and with a somersault that the druidess taught him in the garden, vaulted gracefully onto the sill. The fire rushed by him, and he leapt into the open room, an unoccupied guest chamber, and raced up the stairs to the roof of the tower.

Aglaca opened the oaken door to the roof, and the stars swelled, and the cold air rushed over him. At the battlements, the mage wheeled about, his eyes flaming with rage, his hands raised for yet another spell.

Remember the last lines, Aglaca told himself, rolling out of the way of a black bolt of lightning that shattered the door behind him. By all the gods, remember!

And then the Voice came to him, one final time, soft and seductive and brimming with promises.

It is all yours, Aglaca Dragonbane. Cease your chanting and release my servant, and it is all yours. . . .

The walls seemed to fall away, though Aglaca knew it was a vision. Before him lay a continent waiting, from Kern in the farthermost east, to Estwilde and Throt, to Solamnia and Coastlund, then west to Ergoth and Sancrist, the island kingdoms. . . .

It is all yours, Lord Aglaca. All this power I shall give you, and the glory of it. . . .

Aglaca laughed. "I have heard it before," he muttered, "and it did not move me then. You cannot stop me!" Rebuffed by his laughter, the dark insinuations fled from his thoughts. His voice strong with faith and assurance now, Aglaca pronounced the song's end in the shrieking, pummeling darkness of Cerestes' futile spellcraft.

> *"Let darkest magic flee, consumed*
> *By Nuitari's ravenous gloom."*

Cerestes panted before him on the battlements. The mage looked smaller in the moonlight, his handsome features drawn and wearied, his once-golden eyes as depthless and dull as firebrick.

"Do not gloat, Solamnic," he threatened, his voice strangely high, thin, void of resonance. "The dragon is confined within me, but I have not been idle in my human form. A formidable mage stands before you, and a thousand magicks wait at my bidding."

"Try one of them," Aglaca urged. "Try your most powerful spell, Cerestes."

The mage lifted his hand, ready to cast a fireball, and breathed the old incantation.

Nothing happened.

"You cannot do it," Aglaca replied calmly. "'Tis as simple as that. Your magic has left you, sorcerer, and we stand here man to man."

"But the one who approaches has power, Solamnic," Cerestes said. "You have not accounted for Verminaard, nor for the mace Nightbringer, which he holds like his own dark heart. You will lose, Aglaca. My spells may fail, my magic falter, but you will lose."

"He will decide that," Aglaca said. "Verminaard will choose."

"Oh, very good, Solamnic." The mage leered. "I would have it no other way. And we will not wait long."

He pointed to the east, where Verminaard moved quickly from the moonlit foothills, trailing a swath of blackness behind him as he turned toward Castle Nidus.

"I have no dragonsight," Cerestes hissed. "You have taken that from me as well. But it can be restored by Verminaard. Here he comes, riding the crest of the absolute night, and I can see far enough to know him."

Chapter 20

The man stalked across the eastern plains, and the first of the winter winds swept up from the south, bearing with it the smell of ash and corruption.

It was Verminaard. That much was certain. Aglaca knew him at once by the broad shoulders, by the blond hair and the tattered black cloak. By the damned mace he still clutched tightly.

He moved swiftly, feverishly, as though something pursued him. And behind him the wave of darkness spread and settled, and the eastern hills vanished into a complete and abject night.

"Here he comes," Cerestes announced, pointing a long, bony finger at the approaching man. "Look behind him,

Aglaca, and tell me this: How can such darkness bode aught but ill for you and for your kind?"

Aglaca smiled. Toward the approaching figure he turned, and he began the second chant.

> *"The light in the eastern skies*
> *Is still and always morning,*
> *It alters the renewing air*
> *Into belief and yearning . . ."*

With a bleating cry, Cerestes leapt toward the young Solamnic, who brushed him aside with a wave of a sinewy arm. The mage teetered at the edge of the ramparts, shrieked . . .

And clutched at the crenels, his legs skidding out over the bailey before he tugged himself back to safety and crouched, rasping and whimpering, on the stone walk. Aglaca rushed at him, pinning him against the battlements with one muscled arm.

Verminaard, approaching below, felt a great and ponderous weight lift from him. Suddenly, unexplainably, Nightbringer loosened in his hand. For a moment, thunderstruck, he gazed down at the weapon, then up to the battlements, where his eyes locked with Aglaca's, and he clutched the mace more tightly, more passionately.

Suddenly he remembered the vision—years ago on the Bridge of Dreed, when he had stood and awaited Aglaca's crossing. Again he saw the blond youth on a windy battlement, a lithe, blue-eyed image of himself. But not me, he thought again. My brother . . . my image. Not Abelaard, but my brother.

The young man gestured. His lips moved in a soundless incantation, and Verminaard felt weaker, felt his own power drain from him, then return as he found himself by the walls of Nidus. A dark force pushed him toward the battlements, and relentlessly, almost mechanically,

Verminaard began to climb.

Looking down into the transfigured face of his brother, Aglaca fumbled with the spell for a moment, the words slipping away in his astonishment. For Verminaard's countenance was sallow and gaunt, and a lost light flickered in the depths of his eyes. It seemed as though nothing lay beneath his skin except air and bone. And Verminaard's eyes . . .

For an instant, Aglaca recalled their first hunt, the turning of the great beast in the box canyon, the dull look in the monster's eye, and he wondered why he was remembering this, why his mind played lazily over the past when the present rushed at him, armed and deadly.

And his own vision, a decade ago on the bridge, returned to him . . . the pale, muscular young man, and the mace descending . . .

So it will be, unless you take this matter in your own hands, Aglaca Dragonbane, coaxed the Voice, again low and seductive, neither man nor woman.

" 'Even the night,' " Aglaca sputtered at last, closing his ears to the disembodied coaxing, his voice gaining confidence as he spoke the second verse of the chant:

> *"Even the night must fail,*
> *For light sleeps in the eyes*
> *And dark becomes dark on dark*
> *Until the darkness dies . . ."*

Verminaard did not stop for an instant. Scrabbling up the wall like an enormous spider, buoyed by a dark, whirling cloud, he slung his leg over the merlon and hurdled onto the battlement, his fingers digging at the solid stone of the crenels as he clambered atop the walls and crouched, the mace clutched tightly in his hand.

"Stop him, Verminaard!" Cerestes cried, fumbling in his

sleeves and producing a long, narrow dagger. "Stop Aglaca before he enchants you with his Solamnic wizardry!" Aglaca slammed the mage into the wall. Dazed, Cerestes gasped for air.

Verminaard stared coldly at Aglaca, waving the mace nervously, like the switching tail of a lion.

Aglaca stood his ground, watching Cerestes out of the corner of his eye as the mage drew hesitantly nearer, the dagger rising and falling awkwardly in his delicate hand.

"Stop him!" Cerestes spat, "or the chant will kill you!"

Serenely Aglaca chanted the third of the four verses.

> *"Soon the eye resolves*
> *Complexities of night*
> *Into stillness, where the heart*
> *Falls into fabled light . . ."*

Color returned to Verminaard's skin, and he took a long breath. Was that lilac in the air? His arms were heavy, and suddenly he was very hungry.

"What *is* your answer, my brother?" Verminaard asked. "Will you choose to be my captain, to serve me in the dignity and honor of our long acquaintance, our deepening friendship, or will you choose to leave the girl with me?"

"If you let me finish, I'll be your captain."

Uneasily Verminaard glanced down to the bailey, which seemed to pivot and rock below. For a moment, it seemed to rush up toward him with a blinding, insensible speed, and he thought he was falling.

He closed his eyes, gathering his courage and balance.

Do not listen to him, the Voice coaxed, rising from the shimmering head of the mace. *He will hoodwink you with Solamnic lies.*

No. Aglaca is trustworthy. That is why I want him as my captain. Ten years I have known him . . . ten years . . .

See. Test him and see.

"Have I ever lied to you, Verminaard?" Aglaca asked. "Would I lie to you now? Would I say, 'Yes, I shall serve you,' and then turn away when a safer moment could take me west to Solamnia, or a moment more dire, more dangerous, might let me betray you?"

But remember the hunt, the Voice insinuated. *Remember the drasil roots, and who returned with the girl. . . .*

With a deep breath, Verminaard leapt onto the battlement and walked slowly toward Aglaca. "It will be one or the other, Aglaca. Choose now. Either you serve me, here and now, or the girl is mine."

"Then there is one more choice," Aglaca replied. "Not to choose from the choices you offer."

"Do not listen to him!" Cerestes shrieked. "Help me! He will kill us both and take your castle!"

"He is the darkness on the moon. He is a dragon," Aglaca said, his voice low and soothing and persuasive. He stepped toward Verminaard on the narrow battlement, extending his hand.

A gesture of friendship. Or to seize the mace?

Verminaard edged forward, then back again.

"Set down the mace, my brother," Aglaca urged. "It holds you in the depth of enchantments. It is loose in your hand already. You felt it as you approached the castle, I know. Let me finish and you are forever free."

"Let him finish and we both are dead!" Cerestes cried, and rushed at Aglaca. Swiftly, with the grace of a dancer, the young Solamnic pivoted and kicked him back, and Cerestes clattered against the stone crenels. Aglaca steadied himself on the battlements between his old companion and the stunned mage.

Quietly, turning to Verminaard with a smile on his face, Aglaca began the last verse.

"And larks rise up like angels . . ."

The image of Abelaard flashed through Verminaard's mind, the pale eyes milky and uplifted, the pale hands groping for the hilt of a broken sword.

This is what Solamnia has given you, the Voice urged as Abelaard's eyes fixed upon his brother's in the twisting depths of Verminaard's imaginings. *It has taken your brother away, and its lies have made you injure the one dear . . . one dear . . .* The words echoed inside Verminaard's head.

"Like angels larks ascend . . ."

The voice went on, urgently, compellingly. *Remember the cave and the strong surge of power. He would take that from you as well, as his father took your mother and your father . . . as he took your true brother Abelaard and the girl you had dreamed when she became Judyth. He took them all, and now he would take me from you . . . I, who am your sole confidante, your friend and lover and family as well.*

Do you remember once, when the two of you spoke of me? He said, "I choose not to believe," and you thought, I choose not to believe Aglaca . . . not to believe Aglaca. . . .

You have chosen already, Lord Verminaard. There is no going back. You are mine, always and forever. You have said.

I have seen Aglaca fight, Verminaard thought. He is swift and powerful. I could not defeat him even if I—

He is yours, the mace assured him. *Be ruled by me.*

Aglaca touched Verminaard's arm, and as he began to recite the penultimate line, the big man recoiled, as if something loathsome had attached itself to him. "Midnight!" he roared, and brought the mace, flashing with dark and cold energy and malice as old as thought, toward the innocent face of his companion and brother.

Aglaca had scarcely time to cover his head when the mace struck his arms full force.

Gundling, standing by the portcullis below, heard the shriek of Nightbringer hurtling through the air and the sound of the impact, the snap of the young man's bones. The old guard raced to the bailey's edge and looked up on the ramparts where Aglaca reeled and fell to his knees, quietly breathing the last lines of the spell:

> *"From sunlit grass as bright as gems*
> *To where all darkness ends."*

Gundling turned and raced toward the guardhouse.

As the chant ended, Verminaard felt the mace let go in his hand, felt the hand straighten and heal. He dropped Nightbringer on the stone of the ramparts as Cerestes rose slowly, still clutching his long dagger.

Time seemed to stop for a long breath, Aglaca's pain-dazed face unblinking, unseeing, as he stared into Verminaard's eyes. Cerestes stood, caught in the moon's dark glow, and Nightbringer looked for all the world like a cold cave rock, formed only of limestone and tears, all presence gone, all magic fled. A slow wailing began deep in Verminaard's throat and rose into the stillness.

He had blinded both brothers.

As Aglaca struggled to rise and failed, dazed and sightless on the battlements, his arms shattered, Verminaard stared down upon him, and for a moment, something like compassion crossed over his face like a brief flicker of flame.

And I have done these things, he thought. So there is no hope for me. No hope. I have chosen.

His howl died away, and he knelt and picked up the mace. Nightbringer awoke with a crackle, and this time there was no pain in his hand at all. The scar ran too deep. Coldly he stood above his dazed brother, who groped for the crenel, trying vainly to stand as Cerestes, with a rustle of black robes, slipped behind Aglaca and plunged the dagger once, twice, a third time into his back.

For a moment, the two of them stood there. Verminaard

stared blankly at the mage, who looked back at him with a sly, exultant smile.

"His spell is broken as well," Cerestes whispered, lifting his dripping hands, and the blood and the red moonlight glittered upon newly formed scales.

* * * * *

Fifty miles away, in the infirmary of Castle East Borders, Abelaard sat upright in the bed and cried out.

He had dreamt of a song—some verse, some incantation—soothing words about day and light and larks and angels. . . .

He lifted his hands to the bandages on his eyes, then sank disconsolately back upon the bed. There was no music in this absolute dark.

He remembered the last of the song in his dream, whispered the words to himself as the door opened in the far end of the infirmary, and he could tell by the footsteps and the bobbing light of the candle that the surgeon was making his nightly rounds.

The candle.

Abelaard sat bolt upright and called to the approaching doctor, called out in joy to guards on the bailey battlements, to the lord in the motte: "The candle! I can see!"

He leapt from the bed and lurched toward the source of the light, tearing the bandages off as he ran.

"Thanks be to Paladine!" he whispered, and lifted the astonished surgeon off his feet.

And to whoever had sung the forgotten song in his dreams, he offered thanks as well.

* * * * *

Judyth waited in the garden, but Aglaca did not come.

Long past the appointed time, she sat in the little clearing ringed with evergreens, marking the hours by the tilt of the moons in the sky. An owl cried ominously from the bare branches of the vallenwood, and when Judyth looked up, it was perched there, framed in the red light of Lunitari like something monstrous, glimpsed on a burning plain.

She felt hollow then, and alone. But not afraid. She had already passed through the country of fear. Aglaca had seen to that.

They had come to meet nightly in the garden, and each meeting had been an assurance. Aglaca had been cheery and humorous and confident, his affections strong and kind. Though the greatest of dangers had loomed before them, Aglaca's faith had bolstered them both. He had hoped in Verminaard, but he had believed far deeper things—that even if Verminaard failed him, there was a power, eternal and good, that undermined all of the weakness and treachery of those in Nidus and everywhere. And no matter the failures of mortals, *that* power would never fail.

Somewhere out in the bailey, a soldier shouted, then another, and the silence of the garden broke with the sound of rushing, scattering feet beyond the evergreens—guardsmen calling for Gundling, for Sergeant Graaf, a muffle of voices speaking veiled words, veiled news.

"Battlements," she heard. And "mage."

"Murder."

Judyth stood, straightening her skirts, her fingers absently brushing her hair, clutching the pendant at her neck. Verminaard would be sending for her, no doubt, for in the confusion of sound and light, she knew one thing instantly.

Aglaca was dead.

She had known it could come to this from that time in

Nightbringer's cavern, when Verminaard had first set his hand to that damnable mace. And later, when Aglaca had resolved to free Verminaard from the dark bondage of the weapon, Judyth had known that large and uncontrollable forces were set in motion, that the time would come when her fate and Aglaca's would depend on a single choice.

And the choice would not be theirs to make.

After a while, someone approached, the dim light from his lamp weaving elusively through the trees. The lamp-bearer stepped into the ring of evergreens. It was the Seneschal Robert, armed and solemn and bleary-eyed from a sudden wakefulness.

"Who are you?" Judyth asked. "I think you bear the worst of news."

"Oh, it is scarcely the worst, m'Lady," Robert replied, his voice grave and sorrowful, "terrible though this news is. Tonight we leave this terrible castle and make for the mountains and safety. Toward Berkanth, and the home of L'Indasha the druidess. You have been called to her service, she says, for there is worse to come from Verminaard and Cerestes."

Judyth dropped her eyes from Robert's concerned stare and fought down a surge of anger and pain. He knew this would happen, she thought. Aglaca *knew* this would be the outcome, but still he chose to let Verminaard choose *again*.

And now I am alone, without him.

When do *I* get to choose? Since I left Solanthus, I've been adrift on plots and wills and plans, all of which mapped *what's best for the girl*. I've followed their roads and followed their banners, and the way has changed so often that I could never get back to Solanthus . . . at least not the place I remember.

Then there was Aglaca, and though he did not ask to leave, he's gone and irretrievable, and Robert is planning for me now. But Aglaca was right to do it. There was the one hope of us all in the way he met his own choice. . . .

"Bravely, quietly," she said aloud. Then she looked at Robert again. "There's something left for me to do here."

"Lady?" whispered Robert, still awaiting her answer.

She looked up again, and tears of triumph coursed down her cheeks. She was smiling.

"I will go with you, Robert," Judyth replied. "But not yet. There is something I must attend to here."

* * * * *

Daeghrefn heard the outcry from his tower balcony. He saw the torches milling below in the bailey, the fractured glint of firelight on armor.

It is the mutiny, he thought. The uprising has begun.

He stumbled into his chambers and lurched toward the bed. The window open behind him, the red moonlight skimming across his shoulders, he sat on the bedside and extinguished the candles. Dressing slowly in the half-dark, his eyes fixed upon the door to the chamber, he paused when he was fully dressed in tunic and tabard.

He turned to his battle gear—first the old Solamnic greaves and gauntlets, and then the newer pieces, the black body armor adopted when he set aside the Solamnic plate and its embossed roses and kingfishers.

They will not see me until they pass through that door, he declared to himself, fumbling with his breastplate and helm. And then they will see me as a knight, as the warrior lord of the castle. I shall be waiting for them. At the very last, when all are marshaled against me, I shall end as I began, under my own standard, in the face of the damned and damning Order.

Ceremoniously he donned the long, black cape adorned with the crest of Nidus.

* * * * *

The armor was too large for him.

Robert noticed at once as he quietly entered the chamber, leaving the two unconscious guards lying in the corridor behind him.

The gaunt, wild-eyed man who faced him was only a shadow of the strong young fellow who had come to the castle lordship twenty-five years before—the man Robert the seneschal had sworn to uphold, to follow. It was as though he was waning, like a sliver of the declining moon.

When Daeghrefn saw who it was, he sprang to his feet and backed into the corner, his dark eyes blazing with anger and fear.

"You!" he shouted, his voice husky and harsh. "I knew when I left you on the plains it would be only a matter of time until you came to this room, weapon in hand! So take your revenge and go. If you're man enough."

Daeghrefn drew his sword. The blade weaved and wavered in his hand.

He's exhausted, Robert thought. He's wearied past sense.

"No," he replied, closing the door behind him. "I come for no vengeance, but for your rescue. I am here to take you from the castle, Lord Daeghrefn. It has become unsafe here. There's a mutiny afoot."

"I know that." Daeghrefn's eyes were haunted, wretched.

Robert cleared his throat. "Perhaps, then, you are also aware that your old . . . acquaintance, Lord Laca of East Borders, is on his way from Estwilde at the head of a thousand mounted soldiers."

Daeghrefn gripped his sword more tightly. In his mind's eye, he saw a burning plain, the South Moraine smoldering and charred . . . saw Robert riding away into the smoke. . . .

"Come with me, sir," Robert urged. "I'll care for you."

"*Very* clever, Robert," Daeghrefn said with a sneer. "You could dupe a guardsman or a falconer with your soothing double-talk, but it's hardly clever enough for the lord of the castle. I shall stay here, thank you. And you shall depart my presence."

Robert studied his old master from across the shadowy chamber. I believe where you are going, I cannot help you, he thought. But I shall try, Lord Daeghrefn.

I shall try.

"You must come, sir," he entreated, his voice hushed and somber. "Verminaard has killed Aglaca, and who can tell what that will—"

Daeghrefn stood bolt upright, his gaze vacuous and distant. "The *gebo-naud*," he whispered, his voice cracking. " 'Truce for truth . . . and son for son.' "

"We must leave now, sir," Robert persisted.

Daeghrefn backed toward the balcony, shaking his head, his hands extended as though he tried to fend something off.

"The *gebo-naud*," he said, his voice cracking hysterically. "My son . . . 'And his hand will strike your name,' the druidess said."

Wheeling about with a shriek, he rushed onto the balcony, Robert trailing desperately behind him. "Laca! Abelaard!" Daeghrefn screamed.

"*Abelaard!*"

And he toppled headfirst from the railing, into a strange and dreadful silence, the dark cape flapping behind him like a broken wing.

Chapter 21

Judyth clutched the bundle tightly as she descended the steps of the western tower.

All of Aglaca's cherished belongings, wrapped in his good green cape, were scarcely enough to burden her as she made the sad descent from his quarters. She had found the naming ring Laca had given him, a book of verse, and a locket that had been his mother's. All three he had brought to Nidus with him nine years ago, keeping them in a little pouch by his bedside.

She placed the dagger among them—the little blade he had given her on the night of the Minding. Once she had asked Aglaca where it had come from, for its gaudy handle—ebony embossed with golden claws, studded with pearls and garnets in a replica of the summer night sky—seemed out of place with the tasteful simplicity of his other valuables.

Aglaca had answered her cryptically, repeating that it was a ward against evil, then changing the subject to insects—or flowers, she no longer remembered—and so the dagger remained a mystery. Judyth took the weapon anyway, on the off chance that someone would know of it and of the story that no doubt explained it. Or at least know it had been his.

As she collected Aglaca's belongings, she collected her memories. Perhaps someday she would go back to East Borders, and there present these things to Aglaca's father. Perhaps the gift would make amends for her miserable failure as Laca's spy. But as for now, Aglaca's belongings were hers—the book, the locket, the ring, and even the mysterious dagger.

Now, as she reached the bottom of the steps, she tucked the package under her arm, feeling the sharp prickle of the blade's edge through the cloak. She stepped toward the door of the keep, toward the moonlit bailey and the spot where Robert would be waiting with a fast horse to take them south.

And a sudden crash stopped her in her tracks.

"Lady Judyth!" the voice called. "Do not leave without a fond good-bye."

She turned and stared through the open archway into the great hall of the keep, where Verminaard sat alone at the banquet table, a plate of roast goose steaming in front of him, a bottle of wine in his left hand. The glass he had been drinking from lay in splinters beneath the arch where he had hurled it, and the slivers caught the torch-light and glittered like broken ice.

He motioned to her with the bottle. "Come in! Oh, *do* come in, Judyth of Solanthus!"

His right hand remained beneath the table. Judyth

knew it clutched the mace.

Verminaard beckoned again, this time more insistently. Her hands shaking, Judyth stepped into the hall, the broken glass crackling beneath her riding boots.

"Where are you going?" Verminaard asked sternly. "I've not given you permission to leave, you know."

"I had no idea your permission was necessary, Lord Verminaard," Judyth replied evenly, pausing halfway to the edge of the table.

"Come closer," the new Lord of Nidus muttered hoarsely and set down the wine bottle. "Join me in a toast to my *precipitate predecessor*, Daeghrefn of Nidus. They're shoveling him under the bailey as we speak." He licked his fingers, one by one.

"I truly must be leaving, sir," Judyth said, backing toward the door. "I shall leave you to dinner with . . . your friends."

Verminaard gazed at her sullenly, wiping his mouth with his sleeve. "Won't you join me, Judyth? Are *you* not my friend?"

Slowly he stood, the wine bottle again in hand, the mace in the other, leering at Judyth as though she were the final course, the dessert to his lonely meal.

"No, sir," Judyth replied. "Nor am I likely to be your friend. You have killed too many who are dear to me."

"I have killed but one," Verminaard said, with a cruel half-smile.

"One is quite enough," Judyth replied.

"Even so. Cerestes' knife did that work," Verminaard explained lightly. He staggered from behind the table, taking a wobbly step toward Judyth.

She had seen that look on faces before—in the leering eyes of the bandits when first they brought her to the Pen in Neraka.

"But you blinded him first," she whispered, the slightest quaver in her voice. "So they tell me."

The wine bottle crashed to the floor, and the big man, incredibly quick, lurched toward her. Judyth turned and ran for the door, but Verminaard grabbed her, his thick fingers greasy and groping. She pulled away from him, holding the bundle to her breast, the hem of her gown smudged by his rough hands.

"I shall be leaving now, Lord Verminaard," she announced loudly and turned toward the door. "Stay here, if you will, and crown yourself king in a fallen castle."

"You are not in great favor with this court, Judyth of Solanthus," Verminaard growled. "But then you were *never* what I imagined. Such a disappointment . . . fit leavings for Aglaca, I'd wager. But now . . . well, now you will do."

He rushed toward her blearily, his arms extended, Nightbringer glimmering like a dark torch in his gloved hand. Seizing her, he drew her close, crudely and violently.

The knife! Judyth thought, instinctively raising the bundle. She brought up the packet suddenly, violently, as the sharp blade of the dagger slit through the green cloak and scored across the face of her assailant, a thin, shallow line from chin to forehead.

Verminaard reeled from her, howling and clutching his face. He banged Nightbringer on the stone floor in a flurry of black sparks, and smoke streamed from between his fingers.

Alarmed, but alert enough to seize her chance, Judyth rushed from the hall and out to the bailey. She dropped the bundle at the threshold, then crouched to quickly gather the belongings.

And shivered as the long cries from the hall became shrill and terrible.

* * * * *

Robert found her, as he knew he would, waiting in the garden.

There, in the ring of aeterna lovingly planted by his old friend Mort, he discovered the girl, her lavender-blue eyes reddened and downcast.

"Oh, Robert!" She smiled up at him and rose to her feet.

"Come with me," Robert urged quietly and took her arm.

Gently Robert attended the girl as they slipped through the topiaries, bright with autumn reds and violets, toward the stable, where the seneschal had kept a roan stallion saddled and ready for the trip to Berkanth.

But as they reached the edge of the garden, the tower bells began to ring.

"They're after us!" Robert hissed, pulling Judyth behind the vine-entangled gate. Together, breathless, expecting torches, search parties, and alarms, they stared across the open courtyard at a surprising and ominous sight: the bailey in the eerie red glow of Lunitari, the soldiers assembled around Aglaca's shrouded body, breathing the Solamnic prayers they scarcely remembered as they prepared to bury him amid the aeterna in his beloved garden.

The commotion came from the ramparts, where the garrison of Nidus rushed to man the walls, the archers hastening to the western gate, where the cry of the sentries rose above the tumult.

"Solamnia! The forces of Laca! Prepare for attack!"

"We're going nowhere now, m'Lady," Robert whispered, motioning for silence. "Even if we could cross that moonlit yard and get to the horse, there's no longer an unguarded gate in the castle. I taught these boys how to wait a siege, and if they listened at all, Nidus is shut tight against the enemy."

"Then just what do we do, Robert?" Judyth asked,

drawing Aglaca's dagger, her lavender eyes flashing with anger.

"Not what you'd *like* to do, lady," Robert insisted, gently taking the weapon from her and slipping it into his belt. "We wait it out. We hope that Lord Laca has schooled his men even better."

* * * * *

Verminaard sat in Daeghrefn's old quarters, looking dolefully in the mirror.

He had slept for days—a strange and fitful sleep, filled with shapeless dreams and dark landscapes. He could tell as much by the moons and the shifting planets, from which he gained his only knowledge of time. For pride's sake, he dared not venture down into the keep, where his soldiers might see the wound the girl had given him.

The cut had never bled—not even a drop—but now, three days after his wounding, the scar was even worse. Jagged and purple-black, spreading from chin to forehead, it had branched and forked like a river in rocky country.

My glory is ruined, he thought bitterly. You would think that a wound such as this would be mortal, but it does not hurt. I can no longer even feel it, and yet when I look in the mirror, the scar has spread even farther, to my ears and lips and my very eyelids. The skin is destroyed. My face is eaten alive by this wound.

I shall find that girl.

As he slipped the black cloth over the mirror, he saw Cerestes in it, entering the door behind him.

In Verminaard's absence, Cerestes had assumed defense of the castle. The spell that had bound his magic ended with Aglaca's death, and now the mage used every charm and enchantment he knew to bind the garrison to his command. But Cerestes had recovered only slowly from his own binding, and his spellcraft was still weak and tentative. Though he kept the soldiers in line for the moment, the mage looked haggard and drawn.

"My beauty is ruined, Cerestes," Verminaard pronounced desolately. "Now those I conquer will remember me for my scar, for my ugliness."

"Not so, Lord Verminaard," the mage replied. "They will remember you for the power of your choices, for your victories and conquests."

Verminaard laughed bitterly. With a sweep of his gloved hand, he pointed to the balcony, to the high overlook and its view of the southern plains. "Look out beyond the walls, Cerestes, and think back only as far as midsummer. Now the plains are growing back, and the forest beyond them is greening with fir and juniper. But how will *this* mend, Cerestes? How will this scar look in a season's time?"

Cerestes backed toward the door. "Wait for me here, Lord Verminaard," he urged. "Your wounds will mend as mine do—slowly but completely. Though I cannot hasten that recovery, I know a little of shape-changing and disguise."

" 'Wait'? How could I leave this cell, marked as I am? And who knows when the *mending* will begin?" Verminaard intoned as the mage slipped through the chamber door. Verminaard sat on the bed, burying his face in his hands. "Has any suffered as I have suffered?" he shouted to the empty room.

None, the Voice claimed as the mace by the bedside sparkled with ebony light. *None have suffered as you have suffered, and yet you are handsome in my eyes, a creature of unforeseen beauty, whose scars have deepened his splendor, for in my eyes, you are a spirit of dark light. . . .*

Verminaard shook his head. He would not be consoled. Not yet.

Go to the balcony, the Voice urged. *Look west over the plains whose greening you mourn. West over the army of Solamnics, toward the Eira Goch.*

Reluctantly Verminaard stood and walked to the balcony railing.

"Light," he said, shielding his eyes against the red glow of the sunset. "I see light, and the crests of mountains."

Dream of what lies beyond them, the Voice urged. *I am preparing you an army in Estwilde—a thousand men strong and ready.*

You are handsome enough to lead them.

"I will not have them see this scar," Verminaard insisted. "It is a wound—a sign of weakness."

No weakness. For Cerestes prepares a mask of mysteries, wrought from Daeghrefn's broken breastplate. You will wear the mask at the head of your armies. You are handsome and splendid, but the mask is better. Now none will know you as I know you. None but I shall look upon your countenance.

When you receive the mask, go to the evergreen copse, to the place of transformations. There we shall commune, and I shall bring to pass the first of my promises.

Your army will wait. Your destiny will abide.

* * * * *

Laca watched the dim arrangement of lights along the battlements of Nidus. It was the tenth day of the siege, and there was still no word from Verminaard.

Long encampment sat ill with Solamnics, as did the waiting.

Even now, the thought of defeating Verminaard was enough to fill his dreams with delight and yearning. Deeply Laca wished revenge on his own son, on the cold young raven of Nidus who had blinded one brother through petulance and spite, then slain the other on the battlements where the lights weaved now in the thickening darkness.

But startling news had come from the castle. The emissary, a grizzled Nerakan named Gundling, brought the story to Laca. Verminaard, who was now, some said, a cleric of considerable power, had vanished from the castle two nights ago. Rumors had it that he was somewhere in the mountains, communing with the goddess and readying himself for the great venture. And while he was gone, the garrison had come to themselves, Gundling said. They had seized the mage, who was near exhaustion, imprisoned him, then voted to a man to open the gates to the Solamnics, to hand over the castle.

As a Solamnic lord, Laca had heard stories such as this before—the hoarded promises of besieged towns, the lies of bandit captains. Strong magic could await them inside those walls, and a thousand lesser ambushes.

"We will wait," Laca said, "until your commander has the courage to come forth and parley."

The Lord of East Borders was not alone in his patience. His knights stood beside him, fivescore times ten strong, and not one of the Order questioned his decision. But the archers grumbled, and the infantry fought among themselves as the legions foraged the countryside, finding little to nourish them in a landscape so recently burned.

Laca slept little that night, his dreams a confusion of fire and betrayals.

On the next morning, before dawn, a mist rose in the dungeons of the eastern tower. It rose unnoticed through the castle floors, wafting past Nidus's vigilant sentries, then onto the plains through the equally vigilant Solamnic infantry.

One of the Solamnics—a lad from the plains, not far from the ruins of the old Castle diCaela—thought he saw a shape in the mist, silhouetted against the glow of the campfire. But he blinked and it was gone, receded once more into the mist that passed through the encampment up to the hills, settling on a spot where the rubble inclined toward a rise, toward a copse of stripped evergreen and a rocky, shadowy hillside.

There, out of sight of the armies, in the midst of the evergreens, the mist took human form. Cerestes stepped from the copse and headed toward the high grotto, where Verminaard awaited him.

* * * * *

At midday, a sudden cloud rose out of the east.

The Solamnics cursed and scrambled for their tents, and the sullen sentries raised their hoods against the prospect of rain.

"Verminaard has much to answer," the boy from the plains muttered angrily. "Not even a cleric can make me wait out a downpour!"

But the threatened rain did not come. Instead, the dark cloud settled on the broken copse, and the foothills vanished in a thick mist. The infantry—commoners from Coastlund and the eastern borderlands—took it as an omen. The darkness, they said, was devouring Verminaard and his mage, and many in their number broke camp for a return to Estwilde. Laca found half of them cloaked and ready, the others packing everything from bows to bottles.

It took four squadrons of armed knights to invite the infantry to wait out the darkness.

That night three moons filled the sky—dark Nuitari in the midst of her luminous sisters, eclipsing both of them in the course of an ominous evening. The horses called to one another skittishly, and the infantrymen murmured of omens and the Cataclysm come again.

Then, out of the cloudy grove, came the sound of fire

and splintering wood. A flock of starlings lifted raucously into the air, and behind them, in a glory of darkness, a dragon rose on wide and powerful wings.

* * * * *

When Laca came to his senses, the encampment was silent.

For a moment, he thought that the great beast had descended upon them, had ravaged his army with fiery breath and ragged claws. All the dragon stories of his childhood returned to him as he crawled warily from the collapsed tent and cast his eye over the desolate landscape.

Five hundred soldiers, he guessed, lay in shock or stupor. Others—knights and archers and infantry alike—rushed toward the western foothills, from the high grass north of the castle and from the blackened plateau of the South Moraine, where they had fled the encampment when the monstrous beast passed over and the Dragonfear engulfed them. They were muddied, haggard, matted with dried grass and leaves.

We've been routed, Laca thought angrily. Routed by that monster . . . my *son* . . . and his damnable mage.

Then he shifted his gaze toward the castle, where the dragon turned in a slow arc and made for the one standing man left on the plains of Nidus.

Laca's breath caught fire before he could expel it on the curse that was his last thought.

* * * * *

The towers of Castle Nidus seemed to pivot below him, crested with fire and milling, panic-stricken soldiers as the dragon banked in the icy, thin air.

It was just as the Lady had promised, there in the cave when he took up Nightbringer. For she had shown him then: a castle, its battlements ablaze, its towers crumbling. A thousand castles—the last lights of the west dwindling, guttering, consumed by the spreading dark.

Above them, he would fly on the back of the dragon, its broad shoulders thick and striated with powerful muscles, the low, forgotten song of its heart beneath him.

Now, Ember, Verminaard thought. Let the Solamnics scatter. What are they to me, anyway? My army awaits me in Estwilde, and I will deal with the Solamnics then. But let us attend to the garrison of Nidus.

The dragon surged under him, responding to his thoughts. Verminaard felt the heat along the scales of the creature as its red wings stretched powerfully.

For they did not follow us willingly, bravely. . . . They were the Stormcrow's garrison, not our own, and we shall have no part of them. Let the girl die with them, and let us go to the east.

But now, dear Ember, let us raze this wretched castle.

* * * * *

The fire struck the tower battlements like a windstorm. Racing over the crenels and merlons, over the startled and doomed soldiers, the breath of the dragon burned hair and bone, wood and metal and stone itself.

The western tower exploded in a blaze, in the screams of the burning sentries. The southern tower as well was burning, flames snaking through the upper windows, the terrible smell of seared flesh on the air.

In the garden, Robert dragged Judyth, coughing, out of the path of a collapsing, burning vallenwood as the handiwork of a dozen gardeners withered in the dragonflame.

"Are . . . are you able to ride?" he shouted.

Judyth coughed, glanced at him bravely, and nodded.

"Then damn the garrison!" the old seneschal said. "Follow me!" Lurching into the bailey, he crossed open ground through flame and billowing smoke, Judyth close behind him.

But the stable was burning, its doors kicked open by the panicked horses who had rushed away, whinnying and shrieking, into the churning smoke. Alone, Judyth and Robert stood in the middle of the bailey, the wooden booths and outbuildings collapsing around them, and the granite walls of Nidus crackling with unnatural heat.

The dragon wheeled then, guided by the sure hand of Verminaard, and swooped for one last pass over the castle. Judyth gasped as Ember's glittering golden eyes fixed her in their gaze, and there, at the last of moments, she clutched the old man beside her as the dragon bellowed and the flames surged forth. Robert thought of the druidess and closed his eyes as the fire rained down and engulfed them like the Cataclysm come again.

* * * * *

It will be as I promised, Lord Verminaard, the Voice soothed as dragon and dark cleric passed over the castle, bound for the Khalkist Mountains and the fertile lands to the west.

Ember swooped low over the abandoned Solamnic camp. Then the great beast banked in the dark sky and rose, higher and higher, until the snow-covered peaks lay faint and white below him, and Verminaard rode alone amid the icy air and the indifferent stars.

Alone, but for the Voice. For the Lady continued to beguile and coax and vow. . . .

I promise you a thousand castles—the last lights of the west

dwindling, guttering, consumed by the spreading dark.
Above them, you will fly on the back of the dragon, its broad
shoulders thick and striated with powerful muscles, the low, for-
gotten song of its heart beneath you. And all around you, there
will be more . . . black and blue and green and red, in sweeping
brilliant colors, glittering like moonlight on the blood-black
mountains, the sky darkened by the sweep of dark wings. . . .

And the path of their flight will cross over a desolate country,
where only the dead walk, mouthing the names of dragons. And
the men in the towers, surrounded and riddled by dragons, by
the cries of the dying, the roar of the ravenous air, will await
your unspeakable silence.

And with the night wind at his back and Nidus a dim
flame on the eastern horizon, Verminaard abandoned
himself to the Voice. He knew that the goddess breathed
through him and that now he would engender destruction far greater than that at Nidus.

He would wear the mask forever—long after his face
had healed. It would be his battle mask, he vowed, and it
would protect him from mirrors, where his features
would reflect as fair hair, pale eyes . . . the precise countenance of dead Aglaca. That was a face he wanted never to
see again.

But that was behind him, below him. He steered the
dragon toward the horizon. Before him, in his imaginings,
a great chaos of crushed and defenseless fortresses would
be the work of his own hand and heart and will.

And he would delight in the fierce, magnificent ruin.

Epilogue

L'Indasha lifted her eyes from the auguries of ice. She had lost the travelers in the shadows at the foot of the mountain, but she knew they would be here shortly. She did not need to augur their arrival.

Nor was she eager to see either of them.

For a brief moment on the night before, she had become troubled. In the ice, she had seen the dragon plummet, Robert and Judyth helpless in the bailey, miles from her spells and saving hand, but then she had remembered the pendant.

She smiled now to think of the accident that had brought the jewel into Judyth's hands.

"*For protection against fire*, Paladine said," she whispered.

And my helper, the girl—"

"Was wearing the pendant!" The voice behind her completed her sentence.

L'Indasha stopped and whirled around. The old man stood there, his threadbare robes replaced by a new white gown, his white hair shining like Solinari beneath his floppy, soft hat.

Beside him stood another man, a dark, powerfully built fellow dressed in forest green. He also wore a green cap, incongruously pinned with a paper butterfly.

"My lord . . ." L'Indasha murmured. "And you, sir. I believe I remember you. . . ."

The old fellow with the soft hat, his silver triangle gleaming very brightly, grinned and raised a thin, gnarled hand in introduction of the man beside him.

"There's not a druid alive who hasn't heard of my apprentice gardener, Mort. Came to me about twenty years ago from Nidus. Too many hornets' nests down there to suit him, and they never gave him enough of an allotment to do a proper job on his roses. Been taking pretty good care of my place here, don't you think?" The old man circled his arm over the verdant hillsides, where every sort of alpine plant flourished. "He does a fair job at wardings, too. Kept the fire away from these. Mort's Magic, I call it."

L'Indasha smiled sadly. "I've missed you, Mort. And, of course, you are the unknown hand . . . that camp . . . and this hillside . . . all the signs laid out in the stones!"

Mort smiled and nodded, then extended his hand to her.

"Thank you for the gift, Lady."

The druidess looked puzzled but smiled back.

"Don't mystify my only druidess, Mort!" Paladine ordered with mock seriousness. "If you'll hasten down the trail and greet our guests when they arrive, I would speak with L'Indasha alone."

The gardener bowed merrily and backed down the mountain trail, seating himself politely out of earshot.

Paladine was left standing with the druidess. He looked upon her, and his eyes shone with love. "You must choose again, L'Indasha."

The druidess knew what he meant and nodded. "It will be hard to lose Robert twice in the span of a day—once at Nidus, when I saw the fire engulf him, and now to know he will be here shortly, and that when he arrives I must bid him farewell forever."

"Living things grow and change," Paladine said. "No matter the length of their lives—one day or all of them. Those who let go of one secret do so in faith of knowing others."

"But I cannot let go," L'Indasha said. "My chance died with Aglaca on the battlements. Huma's kin will never unite, and the rune will never be sounded."

Paladine nodded grimly. "And in the coming storm, keeping the rune safe will be even more dangerous."

"And yet I choose to keep it," the druidess replied bravely.

"You are absolutely certain?" Paladine asked softly. "A choice such as this is often . . . final."

"I have chosen," L'Indasha insisted. "Only let *me* tell Robert. I hear him approaching."

On the trail below them, Mort stood and bowed to Robert and Judyth, who ascended slowly, weary after the long day's walk.

"Robert, my old friend!" Mort called out. "Do you remember me? It is very good to see you are well . . . and happy." Mort broke into a bigger smile.

"I am both, you old ground-grubber." Robert lunged toward him in a rough embrace. "I never did find another chess partner, you know." They ascended together a little way, discussing excitedly the fall of Nidus, the years of Mort's absence, what they reckoned the future held for them.

Her eyes brimming with tears, L'Indasha looked at Paladine. He returned her gaze serenely, lovingly.

The druidess took a deep breath. "Robert . . . " she began.

The seneschal stopped on the path. His smile faded and his shoulders slumped a little, but he recovered quickly, gathering himself to a firm, military stance.

"I have heard ill tidings in my time, Lady," he said to L'Indasha, his voice unwavering, "and I have lived through them all."

"It's ill tidings to me as well, Robert," L'Indasha said. And she told him that she could not leave her post as guardian of the rune. For three thousand years, she had served Lord Paladine, the sole druidess in his vast command. In that time, she had hidden the rune well from the curious, the greedy, the malign, unto a moment arranged for a thousand years, when Huma's line would devolve unto two young men violently different, almost opposites. As the rune had two sides, so should its sounders.

"But the moment has passed," she said. "Takhisis will grow in power, and there will be war."

"And we shall win," Robert proclaimed gallantly.

"If the guardian keeps her post," Paladine added softly, "and her solitude."

Robert nodded. "I'll rest here tonight," he said, "and then, tomorrow—"

"Lord Paladine?" Judyth asked, and all eyes turned to her. They had forgotten she was here, so absorbed they were in the sadness of wars and departures. Judyth gasped when the god's eyes turned to her. She felt bathed in a love and peace beyond her understanding, and she knew that what she was about to ask was fitting and right.

"Is there any rule that says *this* lady must be keeper of the rune?"

"What are you asking, child?" Paladine whispered, and it was Judyth's turn to smile.

"I came over these mountains to gather secrets," she said. "In doing so, I met Aglaca, so I know a little of what Robert must be feeling . . . of what the druidess must know."

"And?" Paladine asked softly.

"And I shall be glad to keep the rune, if Lady L'Indasha Yman would entrust to me its keeping."

L'Indasha frowned. "But you're to be my helper. . . . "

It was Paladine's turn to speak. "Judyth, there is no rule. You may offer yourself, but your choice would be a binding one. Would you become the keeper of the secret of the blank rune? The keeper continues without age, without death, without the company of a spouse, so long as the rune holds power."

The girl looked far off into the night. Paladine himself was asking her to be his servant. But not demanding it. It truly was her choice.

"I choose . . ." she began, relishing the words, "I choose to become the keeper, my lord." And then she chuckled. "Because I want an adventure of my own choosing. And because you have *asked* me my mind. How could I refuse your respect, your love?"

"You could," the god said. "Many do. And you, L'Indasha? Your choice returns to you, if you will have it."

"I choose Robert," the druidess said. "I choose to let go of the one secret in faith of knowing others."

"You are absolutely certain?" Paladine asked softly. "You will be mortal again. You will die as others die."

"And I will live as others live.", said L'Indasha. "Yes. I have chosen."

* * * * *

Paladine laid his hands on them and spoke the words of forgetting to L'Indasha, of remembrance to Judyth, and the exchange was complete. Judyth wore the flower pendant with the blue-purple stone. Now it was truly hers—chosen with full knowledge.

As Robert and the druidess made their way down the mountainside, L'Indasha stopped short and crowed with delight. "Look! My daylilies! They were all burned in the fire except this patch, and it was so small and I planted it so quickly—well, just look!"

Before her spread an enormous clump of bright green fans, each one with several scapes rising into the night sky. Beside it lay the signs of warding. Logr and Yr. Water and Yew bow.

Journey and Protection.

"Mort. Of course," L'Indasha breathed. " 'Thank you for the gift,' he said. Bless him."

Judyth heard the last of the druidess's laughter floating up on the mountain breeze. She turned to bid Paladine and Mort good-bye, but they were already gone. She started down the mountain herself and came quickly upon the clump of daylilies. One blossom remained open in the advancing night. In its center, behind a blue-purple eye area, a risted rune-staef, now visible to her in the veining of the flower, spelled the blank rune's symbol. It was now her turn to guard this key to augury against enemy eyes—for a thousand years, if need be—until the coming storms were calmed.

Sothonsien, the rune-staef read, in the old language: The True Face. Revealed Knowledge.

Judyth thought of Aglaca, and then of a ruined face. She wept as she understood. The rune's reverse—its opposite—was *Heregrima*: The Mask.